LUCKY FOR SOME

By David Hoggard

September 11th 2017

Prologue

Out of a Clear Blue Sky

It seems that many truly historic events – the ones that change the world - come, metaphorically, out of a clear blue sky. And those days that utterly change your own life, instantly? Often, the same thing. A clear blue sky.

The sky high over New York City on that crisp morning back in September 2001 was just such a sky. On that day, the day that starts my story, the morning sun shone down out of a pale blue sky onto thousands of people like me in lower Manhattan. There was a promise of afternoon warmth and there was a late summer bounce to everyone's steps. The bright sun threw sharp shadows between the buildings, and the warmth of the sunlight was palpable.

The dusty sidewalks and the noisy, determined bustle were some of the things that I loved about New York. Like a flock of starlings, mysteriously choreographed, we were all going about our individual lives, consciously acknowledging each other hardly at all - flowing along the sidewalk at slightly different paces, to our different destinations, but, if seen from above, moving as one body.

But I wasn't in such a hurry. I'd re-scheduled my appointment. Instead of the 8:30 my boss had told me, I'd called and changed the meeting time to a relaxed 10:30 AM. So, all I was looking for right now was a coffee and breakfast, rather than an office desk and workstation.

The diner was on a street corner. The window counter tables featured a great view: the people on the sidewalk, and the high towers of the cityscape. Rising above all the rest, the twin towers of the World Trade Center, where I was due to make my delivery after this leisurely breakfast, were about a mile away. I ordered coffee, eggs: 3, over-easy; bacon and toast from the busy waitress. After I'd paid, I indicated a free space by the window. "I'll be there – can you bring it over?"

"Sure, honey," she said. "Here, take your coffee." I took the mug, added a dash of cream and carried it and my large briefcase over to the window counter. I glanced at the clock above the door. It was twenty minutes to nine. I still remember every detail of this breakfast. I didn't know it then, but in about 10 minutes' time, the world would change for ever. And my own life would take a radical change of direction.

My breakfast took 5 minutes or so to arrive, along with a top-up of the coffee. I took a moment to arrange the eggs on top of one of the toast slices and picked up a rasher of bacon in my fingers and popped it in my mouth. Then I concentrated on the eggs and toast for a while. Breakfast always made me hungry.

I watched the show outside the window, where it seemed that there had been some sort of disturbance. The traffic, never exactly speedy, had ground to a complete halt all around us. People were getting out of their cars and staring up. Peering out of the window, I tried to see what was causing the distraction. It took me a moment to see what everyone was staring at. I had to crouch, almost, to look up at the looming height of the World Trade Center.

At first glance, it was hard to take in. There was a big black jagged hole in the side of the World Trade Center, about two thirds of the way up. How had that happened? Smoke was pouring out of it, and people were standing and staring at it, transfixed. The hubbub had ceased, and in its place was an eerie silence, broken by gasps and screams.

A city worker, judging by her smart suit, stepped into the diner. "A plane!" she shouted. "It was a plane. I saw it. Oh my God!"

The waitress had just delivered another breakfast. "What?" She hadn't seen the view outside the window.

"There! I saw it. A plane. It just flew straight into the side ... Exploded ... There's people in there." The waitress and most of the diners ran to the door or a window to see what was happening.

We had a grandstand view. The tower was billowing smoke now. It looked like a movie, and I think that's how I saw it for a moment. It was simply too enormous to accept as reality.

Then it struck me that my new friend Brett was in the smashed, smoking tower. He was having an interview – it must have just started. Foolishly, I wondered if he was okay. I remembered his location. "Fairly high up," he'd said. Christ, he's had it, surely? My own meeting was in the other tower, which was intact. So that was OK. Maybe.

I wasn't thinking clearly. I doubt anyone was. Abandoning my breakfast, I grabbed the payphone on the wall and called Brett's mobile. Cellphone, then. I got the "Out of service" tone. What would his phone do if he was in the middle of that? Yes - melt, probably. If it wasn't smashed. There again, he'd probably have turned it off for his interview. I thought they'd start to evacuate the bottom of the damaged tower – and possibly the other one, to be safe.

What to do now? I tapped the cradle and waited for a new dial tone, then called my client, Finklestein.

"Finklestein." He seemed surprisingly cool. His office was in the other tower, and that's where I was heading. Probably.

"Hello, Mr Finklestein. It's Joe Best. The courier." Yes, that's what I was. I used my Roger Moore voice.

"Yes?"

"Mr. Finklestein, in view of the unfortunate accident, I wondered if there would be a change of plan – maybe a new location?" According to my office, my large briefcase had been due to be handed to him, originally at 8:30 – about now, in fact. But I'd rearranged for a slightly later time. So, were we still meeting at ten-thirty?

"What? Why? This tower's fine. Apparently some damn fool's flown a plane into the other tower, but this one's fine. I can't even see it from here. There's no danger."

"Ah. Well, if you're sure..."

"Sure I'm sure. There's no danger."

"Okay. It may take me a little longer to get to you, what with the emergency traffic and so on..."

"Yeah. Just get here. Ten thirty, as we said, or as near as you can. I must go – my first meeting's started." And he rang off.

So, the delivery was still on, in the second tower. I wasn't sure whether or how that was going to happen. But there was at least an hour to go before I had to be there. Wait and see, I thought. Most of the diner staff and clientele were glued to CNN on the TV in the corner. Yes, we watched it on TV, even though we could see it quite clearly, live, out of the doorway. The TV acted as a sort of buffer, giving a sense of unreality. And there was a commentary, although it wasn't much help. The TV guys were clearly as stunned as we were. Like everyone else, I watched, mesmerised and horrified.

I really didn't want to go any nearer. In fact, I doubted I'd be able to. Whatever I was carrying, it wasn't worth getting killed for. Even if I couldn't get it to them today, I didn't think the world would stop.

And then ... well, it did. A second plane hit the other tower. There was a thump in the air - physical as well as audible, or so it seemed. Instantly, the second tower started to burn. The shrieks and gasps in the diner were followed by an eerie, unbelieving silence.

People were weeping now - both men and women - in the diner and on the streets. I was dumbstruck. The TV played on, the CNN pictures seeming to have a life of their own. There could be no doubt now. This was not an accident. And I wasn't going anywhere near the World Trade Center today. If ever.

The howling of emergency vehicles was overwhelming. The sound would have drowned out the TV and the voices in the diner anyway, but I don't think anyone spoke. There was nothing to say, no words that could possibly make sense of this.

This was not my country. Not my city. But I realised then that I sort of loved it, like a bumptious, cocky younger brother. It irritated me beyond measure sometimes, but I didn't want it hurt like this. And I felt for the people in it. And I'd spoken to two of the people in those towers only that morning. I'd had a great night out with one of them just last night. They didn't deserve this. Nobody did.

We all simply stood there, mesmerised by what was happening in front of us. We could easily step outside and see it live, but it still seemed easier to take in on the TV. That way, there was still a chance it wasn't real; it was just on TV. We could see people jumping out. Some were holding hands. God, the poor bastards.

Eventually, I did step outside; I was there on the sidewalk when the first tower collapsed. I was close enough to see and smell the dust after a minute or so, but the immediate effect was a shudder that seemed to run through the air. I don't know what it was, perhaps everybody's horror becoming palpable. But I felt it. And I soon saw - and smelled - the dirty wave of debris. My eyes stung with the dust and smoke.

I had to get away. This was like watching a tragedy in someone else's family. I felt like a voyeur. I walked uptown, carrying the briefcase, and found a small park, I don't remember where. I sat down on a bench to think.

As my thoughts started to organise themselves, it occurred to me that I should have been in there. According to the timings Clive, my boss, had given me, I was supposed to be there at 8:30. Relief was followed by anger: what was he thinking of, sending me in there so early? He could have got me killed.

Then the really big thought hit me. He would think that I actually was there. He didn't know about my habit of amending his instructions by talking direct to the client. I was never reported late, the time given to me was half past eight. Ergo, I was in the second tower on time. And I was dead. Bugger me. Now what?

But let's go back a bit – to the day before this, when the world was different.

Chapter 1

Nothing New

I can still remember the day before The Day. It began with the buzz of my alarm clock, like any other morning. I reached over to stop the noise and checked the date and the time. It was eight o'clock on an unremarkable early September morning in Chiswick, west London, and I had to get into the office in an hour or so. Easy enough, but I then had to get to Heathrow, get on a plane and fly all the way to JFK.

I gave my razor a glance and left it at that. I'd shaved at four o'clock yesterday, Sunday, when I arrived back from Milan and before I went out to see who was in the pub. After a quick hot shower, I jumped into clean clothes: my usual all-purpose uniform of chinos, polo shirt and "smart casual" Gap cotton blazer.

Oh. Let me introduce myself. My name's Joe Best. At this time I was a courier. That meant flying around the world, delivering parcels, envelopes, briefcases and sometimes suitcases, containing stuff that needs to be taken by a real human, sitting on a plane with the stuff in the overhead bin, or maybe as checked luggage.

Usually, I had no idea what was in these packages, but I guess it was nearly always some sort of papers - contracts, pictures, money sometimes. The larger stuff might be prototype components for new electronic devices. Sometimes it was film or disks. Point is, this stuff was worth much more than I was, or at least, my time. And it's worth sending me with it, to ensure it arrives on time and is signed for.

Apart from a clean record, of course, the only qualifications you really need for a job like that is to be reliable, fit enough to travel a lot, and ideally, free of domestic ties so that there's no hassle from a frequently-abandoned family. And I tick all the boxes. Most of the time, anyway. I've managed to be reliable so far, although the boss doesn't see how close it gets sometimes. I still don't know how I stayed fit enough to deal with the time-shifts, crap food, or the strange hours, or of course the time I needed – ok, chose - to kill in iffy bars and clubs, nor how long I could go on doing it. I guess every job has its own stress points.

But, like any job, there are ways to make it easier. Take reliability, for example. The boss commits to a time. On the face of it, I need to deliver to that time. But I would always check with the client. Often, the time the boss has told me is just his idea of how quickly we can do it. But the customer's satisfaction depends on me getting there in his timeframe. Usually, the boss being keen, he over-commits. The customer will give me the actual timeframe, and it would often buy me an extra hour or more, asleep or lingering over breakfast or lunch. It helps. In fact, it kept me alive this time.

So, when my story starts, I'm a courier. But none of us is defined by our job, or at any rate, we shouldn't be. What am I really, then? At this time, I was 39 years old. No one ever believes you when you say you're 39. You must be 40-odd, they think, and lying to hold back the years. No, I really am 39. Or I was when my story begins.

I lived alone in my small flat in Chiswick, which I bought outright a while ago, and I probably drank too much, but that's okay, because I tried to eat sensibly, and cook my own food with proper ingredients whenever I could, and I've never smoked. I'm just under six feet tall, about thirteen stone, and I have brownish hair and light brown eyes. I don't think I'm particularly good-looking, but as far as women go, I do okay.

Before becoming a courier, I had a very well-paid sales management job in the IT sector. I invested some bonus money in shares that did quite well, and in property that did very well. At one time, my house and shares were earning more than I was, which was saying something.

Then, I pulled the plug. They call it "executive burn-out" now, but to me it just felt as if I'd done enough, and I simply quit, just after completing the biggest deal I'd ever done. It felt like the high you're supposed to leave on, so I left. Soon after that, my wife also left me. But let's not dwell on that.

So, after a long, sunny and self-indulgent holiday in Spain, I walked into the courier firm we used to use now and then and asked for a job. The biggest problem was persuading them that I was serious. Of course, they needed references, and they checked me for criminal records and so on. And I had just done a flaky thing, chucking in a "good job" and all that. Persuading them that I was serious and not a nutcase was just a sales job, though: probably the last deliberate one I did.

This turned out to be a great job. Being a courier gave me freedom, involved paid travel to places I mainly knew and enjoyed, and hours I more or less chose for myself. Beyond getting the consignment to the right place at the right time, I had no responsibilities, and there were no politics or targets. It paid a lot less than I'd been used to, but I spent much less now, compared to the old days. And I had some money left from the high times - easily enough to fund the odd week off work, anyway.

When I met new drinking buddies, or girls, around the world, I could be whatever I wanted to be. I was pretty convincing; after all, I knew all the right moves and all the buzzwords. Anyway, that's all that matters about me at that time, for now.

I re-packed my overnight bag, locked the flat behind me, and, in bright crisp sunshine, walked down towards Chiswick High Road to catch the tube. The station near the office was 3 stops short of Heathrow, and I strolled in to find things as busy as usual. As I waited for the boss to appear in response to her announcement that I was here, I exchanged banter with Lizzie on reception.

Ah, the lovely Lizzie. Last Christmas, after the office party, I'd had a brief liaison with her – a cliché, I know, but there you are. She was a bit older than my usual squeeze: about my age, and married, albeit somewhat loosely – her husband, she confided, was serving time in an open prison somewhere for a timeshare scam. He was what they used to call a "bad lot." She deserved better, although I wasn't sure I qualified.

No-one else in the firm knew about the prison thing, or so she said. Naturally, I said nothing to anyone. We didn't think they knew about our liaison, either. She was strawberry blonde, freckled and a lovely shape. I think we both fancied a repeat performance sometime, but the husband represented too much baggage for my liking. Without that, well, who knows?

The phone buzzed. Lizzie picked it up and exchanged a few words. "OK, Tiger, he's ready for you." She leant forward and lowered her voice. "So am I", she winked.

I grinned back at her. "Bet you say that to all the boys."

"No," she smiled. Hmm. Later, maybe, I thought.

I knew that Clive Cook, the boss, was about 50, but he looked more like 60. He was too fat for his own good, and too lazy to follow up on his own designs on Lizzie, who regarded him with amused disdain. As I entered his scruffy office, he was engrossed in the racing pages of The Sun, deciding which unfortunate nags were going to saddled with his daily fiver in his regular combination bet, which he swore would make him rich one day. Yeah, one day ...

"Hi Joe." He gestured towards an aluminium case on the floor beside him. Depending on your point of view, it was a small suitcase or a large briefcase. Cabin-baggage sized, anyway. With combination locks either side of the handle. "There's your package. Lizzie has the paperwork." Not a man for small talk, our Clive. I picked up the case, and he told me that I had to get to a bloke called Finklestein in a suite on the 65th floor of the World Trade Center in New York, at half past eight next morning.

"Don't overdo it tonight – get there on time in the morning. 8:30", he said, and went back to his equine research.

"Thanks Clive. Give those bookies some stick," I said and left him to it. He may have grunted a reply; he may not.

Clive – or more likely Lizzie - had booked a cab to take me to the airport, which was unusual but handy, and it was waiting outside. Lizzie handed over the job papers in an A4 envelope. I blew a kiss at her, in reply to which she blushed, which was really rather cute, and I stepped outside and jumped into the cab.

As the taxi ground its way through the traffic and out to Heathrow, I thought about Lizzie. She had baggage in large amounts, as I said, but as a wise man once told me at a bar one evening, "When you get to our age, and you meet someone who you think you might settle down with, and she hasn't got baggage, well, *that's* the baggage." Very true.

Smoothly checked in through the Business Class express desk, and comfortably installed in the lounge, I collected coffee and a bacon sandwich and read The Times for an hour. The plane was on time for once, and I boarded as soon as possible to ensure I had access to the overhead locker directly above my seat. Once I'd stowed the briefcase and settled into my window seat, I watched my fellow passengers organise themselves and the cabin staff bustle about looking busy. I wondered whether they were staying over in New York. Particularly that pretty brunette with the nice smile and empty ring finger.

Chapter 2

Same Old New York

We touched down at JFK pretty much on time: 2 PM local time, Monday 10th September; a warm, blue-sky afternoon. I was, as usual, amazed at the Immigration Officers – how and why did the US manage to select the most obstructive, humourless, suspicious types for visitors' first official encounter with the country?

The first taxi in line when I finally reached the rank outside the Arrivals building was a typical NYC taxi: beat-up, worn out and driven by a guy who spoke a variation of English known nowhere else. I told him where I wanted to go, and that I wanted to take a bridge rather than a tunnel, then sat back. No matter how bad the taxis were, I couldn't bring myself to arrive into Manhattan any other way. I needed to see that amazing skyline to psyche myself up for the frantic pace, somehow. And it looked easily as stunning on this sunny afternoon as it ever had.

The Belvedere was a scruffy but clean hotel on the extreme east side of Midtown. I'd done a deal with them a year or so ago whereby I paid cash for twelve nights upfront at a time, and they gave me a handwritten receipt for my maximum hotel allowance each time I stayed. The substantial difference between these amounts, plus my "subsistence allowance", which was a predetermined amount, no receipts needed, went on the evening's food and drink and whatever entertainment presented itself as the evening progressed.

I paid off the taxi and made myself known at reception. Ramon nodded a greeting and passed me a key card without breaking off from checking in a bemused Japanese honeymoon couple. God knows what they were doing here. My room was 343 - at the side, slightly away from the noise of the main streets. Good.

After finding the room, the first task was to stash the big aluminium briefcase. It was much too large for the room safe, and I wasn't going to trust Ramon's office "safe." So I hid it in the fitted drawer unit. Pulling the bottom drawer right out and removing it revealed a large void below, where I put the briefcase, and put the drawer back. It wasn't all that safe, or original, but it had worked fine so far, even when my room had been robbed a couple of times in much less salubrious locations.

I yawned. I may have slept in my seat for an hour or so, but I always found flying any distance quite tiring. I had time for a kip, before going out in the evening. But first, I decided to call the client. I got the papers out of my pocket and looked again at the label on at the briefcase under the drawer. The names matched, which wasn't always the case. I rang the number of the guy's office.

Joe Finklestein was his name. I'd almost given up when he answered. "Finklestein."

"Ah, Mr. Finklestein. This is Mr. Best from the courier service."

"Yeah? Something wrong? You'd better not ..."

"No, no, Mr. Finklestein. Not at all. I'm here in New York now, all ready to deliver to you tomorrow morning."

This was my posh voice. New Yorkers who knew the difference were always impressed. They only knew Michael Caine and Roger Moore as English accents. The rest were just not English. A Yorkshire friend of mine had given up, and, to save time, admitted to being Australian as often as not. I could do both acknowledged English voices. I could do a fair American accent as well. Not regional, but accepted in most places. Anyway, this evening, I was Roger Moore.

Finklestein calmed down. A bit. "You're early. I don't want the documents now. You do have them?"

"Yes, sir, I do. No problem. I just wondered what would be your best time tomorrow morning. We like to be convenient. Helpful." You could say any old nonsense to these New Yorkers if you were Roger Moore. You could even make lots of dodgy films, I reflected.

"Oh. Well, not before nine." No danger of that, sunshine. "But by eleven-thirty, latest. I need it for a morning meeting."

You see? The boss had said "Half-eight. No later." Now I had longer in bed. Well, longer out of it, more like.

"Very good, Mr. Finklestein. I'll be there by ten thirty, if that's ok? I look forward to seeing you."

"Yeah. Sure." Click. Brrr. Rude bugger.

Good, then. There was time for a good night out and an easy delivery to the client's satisfaction tomorrow. I lay on the bed for some sleep. Two hours, I told myself. To be safe, I set the alarm on my clever but cheap (i.e. okay to have stolen) watch to give me the two hours' kip, and settled down. As usual, I was asleep within 5 minutes.

I woke just before the alarm, it seemed. It took me some time to shake off the sleep: I could have slept on, but that would be no fun. I showered and changed my shirt and underwear. I would always do this in a new town, especially if I've time-shifted. It feels like turning a page, somehow. I put on a blue and white striped shirt I'd found in a Tommy Hilfiger outlet store, my chinos and Gap blazer again, and buttoned my wallet into my hip pocket with a couple of hundred dollars and a credit card in it. The look was preppy, as they used to call it, but local.

Down in the lobby, Ramon was watching a basketball game on the TV. I had told him that, in England, it was mainly played by schoolgirls, but he thought it was my Crazy English Sense of Humour. "Ha-ha. Benny Hill." Yeah, OK. In search of a taxi, I walked up towards the main drag and, this being New York, soon found one. The driver spoke reasonable English, and I told him to take me to the bar of a well-known upmarket chain hotel I knew, not far from the park. Slumming it at my own hotel was all very well, but right now, I wanted a reasonably posh bar, with reasonably posh birds.

A good chain hotel was better for this than the really upmarket stuff, where they were too snooty to engage in bar banter. And airlines didn't check stewardesses in at the Plaza, but they did sometimes use the better chains in town, if they had a longer layover.

The first-floor cocktail bar seats looked out over the street and back down across the bar and over the cavernous foyer. It was bustling with the after-work crowd, but I found a seat at the bar. There was a Bartender there at once. That was something I liked about New York. They actually wanted to serve you stuff. "What can I get you, sir?" asked the uniformed young man. What indeed? Hmm. Nothing too strong, but I hated American beer.

"I think I need a Bloody Mary", I answered. "Not too strong."

The Bartender stared. "You want a weak one, sir?" Clearly an unusual request.

"Yeah. Had a bit of a heavy night, then flew in here today. Need to start slow, you know?"

"Ah. I see, sir. Would that be Absolut Vodka, easy on the Wor-ses-ter-shire sauce?"

"Yup. Exactly." We understood each other perfectly. He mixed it and passed it to me. Grabbing some peanuts from a bowl in front of me, I sat back and looked around, looking for likely crumpet, or at least a drinking pal.

In fact, he found me. A voice from the next seat said, "Had a bit of a wild one, buddy?"

This was a bloke, about my build, which was "average", so no surprises there; maybe a bit older as far as I could tell. He was grinning at me. Not gay, I guessed. Just from out of town and having a drink. OK. I'd see where this went.

"Yeah. In London. Then I had to fly here at short notice." I shrugged, a simple Global Villager. I decided that I would be a big hitter for a while, subject to flying round the globe at a moment's notice, to deal with otherwise insoluble problems.

My new pal nodded his understanding and recognition of a fellow big hitter. He handed me his card. "Brett Foster", he announced. His card confirmed this, and added his title "VP, West Coast Sales" and a name of a firm I'd never heard of, with the phrase "Oil Exploration Equipment." Ah. Should have an expense account then.

"Hi, Brett. I'm Joe. Joe Best. Sorry, I left my cards in my room." We shook hands. He offered me another drink, then in due course I offered him one. He was more forthcoming than I was, in the American style. He was going to the WTC himself tomorrow morning, for a job interview. He intended to be there at 8:30, and then had a crunch meeting later with his current firm, at one, uptown. He seemed to think he could jump ship before he was pushed down the plank. I wished him luck and we had another drink.

Then he started to tell me about his wife. I drifted off a bit, but I think he said that she was early forties, to his late forties, and had been a cheerleader but had gone to seed a bit, and that she was angling for a divorce, which he was okay with but didn't want to get ripped off. By the wife or 'The Lawyers'. I could empathise with that. I guess we passed an hour or so in unremarkable man-chat, as the after-work vibe slowly changed and the more serious early evening cocktail and dinner crowd moved in.

He had to be up earlier than I did to get down to the WTC, but he was game for a bit of fun. He nodded briefly towards a table in the middle of the bar area where two girls were sitting, sipping some sort of cocktails. "You wanna give those two the once over?" I took a quick glance, and decided that they would definitely do for me.

One was classically blonde and beautiful. From the top down, she had shoulder-length honey blonde hair, toothpaste ad teeth, and as far as I could tell, a pert trim figure with natural breasts. She was wearing a short dark blue tailored skirt and cream satin blouse that showed just the right amount of cleavage. She looked too expensively dressed for a secretary, but slightly too well turned out to be an exec winding down at the end of the day. And anyway, this was not your typical Manhattan after-work bar.

On that quick glance, I thought they could be hookers, but somehow it was the other one that convinced me. She was small and dark, possibly some Asian blood in the mix. She was wearing a dark red satin blouse, again just the right amount of cleavage, and tight black trousers. She was smaller than her friend, more petite all round, but somehow more blatantly sexy. Call me sexist by all means, but if this girl was not very available, either for money or otherwise, I've completely lost my touch, I thought.

They had that skill that some girls seem to learn quite early in life, where they could scan the entire room, making sure that were having the maximum effect on every male present, without overtly paying any attention to anything except to their own conversation. I turned to the Bartender. "Those girls behind us, at that table. Are they regulars?"

"You could say that, sir. They often come here at the start of the evening."

"Do they, now? Good-lookers, aren't they?"

"I guess you need to be in their line of work, sir," he said archly, and went to serve a couple further down the bar.

So, that confirmed it, pretty well. I grinned at Brett. "Looks like we'll need some funds, but I'm up for it if you are."

Brett caught the blonde girl's eye and smiled. She smiled back and changed position slightly, moving away from the other girl slightly and making their table seem more open for us to join them. It was subtly done, polished. It reeled us in, anyway. We walked over and sat down, Brett, the blonde, me and the dark girl, in a semicircle at the round table, in that order. I waved a waiter over. We ordered drinks and introduced ourselves. The girls were Mandy, the blonde one, and Cherry. Or so they said.

We chatted about nothing much as we brought the subject subtly round to the main business of the evening. They laughed enthusiastically at our witticisms and were just slightly too interested in our jobs and our lifestyles. Mine was pretty well all fiction anyway. It was Cherry, the darker girl, who made the first move.

"So, you guys have lots of money to spend on partying, then?"

"Well, yes, if we're having a good time. But we do like to bet on certainties", I countered. "Another drink?"

"How about some champagne?" asked Mandy, the blonde, leaning into Brett, just enough to make a refusal impossible. It seemed that they'd already decided who was having whom. And vice versa.

Brett smiled. "I have an idea. I have a suite here. Two connected rooms. Why not get some room service and have a small party, just the four of us?" Oh. That was handy: a suite had possibilities. This was working out well.

The girls exchanged a glance. "We'll just go to the Ladies Room", said Mandy. "Then we'll talk about that."

I turned to Brett. "Brett, do you know the drill here? I mean, how much is this likely to be? They don't look cheap, do they?"

"Well, who wants cheap? I'm sure they'll be working that out now. You are up for it, aren't you?"

"Oh, yes. Definitely. I only have a couple of hundred in cash and my cards, that's all. I may need to go out to an ATM."

"Don't worry. Look, give me the cash and I'll deal with it. You can get more later if we need it. I've got a pile of cash in my room safe. I was hoping something like this would come up." He was evidently an old hand at this.

"Okay, thanks. I'll let you fix it up and I'll pay for these drinks and the bar tab with my card." I gave him my cash and waved the waiter over, as the girls sashayed over from the restrooms at the far end of the bar. Every male eye was watching them. Most female eyes were as well, with a range of emotions: jealousy, envy, outrage, and probably lust here and there.

Brett stood up to meet the girls as I went to deal with the waiter, who took my card off to process. They were ready to go upstairs, and Brett told me the suite number and took them off while I waited for the waiter to return with my card and the slip.

When I got to the room Brett was on the phone to room service. He winked at me, which I took to mean that he had sorted out the commercial aspects. He ordered two bottles of champagne, a bottle of vodka and some tonics, checking with a glance that that suited everyone. "Can we get something to eat?" asked Mandy. Brett added steak sandwiches to his order.

There was a small sitting area with 2 sofas and an armchair and TV. Doors led to a bathroom and two bedrooms. I looked round with Cherry. The bedroom Brett had chosen on arrival was naturally the biggest, but the second room was fine, with another TV. For a Manhattan hotel, this was very spacious. I turned the lights on low, and we went back to the central lounge area.

"Nice suite, Brett", I smiled.

"Yeah: I use my loyalty points, and they have to give me an upgrade if they have one. I chatted up the bookings clerk on the phone and she gave me this."

"Nice", smiled Mandy, putting her arms round Brett and kissing his cheek. "How about some music?"

Brett found a CD player and an assortment of CDs. He selected some smoochy piano jazz I didn't recognise, and it oozed out of hidden speakers, low and sexy. There was a knock at the door and the waiter arrived with the drinks and sandwiches. Brett signed the slip and put the tray on the table in front of the sofa.

I took my jacket off and dropped it over the back of the sofa, then eased off the cork and poured us a glass of champagne each. I put my hands round Cherry's waist as I did so, dancing her slowly into the second bedroom with the open bottle in my spare hand. The music followed us through speakers in the ceiling. I turned and winked at Brett and kicked the door shut behind us.

Cherry giggled as I ran my hands over her lithe body as we danced. She stood back and reached behind her to unhook her skirt. It dropped to the floor, and, swaying with the music, she slowly unbuttoned her blouse and dropped that as well. This left an expensive-looking satin bra and panties set. She sashayed up to me and pushed me down so that I was sitting on the bed. She sat facing me on my lap, legs either side, and reached behind her to unhook her bra.

It was about one in the morning by the time Brett called time on the session. It was a bit early, but that was okay by me. He wanted to get down to the WTC for his interview in good time in the morning, and he needed some sleep if he was to do well at the interview. I'd had a fun time – well, two fun times, actually; once in the shower. We'd had a lot of fun.

Brett had already paid the girls the agreed amount upfront, but he picked up his wallet from the coffee table and gave them another fifty dollars each, as a tip. He put his wallet back in his jacket on the sofa, and asked them if they needed a cab. They said they'd manage, kissed us again and left. I think they wanted to try for one last punter downstairs: they may just have had time.

After visiting the bathroom, I came back into the sitting area. Reaching out and shaking Brett's hand, I said "Well, thanks for a great evening", I laughed. "How much do I owe you?"

"Hey, Buddy, forget it. We had a great time, didn't we? Look, be sure to call me when you're next over here. My cellphone number's on the card I gave you. It's my own, so it'll work even if I get iced today." He grinned.

"Ah, I'm sure you'll get the new job, anyway," I grinned back. "I've got your card," and I tapped my wallet in my hip pocket to reassure him. I picked up my blue jacket off the sofa, shook his hand again and left the room.

He slept well, I hope. It was his last night on earth. Mind you, it had been a bloody good night.

Chapter 3

The Whole World Watches

Having handed my money to Brett, I was out of cash, but there was a convenient ATM machine on the corner, so I took my wallet out of my hip pocket and took $200 out, and then found a late cab.

We got to the Belvedere quickly. Ramon was still on duty as I went through the lobby – I wondered in passing when he ever slept. I went straight to my room and put the 'Do Not Disturb' sign on the door and double-locked it.

Just to settle my mind, I checked the briefcase. Still there. Having brushed my teeth, rinsed my face, set my alarm and dropped my clothes on the floor, I got into bed, and fell into a happy but dreamless sleep.

I woke quite early – about 7 - feeling pretty good. I hadn't had that much to drink, and I'd had lots of sex. Plus I had been dog-tired. So, I'd managed six or seven hours of quality kip. That felt like enough, and I decided to get up and beat a leisurely path downtown to make the delivery. There was time to grab a New York diner-style breakfast on the way – I was certainly hungry.

After an unhurried shower and a shave, I dressed as usual and threw on my blue jacket from the previous evening and made for the lift. Elevator, then, since we're in New York. It came, with the Japanese couple in, silently gazing into each other's eyes. Looked like they'd had a good night as well. We arrived on the ground floor and I made straight for the door.

That's strange. There was something in my top inside pocket. I felt for it and took out a black leather wallet. Opening it, I saw that it was Brett's. It had half a dozen credit cards, a California Driver's licence and about five hundred dollars. Now, how had that happened?

It was my jacket all right, but I did remember that Brett had a similar one. Then I remembered him getting his wallet from the table to give the girls a hundred each, and then putting it in his jacket on the sofa. Except, in fact, that had been my jacket, not his. Why hadn't I noticed it last night? Because I was shagged out, I suppose. Literally, you might say.

So, what would happen when Brett woke up and looked for his wallet? He would probably think he'd been robbed: either by the girls or perhaps even by me. And how had he got to the WTC for his interview? Had he managed to go at all? I decided to call his hotel, in case he was still there, stranded. He was a partner in crime, after all. I felt responsible to some extent. There was a payphone on the wall in the lobby - no point in paying International cellphone charges for a cross-town call. I put a few coins in and phoned Brett's hotel.

The switchboard answered almost at once and put me through to 'Mr Brett Foster's room', as requested. No answer. The girl came back on.

"Would you like voicemail, sir?"

"Erm, no, thanks. Is the concierge available?

"I'll put you through."

Why didn't I leave a message? I don't know. For one thing, he may have checked out. Yes, I had his wallet, but he would probably have used the hotel's Express service anyway: they'd have swiped his card when he checked in, so that was covered. But he would have had to use the concierge to get a taxi without any money. The concierge came on the phone.

"Yes, sir. Can I help?"

"Yes. Mr Brett Foster. He had to get down to the World Trade Center this morning. Did he ask you to call a cab?"

"No, sir. I don't recall that."

“Ok. I see. No problem, thanks for your help.” I rang off. Then I had an idea. I checked my watch. 8:05. His interview was at half 8, as I remembered. Putting some more coins in, I rang Brett’s cellphone. He answered, sounding slightly hassled.

“Foster.”

“Brett, it’s Joe Best. I have your wallet.”

“What? You do? Why?”

“Well, I think you must have put it in my jacket instead of yours by accident last night. You have a blue cotton Gap jacket, don’t you? Well, so do I.”

“Oh. Yeah, I do. I see. Well, hey, that’s a relief. I thought those girls had robbed me. I was about to cancel everything – all the cards. Good job I didn’t, I guess. Can you get it back to me? I’ve just arrived at the building. Didn’t you say you were coming here as well?”

“Yes: I’m about to set off. Where are you? Which tower? What floor?”

He told me – it was the other one - the North Tower, quite high up. “OK,” I said, “How about we meet after our meetings? Early lunch, maybe?” He suggested that we meet in a diner he knew, at street level. I had plenty of time. “OK, I’ll get there as soon as I’m free. Wait for me. My call for lunch.”

“Right, thanks, buddy, I’ll see you then … I have to go into the building now. It takes a while to get to the higher floors.”

“Okay. Good luck.” I rang off. His interview hadn’t started yet, but he’d obviously arrived at the building safely, so that was OK.

I walked out of the hotel and hailed a taxi and asked to go towards the World Trade Center. We were in traffic, and it was the rush hour. But I was in no hurry. I’d get breakfast somewhere near the WTC and deliver the briefcase in good time, and then give Brett his wallet back. It would all be okay. I sat back and relaxed, everything under control.

Of course, as everyone now knows, things were about to spiral very much out of control ...

Chapter 4

One of Our Agents is Missing

Two hours later, back in London, a silent, shocked audience was staring at the TV screen in Clive's office. Clive's initial refusal to relinquish his habitual racing coverage to the news programmes had quickly given way to fascinated horror. The events that were unfolding there put the regular shredding of his dreams of the big win in a new perspective. He was glued to the global drama that was playing out for all the world to watch, along with the entire staff. They all knew that Joe was in New York, but only Clive knew where the drop was.

Clive had a feeling that there was – or anyway, had been, something between Joe and Lizzie, and he was wondering whether and when he ought to let her know just how close Joe had been to this horror.

"Lizzie, would you phone Joe's mobile for me please?" he asked.

"Do you think he's OK?" Lizzie was already on the brink of tears. "How close was he – where was the delivery?"

Clive swallowed. "There." He pointed at the TV screen. "About 2 hours ago, though. He should be out by now. Just check he's OK, will you?"

Almost without noticing it, Lizzie started to cry. She had a bad feeling about this. She left Clive's office and sat at her desk, where she dialled Joe's mobile number. As she listened to the single ring tone, unlike the UK double-tone, she reached for a tissue from the box on her desk. The ring-tones stopped and she heard Joe's voice.

"Hi, it's Joe", she heard.

"Oh, thank God you're all right ..." she started, but stopped suddenly as the voice went on "... sorry I can't take your call, but please leave me a message and I'll get right back to you as soon as I can," Joe's voice continued.

"Oh, Joe, please let us know you're OK. Please – as soon as you can. Oh, God ..." Lizzie was crying hard now. She burst back into Clive's office. All eyes turned to her – she was clearly distraught. "I can't find him. It was his voicemail ... I heard his voice." she wasn't making much sense even if you could make out what she was saying through her anguished tears.

Clive motioned for Preeti, the accounts controller, to look after her. "Look, he was supposed to be there at 8:30. Simple handover, sign the docket, away. He'll be well away from there by now, I'm sure."

"Oh, Clive, for God's sake!" said Lizzie. "Didn't you know? Joe always checks with the client to see when he really needs the stuff. He never pays attention to your timeframes. He delivers when it's needed, not whenever you think he can get there. Hadn't you realised that? He'll probably have moved it - a bit later. And anyway, it was just half an hour after that when the plane hit. Even on your times, he'd still be in the building. On his, he certainly would."

"Well, the cheeky sod. He always gets good feedback. You wait till I see him."

"If you ever do," added a lugubrious voice from the back of the room. It was Pete, one of the van drivers. He'd just returned from dropping a consignment of domestic effects at Heathrow air freight depot. "They say one of these planes is on its way across the Atlantic to London. They're evacuating the big buildings in the City."

"Don't be ridiculous," said Clive. "That couldn't happen."

"Neither could this", said Pete. "But look. It's happening."

At this, Lizzie broke down completely, and Preeti took her out to the ladies, while Clive lapsed into a contemplative silence. The TV kept on showing the pictures and running a baffled commentary.

"OK, said Clive after a few minutes. "There's nothing we can do. Someone keep phoning him, and if any of you are religious, you can pray that he's all right. He would be if he'd followed my instructions properly," he added defensively.

Preeti ordered a taxi to take Lizzie home, and at the last minute decided to go with her. Clive watched the TV for another 3 hours, then went to the pub and drank far more than he expected. It seemed that he had a heart after all, and he was wishing he hadn't.

Chapter 5

To be - or Not to be

I needed to think about this - to sit down quietly and work it out. I still had the briefcase. That probably held a clue as to what to do next, so I obviously had to open it. Should I have called the office? Probably, but I wasn't thinking very clearly. It seemed obvious that I needed to get back to the hotel.

The subway had shut down. The station under the WTC was obviously wrecked, and the trains couldn't run there, even if the authorities hadn't decided to close the whole system. I saw gates across all the station entrances as I walked north. So, I walked all the way back to the hotel. There was none of the usual bustle. Everyone was in bars or shops, glued to CNN. Some of the smell and the dust had got this far up by now.

As I walked through the foyer of the hotel, I saw that Ramon was – at last – taking some time off. There was a small squat Hispanic woman at the desk, riveted to the TV screen, with some guests watching from the customer side of the counter. I don't think anyone would have noticed me if I'd been riding on a camel, to be honest, but I had put on dark glasses anyway. If I was indeed dead, I didn't want anybody seeing a ghost.

My key was in my pocket, so I went through reception and up to my room without attracting any attention. The Do Not Disturb sign was still on the outside. I'd forgotten to take it off. The maid had left the room alone. I double-locked the door behind me and turned on the TV. Both towers were down now. The commentary was disjointed, and they kept showing the whole sequence, from the first strike to the second collapse. It was compelling, awful viewing. They were showing people walking and running away from the area, covered in dust. They looked like ghosts. I'd been on the edge of that. And nearly in the deadly centre of it.

I took out my information pack and put the briefcase on the bed. Up to now the briefcase had been, well, just a thing I had to hand over, safe and sound. Now, it was a piece of a puzzle. It was an aluminium case, larger than a briefcase, more like a small suitcase. It just qualified as hand baggage and I'd stowed it in the overhead bin: it fitted in there quite neatly. There were two combination locks, one on either side of the handle, with three numbers each. The locks didn't look like they'd force easily, but I had the combination.

Of course, we didn't just write down the combination in our notes. We had a code for the odd occasion we needed to open our boxes or briefcases, when the client forgot or didn't have it, for example. Or when airport security wanted to see inside.

For really valuable stuff we usually used electronic locks that shut out for up to an hour after each unsuccessful attempt. And of course, there were cases with explosive dye canisters and spikes if the locks were forced. We didn't usually chain the cases to our wrists. That would be advertising the fact that we had valuables with us. I preferred not to, anyway.

This case looked pretty strong: it may well have dye or something. My notes said the combination was 3,4,3,6,5,8. That was the usual "up and down" code. So, I set the counter to 2,5,2,7,4,9. The locks sprang open. I opened the lid.

Bloody hell.

There was a selection of paper in the case. The most immediately astonishing was just beneath a sheet of brown paper that lay immediately on top of everything. There were neatly stacked dollar bills apparently filling the entire case. All used, and of various denominations, but I could see some hundreds. I lifted some out. In fact, they filled more than half the case, stacked in bundles, three by six. I took them all out and counted them. Eighteen bundles. All used, mostly high denominations. I flicked them all to see. I couldn't guess the actual amount at a glance, but I reckoned it had to be a million - probably more. In something of a daze, I looked at the other stuff.

Below the cash there was what was obviously some sort of contract. I speed-read it, trying to make sense of this package. I quickly saw that it was for the sale of a company from one organisation to another. I didn't recognise either one, but I thought I saw an Italian name. Scanning the pages, looking for the price, I found it on the second page of about thirty. Twenty-five million dollars. There were some signatures on this page, but space for more. I set the contract aside.

The rest of the case was full of Bearer Bills. These were in various amounts, but the ones I could see were all high tens of thousands of dollars. There was no named payee. I knew what these were. They were irrevocable and they were as good as cash. But they had to be passed through a bank, so their encashment was traceable. They were like cheques, signed and ready to deposit to another account. But they could not be cancelled.

So, I had probably a million or more in cash and a lot more in Bills. Maybe – no, probably - the entire twenty-five million. I was dead, as far as the world was concerned, and this briefcase was most likely crushed, burnt or otherwise irretrievably lost for ever. So were the main principals of the deal, probably. Certainly, the middleman was, or whatever Finklestein was.

I had to decide what to do. Firstly, I repacked the case, locked it and spun the combination numbers. Tucking the coded combination in my wallet, I put my jacket back on. Brett's wallet was in the inside jacket pocket, and my own was in my hip pocket. My passport was in the room safe, and I took it out. I had about $500 between both wallets. My small overnight case was still on the dresser, and my wash bag in the bathroom. I wasn't going to need any of this stuff, so I left it where it was.

Although it all looked as if I was coming back, I felt sure I wasn't. The room maid had not been in since I left – it was lucky that I'd left the

Do Not Disturb sign on by accident. I left the room, locking the door again and leaving the DND sign on. They would sort that out later. Not my problem. I was dead.

Then my phone rang. It was eerily normal. The phone was in my top jacket pocket. The moment of time needed to reach for it delayed my instinct to answer: I simply picked it up and looked at it. The caller was "Unknown" – that probably meant it could be foreign – most likely, the office. As I hesitated, it stopped. The voicemail had evidently cut in, and the phone went dead again. If I had answered, or if I checked my voicemail, I was alive. If I left it, I could decide later. But really, I suppose I had already decided.

Reaching the lobby unnoticed, I went out the back way with the case. They were all glued to the TV anyway. For some reason, I felt I needed to get out of NYC. Making my way towards the subway entrance, I saw from a distance that these gates were closed, like all the others. So it wasn't just the local system to the crash scene - it seemed that the whole subway system was suspended.

On a hunch, I walked westwards, over to Penn Station. It seemed from the movement of people and the signage that some trains were still running. Locating the ticket window, I bought a single to Philadelphia. First Class. Cash.

The train was at the platform, and it left in half an hour. It rolled out, dead on time, with a dead man on board. A very rich dead man.

Chapter 6

A time to think

Why was I going to Philadelphia? Well, NYC wasn't working properly, and wouldn't for quite a while, I reckoned. Plus, I had never been to Philly. No one knew me there, and I reasoned that they wouldn't know Brett Foster there either. If I was going to create a new life, and that was a clear possibility, I needed to get out of New York and disappear. I needed to be sure that no one could follow my tracks. No one would think of looking for me in Philly. Plus, it was the nearest big city I could go to without checking in through an airline desk that might have needed my ID. Although I wasn't sure what I was going to do, I was sure that I needed to leave no footprints.

As the emergency situation and official reaction to it quickly spread, all flights within, into or out of the USA were cancelled, eventually for a week. I had seen on a TV at the station that the Pentagon had been hit as well, and there were all sorts of rumours about other targets. It was getting pretty scary, even for a Brit, used to the IRA's atrocities over the last twenty years or so. This made that look like kid's stuff.

The train was scheduled to stop at Newark and Trenton, N.J., then on to Philly and then Washington D.C. Just under 2 hours to Philly. Plenty of time to think. The case was beside me, on the seat by the window. I took the aisle seat. I would have to take the case with me if I went to the loo, of course. Unconsciously, I put my hand on the case, closed my eyes and concentrated. I used to be a good strategic thinker back in the old days.

Facts first, then. I had, say, a million dollars plus of untraceable cash. I had a feeling that the whole contract amount was actually in the case, so let's say another twenty-odd million dollars in irrevocable but visible instruments. Visible, meaning that when, or if, I turned them into usable funds, I'd leave a trail.

There were also the credit cards and ID as Brett Foster. Question: was the ID any use? Taking the wallet from my jacket, I looked at the licence and the photo. The licence had been recently renewed. The photo showed Brett with possibly slightly darker hair than me and square brown-rimmed glasses. He must have been wearing contacts last night. It wasn't a great picture, or even very clear. I thought that if I brushed my hair like his and got some reading glasses, I could use it in most places. OK, good.

Looking through the rest of the wallet for the first time, I saw several credit cards. Personal and Corporate Amex and two each of Visa and MasterCard, all personal. The signature wasn't complicated. I thought I could do it with a little practice. I looked for a family photo. None. He hadn't been acting like a family man, but you never know. There was an address, "if found", on a card in the picture window. In San Diego. Was that his own address or a service? What would an oil man be doing living in San Diego? Well, he sold engineering stuff. Maybe he wasn't an oil man as such. Useless to speculate. Leave it for now. Apart from the five hundred dollars, five hundred and twenty, in fact, that was it.

Ok, facts again. I had a workable ID and credit cards – Brett's - that hadn't been cancelled. Brett had said so in that fateful telephone call, and he hadn't been sacked yet, so both company and personal cards were probably still live. But using them would leave a trail that would ring some bells somewhere eventually. In any case, they would be cancelled sometime, once the dust had settled and Brett was acknowledged, or even suspected, to be dead and gone.

The ID would work, casually, for quite a while. But if anyone investigated it, that would ring bells as well. But there was no traceable link between me and Brett.

Or was there? Let me think. The two girls, Mandy and Cherry – or whatever their real names were – knew that we were linked, at least casually. But they probably didn't know our names, and anyway, who could find them?

Well, the Bartender would probably remember us picking up the girls, and the bar bill was on my credit card. And the room service waiter might possibly remember the four of us in the suite. So it would be possible to link me and Brett if anyone had a reason to dig deep enough, and did it before the Bartender and waiter forgot us in the shock of today's events. If anyone really needed to, and the Bartender did remember, they could also find the girls, I supposed. But this was all a very long shot. And why would anyone bother?

So, what about the phone calls? The concierge might remember that someone had called concerning Brett, but he would have no idea who it was or why he phoned – if he recalled it at all. That could be important, if anybody investigated Brett thoroughly. And if Brett, a dead man, started to use his credit cards, they might well do that in due course.

My call to Brett would be on his cellphone record. At any rate, I had to assume that it could be recovered from the system, if anyone had a reason to try. It would show a call from a payphone in the lobby of the Belvedere, where Joe Best, another WTC victim, was staying. So what? All this was genuine coincidence, no more. Unless you were trying to find a link. The call to Finklestein from the downtown payphone would mean nothing. I doubt anyone would even find a record of that.

So, if anyone was given enough reason to dig deeply and carefully enough, and was really lucky, they might eventually discover that Brett and I had met in the hotel, had drinks and taken some girls up to his room. So what? And why would they dig? If they needed to find out whether either or both of us were really dead, for one thing. They would have no reason to think Brett was still alive, unless I used his credit cards or driving licence.

I suppose the owner of the briefcase would want to check that I was dead, but he could probably only look for proof that I wasn't. Eventually, he'd have to accept that I was dead and gone without trace – along with the money. It seemed almost certain that they wouldn't find and identify each and every body, nothing like.

So, I couldn't use my own passport and credit cards. They would leave a clear trail, and that would be worse for me than a "Brett" trail. I could see no reason at all to use my cards, and plenty not to. Apart from the company one, they were all near their limits anyway. I'd get rid of them. But I'd keep my passport. I might need credit cards, at least in the next few weeks, and if so I'd use Brett's and then dispose of them as well.

Next question: had I left a ghostly presence anywhere after the second plane hit? Well, no one would remember me in the diner or on the street on my walk back to the hotel. Everyone was either panic-stricken, catatonic or glued to CNN. Or all of the above. What about the Belvedere? No, that was fine. They were all watching TV and had their backs to me. No one knew me to recognise me anyway. I hadn't done anything in my room that would have suggested that I had returned there after the strike. It hadn't been cleaned, so there were no new traces, and my personal stuff was still there.

So the chances were I had passed through and out of NYC without leaving a trace after the WTC disaster. Cash for the train ticket. No ID needed anywhere. Thanks to a series of coincidences, good and bad habits and good luck, I had vanished along with millions of dollars, and no one would come looking for me. At least, not for ages, if ever.

I could see no way that anyone could ever suspect that I never made it to the WTC. They would surely never find all the bodies and be able to say that I was not in that number. I wasn't sure just how I would convert the Bills to cash and disappear, but I was fairly sure that I could do that before anyone picked up my very faint trail of my movements after the WTC and the people in it were destroyed.

So, I could probably pull this off. I was away. The game was on.

However ... I still didn't have to play. I could still call the office and let them know I was safe. Maybe I could possibly keep the money and still go home as Joe Best. If I told them that I'd delivered early and got out just before the plane hit, I could stash the briefcase somewhere and come back for it when the fuss died down.

So, let's work that one through. I would need to show the receipt, signed by Finklestein, for the briefcase. I couldn't fake that: I'd never seen his signature. And the client would want to see it, and that would be someone who did know what it looked like. Okay, I could have lost it, with my jacket, in the blast, and only emerged in my tattered chinos. Plenty of people had, judging by the TV pictures.

That would be a bit suspicious, though, especially when I turned out to have a million dollars or so hidden away. And I would have to destroy the Bearer Bills, because there would be no doubt who'd cashed them in. To use them, I'd need a new ID anyway.

No, no good. Either I came clean, took all this stuff back and forgot all about it, or I stayed dead, reinvented myself and started a new – rich - life. Not much of a choice, frankly. I wasn't leaving much behind: a job I couldn't do forever, a few drinking mates, and one or two casual girlfriends. And Lizzie, of course. But, bless her, she wasn't really a good reason to turn my back on a fortune. Apart from anything else, she was still married. My dad had cleared off when I was two, and my mum had died three years ago. I had other relatives, but none I needed to keep. There was no argument. Not against squillions of dollars, anyway.

Right, then. The decision seemed to be made, for now, anyway. I knew what I wanted to do. I knew that I had the chance to do it. Now I needed to figure out how to do it.

The main problem would be ID, I figured. I didn't know how long Brett's licence would work. Probably forever in casual use, but could I open a bank account with it? And if I used the credit cards, or let anyone take a permanent note of the ID, I'd be risking ringing those bells somewhere. If anyone was listening for them.

How do you get a secure, fake ID, anyway? I had never moved in the sort of circles where it mattered. Hmm. Leave that for now. What else?

Well, I couldn't keep carrying all this cash around: I had to stash it somewhere, and I couldn't pay cash for everything. Like, I needed a car, a place to live, all that sort of stuff. To get these things, you needed to have an official existence. And you didn't pay cash for a nice new Jag, did you? Or a house by the beach? Well, I suppose you could, but it would look odd. And I didn't want to attract that much attention.

Anyway, how much cash was there? I'd said a million to myself, but I didn't really know. I needed to count it properly. Not here on the train, of course. But say it was a million. That wasn't much, in fact. Renting or buying a place to live, living well, some wheels, partying ... it would soon vanish. So I would eventually need to cash the bearer bills.

Another thought: whose cash was this, anyway? It seemed a bit odd, buying a company with used notes and bearer bills, didn't it? Surely you used banks and company cheques, not suitcases full of cash and bearer bills? I needed to look again at the contract in the briefcase, to try to figure out what was going on. One thing, if it was dodgy, or even if it wasn't, then as soon as they knew I'd cashed the bearer bills, they'd come looking. Hmm.

I had another thought. Did I have to stay in the US? What about Mexico, or the Caymans? Didn't they have some interesting banking privacy laws?

By now we were approaching the outskirts of Philadelphia. My thoughts turned a bit more short term. I needed a hotel, some fresh clothes and some more thinking time. And, I realised, some grub – I was starving.

Walking through the station, following the signs to the taxi rank, I was regretting my decision to go to a city I didn't know. I had no idea what to say to the driver. As I got into the back seat, the briefcase at my side, I decided I'd just wing it.

"My plans are all screwed up today, with this terrorist crap," I said in my non-specific American accent. "I need a downtown hotel. A Marriott or something."

"You want de Marriott?" asked the driver. Oh, God, another no-speakee.

"Yeah. Downtown."

"You gott-a address?"

"No. Just drive downtown. The hotel district."

The driver seemed to think I was mad. I was missing London already. He set off, anyway, and I kept an eye open for a familiar sign. In fact, I soon saw a Hilton sign on a big square building.

"There!" I yelled at him. "Hilton. That'll do"

"Okay. Hilton. I see it. Not Marriott?"

"No – Hilton's fine."

I wondered if I'd need ID to check in, unreserved and with no credit cards. I got Brett's Licence out of the wallet, and some of the cash, and transferred it into my trouser pocket. I really didn't want to be forced to use this ID just yet, but I had to be ready.

The taxi dropped me at the front door to the hotel. I paid him and walked to the front desk with my briefcase. The receptionist was brunette, young and pretty. Her uniform white blouse fitted her perfectly. She saw me check it out. Not sure she liked that. Anyway, here goes.

“Hi. I don’t have a reservation. In fact I hadn’t intended to be in Philly at all tonight, but I can’t get a flight. Do you have a room?”

“Yes, sir. We have a room with king-size bed, or with two queen-size.”

“Great. King-size. Non-smoking.” I had to remember not to say “Please” all the time. Too English.

“Okay, sir. Name?”

“Oh, there is one other thing. I need to pay cash. I didn’t bring my pocket-book with me. Didn’t think I’d need it.” Careful. Nearly said “wallet”: too British.

“That’s okay, sir. I’ll need a deposit. It just means that we can’t give you charging facilities at the bars and restaurant.”

“Oh, fine. It’s Stein. Rick Stein.” Where did that come from? I wasn’t a chef. Peeling off two hundred dollars, I asked “Will this be okay?”

“That’s fine, sir.” She handed me a registration card. I had to think of an address, quickly. I put: Rick Stein, 120 William Street, Trenton N.J. I couldn’t think of a Zip Code. “I’m sorry, I can’t remember the Zip. Just moved in last month,” I smiled my most charming smile.

“No problem, sir. I’ll just put nines. It doesn’t check.” She keyed in the entirely bogus name and address and handed me a key card. I was in. Ironically, after today’s events, it would soon be impossible to do this in any decent hotel. They would all ask for ID. But they hadn’t had time to think about that yet.

“We have a bar and a restaurant, sir, down the hall there. Your room’s 646, and the elevators are over there,” She smiled a professional smile. My return smile cut no ice, so I made for the elevators. The room was fine. Standard Hilton, the same the world over. I put the DND on the door, double-locked it and flicked on the TV.

There was no escaping the pictures. Now there was also commentary and analysis from any talking head the studio could find. The consensus was that it was organised by some bloke called Bin Laden, and we had a picture of a genial looking chap wearing a dodgy looking beard and a turban, to show us who he was. Apparently, he'd had a go at the WTC before, with a bomb in the car park. I remembered that. The building must have annoyed him. The restaurant on the top floor had closed as a result of the first bomb. Well, it wouldn't be opening again.

It was half-five. I had been quite a day. I lay on the bed and thought back. It was too much to take in. I needed a bath and a shave. Then I realised that I had no luggage. Well, only probably twenty-five million in cash and bills. But no clean clothes, toiletries, nothing I actually needed right now.

I did the usual trick with the briefcase under the bottom drawer and moved the cash from both wallets into my trouser pockets. I slid the wallets and my passport into the room safe. I pocketed the key card and went out to the elevator again, leaving the DND sign on the door.

Back to the desk, the same girl was there. A badge on her left tit I hadn't noticed before said she was called Tracy. She caught me looking at it. Bet she thought I was staring at her tits. "Hi, Tracy", I said, to show I wasn't. Much. "Is there a store in the hotel?"

Tracy gave me the icy smile again. "Yes, sir. Just down the hall, past the bar." She looked at her watch. "It closes at six." Soon, then.

Thanking her with a hopeful smile, I went past the bar into the shop. It sold toothpaste, toothbrush, disposable razors, deodorant and aftershave, so it wasn't too bad. No clothes, though, unless I wanted a "My folks went to Philly and all they got me was this T-shirt" T-shirt, which I certainly did not.

Back in room 646, all was as I left it. From the room service menu, I ordered steak and chips and bottle of Californian Pinot Noir. I paid and tipped the room service waiter in cash, and put my meal in front of the TV. An old movie was about to start on a channel that was not showing today's events, and I set about a very good sirloin steak. The wine was good, and I realised that I was very hungry.

There was one matter I needed to resolve before I finally closed off this shocking day. To ensure I wasn't disturbed, I put the tray and plates outside the door, keeping the wine bottle, as there was at least a glass left in it, and double locked it again. I got the briefcase out, decoded the numbers and opened the locks. After removing the bundles of notes I closed it again.

The eighteen bundles almost covered the table, where the tray had been. There hadn't really been time to look very closely at it in the Belvedere. Was the money real? I picked up a bundle at random and extracted a note.

It certainly looked and felt all right. It had the watermark, and the paper seemed right. It wasn't new, but not particularly ragged. Fake notes didn't last long, as the paper and print were usually poor quality and didn't stand up to the wear and tear. Or so my airport novels had told me sometime. And I'd had the odd dodgy tenner given me in change now and then. Once by a London cabbie, who was very abusive when I wouldn't take it. If these were dodgy, they were very good. I checked a few serial numbers: all different. I took the note through to the bathroom and soaked it. It held up okay. I decided they were the genuine article.

Each bundle was three to four inches thick, secured with a thick elastic band wrapped over the middle. Very neat. The work of an accountant, probably. Someone had counted them and, possibly, neatly put them into equal value bundles. Count them, I said to myself.

It took me quite a while. I was right. Each bundle was exactly $100,000. No bills less than twenty, mostly hundreds. All used notes, all seemed genuine: I handled every one. More than I thought: one million, eight hundred thousand dollars. I had finished the wine. I needed more, really.

Opening the case again, I put the cash to one side and removed the bearer bills. They were all A4 sized, and in two single piles. About a hundred, I thought. I took those out and put them on the table.

These looked kosher as well, not that there was any test except for trying to cash one. All on the same bank, in the Caymans. I took the notepad and pen from the phone table and listed each amount. These were much higher denominations: one or two were actually for a million and one for five. I added up the figures. I checked, but it was the number I expected: twenty-three million, two hundred thousand dollars. Including the cash, the whole contract amount was in this case, in one form or another. I replaced the bonds and the cash in the case.

Now for the contract. I sat back and tried to make sense of it. Although I'd been involved with some contracts in my old life, this sort of thing was new to me but I got the general gist of the thing.

It seemed that a company called Wavetree, registered in the Caymans, was selling a company it owned, called Pinkfoot, also registered in the Caymans, to a company called Fastlake, registered in Belize. The price was twenty-five million dollars, payable on signature, and the signatories were a bloke called Costello and another bloke called Richardson.

Earlier, in my shocked state, I'd thought Costello was an Italian name when I glanced at the papers earlier. I remembered now that it was, in fact, Irish. That was certainly food for thought. Anyway, I guessed they would be dead and unidentifiable now, in the rubble of the WTC. Like me.

There was a lot of other legal wording, but I felt sure that I had understood the main thrust. That was what this document was about. It could all be above board, but it looked strange to me. It was hard to see how this deal would require the payment in cash and bills if it was all above board. Added to the Cayman and Belize registrations, it looked like money laundering to me, not that I knew anything about that. But it struck me that I was going to have to, soon.

That really was enough for one day. I had been killed, I was a millionaire several times over, and I had a new life to plan. It was all very tiring.

My last thought, before I went off to sleep, was that I would probably have done a runner just for the $1.8 million cash, and it would have been a whole lot easier. The bearer bills were a bonus. A big bonus - and a big problem. But obviously, I couldn't just destroy them. It was too much to lose.

Chapter 7

Cross-country

My first thought when I woke was that I'd forgotten my name. Not my real name: the one I'd booked in under. I knew it was a chef. It wouldn't be Ainsley Harriot. It wasn't Anthony Worral Thompson. I thought it was a posher one than that, more up-market: Gordon Ramsay? Nah. This was a bit of a worry. Maybe it wouldn't matter anyway.

I felt as if I'd slept well again: the right amount of booze and a tiring day. No nightmares. I looked at my watch: half-eight. After the usual ablutions, I sat on the bed and thought. The first thing I needed was a reliable ID. Nobody could operate without one, no matter how much cash he had. And I was going to have to get myself a comfortable and respectable base - for a few weeks, at least.

Reluctantly, I decided I needed to break cover with Brett's ID. I needed to make some preparations. I called down to reception.

"Good morning Mr. Stein. This is Nancy. How can I help?"

Ah. Rick Stein, that was it. Thank God for fancy phone systems. I wrote it down as I spoke. "Hi. What's your check out time?"

"Would you like a late check out?"

"I don't know. What's the usual time?"

"Twelve o'clock, sir."

"Okay. That'll be fine."

"Thank you sir. Would there be anything else?"

"No. Thanks." I rang off.

I showered, shaved and dressed in my old clothes. I hated that. Leaving the DND sign on the door, I went down to the lobby and found the concierge's desk. He directed me to a department store, and I went out into the street.

In the store, I bought four pairs of store brand chinos in two different colours, some polo shirts and Oxford button-downs, underpants, socks, Timberland deck shoes, a pair of boots and a baseball hat. I added a light linen and cotton jacket that looked as if it would travel well. I found the drugstore section and bought a nicer deodorant and matching aftershave, a better razor and shaving foam, some hair gel and a pair of dark-rimmed reading glasses as close to Brett's style as I could. And a driving map of the USA. In the suitcase section, I bought a good suitcase that swallowed all this lot with room to spare.

This took care of quite a lot of the cash that had been mine and Brett's. Clearly, I'd soon be starting on the millions. Taking my shopping the block or so back to the hotel, I locked myself in my room and packed the new case properly, removing labels and bags. After laying out a clean set of clothes, I showered and shaved. That, and putting on the new clean clothes, made me feel much better.

Rubbing in some gel into my hair darkened it somewhat, as well as allowing me to brush it into something like Brett's style on his photo. Adding the reading glasses, I peered into the mirror, then back at the photo. It worked. In the mirror I was looking at a semi-familiar stranger.

Now I needed to forge his signature. His licence and the cards were not quite all the same: they wouldn't be. He had a curly style. Mine tended to go up and down, a bit spikier. I filled a page of the notepad with practice attempts, and eventually seemed to be getting close.

Feeling I'd done enough on that, I took the briefcase out of its hiding place. It was time to use the cash. I took out a bundle and peeled some notes off the top. I packed my own wallet into the briefcase and put the cash into Brett's.

One more time, I took out a clean sheet of paper and did the signature again. It was good enough, even without the original to copy. I put the stuff back in Brett's wallet and put that and the glasses into the jacket pockets. I was ready for off.

Before I left, I tore the notepad sheets into strips and flushed them down the toilet, both the adding-up from last night and the practice signatures. I looked around. Nothing untoward. I chucked the DND sign back into the room, picked up my new suitcase and the briefcase and went to check out.

But at the desk, another standard-issue blonde told me that there were no flights anywhere into, out of or within the US at least today. I hadn't thought of that. "I see. Can I keep the room for a while?"

"Let me see." She rattled the keyboard. "Yes, we've had some cancellations from a conference that was booked here over the next 2 days - that won't now happen. Would you like to keep the same room?"

We agreed on that, so I extracted some more cash to cover a few more days. The receptionist re-validated my key card, and I returned to the same room and stashed the briefcase again. Eventually, I spent 5 days in Philly. 2 were easily enough to see all it had to offer, in my opinion.

Looking back, the time I spent in Philly was almost like an out-of-body experience. The whole country was in a sort of daze after the terrorist attacks. And so was I, not only due to my proximity to one of them – after all, I was nearly involved in it – but also my unexpected possession of such a huge amount of money. Those 5 days were really my last chance to come to my senses and call the office. The delay, had I called during this time, could easily be explained – shock, fear, even disorientation – any of these excuses would probably be understandable.

But I have to be honest. I never got close to calling the office. I considered it once or twice, but for less than a minute. The money – or the opportunities I imagined it would give me – appealed much more than the return to normality. At that point, I had no clear idea of what those opportunities were, or what I'd need to do to get completely clear. But I knew for certain that if I just gave up and went home, I'd regret what could have been for the rest of my life. Even if I came to regret disappearing with the money, which I doubted, that regret wouldn't compare with the daily regret of what might have been. The die was cast.

I had decided to fly to San Francisco as soon as flights were re-opened. Firstly, I liked it there. Secondly, I thought I might know someone there – a pal from way back. I might decide that I needed some help and advice. And I might trust him enough to ask for it. Thirdly, I felt that it would be a good idea to lay low for a while; I preferred to do that a long way from New York – and where better than good old San Fran, anyway?

The airport was chaotic on the day the flights started again. All flights had been grounded for 5 days, and it seemed that people and planes were all in the wrong places. Everybody wanted to fly home or to pick up their schedule, and the clerks had little idea which planes were going where.

Standing in line at the Delta desk, I put my new glasses on, and at the desk I asked for first class one-way to San Francisco airport – SFO. Name? Brett Foster. Would it be OK if I pay cash? Yes, that was fine. I still wasn't used to laying out cash like this, but the gate clerk didn't hesitate. She just counted it and gave me change.

That was all I needed, and I was ready to go. Being First Class, both of my bags were acceptable as cabin baggage. As soon as there was a flight. Oh, by the way, I'd need photo ID at the gate. Was that okay? Could she check that? Fine, I said. I hoped so, anyway. I showed her the licence. She glanced at it, then at me. She nodded. No problem. She obviously hadn't seen my insides churning.

To calm down, I found a café, and picked up coffee and a donut. It seemed that I'd passed the first test: the ID apparently worked. I sneaked a look at the licence. It was probably going to be all right. But of course, I had started to leave a trail, just by using Brett's name. I waited for two hours or so, drinking too much coffee and reading the for sale ads in a copy of a yachting magazine I'd picked up on a whim at the news stall. Well, I was a rich man, wasn't I? And I had an idea about how I could sort out a place to stay.

The ID worked again at the gate. I got onto the plane without any undue attention, and sat in a nice comfy seat. We left at 2.30, and we would be into San Fran at 4.30 local time. Internal flights in the US were pretty spartan, and Delta wasn't the most luxurious airline in any case, but first class was pretty good and I made the best of it. I drank to Brett's memory with a gin and tonic and enjoyed free wine with my lunch, which wasn't bad.

I rented a Mustang in San Fran Airport, or rather Brett did: I was using his credit card for the first time. There was no way they would rent a car against cash – it would be foolish to try, and anyway of course I'd used his driver's licence. I couldn't help it; I left another footprint here.

Sausalito was – is - a pretty resort with a few chi-chi hotels and a yacht marina. Not the first place you'd look for a dead man, I reckoned. So that's where I was heading.

Frederick's was a nice small hotel a couple of hundred yards along from the marina. The desk clerk's only concern was that he only had a small room at the back. I said it was okay and dropped my stuff in the room. There was no room under the bottom drawer, but there was at the bottom of the wardrobe, so I put the big briefcase there and my suitcase on a low table.

I picked up the phone and called directories. My mate was called Ronnie Wimpenny, and I thought there would only be one or two Wimpennys at most in Oakland, where he was living when last I knew. That was ten years ago: it was a long shot. No luck. No Wimpenny in Oakland. He could be anywhere, in fact: the software business was shot to pieces nowadays. I picked up the local directory. No Wimpennys there either. Didn't think so. Forget that plan, then. I went for a walk, to do a bit of a recce.

Down in the marina, the air was full of the sound of ropes pinging on aluminium masts, flags flapping and gulls screaming as they fought over scraps of food. I walked along the path leading to individual jetties, looking at the sailboats and floating gin palaces. Access to each jetty needed a pass key to open a steel gate, but it was easy to see the nearest boats. It was strange to think that I could probably afford any of them; two or three if I felt like it.

There was an Italian restaurant over the road, overlooking the marina. It had a small bar area, but I got myself a table near the window. The waitress approached with a smile and a menu. I was hungry, despite, the airline lunch. I ordered a penne with tomato sauce starter, followed by a chicken cacciatore, and a bottle of Californian red, and looked out over the marina.

There was quite a bit of coming and going, and it looked as though some of these boats were lived on, rather than just used for pleasure sailing. As I'd walked around, I'd noticed that most of the boats showed their home ports as San Francisco, although there was a smattering of visitors from up and down the west coast and elsewhere.

The waitress came to remove the pasta starter. She was not devastatingly pretty, but she had a trim figure. And a nice smile. She pushed her chestnut hair behind her ears. It had sunshine streaks of auburn, and was just short of shoulder length. She looked about thirty, I thought. Probably looking better than she'd been at twenty, if you know what I mean. She gave me a friendly smile. “Hi. You off one of the boats?”

“No, I just flew in. I’d have more of a tan if I was a sailor, wouldn’t you say?”

“Oh. Yeah, I guess so. So what brings you here?”

“I’m thinking about buying a boat. Thought I’d see if there were any to sell.”

“There usually are, especially at the end of the season. You should check at the harbour office. There, by the flagstaff.” She leant nicely past me to point the office out for me.

“Can you live on the boats in there?”

“Sure. You want to live here in Sausalito?”

“For a while, I think. It seems like a nice place. And I need to stay somewhere for the next few months. Somewhere nice and quiet.”

“That’s Sausalito. Nice. And Quiet,” she smiled, and walked off with the empty plate. And a nice sashay. If that’s the word I want.

So, why a boat? What’s the point of that? Well, consider this. If you wanted to sell a boat in September, you’d have to pitch the price lower than in, say, April. You’d probably be starting to think your window was closing. You’d listen to an interesting deal, especially one that had a cash dimension. And I didn’t think I could rent a house for cash right now. I needed a more flexible sort of market, one that was less inclined to keep records, or create so many footprints. And a quiet cash deal to rent a live-on boat for six months might fit the bill very well. I couldn’t drive one to save my life. But I could sleep on one.

She came back with my chicken. And that nice smile. I thought I might stand a chance here. “So, what’s your name?” I asked.

“Sally,” she grinned. “What’s yours?”

“Brett”, I replied, and we shook hands. Hers were warm, soft, just enough grip. She left me with my chicken and my thoughts. I was starting to warm to the idea of living on a boat. I didn’t think it would get too uncomfortable, here in the marina, even in winter. And I didn’t intend even to untie the thing, let alone set off into the sea. Ocean, rather. It would work quite well as a bachelor pad as well, I thought.

And that brought me back to Sally. The restaurant was quiet. I wondered what time she would finish work. And then what she intended to do. Finishing the chicken and putting my eating irons down, I filled my glass with the last of the wine and sat back. Sally strolled over. “All done?”

“Yep. That was great. Thanks.”

“Good. Anything to follow?”

“What you got in mind?”

She smiled. “Well, what would you like? Tiramisu? Coffee?”

“I thought maybe cocktails somewhere?”

She raised her eyebrows quizzically. Hazel eyes, I thought. “Hmm. Maybe. It looks like I’ll soon be finished here. Have a coffee.”

“Fine. Coffee, then.” She winked and strolled back. I watched her go. Since I reckoned I was in with a chance, I watched her a bit more carefully. She was short and cute. Nice bum. Ass, then. I was sure she was swaying it a bit more than strictly necessary for mere locomotion. It looked like I was going to like this little town.

I dawdled over my coffee and Sally finished serving the other few diners, took their payments and saw them out. She sat down at my table. The proprietor looked at us from the back of the room, not altogether friendly. Sally looked quite friendly, though.

"Cocktails, then," she said. "I could use one. But that's all," she had a look that said she meant it. That was fine: I intended to be here for some time.

"Deal," I smiled. "You can tell me all about Sausalito. For a start, you can find us a cocktail bar."

She took us to a bar across the road from the marina, with a stage for a band, not being used, early Eagles music on the PA, a few customers scattered around booths, and a girl serving more customers at the bar. This one was a redhead, tall and skinny. Unlike "my" redhead, Lizzie, who was shortish and, well, not skinny at all. It struck me, again, in a flash of reality, that Lizzie must be thinking thought I was dead, and I wondered how she was taking it.

Anyway. This redhead was redder as well as skinnier. She wore what looked like the official T-shirt: "Daisy's", it said across her pointy chest in a curly Cheers-like script. It matched a sign at the back of the bar, which then said "Welcome to Daisy's, where we expect the men to be Gentlemen and the Ladies to be ladylike." I guess this was a warning, but it didn't seem like a bar – or even a town – where raucous behaviour was much of a problem.

We sat at the bar. "Hi Sally", said the redhead.

"Hi", said Sally. "Red, this is Brett. He's looking to buy a boat."

I shook hands with Red and ordered drinks. One for her as well: I needed some friends here. Actually, she was rather cute. Nice smile, anyway. I remember a very attractive strawberry blonde, a model, who I took out to dinner in London - Langans, as I recall – once suggested that ginger girls were either very good looking, or not at all. I had to agree with her at the time – she certainly was very good looking, if impossibly tall. And I still think she was right.

"Buying a boat? Plenty for sale here. You planning a cruise?"

“Maybe,” I said, taking a sip of my Martini and trying not to gasp. I would never get used to these measures, I was sure. “I may live on it for a few months. Get used to it.”

“Yeah”, said Red. “That would be cool. It’s a nice place to live, down in the marina.” She went off to serve some more customers. Sally settled at the bar, so I couldn’t remove her to a booth to test her resolve. Ah, well.

“So, why would you want to live here in Sausalito?” she asked. Fair question, really.

“Well, I like the west coast and the Bay area, but I don’t want to live in town, or somewhere like Palo Alto. I like it here: handy but different.”

“And what’s happened to Mrs Brett whoever? You done her in or what?” She was smiling, but it was a genuine enquiry. I decided to use my own back story.

“Nope: long gone. Divorced, paid off and vanished. No idea where she is now.”

“Ah. I thought you’d come to spend the insurance on a boat.”

I laughed. “Oh, no. This money comes from a company sale.” That was true, wasn’t it? “I’d rather the IRS didn’t get to hear of it. Maybe I’ll sail away with it. Spend it on having fun in the sun.”

Sally smiled, her eyes far away. “Yeah. That would be good. Isn’t there anyone wondering where you are, then?”

“Not really. Maybe I’ll tell you some day. Another?”

Sally looked at me full in the face for probably the first time. I looked back. She was getting better looking, really, unless that was the booze. Girl-next-door, rather than in-your-face. Maybe I’d got too used to more dodgy “ladies” recently. This was a real girl, and real girls were different. To begin with, anyway.

We had another. I switched to a Cuba Libre to try and dilute the alcohol. She had another martini. "Just one more. Really", she'd said. I believed her.

She was a mature student, studying Politics on a remote course from a university in San Jose. She went to residential courses every month, for about four days, but stayed here in Sausalito with her "mom", who was a widow and inclined to be lonely. That way, she lived for free while she studied and the waitress job covered her need for cash and paid the college fees. I learned this over the next drink. Red came back and chatted with us as we finished our drinks.

We talked about buying boats. Sally said she'd come with me next day, lunchtime, to look around, if I liked. I said I liked. She knew a little bit about boats, she said. I told her I knew nothing. We left it at that for now. My hotel was the other way from her mom's house, so after arranging to meet at the same bar tomorrow, and a peck on the cheek, we went our separate ways.

I made my way back to my hotel room. I checked the wardrobe for the case: still there. I was tired, and with a bottle of wine and the cocktails we'd had, somewhat mellow, plus I had a bit of jet-lag. As I drifted off, I thought again about this boat idea. I still thought it was a good idea, certainly better than anything else I could come up with. And it would be good to stop moving for a while. I fell asleep and, for all I know, dreamt of boats, or Sally, or even Red. I can't remember.

Chapter 8

A Place to Stay

Next day, I got busy. With about two thousand dollars in my hip pocket, I took another twenty grand out of the pile I'd started yesterday. Splitting the twenty into stacks of five thousand, I put them into various jacket pockets. Then I put the rest back in the case, locked it and hid it again. What I now needed was a bank, so off I went into the town in search of one.

It was a typical west coast September morning. The view across the Bay was obscured by mist, but looking straight up at the sky, I could see the palest blue. It promised to be a great day after about eleven, I guessed. Good-looking men, women and girls flitted about on the pavement – sidewalk – and made me feel just a bit dowdy and pale. I felt very much the outsider here. Well, I was going to change that.

I had no idea how this was going to work, but I couldn't keep the money and bills in a hotel wardrobe forever. Or in a locker on a boat, for that matter. The first bank I found was a branch of Bank of America. There was a clerk at a desk in the main office, customer-side of the counters.

"Excuse me", I said. "I need to open an account. I have some cash to deposit, and an item I want to leave in safe deposit. Can I do that?"

The clerk, a grey-haired man of about fifty in a shirt and tie, and glasses, looked at me wearily. "Do you have ID?" He was short and stout, and seemed to regard customers as an intrusion to the smooth running of his bank.

"Yes, my passport. Will that do?"

"Let me see it." I gave him my passport. British, of course. He looked at the front pages. "Does it have a photo? You need photo ID."

I took it back and showed him the photo page at the back. "There. Okay?"

He took out a form. "What's your address?"

"Well, I've just arrived here from England and I'll be buying a boat. That's why I need an account. Will my address in England do, or how about my hotel?"

"We need a US address."

"Okay then." I used the hotel address. "Frederick Court, Frederick Street. Here in Sausalito. That's my hotel."

"No, we need a permanent US address."

"Won't my UK address do instead?"

"No, we need a permanent US address."

"Right then. I'll come back when I have one. Okay?"

"Thank you sir." He went back to his paperwork, happy with a speedy resolution. Sod them. I went out and looked for another bank. This time, I would try Brett's Drivers Licence as ID. Any valid photo ID seemed to be OK.

But in fact, I realised, I'd had a lucky escape. Using my own ID would have been very silly. I'd have to be much more careful. The lazy clerk would quickly forget the entire episode, I thought, but still ...

About 50 yards up the street I found a smaller, more local bank. California Saving and Checking. Deep breath; try again. This time, I was Brett, in my all-purpose American accent.

A more interested, younger clerk was keen to help. Wearing chinos and a short-sleeved shirt, no tie, he didn't look like a typical banker. Tall and tanned, blond hair ... he looked more like a surfer. But that was fine.

Brett's licence was accepted as photo ID without demur. They took a note of the address on the licence, but the hotel was okay as the main address. The cash I took from my pockets was deposited, receipted and tidied away. I now had a checking account with twenty grand in it and a temporary checkbook, all in Brett's name. And they had safety deposit facilities. I said I'd be back this afternoon with the items for the safety locker, and to make a larger cash deposit, and that was that. Easier than I'd expected, really.

Now for the boat. I'd agreed to meet Sally at a coffee shop on the marina at twelve, and she came into view at five past, as I sat in the window with a coffee and donut. She accepted a coffee and we sat and looked out of the window at the boats.

I'd had time for another quick look round before I went to the coffee shop, and I'd seen a boat that looked about right with a "For Sale" sign on the rail at the back. It was quite close to the gate, so I was able to see quite a lot from the public path. It was what I'd loosely call a largish yacht: what the Americans called a sailboat. It was quite wide across the middle, so probably plenty of room. And there was a big sitting area at the back, where the wheel was, with a fold-down table and benches moulded into the sides. It was easy to imagine myself sitting there in the Californian sunshine, taking it easy. I pointed it out to Sally. She nodded.

"Looks good from here. Let's take a look." We finished our coffee and strolled over to the marina offices and chandlery/souvenir shop. There were two middle-aged ladies in the offices. One seemed to be in charge of the shop, while the other was doing something in the offices.

One of the ladies – the one in the office - said "You really need to talk to George, the Harbourmaster, but he's just popped out for a haircut. Quite a rare event, so we can't complain. So I'll take you over", she smiled. She took us out and across to unlock the gate, while the other stayed behind to mind the shop.

The boat was registered in San Fran, and was called "Mystere." Seemed a good omen to me. I was likely to be a bit of a mystery. "Ah. A Hunter 460," said Sally, reading the model number on the side. "Nice. About a quarter of a million, I should think. Maybe more, if she's well-equipped. Comfortable and classy." So she did know something about these things. She checked the telephone number. "Local owner, if that's his number." That was good, too. I needed someone not too far away.

We walked back and forth on the quayside to get a better look at Mystere, but couldn't see much more, as it was tied up end-on, as they all were. It looked fine as far as it went, though. Sally suggested we take a note of the telephone number, but walk around a bit more to see what else there was.

My experience of yachts and boats was very second-hand, in that I knew people who knew people who had boats. But I'd been to some pretty classy resorts in my high-earning days, and, like anyone else, I suppose, I'd strolled down countless marinas looking at yachts and cruisers and idly wondering which one I'd buy if I could be bothered. I'd also picked up some of the boating magazines in airports, as recently as yesterday, in fact, but they all seemed a bit esoteric. Except the classifieds, that is, and the ones I liked cost serious money. Which I now had.

There were one or two smaller sailboats with sale signs up, and a couple of motor cruisers, one huge and one a bit smaller - about the same size as Mystere - but I didn't like them as much, really. Less classy, I thought. The nice lady said the harbour master might know of others, for sale but without signs, which made sense to me. So we went to wait for him in the offices.

In fact, he was already drinking coffee outside his office, stroking his newly-shorn head as if wondering whether he'd ever get used to it, but he seemed pleased to see us when we strolled up and were introduced. "George", he introduced himself, taking over the discussion from his staff. If you can imagine an old sailor, well that was George. A walking cliché. He had the full beard, now neatly trimmed, the piercing blue eyes and an instantly obvious easy-going approach to life. I liked him on sight.

"Hi," I replied. Brett, and, er, Sally." We shook hands and he asked how he could help. We explained our mission and asked him about Mystere. He was eager to help. It was a quiet day on the marina, midweek at the tail end of the season, so he was clearly at a loose end. He suggested a seat in the bar area, and poured us some coffee from a filter jug on the counter.

He knew the owner of Mystere, and was probably more forthcoming about why it was for sale than the vendor would have wanted. He told us that the owner had made his money in the dot-com boom, and was in trouble now. Not deep trouble, but a recently-ex-wife was adding to his cash crisis. He phoned him for me, and we arranged to meet at the boat in an hour. So, he was keen, it seemed. So was George. He said that Mystere was the best boat currently available, that she was a bargain, and should be snapped up. He was probably a drinking buddy of the owner, but I didn't mind that. I wanted to see inside the boat.

Sally and I had had another wander about the marina and then went back in the bar/coffee shop to wait for the owner. She asked how come I could afford this boat, and why I wanted one when I knew nothing about them. I dodged the questions for a while, but promised I'd tell her "the whole story" eventually. She wasn't really happy with that, but it would have to do for now, really. I said that I wasn't a bank robber or drug smuggler, and that I hadn't murdered anyone, but I don't think she was entirely convinced.

The owner, Ken White, was short and solid. I couldn't really say whether he was just overweight or used weights. Maybe both. He had a hurried manner, and clearly wasn't used to wasting time on small-talk. "So. You wanna buy my baby. You got the money? I'm a busy man." Well, I thought, you can't have been too busy this afternoon. Then I was astonished to see him pick his nose. Not casually, but a serious root up the right nostril, as if he'd lost something important up there. He didn't seem to notice he'd done that. Sally was staring at him. He winked back, unabashed.

"Oh, yeah," I replied. "I have the money. I may have a proposition for you involving cash, in fact. But let's have a look first." He nodded and led the way, short but quick steps. I winked at Sally. She was trying not to giggle. I liked her.

Despite my casual interest, Sally was pretty well right: I actually know nothing about boats. I didn't even know the terms: "aft" and "forrard" still seem pretentious to me, and pointless. Why invent "aft", when "back" already exists?

It was indeed a Hunter 460, 48 feet from front to back, White told me. We went up the gangplank (probably some other daft name, but you know what I mean) and there was the steering wheel thing, on a sort of stand, with some dials and a compass and so on. A big stainless steel thing, the wheel. Very impressive. It came off and stowed away to the side when you weren't actually moving, which was where White put it now.

I imagined myself posing with G&T, or maybe Pimms if I could find it, in this part. A folding table opened out like a gateleg dining table, snug for eight but easy for six, especially with the wheel removed, which was clearly easy to do. With the table closed down, it would be easy for a fair number of people to sit about here. Or rush about winding winches and pulling on ropes, I supposed.

There was a run of benches with padded seat covers and backs around the sides. Ideal for doing nothing much on. Or applying smooth chat and sun cream to bikinied lovelies. There was a canvas roof to this bit, to keep the rays off.

White conducted a rapid tour of the inside of the boat. Further on, inside, White told us that there was a big bedroom called a "stateroom" and some "cabins", which were smaller bedrooms – two of these. The kitchen was a "galley", the loos were "heads" and the inside lounging-about area was a "saloon." The area outside where the wheel was, and the table, was the "cockpit." And there was a whole load of equipment that was a complete mystery to me, radar, chart plotters, depth finders, God knows what.

But there was equipment that I did understand. A hob and cooker. Fridge, freezer, heating and cooling, TV and DVD. A decent CD stereo. More importantly, the boat was spacious and comfortable. Money had been lavished on it and it showed.

The saloon was a sort of sitting room with the kitchen down one side. White fitted leather sofas, TV and so on, low table in pale wood. Panelled walls in the same wood, except the kitchen side, which was stainless steel. All very couth. It would look daft in a house, but it looked just the very thing on this boat.

Back towards the blunt end, under the cockpit, there were two of the bedrooms, erm, cabins, big enough for double beds, just, each with a shower and loo. I was deciding which one I wanted as White led us back through the saloon and towards the "Stateroom" at the sharp end.

Wow. I didn't expect this: I thought it would be another small cabin, but it was relatively large: a cosy and well-fitted bedroom. The same pale wood panels on the walls, a huge bed, sort of a blunt triangle shape to fit into the pointed end, but dead sexy. The bed was quite high, on a sort of platform, with drawers underneath in the same pale wood. The ceiling was low over the bed, and again panelled. Very cosy.

There was more stainless steel and pale wood on the walls, wardrobes, well, clothes cupboards, and some wall lighting, and drawers and so on in the corners. And a zebra skin rug on the floor.

White seemed very proud of this set-up. For some reason, I suspected his wife hadn't actually seen any of this.

That concluded the tour. Sally had followed us around, but hadn't spoken. Gobsmacked, I reckoned. I know I was.

We went out and sat at the table in the cockpit. I loved this boat. I had to live on it, here, in this marina. The sun by now was twinkling on the water, just to make the point, and gulls wheeled in the blue sky. Those ropes pinged on those masts.

White opened up the discussion. "Okay, Mister Foster. You obviously don't know Jack Shit about boats. So what's the deal here?"

I smiled. Keep cool, I thought. "No. This is possibly my first time on something like this. But I need somewhere to live for six months or so. This is exactly what I want. I can offer cash, upfront, right now for a six-month lease."

White rose to his feet. "Nope. This is a waste of time. I need to sell the boat, not let it. What good is that?"

I stayed put. Sally sat and watched. I would buy it if I had to. No problem. But I wasn't entirely sure I could do that without leaving footprints. There'd be paperwork and so on. "Mr. White," I said, all calm and collected. "How many people have you shown round this last two weeks? And how many more do you expect before the winter season?"

White sat down again. "You obviously know nothing about selling sailboats either. It's on the Internet, worldwide. People sail all year round here. And it's a very fine boat. It'll sell."

"I'm sure it will. In fact, I'm sure you'll get top dollar - next spring. Here's my proposal. I'll pay you cash, upfront, now, well, in one hour, ten thousand dollars just for the right to live on your boat for six months. You cover port dues and so on. I'll pay mooring and utility bills. You insure it. You can keep the keys if you like; I'll not be sailing away. And I'll not tell the IRS, your wife, or anyone else about the deal. Just take it off the market for six months. A sensible thing to do anyway, actually."

He looked at me. I had him. He needed the cash. And I think he knew that he'd have a far better chance of a sale at a good price in spring.

"Fifteen thousand", he said.

I thought for a moment. "Twelve. But, for that, I need you to show me how all the domestic equipment works, and come down and keep an eye on maintenance items once a month. And I want an option to buy before ... let's say May thirtieth next year, for two hundred forty thousand."

"Option at two-fifty."

"Two forty-five. My option, by the way, not yours."

"No paperwork?"

"We'll write a note now. A memo only. Two copies, one for you, one for me. Return them, tear them up, on May thirtieth, whether I buy or not. And I want you to take me – us - sailing on it one afternoon."

He sat, silent with his thoughts. He had another root up his nose. Appalling. Then he reached across the table and smiled. It made him look almost human. "Deal," he declared. Reluctantly, in my case, knowing where his hand had been, we shook hands. "There's an inventory also. You need to check and sign that. And the rental isn't part of the sale price."

That seemed fair. "Okay," I said. "I'll see you back here, on the boat, in one hour. I'll bring the money, you bring pen and paper, the inventory and any manuals I might need. Then you can show me how everything works."

"Fine. I'll see you here. What about the young lady?" We both looked at Sally.

"I'll go check on my mom," she said. "I'll see you here in an hour?"

"Fine," I said. We left White on his boat and walked back along the concrete jetty.

"Brett. You really are gonna have to tell me what you are all about," said Sally. "This is kinda weird."

"I know. I will. Soon."

"Hmm. We'll see. I'll catch you in an hour or so." And she was gone, into town, as I walked two blocks the other way to the hotel.

Retrieving the case from the wardrobe, I took stock of my cash situation. I needed fifteen thousand for White, but I had already paid in the twelve thousand. Another thousand walking-about money made sense. Having counted the cash out, I closed the case and spun the dials. Although I hadn't really unpacked, I gathered up my stuff and packed my suitcase. As I left the hotel, I put my head into the reception office. "I'll be checking out this evening. I've found a place to rent. A boat, actually"

"Oh, that's nice. We'll see you later, then. I'll make up your bill."

"Okay. I'll be back in an hour or two."

"Thanks. See ya." It seemed all very west coast and laid back.

I took the briefcase to the bank and they showed me to a strongroom with drawers along three walls, the door and steel fittings taking up the fourth. After removing all the remaining cash, I put the case with the bonds in a steel-lined drawer, locked it, signed the agreement and left the vault, feeling a lot safer.

After removing the cash for White and my pocket money, I could now deposit some of the cash in my new account. I decided on a quarter of a million. This was obviously a much larger amount than they generally saw, and I felt that an explanation was in order. "I've just sold a lot of antiques over in New York. These dealers like to pay cash, and I'm glad to get it deposited, to be honest." That seemed to satisfy their unspoken curiosity, and after counting and double-counting, I was given a receipt for the deposit, followed by a very healthy balance read-out.

Just as I turned to leave, the manager appeared from a back office. Uh-oh, I thought ...

In fact, he was being very helpful. "Mr. Foster. As well as your check book, it might help if we gave you one of our debit and ATM cards to access your funds. The debit card uses Visa, but payments are made directly from your account. And of course we'll set the daily ATM cash withdrawal limit as high as we can – say 1,000 dollars?"

That sounded eminently sensible. I said so, and the manager asked me to come in in a day or two, sign the forms and collect the card. All very convenient.

I then made my way to the marina and Mystere, ready to conclude the arrangement. White was there, with a bag of personal belongings he'd gathered up from the lockers and wardrobes. He welcomed me into the cockpit.

"Okay", he said. "First things first. I've written your memo. Read that, and sign if you're happy with it. I've left your name blank for you to fill in." It was handwritten, but looked fine, and he'd signed both copies. I remembered to sign my name 'B. Foster', and we pocketed one copy each. They were both the same: I checked.

Then we went through the inventory. That looked like taking a while as I started to count cutlery. I soon stopped that and checked for, say, a stack of plates rather than counting them. I took his word about the electronic stuff. It seemed to be all there.

I passed him the money. "You'd better count that now." He did, and of course, it was all there. He pocketed the pile, in three bundles.

"Mister Foster, I really don't know why you need to rent this boat right now, and I don't care, but I guess it will suit you as well as me if we keep our little arrangement off the radar?"

"Yup. I guess that would suit us both." I watched Sally walk down the jetty and up the plank.

I watched White watch her as well. "Nothing to do with me, but would this little lady be a reason for this?"

"No, it's a not-so-little lady who's after my ass for a divorce. Do her good to lose sight of me for a while, you know? Her and her fucking lawyer." I was making this up, of course, but White picked up the thread.

"Okay. I get that sure enough. Well, you can rely on me. Yes, I know all about that." Once Sally was on board, he continued: "Now, I'll show you how this thing works when it's tied up." It didn't take long, really, and it wasn't difficult. He seemed to think that Sally was going to be involved in using the cooker and so on. She took no more than a polite interest. Then he was at pains to show me all the sailing electronics. "I'm telling you, this is some great technology." I couldn't care less, but showed the same polite interest as Sally had in the domestic stuff.

He agreed to come by in a week or so and take me out into the Bay, then to pop in every so often after that, to keep an eye on the maintenance things, like the generator and the waste disposal system. He gave me his phone number and I promised to give him my cell phone number when I got my new one. Better do that tomorrow, actually, I thought. One of those with cash arrangements – no traces.

We walked off the jetty with him and, not knowing that we'd already met, White introduced me to George, as Sally went into the store. White explained that I was going to stay on Mystere for a few months and told him to look after me. George winked. "Welcome to the marina, Mr. Foster. Anything you need, you just ask me," he smiled. It was nice to feel welcome.

I strolled back to Mystere and walked up the plank. I sat down on the cockpit and watched the sea twinkling in the sun. I needed some provisions, I reckoned. Sally would tell me where to get stuff.

She arrived back from the store with a bottle of Napa Valley "champagne", which she put on the cockpit table with a grin. "You should launch your new boat, don't you think? Go get some glasses from the galley."

"Hey, thanks." I was quite touched. There were some champagne flutes, engraved 'Mystere' with an anchor logo, in cupboards in the galley, and I took two back to the cockpit. "Look at these. This boat really is properly equipped." She opened the fizz and we drank to my new home.

We sat back on the benches and sipped our champagne in silence, looking out at Sausalito and the hills behind, across the marina's shimmering waters. I don't know what she was thinking. I guess she had a head full of questions. I was thinking that, even if I got caught - and no matter how tricky it was, I was determined not to be - I had made the right decision.

In any case, I'd well and truly dived into the hot money now. The morality of using money I'd effectively stolen didn't really bother me. I was fairly certain it was ill-gotten in the first place anyway. There was obviously a bunch of people somewhere who would be sure they'd just lost all this money in that huge globally-observed catastrophe. I couldn't really imagine them shrugging their shoulders and simply writing it off – and I doubted they could simply make an insurance claim. But I was quite sure that there was no link to me, here, now, on the deck of this lovely boat.

Although the morality didn't bother me, the potential danger was a bit more of a concern, considered over the longer term. I might just get away with being Brett Foster, doing cash deals with equally publicity-shy characters for a while, but I was certain to set a chain of events in progress when I started on the bearer bills, and I was bound to want to do that at some point. Not yet, but sometime not too far away. The owners of the money would get very interested in it again at that point. Whatever, there was no going back now. Not that I wanted to.

Sally topped up the fizzy wine. "Come on. Let's explore." We took our glasses and walked around the deck to the front, where there was quite a large sunbathing area and some hatches giving access to space below, in front of, I supposed, the big bedroom. Stateroom. There was a small boat – dinghy – strapped to the roof, but still room to sit, if you weren't sailing and charging around.

Going back again and down, the sitting room – saloon - and galley was quite spacious, stretching as it did from side to side at the boat's widest point. We checked the telly; we found CNN via a small satellite dish up at the top of the mast. It was still talking about the terrorist attack and endlessly showing the footage I'd seen all too live, and I quickly turned it off.

The kitchen area was fine for cooking for four or even six at a push: there were four hob rings and a small oven. There was also a microwave built into a cupboard above the sink. Not that the cooking facilities had seen much use.

The fridge was empty, as was the freezer. So were the food cupboards, although there was china and glasses for six, all engraved or monogrammed with "Mystere" and an anchor motif, as I already knew from the inventory. "You need to do some shopping for provisions, skipper," said Sally, poking around.

"Yeah. You need to tell me where to go for that."

"Mmm. You'll need to make a list, I guess."

We passed on, out the back to the two smaller bedrooms. There were pillows and a duvet in each room, and bed linen, embroidered with the same motif as the glasses and crockery, as were the towels in the cupboards. “I guess I need toilet tissue.”

“Get the right stuff. Biodegradable. The system will get blocked if you don’t.” Oh, I thought. Who’d have guessed that?

Between the smaller bedrooms, cabins, rather, there was a hatch. I lifted the rings and peered down. The engine was down there – it more or less filled a sort of cellar, with just enough room for a mechanic who, ideally, had once been a jockey - or perhaps a contortionist. It all seemed to be there, so I shut the hatch. Not my scene.

We went forward, through the saloon, to the big stateroom. It was easily as impressive as the first time I saw it, compact but clever, with all the available space used for storage. There were small windows, high up on the walls, and low level lighting on sconces and screwed to tables. There was a pile of pillows and a huge lightweight duvet on the bed.

Nothing in the clothes cupboards, of course, but they were lit by internal spotlights when the doors opened. “I’ll need some more clothes, too,” I grinned, when I’d opened them all.

I lay down on the bed and surveyed the room. It looked fine – neat but luxurious. I could certainly live here for six months, no problem. Sally sat down on the edge of the bed.

I sat up and made to put my arm round her. She pulled back, slightly, just enough to stop me. “Hey, Mister Mystery. Let’s hear your story first. I bet you’ve got a wife somewhere, like you told that nose-picker guy.”

I laughed. “That was something else, wasn’t it, that nostril-mining?” Sally giggled again. I liked that giggle. “No, really - no wife or anything like that. I was just spinning him a line. Like I said, I'll tell you all there is to tell, sometime. Just not yet. Let's take it easy for a while, yeah?"

She laughed. "Okay, fair enough. I guess things are moving quite fast enough. You are, anyway." She kissed me on the cheek, but before I could grab her, she skipped off the bed and grinned back at me. She went to check the shower room and loo - the heads. The shower was big enough for two, fully lined with marble effect Perspex stuff, with a sliding glass door. There was a small space between it and the door to the bedroom, with a wash basin and cupboards below and above. There were monogrammed towels, like the glasses, but no soap or shampoo of course.

"Looks like I need bathroom stuff as well."

"Okay. Let me use the facilities. Then we'll make a list."

I went back to the cockpit table and started writing out my list. Sally joined me and added a touch of the practical. It was close to five o'clock by now, but Sally said there was a household store in Sausalito where I could get some bits and pieces, and of course plenty of supermarkets not far away.

The wine finished, and the list complete, we locked up and walked down the plank onto terra firma. Sally showed me the supermarket and told me where the household store was, pecked me on the cheek again and strolled off towards her place, but not before she gave me her telephone number.

I went straight to the hotel and paid the bill, cash, then picked up my suitcase and put it in the boot – trunk - of my rental car. I'd need to lose that soon as well, I thought.

I stopped off at the supermarket and got pretty much the entire shopping list, plus, on impulse, some luxuries. I drove to the marina and was allowed to drive close to the boat itself to unload, then parked in the owners' car park.

I busied myself with putting things away in cupboards, making the bed, generally poking about. Just like anyone in a new home, I suppose. To get used to the kitchen, I made an omelette with a salad and opened a bottle of local beer. Then I settled down to watch the sun go down across the bay.

This was a moment for the mental photo album. Phase one was complete: I had detached myself from one life and started another, much better one. And that one looked good from here.

Chapter 9

Meanwhile ...

The view from The Lawyer's office window on that sunny September afternoon was of a small, drab city and a sparkling sea beyond. The city had been much rebuilt in places, partly due to the depredations caused, directly or indirectly, by one of the two men in the room. The police stations and the army barracks still bristled with defences and communications aerials, but life in this Northern Irish city was slowly, cautiously, returning towards a sort of normality.

The office itself had an air of prosperity, as well it might. The tall, sleek man, with his rimless glasses and a luxurious mane of grey hair, his well-cut suit, silk tie and antique enamel cufflinks on a sea-island cotton shirt, looked, and was, extremely prosperous. He had done well during the "Troubles." He had defended, often with uncanny success, terrorists, murderers, burglars, thugs and petty criminals. His opposition had been a Crown Prosecution Service that was obliged, above all, to be scrupulously fair and open, and seen to be so. The same Crown service that paid the prosecution lawyers often also paid him, in the form of Legal Aid. These relatively puny fees were usually topped up handsomely by the tall, thin man looking man sitting opposite him in his priest's day-clothes.

Not that this was the extent of The Lawyer's services to this client. Recently, for example, he had arranged, at arm's length, a series of transactions designed to secure untraceable access to a very large sum of money. This money had come from large and small donors located around the world: from the USA but also Libya as well as Russia.

The money had, on the face of it, been given to support charitable activities in deprived and devastated Northern Irish towns and cities. However, it had in fact mainly been used to fund further acts of horror, whose main effect was to perpetuate the misery of the ordinary citizen, and to instigate and sustain the bitter, low-level, casual, everyday violence that had been Northern Irish life. Some of these donors knew that, and had rejoiced in the knowledge that they were sponsoring the "spectaculars." It was the least they could do for the old country. The Libyan donor, and from time to time, the Russians, were simply happy to disrupt British life and cause pain – 'My enemy's enemies are my friends'.

Recently, this process had been changed by radical political "interference" from the London and Dublin Governments, and it no longer made sense to spend the money on hugely expensive showcase campaigns or missions to the mainland. The petty stuff funded itself, of course. There was a large sum of money left – much larger than the authorities could have guessed at. It was deeply hidden but not untraceable, and The Priest believed that only he, The Lawyer and one other man knew where it was.

The Priest and his colleagues knew very well that the money, as it had been deposited, would eventually surface. Then the organisation, the church and the governments involved would all be embarrassed for their own reasons. The organisation was not supposed ever to have had such funds available, and what funds and other resources they once had were supposed to have been declared and surrendered.

Not that that bothered the leaders. They had their own plans for the money. They'd be damned if they were going to throw away over 25 million bucks.

So, The Priest had instructed The Lawyer to arrange to move the money around, in and out of hiding places, through a series of countries and companies, so that it emerged, free of suspicion, and camouflaged from the original generous donors, in a location where it could be shared out. The Priest intended to enjoy the life he had apparently forsworn many years ago. This process would mean that the money would lose small but not insignificant slices every time it moved and adopted a new disguise, and The Lawyer opposite had taken the first sliver before initiating the process. But there would be a tidy sum left for The Priest's retirement and, unless he could avoid it, his old brothers in arms. It would allow them to look after themselves and their families in fine style, and they were looking forward to that.

Only The Priest had known just where the money could be found, and how it could be released to start this journey to anonymity. Once the journey started, he knew that the money had to move quickly. He would then need to catch it at the other end, split it up and disappear from sight. Some of the larger donors and other colleagues at the top of the organisation would be very interested in these funds once they knew they existed. So would both the Irish and British Governments. Once the funds moved, he had to move. The money was likely to become noticeable once it completed its journey.

And the next move had been planned for yesterday, September 11th. The New York lawyer was meeting two of The Priest's inner circle, and they were in the final stages of collecting the bulk of the money, less The Lawyers' share, after a vortex of transactions and transfers that had emerged nice and clean in the Cayman Islands. And The Priest was expecting to become a wealthy Irish property developer looking for a comfortable retirement home in the sun. That future was now looking slightly cloudy.

"So, my friend, what's happened to my money?" asked The Priest, in a reasonable, level tone, after Mary, the secretary, had left the tea on a mahogany side table and closed the door behind her. He sipped his tea and took a plain biscuit.

"It's hard to say, frankly," replied The Lawyer. Sweat was starting to bead his upper lip, and he too sipped his tea, to disguise it. He knew this mild-looking man didn't accept bad luck, or even acts of God, ironically, as valid excuses. "I can't reach Finklestein's office, of course: it's, well, it's vanished. And his home number seems to be unplugged. I fear the worst, frankly."

"And what is the worst, Peter?" asked The Priest, quietly.

“Worst case is that the money and bonds, Costello and Richardson, and Finklestein, were all burnt to ashes and beyond by the accident yesterday. That’s what I think.”

“Hardly an accident, would you say?”

“Well, no. Terrorist action, then.” The Lawyer wanted to smile. The Priest knew all about terrorist action. He was sure the irony was not lost on him. “But the meeting was set up for first thing yesterday. In the World Trade Centre. I don’t know exactly where Finklestein’s office was, but it’s not there now. The plane would have hit during the meeting. I can’t see anyone – or anything – surviving.”

The Priest sat silently for a moment. “And do we know they got there? Do we know the money got there?”

The Lawyer grimaced. He couldn’t be sure, in fact. “Well. I suppose not. Our men seem to have left their hotel on time and never came back. I checked, as far as I could. It’s all a bit chaotic over there, as you’d expect.” He looked at The Priest, who stared back with hypnotic blue eyes. “I don’t know about the money: we used a London courier company. We’ve used them before – very trustworthy. They had no idea what the consignment was. They never do.”

“I think we should speak to them, don’t you?”

“No reason why not.” The Lawyer picked up the phone and called his secretary. “Mary. The courier company in London. Yes, them. Call them for me, will you. I want the boss. Clive something.”

Neither man spoke until the phone rang again. The Lawyer didn’t look into those eyes. He never did unless he had to - they always frightened him. Instead, he looked at the notes on his desk – the sparse notes he needed to manage the process and no more.

The phone rang. “Thanks, Mary. Yes, hello … Yes, it is. Is this, erm, Clive? Good. We were wondering about our delivery yesterday to the World Trade Centre … Yes, terrible. We watched it on the TV here as well, of course. Awful ... Yes, we thought it would be about that time. We were very worried ... About your man as well - quite. Yes ... Nothing? ... No, I suppose not. So you've no clear idea, then? And not heard from him ... No, I see ... Yes, as soon as you have any information. Thanks."

He replaced the phone and chanced a look at his visitor. The eyes boring into him now. "Well, they don't know for sure. They know he left the hotel, but nothing else. It's all speculation – assumptions. They say he would have called if he could: he usually did, in case there was a return package or anything. Nothing. No sign of him after he left the hotel in the morning"

The Priest was silent again. He showed nothing. "Right. I think we need to find out for ourselves. Do you have anyone who can help us with that?"

"In London, certainly. In New York, well, possibly. I'll need to make some calls."

"Do so. Find out the last known movements, the last telephone call, the last piss, of these people. I want to know where my money is."

"Do you want it quick or thorough?"

"Both." The Priest gave a smile, which was even more unsettling. "A quick pass, to look for anything obviously wrong, then dig a bit deeper. Get back to me in 3 days, then 3 weeks. You know where." He stood up and walked to the door and turned back. "I want my money back, Peter."

The Lawyer opened his mouth to – what? Protest? Argue? Reason with him? But he was gone.

He picked up the phone. "Mary. Get me Mr. Edwards."

Chapter 10

Private Investigations

"Mr. Edwards", announced Mary, two days later at three o'clock on a drizzly Ulster afternoon. A Private Investigator walked in. In a nondescript dark blue chain store suit, plain shirt and no tie, he could have been anything. Of course, he could also look like a bank manager, a tramp, a football hooligan, or anything else his case needed. Right now, it needed him to look like a competent Private Investigator, so he did. He sat down and smiled at Mary. "Tea?" she asked. He nodded.

"Thank you", he said as Mary brought a second cup from the cupboard and poured him a cup from the teapot on the table, and left them to it.

"So," The Lawyer began. "What's happened to our friends and this consignment?"

"Can't say yet for sure," replied Edwards. "But the chances are that everyone's vanished off the face of the earth. I went to their offices yesterday. I spoke to the boss, Clive. And not just the boss – everyone I could. I said I was press: they seemed to accept that. I said I'd got hold of a story that one of their men was missing." He paused as Mary brought the tea in and put it on the table.

"Go on", said The Lawyer, as she closed the door.

"Well, that was it, really. The courier on your job was called Joe Best." He was looking at a notebook. "Lives fairly local to the office. I checked his home address: no sign of life there. Neighbours don't really know him, but they're used to him coming and going, away for days, sometimes. I checked the pubs. They know him, but he hadn't been in for a few days. Again, nothing strange there. No close family as far as I could tell quickly. The office confirmed that." He turned a page. "Not your usual courier type: used to be a bit of a high-flyer but jacked it in. Been there a couple of years now. A bit of a loner. Divorced, apparently."

"Is that significant?"

"Probably not, but he might be more capable of deliberately disappearing than a close family man, life and soul of the neighbourhood, I suppose."

"Hmm." Particularly, thought The Lawyer, if he'd looked in the case and seen the contents. "Did they say he was honest? No trouble before?"

"Absolutely. Just did the job, never any complaints about him - or from him, come to that. Model employee, they said."

"I see. What about New York?"

"Well, I phoned the hotels. It's all a bit of a mess over there, but the stories check out. Best seems to have left his hotel in the morning, but they're not sure of the time. Costello and Richardson checked into theirs okay the night before and checked out on time to get their taxi."

"Someone actually saw them leave?"

"Costello and Richardson, yes. The receptionist remembers them checking out. As for Best, his room had been slept in and was empty when the maid eventually went in. I spoke to the desk clerk."

"'Eventually'?"

He checked his notes. "Yes. He'd left the 'Do Not Disturb' sign on when he left, apparently."

"Is that significant?"

Edwards shook his head. "I doubt it. We've all done it, especially when our hands are full. No. All the evidence says they've all been crushed or burnt to a crisp, along with whoever they were meeting and the goods, whatever they were. What were they, anyway?"

The Lawyer looked hard at him. "A very great deal of money. Quite a bit of it cash. All of it cashable, if you knew what you were doing."

It was Edwards turn to go "Hmm." "That might change things, maybe …"

"Why?" asked The Lawyer.

"Well," replied Edwards, thinking as he spoke, "There's nothing I can see at the moment in Best's life to keep him anywhere in particular, but, so far, nothing to run away from, either. Lots of money, well, that might be a reason to scarper and start a new life. How much money?"

"Plenty enough to start a very exciting new life," replied The Lawyer, thinking. "What about Costello and Richardson?"

"Well, you know about them," replied Edwards. "Irish-American, families in Boston, wives already going frantic – they knew where they were going and they fear the worst. I've been on the phone to them. Pretended I was with the church. No, I can't really see them doing a runner. You have their files here. Yes, if anyone's scarpered, it's Best. But there's no reason to think anyone has. No evidence. Not yet, anyway."

"What would give you reason to think so – what evidence?"

"One of the guys' credit cards being used, maybe. Passport controls. We could watch the houses?" A thought struck him. "What form was this money? Cash or Bills?"

"Some cash – say a couple of mill or so. Dollars. The rest in Bearer Bills. Quite a few Bills. High value."

"Well, that's your best bet. Sooner or later, if those bills weren't burnt to ashes, someday, someone will try to cash them. You find out where and when, you've got a trail again. Right now, it's impossible. It's, well, biblical. There are thousands dead, they'll never find and identify all the bodies. If you want to disappear, this is the time. Unless you leave a positive mark somewhere, you're gone."

The Lawyer thought about this. Edwards was right. As long as nothing happened, there was probably nothing to follow. And anyway, chances were that they were all dead; the money too. "Any point in going to New York?"

Edwards shrugged. "No. Not now. It'll be crazy over there, for one thing; nobody can give any reliable information. Look at the President, for God's sake. Even he doesn't know what to do next. And we're looking for 3 or 4 probably very dead men, in case one or all of them happens to start leaving footprints somewhere. This is the coldest trail imaginable. The probability is that there's nothing to find, and even if there is anything, it's needle-in-a-haystack stuff. There's no point at all right now. Anyway, I doubt I'd get a flight for a few days."

"Our friends who are, erm, interested in the money want to be certain they haven't been ripped off. They'll want you to go there, I think."

"Well, I'll go if they insist, but there's no point yet, as I say. And they might never be certain, until they find and positively identify all the bodies. All four – Best, Finklestein, Costello and Richardson. Or the bag or case or whatever it was. Which they might very well not manage to do at all. But not finding them proves nothing. If you have been ripped off, then there might be a chance of proving that. But not yet. There's a lot of dust to settle. Literally."

"So, what do I do?"

"Nothing. Really - there's nothing you can do. Get the bank to let you know if any of the bills are cashed, as soon as it happens. Wait for bodies to be identified, names given. Register the names as missing." He paused. "Did they have credit cards?"

"Don't know. I guess so. Who doesn't?"

"I mean in their own names."

"Oh. Yes, I expect so. No reason not to on this trip."

"Well, we could try to get the card companies to let you know as soon as one of their cards is used, if it ever is. And you might be able to get someone in Customs to check border crossings and so on. But officially, you'd need more than a suspicion to get them to do that."

"Like the Bills being cashed?"

"Yes. That's your only hope, really, short of them pulling one of them out alive. Dead but not forgotten, I'd say they are."

The Lawyer stood up. "OK, thanks. Well done. We'll be back onto you if anything breaks." As Edwards closed the door behind him, he dialled a number. Mary didn't know this one. The Priest wouldn't like this.

It was an easier call than he'd hoped. Edwards' logic was faultless. There really was no point in rushing off to New York right now. Anyway, The Priest had more immediate problems. Wherever the money was, it wasn't where it was supposed to be. Not that The Priest himself wasn't dangerous.

The Priest decided to make a journey. Not to New York – to Boston. There were some people there he needed to talk to. And he would visit the Richardson and Costello addresses. He knew very well what recently widowed women looked like, and he'd check that these two looked like that. And if not, find out why not.

Chapter 11

Digging In & Lying Low

An unaccustomed noise roused me, and for a moment, I wondered where I was. It came back to me in a pleasant rush as I recognised my surroundings. There'd be a few new sounds to get used to, I reckoned. It was half past seven. I lay there for a few minutes and thought back over the last few days. The change in my life had been beyond imagining: instant and totally unexpected. I was sure I'd done the right thing. But looking forward, there was a lot to do to complete the process. And there was no going back now.

I got up, fixed myself some breakfast and contemplated a day with nothing to do and no-one to answer to. It might get boring eventually, but it felt good for now.

I had moved quite fast since fate had suddenly dealt me a new hand, and I felt a need to settle down for a while. It was quite surprising to realise that it had only been ten days since the attack. As a newcomer around here, and probably a mysterious one at that, I was naturally going to attract some attention, which I reckoned would pass with time. And I needed to catch my breath and come to terms with my new circumstances and new opportunities. Plus, I needed to make plans – careful plans with no footprints, if possible.

I spent the next few weeks pottering about on the boat and in the town. I ate lunch or dinner in various restaurants, but kept popping into see Sally and went to Daisy's for cocktails now and then. George, the harbourmaster, and I had a few cold beers once or twice a week, and I met some other salty types in the marina bar. I started to become a local. It occurred to me that Americans make friends quicker than we do in the UK. I suppose a more mobile population would do that anyway, but there seemed to be a willingness to accept people at face value.

That said, I think it might have been different if I'd been Middle-Eastern in appearance. America was hurting badly after the hit on the WTC and looking for vengeance. It was agreed all round that Afghanistan was going to get it in the neck, and probably Saddam Hussain in Iraq, but nobody seemed to be asking how and why that made sense. I got the feeling that the US was just lashing out at any suitable target. The assumption was that Bin Laden was living there, and the idea they could hit back significantly this way was not really challenged. I didn't raise my head by arguing with this, but it did seem like a knee-jerk to me.

Not that I had any sympathy for the Afghan regime, and I did think that most of its benighted citizens would welcome the removal of the Taliban, who seemed to be suffering from a collective religious madness. But the USA seemed just like the school bully who had been hurt by surprise and was picking on the least popular boy in the classroom to punish, simply in order to restore his pride.

Maybe it was too soon, but I did feel – I still do – that it would be a good thing for them to try harder to understand why these people hated them. Some people were saying this in the media, but they were more or less drowned out by the gung-ho brigade. Everybody was talking about what had happened, but it seemed to me that not many people were really thinking about it.

So, I kept quiet in these discussions. I was still playing the US accent and, I think, getting away with it. It got easier every day. But I didn't want to draw attention to myself any more than was necessary. It made more sense simply to go along with the conversations and try to blend in.

Another development directly following on from the attack was that most security systems were apparently being tightened up. This included the need for good ID on airlines, even domestic flights, when making reservations. Hotel check-ins and banking transactions were also being scrutinised more carefully. That was not good news for me.

I went over my ideas for getting at the big money and watched the press for more details on the new security arrangements. I wondered how long my Brett Foster driving licence could – or should – be used as ID. I thought I had a few more weeks at least. I hoped so, anyway. There was a book I'd read once, on a plane, about money-laundering. I could do with that book. I wondered if I could find it again, in San Fran, if I looked hard enough in a big enough book shop.

I'd taken the rental car back. I had paid for it with Brett's ID and his credit card, so it was a clear footprint, and the longer I had it and used it, the deeper those footprints got. After dropping it off, I returned from the airport via the BART underground system and the ferry. I'd never used BART before, but Sally told me that it was the best way to travel in San Fran, assuming it went where you needed to be. It wasn't anything like as comprehensive as the tube in London, but it went straight from SFO to the ferry dock at Embarcadero. Quick, easy, cheap. I wished I'd known about it when I first arrived it would have kept some of those footprints off the map.

Anyway, one sunny morning I got the San Francisco ferry from near the marina. I was there in just over half an hour – much easier than driving and parking, even if I did have a car. Which of course I didn't, yet. San Fran was more like a European city in many respects than, say, L.A. More foot-friendly, especially with the cable cars and, of course, BART, to move around on.

There was a bookshop just off Union square, and I wandered about the business section, looking for the book I remembered. Could I really ask the assistant for a book on money laundering? I took a chance and approached an assistant, I said that I was a writer and needed to find a book to help my research. On money laundering. He didn't hesitate.

"Oh, how exciting! A writer! Would I have read anything you've written? What name?" Ah.

“Er, no, I write scripts, mostly. For TV, you know.” I was tap-dancing here. “Part of a team. Detective stories, usually. I don’t get personal credits.”

He wasn’t easily put off. “Gosh! Which show?”

“A new one. We hope CBS will take it. It’s about a lady cop who, er, who’s in a wheelchair. Works mainly on the internet and so on. A female Ironside, I suppose.” I couldn’t keep this up much longer. “So, money laundering ...”

He camped up a “Hmm, let’s see” pose, finger to his temple. “Ah, yes. I know what you need.”

And he did, too. It was the same book I’d read, half-heartedly, about three years ago, and then it was only just interesting enough to keep me awake. It would be riveting now, I thought. Using my new debit card, I paid and left with it.

While I was shopping, I decided that I needed more clothes, so I spent an hour or two in various stores and bought a rain jacket, more chinos, jeans, shorts, shirts, polos, a couple of pullovers, deck shoes, underwear and so on, as well as a suit and formal shirt and tie. A complete wardrobe, I thought. Not far from the ferry dock, I found a shop selling the cash-based mobile phone I’d decided I needed. So I bought that – cash of course, and put $100 on it.

The last ferry wasn’t till half-six. I decided to have a late lunch or early supper before I caught the ferry back. I found a sports bar and had a burger, fries and salad and watched the TV. It was mostly sport, of course, but some sets were still showing the news. Burdened with all my shopping, I hailed a taxi back to the ferry terminal and made it home just ahead of the rain, which had followed us across the Bay.

I started to see more of Sally on her days and evenings off, and found myself really looking forward to seeing her. She still didn’t entirely trust me: she kept saying that she wanted to know my “guilty secret”, and I kept insisting that I didn't really have one. She was half-joking about it, but she wasn't going to go much further with me until she got the truth, or at least something that would pass for the truth. And I wasn't sure how far I wanted things to go, either. For the time being, we simply enjoyed each other's company.

Ken White came, as promised, to show me how to sail the boat. Sally came as well, of course, and we had a surprisingly good day out. Ken was less aggressive now that he'd done the deal, and he proved good company, if you like the matter-of-fact business type. Which I did: it took me back to my days in the IT business. Sally took to sailing like a veteran: she had done it before, and she understood what was going on most of the time. I was a complete novice, but enjoyed the feeling of zipping through the water in my home.

We got back to the berth in semi darkness, having spent longer out at sea than anyone had planned. We had all enjoyed ourselves and promised to do it again, which we did, twice, when the weather allowed, and I started to get the hang of things. I started to think that, with Sally's help, I might be able to sail this thing properly, one day – or one like it.

Sally had an old Volvo, and we went on trips out to Sonoma, which was a bit nearer than Napa, where we picnicked and bought cases of wine, or over the bridge into the city where we shopped, had lunch, went to the theatre or the movies and so on. She ate with me on the boat a few times, and eventually I met her Mom, accidentally, when we were out in town buying groceries. I was my charming self, and she was politely curious. But the ice, if there was any, was broken.

Sexually, Sally drew a line. The inference I took was that things were not going to develop much beyond the brief kissing and cuddling stage until she had unearthed my "secret" and decided that she was happy with whatever it turned out to be. I suppose it was a matter of trust for her, and I had to accept that limit for now. But I knew that things couldn't stay in the holding pattern for ever.

Of course, it was a matter of trust for me as well. If I told her the truth, I would need to know that she would keep it to herself. In fact, I wanted her to be at least fully aware of my plan, if not necessarily an active participant. So I needed to figure out what kind of person she was: was she resourceful, reliable, pragmatic, adventurous, or was she scrupulously honest, timid, over-moral, plodding - and so on? She seemed to be somewhere between the two; probably more the former than the latter. And I felt that it would be good secure her involvement in the next stage, at least on a sort of business partnership basis, if nothing else.

As November came in and the Northern Californian version of winter started to make itself felt, I started to think of the Caribbean sunshine I could easily afford. But even a trip to Florida realistically meant a flight and the use of my – Brett's - ID, leaving footprints again.

I had become impatient to be moving forward. I might have been a bit bored as well. I suppose I decided I had lain low long enough. I wanted to be ready to start to make my moves in the New Year. It was time for Sally to opt in – or out. Over cocktails in Daisy's, I suggested a "special dinner" the following night on the boat. "It's time you knew my history", I said. "I just hope you like it. And my cooking, of course."

Chapter 12

Coming Clean

My plan, such as it was, was based on the idea that you could move money around by buying and selling companies with the money attached, if you used the right countries and the right lawyers. My research, using the book I'd bought, seemed to support this. I hoped that I could still do that after the new security processes had been implemented. The sooner, the better, I decided. It was probably a good idea to buy a car that couldn't be traced back to me, as well. That might involve Sally, if she wanted to get involved.

In any case, I felt certain that I would need an accomplice to help me do this, although I wasn't sure exactly what this would involve. Sally was intelligent and sort of ordinary, in that she was pretty but not stunning, and didn't stand out in a crowd too much, depending on how she was dressed. Not very gallant of me, perhaps, but that was actually a positive aspect.

She wasn't my usual sort of girl, in fact, but that was probably no bad thing. I'd not enjoyed a great track record with women over the years: mostly opportunistic, short-term or even commercial relationships with women chosen exclusively for their physical attributes, and my failed marriage, were all I could look back on. And of course my brief dalliance with Lizzie. I still wasn't sure what I wanted from this relationship with Sally, and until I'd come clean with her, I didn't know what she wanted either.

Well, I would soon know. Dinner tonight. I realised that I was really looking forward to it. Showered and dressed, I walked into town and stocked up with food and groceries, with the evening meal in mind.

I phoned Sally. She had taken the night off, and said she was looking forward to dinner on the boat. "And you're gonna tell me all about who you are and how you got here", she warned me. We settled on 8 o'clock, and she rang off. I had four hours to decide how much truth to tell her, and to cook dinner.

Although I say so myself, I'm quite a good cook. To start with, I put a chicken in the oven in a covered roasting dish with lots of lemons and some tarragon. Leaving it to cook, I made a cup of tea and sat down in the cockpit in the September afternoon sun to read my book on money laundering. The plan wasn't all there yet, but it felt like the right idea. Now I needed to decide what to tell Sally. I went in to complete the dinner.

As I chopped, shredded and cooked, I worked out what I was ready to tell her. It was probably best to stick to the truth as far as possible, and, obviously, to tell no outright lies. I was sure I needed her for my plan, I liked her, and, well, who knows where this might lead?

My menu opened with a Greek style starter - humus and taramasalata with pitta bread. It was a good way to start, using our fingers and sharing bowls and so on. Then the cold lemon and tarragon chicken, with a green salad and hot buttered new potatoes, followed by an open apple pie, but sort of French style, on puff pastry with an apricot jam glaze and mascarpone. A Tarte Tatin, really. It was something I'd made in the past, and it was always simple, tasty and impressive, I thought. "Result cooking", usually. The little supermarket had stocked all the ingredients, and it was all great quality - I knew it would work well.

Once this lot was prepared, and the wine was in the fridge, it was easy to concentrate on being the perfect host. Sally arrived at five past eight and we sat and drank wine and watched the lights in the marina twinkle into life.

I brought out the first course and we ate in the cockpit, in the open air beneath the canopy. It was a warm evening – warm enough to sit outside anyway, with a sweater on. I lent Sally one of my new ones, which she put round her shoulders. We went down below to collect the chicken, salad and potatoes, and brought it back to the cockpit. It was all as good as I'd hoped. I thought Sally seemed impressed, and maybe surprised, but she made only the usual polite noises as she started each course.

She wanted me to tell my story as we ate, but I said that I would rather wait until we had eaten, so it was just before 10 o'clock when we sat opposite each other at the cockpit table. The sound of the water against the side of the boat was comforting, and the level in the bottle of Chilean Sauvignon Blanc was well down the label. It seemed that we were suitably mellow.

"OK. Before I start", I said, as I topped up our glasses, "I promise you that I'm going to tell you as much truth as I can. It won't be the whole truth, but everything I tell you will be true. And I need to know you'll keep all this to yourself."

"Okay", grinned Sally, and she giggled a bit as she settled back on the cushions and pulled on my cashmere sweater. "I'm listening. And I promise not to tell."

"Well, for a start, I'm not actually Brett Foster, and I'm not American. I'm English. My name's Joe. Joe Best. Everyone who knows me thinks I'm dead. And I think his friends and family believe Brett Foster's dead, as well. Which he is."

Sally had stopped giggling now. She looked at me intently. I went on.

"I've accidentally come into possession of a great deal of money. Millions of dollars. Nobody knows I've got it: as I say, I'm supposed to be dead. I don't know for sure whose money this is – well, I think I do, but if I'm right, I don't think they got it legally. They probably think they've lost the money for ever."

Sally sat up more upright. She looked uneasy. "So who's Brett Foster? Is it his money? And who killed him?"

"No, it's not his money. Listen; you'll get the gist." I told her that Brett had been killed in an accident, and that I had found his wallet and ID, innocently, just before the accident. I didn't want to bring up the link with the World Trade Centre disaster if I could help it. I said that the money was thought to be physically destroyed, and that it was partly cash, but also bankable papers that needed to be turned into cash, which would be risky.

I talked about my past life in London, my marriage and divorce, and my old job in the computer business, but I didn't mention my courier job. Too much of a clue, really. I explained that I had decided to give up my old life completely to take advantage of the money I had "found." "I've burnt my boats," I said, looking at my new boat.

She said nothing for a few minutes and sipped her wine. I moved to top it up but she shook her head. "Christ. That's quite a story. Is it really true?"

"Yes. I told you, all this is true. Not the whole truth, but it's nothing but the truth."

She looked thoughtful for a while. She was still sitting upright, almost uptight. Had I misjudged her? "So, tell me. Truly. Did you steal this money? Or is it a drug deal, or what?"

"Well, as I said, I came into possession of it. Found it, if you like. The owners don't know I have it – they probably think it's burnt to ashes. Or something." I thought she'd leap to conclusions at this: the WTC disaster was the obvious place for a catastrophic fire recently, after all. But she didn't. Not just now, anyway.

"Isn't that stealing it, though?"

"I suppose so, in a way. But I didn't – I don't see it like that. The owners – whoever they are – think it's vanished. As far as I can tell, well, I guess, anyway, it's dodgy money. If they got it back, I don't think they would use it for legal reasons. Or to help the poor. I think it came from, I don't know, drugs or extortion or whatever, and I'm sure it will stay there if it goes back, in that world, funding that sort of stuff."

She gave a short laugh. "Right. So, what do you propose to do with it? Build an orphanage?"

"No, Sally. I'm going to try to make myself a new life. One with, I don't know, yachts like this and tropical beaches, nice houses and cars. I'm going to spend it on having a good time. I think that's better than funding more gangster stuff or drug deals, don't you? Maybe I'll set up a business or two. Employ some people. Anyway, I'll put it to good use – better use than the original owners would, I'm sure."

She looked me in the eye, and I realised that she had avoided that since I started the story. Maybe I was getting somewhere. "So you don't see this as stealing?"

"In a way, it is, yes. I said so. But what's the right thing to do? Hand it in to the police? Say 'Hi. I just found millions of dollars. Do I get to keep it if the owners don't come forward? I think they may be gangsters, in fact. Will there be a reward?' What would you do?"

She thought about that. She relaxed her position a bit. "I really don't know. How much did you say there was?"

"I didn't. Let's just say it's a life-changing amount. Several million dollars. So the amount matters, does it?"

She took another sip of wine, then emptied the glass. "No. Not in principle, no. Finders isn't keepers. But I do see the point about not giving it back to the original owners. I don't know ..."

She allowed me to refill the glass, and mine, which emptied the bottle. I said, "Look. That's not the point, actually. I've burnt my boats, as I say. It was my decision to make, and I've made it. I've left my past life forever. I can't go back. So the real point is, where do I go from here?"

Sally stood up. "I need the heads," she smiled, and made her way below. I considered: had I gone too far? Had I really needed to tell her anything at all? I did need an ally, and having one who was clever and quite pretty, and, well, simply good to be with was a better bet than otherwise. I had to trust someone – and I had to make fairly instant decisions: all my old mates were in the unreachable past.

It suddenly struck me: had there been any sort of funeral back home – back in London - and if so, who'd come? Lizzie, surely. Clive as well, probably. Had my mate taken charge of the convertible Beemer? I hoped so.

Anyway, back to the here and now - as far as I could tell, Sally was clever – and honest, which was possibly proving to be a problem for her. But if she did decide to fall in with me, I thought she'd be straight with me. So, would she?

She came back with a new bottle that she'd got out of the fridge, which I thought was a good sign. She sat down - next to me - another good sign, I thought. "Well, Joe." She smiled. "It's a nicer name than Brett, anyway. So, as you say, what now? Do you have a plan?"

"Yes, up to a point. I think I know how to get the papers converted into cash, and vanish with it. And I think I know what I want to do with it – where I want to go, what I want to do. I don't know all the details, but I can work it out."

"And where do I come in? Why tell me?"

"Good question. First, though, am I still on trial, or do you agree that I was right to take the money and run?"

"Hmm." She smiled at me. "If you're telling the truth, I think you're in the clear. I can't say I wouldn't do the same in your position. And you've trusted me, so I'll trust you, I guess." Then she kissed me. Properly, for the first time.

“That was nice,” I grinned. Was that it, then? Sealed with a kiss? Had I won her over to my point of view? I thought back over the last half hour. The objections had been natural but her conversion to my point of view seemed genuine, based on, I thought, reasonable argument. Of course, it’s always easy to accept that someone would be swayed by your own peerless logic.

Taking her at face value for now, I said “Okay, partner, first thing is, you’re going to get yourself a new car.”

“What? I don’t need a new car.”

“No, but I do. And I don’t want to go on record anywhere, for anything, if I can. As Brett, or Joe. So, you get a new car, your insurance names me – well, Brett, since I have his driving licence - and I drive it, mostly.”

“But it’s my car? So I can just take it and go? And there’s nothing you can do about it?”

I nodded. “Yup. But that’d be the end of it. No more to come.”

“Oh. And if I stay in the game?”

“Lots more to come. I need – well, an accomplice. And I’ll share the proceeds with you if you help me.”

“Fifty-fifty?”

“Ha-ha. No: we’ll agree a share. We can discuss that when I work out exactly what I need you to do. But it won’t be dangerous. Or illegal, I’m sure. In fact all I can see now is that I need a buddy who knows what’s happening.”

Sally took a long drink of her wine and I topped up the glasses while we both thought our thoughts.

"Okay," she said. She swung her feet up on the seat, laid back and put her head on my lap, and looked up at me with a grin. "What kind of car am I going to buy?"

I laughed. "Well, something not too ostentatious, so not a Porsche, I'm afraid. Not yet anyway. A Lexus, maybe. Or a Merc. Comfortable, discreet and fast. No need to slum it, is there?"

"I see. And just how do I explain how I get to buy a new Mercedes?"

"You don't. I buy it for you with cash, I keep it. But it's registered to you. If you take it, I can't do anything about it, but you would have to explain it to your friends."

"Oh. And can I drive it? Do I get to keep it in the end?"

"Oh, yes. It's part of the deal if you like. We'll work out how to explain it before we get there. Rich Aunt Doris's will, maybe?"

She giggled. "This is all too weird. I was expecting ... well, some sort of 'my-wife-left-me-and-ran-off-with–the-gardener' line and a lunge at my ass."

"Oh. Disappointed? Anyway, if you expected that, why come along?"

She looked up at me. I must have looked strange from that angle, but it didn't seem to put her off. "Well, I suppose I kinda like the look of you. And I've enjoyed spending time with you. You seem like a decent sort of guy. I thought you might have an interesting story. Nothing like this, though. This is weird shit." She looked serious again. "This is for real, yeah? Not some bullshit story to get me into bed?"

"Er, no. But would this get you into bed?" I grinned.

Sally grinned back. "Well, a mysterious stranger, a Mercedes, a quest to win untold millions ... oh, and a great meal, by the way. First class. Do all Englishmen cook that well?"

I was flattered, who wouldn't be? "No. Some are much better, but I think I'm okay for an amateur. Bit out of practice, maybe ... it's all about the ingredients, you see ..."

She stopped my rambling by swinging her legs down and her face up to kiss me again, pushing me onto my back and moving on top of me. I put one arm round her back and one onto her bum. Ass, then. We snogged like kids for a while, but then she extracted herself and sat up, frowning.

"Look," she said. "I need to think about this. It is a bit weird, you've got to agree. And if we're going into business together ... well, I just need to think about it." She stood up and smiled again. "Maybe you should have just given me some lame old story. Maybe we'd have been in that weird bedroom at the sharp end by now."

"Really?" I couldn't keep up with this. I stood up.

"And maybe not." She rose on tiptoes and kissed me again. "We'll see. But you've given me a lot to think about, haven't you?"

"Well, I suppose so. How long do you need – to think about it, I mean?"

"Come round to the restaurant tomorrow evening at closing time. We'll go for cocktails again. I'll tell you what I think then."

There was no choice anyway. "Okay, fine. Around 11 o'clock?"

She kissed me again as she squeezed past. "Fine. And don't worry. Your secret's safe." I went up and watched her as she walked down the plank and turned back to looked at me. "So, is this just a business arrangement, then?"

"Probably not", I grinned back. "But we both need to be happy with the, erm, project, first, wouldn't you say?"

“Guess so”, she said, and she blew me a kiss and strolled away down the quay into the evening. She knew I was watching. She was swaying her arse again. Ass.

I gathered up the plates from the cockpit and locked the door. I poured the last of the wine into a glass and sat back to reflect on the evening. The bet was placed now: I could only wait to see what the outcome would be. I could have waited a bit longer before I told Sally - or someone - the story, but I was always going to have to trust someone. And, although I hardly knew her, it felt right for some reason.

As I dropped off to sleep later, I thought again about what I’d done – opening up, I suppose. I knew what it was: I wasn’t really suited to isolation. It was more than just an accomplice - I needed a friend, at least - maybe more than that. I needed to be part of a team, even of two. I couldn’t operate alone. And, to be honest, I suppose I was lonely.

Chapter 13

Partners

Next day was a miserable day, weather-wise - drizzly and cold. Just like England, in fact. I made myself cosy in the inside cabin and read the money-laundering book again. I walked into town at lunchtime and shopped half-heartedly, but achieved nothing, really. I was keen to start moving again. At seven o'clock, after a dinner of leftovers from the previous evening, I went over to the marina club. George was at the bar. "Hi. How're you doin'?" he asked, as I sat down on a stool made up to look like a capstan.

"Fine, thanks", I told him, and bought him a beer. The TV was on. We chatted about the latest terrorist theories and what the President ought to do next. Afghanistan was going to get a pasting, it seemed, according to George, who claimed to know some influential people. We talked about other stuff: sport, boats, women. Or he did: he was a good talker and I was happy to let him ramble on as I watched the other boat owners come and go. He had something to say about most of them, not all complimentary. I wondered what he would be saying about me.

Soon after half past ten, I paid my tab, said good night to George and set off to the restaurant to meet Sally, as arranged. The restaurant was still quite busy.

"Hi. You're early", she said as I walked in. "Wait for me in Daisy's; I'll see you there."

"Okay", I said. "Will you be long?"

"Twenty minutes, maybe. Thirty at the most." She winked. "Have a cocktail ready for me."

Red was behind the bar as I strolled in and took a bar seat. "Hi", she said, wiping the bar top and putting down a coaster. "How're you doing?"

"I'm good", I said. "You?"

"Yeah, fine, thanks. So, what are you drinking?"

"Gin and tonic for me, please. You having one?"

"Thanks. Just an orange juice. You expecting company?"

"Yes: Sally. She wants me to have a drink ready for her. A martini. After I've had this one."

Sally came in as I was getting myself another G&T and her martini. "Hi, Red. How's it goin'?"

"Good. You?"

"Just fine." She looked around the bar and pointed to an empty booth. "We'll sit there", she said, picked up the drinks and strolled over.

Red winked at me as I paid the bar tab.

Sally sipped her Martini. "Whew. I needed that", she smiled.

"Busy evening?"

"Mmm. Even for a Saturday evening. Plenty of tips, though." She sipped again and sat back, enjoying a quiet moment.

I took a gulp of the G&T. "So. About last night ..."

She put her finger to my mouth. "Shhh. I need another of these first." She drained her martini in one go. My eyes would have been watering. "I'll go get 'em. Same again?" She stood up.

"Okay." Actually, what with the beers in the marina bar and these large measures, I was starting to feel a bit woozy. But I could manage another.

Reinstalled and replenished, Sally was ready to talk. "Right. I figure this is something to do with the World Trade Center thing, yes?"

"Well, in a way, yes. By the way, I may not be able to answer all your questions. As I said last night, 'the truth, and nothing but the truth, but not necessarily the whole truth'."

"Okay. But it is to do with that?"

"Not really, in fact. It happened because of that, but it's nothing to do with the reason it happened, whatever that turns out to be."

"Are you sure? This is important. I couldn't be involved in that. And there's going to be a shitstorm coming for anyone who is involved."

"True. Yes, I'm absolutely sure that this money has nothing to do with the attack. It relates to a transaction that was supposed to happen in an office there, that's all. Obviously, that didn't happen after all."

"And who's going to come looking for it? Surely someone will. And they'll be pretty mean, I guess."

"I don't think anyone will come looking just yet. My guess is they'll assume it's lost for ever. Until I cash the paperwork. The Bonds."

"And then what? Then they come looking?" Sally was quite right: That was when the fun would start.

"Er, yes. And we can assume they'll be very pissed off, to say the least. That's why I – we – need a plan. We'll try to leave a tangled trail that can't be followed, either on to where the money is, or to where we are. Or – especially - back to you, if you're back here. You're safe, I'm safe, the money's safe. Nobody knows who did it. That's the plan, anyway."

"But they will come looking?" she insisted.

"Oh, yes. Once they realise there's something to look for. But not for you. You'll be untraceable. Nothing to do with me, anyway. I might need you to help to cover me, offline, if you like. That's all."

"What do you mean?"

"Well there are some things I can't do without solid ID, like, I dunno, buy a car, that sort of thing. And I'll maybe need someone to be on the end of a phone when I'm elsewhere. Nothing traceable, and certainly nothing illegal. No connection with me at all."

She looked at me, still considering. I tried to look all, sort of, dependable and honest. In the end, she spoke first.

"What if you don't cash in these – these papers?"

"Then I think I'm in the clear. No trace at all, I'm fairly sure. But ..."

"But what?"

I took a moment to think, covered by a gulp of the G&T. "There's a reason. A good one. But I need to know whether you're in the team first. If you say you are, I'll believe you. And I'll tell you the reason then."

Sally did the same as I'd just done – stopped to think, covered by a sip of her Martini. Then she nodded. "Okay. Deep breath here. I'm in. You promise me I won't regret it?"

I grinned. "I promise." I raised my glass to her and drained it. She drained hers. Must have been a hard day, or maybe she needed some Dutch courage.

"Come on, then," I said. Sinatra was working his magic on the sound system. "Let's dance, partner."

"No, tell me that reason. About the papers or whatever." She smiled. "Then we can dance."

"OK, here's the thing. I never told you how much money is involved, exactly."

"You said millions ..."

"Yes. Around 25 million, in fact."

Sally looked stunned. “25 million? Christ ...”

“Yes. But only about 2 million in cash. The rest is in paper. Bearer bonds, they’re called. And when I cash those in, the alarm bells flash in the issuing bank. So to speak. And then the original owners. And then they’ll know for sure that it wasn’t destroyed - that someone has their money.”

“I see. Hmm. And I see why you can’t just burn them – these bonds. Pity it’s not the other way round.”

“The cash and the bonds – more cash, less bonds? Yes – that would be an easy decision. But ...”

“But they’re not. OK. Well, partner, you can tell me how you plan to do that – later. Now, we dance.”

I nodded. I had found my partner. We danced for a while as Sinatra gave way to Bob Seger’s Night Moves, appropriately, and then went back to the bar. “I need to get back to the boat, really”, I said. “How about you?”

“Yeah, I’m tired. One for the road?” So we had another at the bar and then left together. Red said nothing except “Goodnight, you guys!”

We walked down the main street, to the point where one way led to the marina and the other way to Sally’s place. She stopped and kissed me, but was clearly not up for high jinks on the boat, so I didn’t push it. Plenty of time for that. Anyway, I was quite full of beer and G&T. “Right, partner,” she said. “Tomorrow you can explain this plan of yours. It had better be good. Tomorrow morning. Ten thirty suit you?”

Tomorrow was Sunday, of course. “Fine. I’ll have coffee on.”

“Okay. I’ll bring donuts.” She smiled again and set off towards home, and I did the same.

I reflected as I stepped onto Mystere and locked up behind me. I was pleased Sally was on board, so to speak, but I still had a vestige of –

not doubt, exactly – uncertainty, maybe. I was sure I could trust her not to drop me in it, and almost sure she could do what I needed her to do as the process unfolded. But not perfectly certain. Well, what the hell. What choice did I have anyway? And when can you ever be absolutely sure of anybody?

She arrived on time the next day with her donuts, as promised. I had coffee ready. It didn't take long to explain my plan, such as it was. She sat quietly and listened; asking questions now and then, but didn't challenge the strategy, and didn't ask for fine detail, which anyway I didn't have.

When I'd finished, I stood up to make more coffee. As I messed about at the sink, she said, "How do you know this will work?"

"Hold on." I went into the bedroom and brought her the book, and said, "It's all in here. I've put a sticker on the section that relates to this. Things will start to change after what happened, but not much as yet. New regulations and so on, I expect. That's one reason to move quickly. Take this and read it, so you'll know what we're doing and why. And bear in mind that we'll engage an expert in this process."

"Okay. And, why do you need me? Can't you do this on your own? It would be much safer, wouldn't it?"

"Well, possibly I could, but I'd just feel better with a wingman. Wingwoman, then", I grinned. "I may need a genuine US citizen with proper ID and so on sometimes, and we may need to be in two places at once for some transactions. I'm not sure, really. I like you and trust you, and I think you'll be good in a crisis, if we have one. Anyway, I work better as part of a team. I'll need someone to check my plans, talk through any problems, just support me. You know?"

"You're taking quite a risk, aren't you? With me, I mean."

"Well, I'm taking plenty of risks anyway; this is just one more risk, I guess. But really, once I left New York with the money I had no choice but to see it through. I think I'm good at recognising people I can trust. And I feel I can trust you. And I'll make it worth your while, of course."

She weighed the book in her hand. "Mmm. I see. And it's all in here, is it?"

"No, but the basics of the financial stuff's in there. The trick seems to be that you bounce the money through complex corporate ownerships really quickly, across different countries, and keep ahead of anybody who's trying to follow you. There are quite a few countries, especially in the Caribbean, whose corporate laws are a bit slack or work very slowly and inefficiently. And Switzerland is still almost obsessively secretive in most things. And, as I say, I'll use an expert at doing just that."

She put the book down. "Right. So what's the deal? What's my piece of the action?" She did that tucking the hair behind the ear thing. Why did I find that so attractive, I wondered ...

This – what's the deal - was a question I'd thought about it for a long time. I thought I had a fair proposition, but I didn't know what she really expected. Of course, if things developed between us, it might turn out to be less important, but we both needed to start with an agreement that would let her walk away at the end, safe and happy, if she wanted to. And I needed the rewards to be sufficient to keep her committed throughout the process and silent afterwards.

"Well. As I said, we need to buy you a nice car – one that I can use. You get to keep that for a start. "I'll give you some cash to cover any expenses and so on. And I think you ought to keep, say, a million dollars. As a thank-you."

"Ooh. Just to keep you company?"

I laughed. "Well, I wouldn't put it like that. It's for your advice, support, being a sounding-board, maybe doing things I can't do ..."

"I see. When does all this happen?"

"Within six months, I'd guess. We need to move fast, as I say."

"And how much do you end up with?"

I thought she'd ask that. "The balance. A lot," I smiled. "I don't know what the expenses are going to be, of course. But all I'm asking you to be is a sort of confidante, if that's the word. There'll certainly be some interesting adventures if you come with me. You may not actually have to do anything. You break no laws, I think, and you shouldn't be in any danger physically, but there is a small exposure. Small, but it's there, I have to admit."

She smiled. "Okay, I'm in. It should be fun, and, well, I think I can trust you to keep me away from any trouble."

"Good." We clinked coffee mugs.

"So. When do we start? What's the first step?"

At least I knew what the first few steps needed to be. "When can you get some time off? About two weeks?"

"Well, we'll be busy in the restaurant over the holidays, so not before then. Say early January?"

"Yes, that would work. I need to get some things sorted before we start to really move, so, yes. So, can you take 2 weeks off?"

"I'll ask. Where are we going?"

I looked at the clock. It was midday on a drab Sunday. "Tell you what. Let's jump in your car and go into San Fran for a late lunch - somewhere posh. I can explain it all then."

She giggled. "'Posh'? How English. You need to watch that. But yes, why not. My Mom's gone down to Santa Barbara for a few days to visit her friend, so I don't have to get back for her. Yes. Let's go. But we don't need to drive – we can take the ferry. It's turning into a nice day."

So we locked up and walked down to the dock. The next ferry into San Fran left in 20 minutes, so we bought return tickets and boarded. As we walked out of the terminal at the dock – on the Embarcadero - forty minutes later, we saw a bus conveniently pulling up outside. Not really caring where it was going except towards the centre, we took it, and then changed for a cable car into Chinatown. We settled on a restaurant more or less at random. Not very posh at all, in fact, but authentic enough.

Over a Chinese feast for two we discussed the details of what we needed to do. Sally was delighted to learn that part of the process required me, at least, to go to the Caymans for a few days, with an opportunity for a holiday for both of us, if she fancied it. It seemed that she did. We didn't discuss sleeping arrangements, though.

We talked about what might go wrong with my plan, and what we could do about it, and how to spend the money once we had it. She was already thinking it was "our" money ... somehow, I was ok with that. The very old and very Chinese waiter seemed to speak little English, but we spoke in low tones, like lovers do, as the song goes. He beamed at us and gave us extra treats in between courses.

It felt good to have a co-conspirator at last, and Sally seemed to relax more and more into it as we talked. We drank tea, and then shared a bottle of wine. The meal lasted nearly two hours, and at the end of it I began to feel that I'd been right to trust her and involve her in this adventure. On a whim, I bought the Sunday San Francisco Chronicle as we walked back to the cable car stop.

The weather had improved a lot after the morning drizzle. We sat outside on the ferry in chilly sunshine and amiable silence and watched Alcatraz slip by on one side and the Golden Gate on the other. It all felt quite familiar now.

Sally took my hand as we stepped down the dock from the ferry. "I think we might need another bottle of wine. I'm going to raid your fridge. You must have some wine in there?"

Of course I did, so we opened another bottle and watched some rubbish on TV before she took my hand again and led me into the bedroom. I must have looked surprised, although not reluctant. "I told you, my Mom's away, and I've no need to go home to look after her. Now that I know your secrets, you're in the clear. We have some catching up to do."

We did, too. I'd forgotten the pleasure of truly connected sex – lovemaking if you like – as opposed to more matter-of-fact fucking I'd got used to in recent years. It was better, of course, but it was also a bit scary. We were entering uncharted waters in more ways than one. But that was what this whole thing was about, when I thought about it. Meanwhile, Sally slept, snuggled into my side with her arm round me.

Chapter 14

Meet the Wife

Next morning was Monday, of course. Sally had stayed the night, and as I watched her fussing over coffee and bacon, I had one of those nice warm feelings I'd almost forgotten. It was the tingly feeling that this could be the start of something really good. And to be honest, it was a long time since anybody had made me breakfast without it being their job.

She said we needed some fresh croissants if I wanted some to start with, so I said I'd walk over to the deli on the marine drive – just 5 minutes. I came back with 2 warm croissants and a punnet of imported strawberries on an impulse. I put the croissants on the worktop and handed her the strawberries with a kiss.

"Ooh, you do know how to charm a girl, don't you? I love these. Very tempting. I'll just have to have one as a sample." She picked a large strawberry and popped it into to her mouth. She made a moan of pleasure and smiled.

"Hmm. I think I've heard that sound before ...," I smiled. Sally blushed and gave me a playful slap.

Over breakfast, I looked over the classified ads in Sunday's San Fran newspaper. Sally looked over my shoulder. "What are you looking for?"

"I said I – you – needed some smart wheels. Look here."

"Merc sports? Nice."

"Mmm. I think we should go and get one, don't you?"

"What, today? Well, I suppose we can – I'm not due at work until seven." She was excited and giggly.

There were 2 Mercs of the right age and price for sale privately. We called both numbers. One failed to answer, but the other answered at once, and said that the car was still available. We agreed to see the seller that afternoon. I went up to the bank and withdrew thirty thousand in cash, which caused hardly a ripple. I came back and handed the cash to Sally. and we set off for the ferry dock.

We arrived at a nice apartment block in Nob Hill and met a forty-something lady of leisure, who was selling her 2-year old Merc 500 SL to buy a new one. Silver, low miles, Merc service history and nothing much to haggle over, except a couple of stone chips on the bonnet. Hood. We haggled bit, mainly on the strength of the wad of cash that Sally pulled out of her jacket pockets.

The lady of leisure maintained her cool in the face of the cash as well as she could, but we were soon the proud owners of smart, discreet but classy wheels. Well, Sally was. We left the car where it was and sorted out the insurance on the phone to Sally's broker, who wasn't fazed by the additional car and driver. She then dealt with temporary registration, which was a mystery to me. But within an hour we were driving away in some style.

And of course, I was driving – it's the same the whole world over – men drive, ladies look good in the passenger seat. And she did. Brett was named on the insurance, and of course I had his driver's licence. I hoped that wouldn't attract any attention – at least on record. I would have to drive sensibly.

There was one more thing I felt I had to do now that I had wheels, and before I started to make my moves with the bonds. I hate loose ends, and I suppose I have a soft streak. And, to be fair, there was something I wanted out of it. I'm talking about Brett's wife. And his Passport.

Brett's address was in his wallet, of course, and I decided to pay her a visit. I could have flown down and hired a car, but I didn't want to use Brett's credit cards, especially in his own back yard, so to speak. And anyway, I wasn't sure they'd still be any good. I asked Sally if she wanted to come along for the ride, but she said it was too short notice to take time off. Especially as she was about to take a lot more time off.

So, early next morning, I set out and drove south, along the coast. Sure, you can fly it in a morning, and it takes at least couple of days to drive it, but if you have time on your hands – and I did – it's a great drive. Roof down, west coast blues playing on the stereo, this was one of those lifetime drives. I stayed in a couple of nice small hotels in little seaside towns, out of season, and ate some great seafood.

I missed Sally. I'd got used to not missing anyone, really. It was nice, though. Meanwhile, I was enjoying being Mr. Nobody; and of course, I paid cash everywhere. Nobody objected to that.

Skirting round the Los Angeles sprawl and heading still further south, I eventually arrived in La Jolla, just north of San Diego, at about lunchtime on Thursday. I bought a street plan at a gas station and looked up Brett's address. It was in a nice location, not far from the ocean, in what looked from the map like a fairly upmarket residential area.

And so it proved. Slowly driving past the address revealed a large ranch-style house, all on one level, with an open front garden and double garage. The same as countless others throughout the warm southern states. Comfortable, probably a pool out back, and about three bedrooms. No car on the drive. It was half-three: she was probably out to work. Or shopping.

Rather than block the drive, and to keep it out of sight, I parked the Merc round the corner on the cross-street, and walked back and up to the front door. Ringing the bell had no effect inside, so I stepped back and looked around. It certainly looked occupied: all was neat and tidy, and when I looked through the windows, it looked lived-in. Furnished, some bits and pieces lying around. Just normal.

As I turned and walked back down the drive, and looked back from the sidewalk, a pink-rinsed skinny old bird came out of the house next door. She was old in a sunshine state way: tiny, shrivelled and brown. She could have been any age north of sixty-five. She was wearing what they called a housecoat: a polyester overall I supposed you wore to do the cleaning.

"Can I help you, sir?" asked the old bird.

"Yes, I hope so. I'm looking for Mrs Foster. Is this her house?"

"Ah yes, that's erm, Peggy?" She seemed to drift into a reverie. She was not quite humming, but not quite singing. Then I realised - it was Buddy Holly's 'Peggy Sue'. Weird. "No, not Peggy. Caroline, maybe?" And we had a scratchy burst of Neil Diamond – 'Sweet Caroline'. "No, not that." Thank goodness she hadn't heard of Status Quo. That would have been too much.

This was really weird. The old bird was clearly barking. Mind you, there were lots of people much worse wandering the streets back home, I recalled.

"Ah!" the old bird squawked. "Mandy!" And we had a burst of Barry Manilow. "Yes that's it. Mandy!"

"Ah, right. I see." I had that slightly unsure feeling you get in the presence of the not-quite-right-in-the-head.

"Yes. Mandy. That's it", she said. "Is this to do with her husband?"

"It may be. Does she live here?" Disconcerted, I had lapsed into my British accent.

"Yes, but she's at work right now. She works at the beauty parlour over on Saxon Street."

"Right. When does she get home?"

"'Bout six usually. Her husband's missing, you know."

"That so?" Maybe this old dear would be usefully indiscreet as well as bonkers. "Where's he gone?"

"No-one knows. He just vanished. Coupla months ago now. No word since. Just gone."

"I see. Anyone know where he might be?"

"Nope." This was clearly a big deal for the old dear. "She needs to find him real bad."

"Why?"

She looked at me suspiciously. "What's it to you, anyways?"

"Oh, nothin'. Just interested. It's Mrs. Foster I need to see. Mandy. Back around six, you say?"

"Yup. I'll tell her you called. Mr ...?"

"No need. I'll come back at six. Take care, now."

"Hey! You're British, ain't you?"

"Erm, yes, that's right. From London."

"Ooh! I love London. All those musicals." And we had a burst of "I had a dream ..." Les Mis, I think. Christ, this was a trip to the circus.

"Yes, very nice. Thanks a lot. Be seeing you." I hoped not.

I walked round the corner and got back into the car and moved off quickly, before the old trout could ask any questions. So, Mrs Brett Foster – Mandy - had no idea where her husband was. Assuming the old bat was up to date, that was: she didn't seem quite the full shilling by any means. But these nosy old bats usually know what's going on.

It was just after three o'clock. A very late breakfast would pass the time for a couple of hours. Driving back into the centre of town, I discovered a diner and ordered sausage and eggs and coffee. Yes - breakfast again: what the American diner does best, really, except maybe for hamburger and chips, which I didn't fancy. Brett's business card was still in my wallet. It had the address - that is, floor and company name - of his last meeting, in the WTC, scribbled on the back when I spoke to him on the phone that morning. I looked again at the company name and memorised it.

The diner had a view of a busy crossroads, and there were plenty of people walking around and in and out of shops. Watching the pretty young waitress and gazing out of the window occupied my time in equal proportion. I enjoyed watching people, not just pretty women and girls, but all sorts.

I watched the typical American suburban scene – struck as ever by the apparent mismatch between the huge cars and trucks being driven by diminutive American housewives. Then, judging by his demeanour as he left the clothes store opposite, I was sure I saw a guy steal a t-shirt from the shop. Sure enough, the assistant came out, looking harassed, a minute after my suspect left, walking smartly, up the street and round the corner. There was nothing I could do, and I was certainly not going to get involved. Just an observer.

Just as I thought I was starting to look suspicious, or like a cop, I paid up and left the diner. It was a quarter to six as I arrived at the Foster house and parked around the corner, where I could just see the drive across the open-plan front lawns. At ten past, a black Ford SUV turned onto the drive and a trim blonde woman got out. She went round to the back of the truck and opened the door, then reach in to get some shopping bags. Short blonde hair, nice shape, knee-length white coat - from the beautician's, I supposed. She took the first armful of bags to the house, unlocked it and went in, then came back out to the truck again.

"Excuse me", I said, walking up the drive. "Mrs. Foster?" I had decided to be Roger Moore again. Don't ask me why – maybe I thought it would be more credible. And, of course it was consistent with what the bonkers old dear had heard.

She turned round and looked at me. She was pretty, and I remembered that Brett had said she had been a cheerleader. I could see that. And she clearly knew how to keep her looks. Tasty. And not at all "gone to seed", as Brett had said.

She gave me a quizzical look. "Who wants to know?"

"My name's Johnson. Bruce Johnson. It's about your husband."

"He's not here. In fact I don't know where he is." She turned back to the truck. She picked up a bag of shopping in each arm, leaving two more in there.

"No. I know. I have some news for you. Perhaps we should speak inside. Let me help you with these." I picked up the last two bags.

She looked at me again and turned towards the door. "OK." I followed her into the house and on to the kitchen area, where she set down the bags on the table. I did the same. She walked back and shut the front door. "So, Mr. erm ... Johnson, did you say? Who are you?"

"Well, for now, let's just say that I'm someone who knew your husband. Who knows what happened to him."

"'Knew him'? 'Knows what happened to him?' Is he dead then? You're English, aren't you? What's going on?" She was quick on the uptake, but she was flustered and flushed. She was very pretty, I was still aware of that.

"Mrs. Foster, what do you think has happened to your husband?"

"I think I need to know who you are. Why do you want to know?"

"Look ... may I call you Mandy? It is Mandy, isn't it? I'm working with your husband's employers. Klein and Son."

"Er, yes, it's Mandy. I've already talked to them when he disappeared. They had no idea what happened. Why would they send you now?" I hadn't thought of that. Of course, they would have dealt with this straight away.

"It's a new line we're following. I approached them with certain ... information. I happened to spend an evening with your husband, just before he disappeared. I know what happened."

"So, what did happen?"

"Mrs Foster ... Mandy, I have to ask you again. What do you think has happened to your husband?"

"You said you knew."

"Yes. I need to know what you believe."

"I believe he's dead. He would have been in touch somehow if not. We ... we had things to deal with ..."

"Ok ... look, is there anywhere we can be more comfortable?"

She nodded, and led me through to the sitting area in the open-plan centre of the house. It was well furnished, but a bit dated, somehow. As if money had been spent once, but not recently. When we were sitting down, I said, "Mrs Foster, I have bad news. I'm afraid that, well, your suspicions are correct."

"He's dead?" I nodded, looking grimly sympathetic. Not my best look, but it didn't matter.

Her earlier poise collapsed and, slowly, tears ran down her face. She looked away for a moment. She walked over to a low table and took a tissue from a box. She blew her nose and composed herself. "How?"

Deep breath, honest face. "Mandy, I have to confess to misleading you a little earlier. I'm not an investigator; at least I'm not officially investigating your husband. And I'm not working for Klein and Co. I apologise for that. I needed to gain your trust. But I assure you; I'm telling you the truth now. I did spend some time with your husband the evening before he died. And I do know what happened. And I had a feeling you might have guessed."

"I see. Go on." She was composed now, and prepared for the news.

"We were staying in the same hotel in New York", (not quite true, of course, but easier) "and we met in the cocktail bar there, on the evening of September 10th. I was in New York on business, and I happened to sit next to him at the bar. We got talking, as you do. Did you know he was in New York?"

"Uh-huh," she nodded, her eyes fixed on me. "He had to visit the Klein and Co offices there."

"Quite. Well, we went out for a change of scene, and had quite a lot more to drink. Somewhere along the way, he lost his wallet. I lent him some cash, and he gave me his business card. He was insistent he paid me back. I wasn't too bothered. It wasn't a lot." Not quite the truth: better than the truth.

"So you want me to pay you back?" She half stood up.

"No, no. That's not it at all." I gestured her to sit down. "As I say, it wasn't much. I can't remember how much: a couple of hundred maybe. Not a problem."

"Ah. Okay, go on," she sniffed.

Well, as I say, he gave me his card. He insisted that we met for lunch next day and he would pay me back. You see, we were both due at the same place the next day. The World Trade Center."

She went pale. "No. You must have made a mistake. He had no reason to go there. His New York office is – was - uptown." But her face said that she knew it must be true.

"I know. But he had a meeting in the Trade Center. At half-past eight, as I recall. It was with a recruitment company. Obviously, Klein and Co didn't know about that."

"Oh, God." Her hands went up to her mouth, her eyes stared. "So ... he was in there, when ..."

"I'm afraid so, yes. There's no doubt about it. You see, I phoned him just before it happened. He was there for certain. I'm sorry, Mandy."

She was still staring, shocked. "But what was he doing in there? Why was he there?"

"He was being interviewed for a new job. By a recruitment agency. He told me all about it. I had business there later, as it happened, in the other tower, which of course I didn't get to. A coincidence. Just luck, I suppose. I really am sorry to have to tell you this."

"Is there proof? I mean, how can I, erm, settle things?"

"I think I can help you prove it. Erm, look, if this helps you believe me, well, I understand that you and Brett were contemplating a divorce?"

"How could you know that?" She blew her nose. "Well, yes, you must have met him if you know that."

"Exactly. He told me. He was quite drunk later on, in fact."

"Were you picking up hookers? He usually did." She looked angry, with Brett, I thought, not with me. I saw no reason to tell her about that. I was telling the truth, well, mostly - as far as I could, but there was no need to be cruel.

"No. Not my scene, I'm afraid," I lied – a white lie, but again, better than the truth. "We had drinks and a bite to eat. He was talking about his work and said that he had arranged this meeting – interview, really - because he thought Klein and Co might be thinking of giving him the push, as we might say."

"That's true, I guess. He didn't like it much, anyway. And you say he told you about the divorce?"

"He said you wanted to divorce him, yes. He seemed quite resigned to that."

"Hmm. Well, I wouldn't wish this on him, no matter how much of a cheating son-of-a-bitch ..." She tailed off, not sure what she ought to feel, I thought. "Did you see what happened? God, he wouldn't have been one of the jumpers, could he? I couldn't bear that."

"My guess is that he would have known very little. He was very close to the site of the first impact. Instant, I'd say."

"Well, I guess that's something. He was a cheating son-of-a-bitch, but hell, this ... no-one deserves this. And you escaped?"

"Yes. Well, I was due there a little later, so I didn't get there at all as it turned out. Lucky, I suppose."

"Hmm. So, who were these people he was meeting? Can I prove he was there?"

"I can help you with that, as I say. But I'd like you to help me as well, Mandy."

"Oh? How?"

"Do you have your husband's passport? I assume he had one?"

"Yes. I looked for that earlier, when I thought he'd disappeared to some place in the Caribbean or somewhere with some bimbo... I'll show you." She walked over to a bureau against the far wall. I couldn't help watching her arse – ass – as she walked. She was still wearing her white coat, and I could just make out her underwear through it. I know I shouldn't have been so carnal at that time, but there you are. Old habits. She was a pleasant sight, when it was safe to look.

She passed me the passport. I looked at it carefully. It had the same photo as on the driving licence, and the expiry date was six years hence. I flipped through the visas. Not many, but some from

Venezuela – work, I suppose – and some from St. Lucia and Grenada. Vacations, probably: nice. I put the passport down near me. I wanted it. That was my real motivation, if I was honest, in coming all this way.

"Mandy, I'd guess that, if you could satisfy the authorities that Brett really is dead, you'd inherit the house and everything, plus some insurance payouts? Possibly his job carried insurance? Altogether, far more than you'd have gained from a divorce?"

"Well, I suppose so, yes. Why?"

"Before I help you get that proof, I want something from you."

"What?"

I picked up the passport. "This."

She looked at me for a long moment. "Why?"

"I have my reasons. You don't need to know. And you don't need this anyway. He could easily have lost it. Or had it with him when he died. So, that's the deal: I give you proof of Brett's death and the key to that money and your freedom, or at least a way to get it, for this." I held up the passport.

She looked at me again. "I don't think you're on the level", she said, and waited a moment, thinking. "But I don't see what it has to do with me. Okay. It's a deal. I do need your proof. And I don't need that passport, I guess"

Reaching into my pocket for my wallet, I brought out Brett's business card, and put the passport in the other side pocket. "Okay then. Brett was meeting a firm called Page and Nash. They're an executive search outfit - head-hunters, an international operation. They have a head office in Chicago. If you – or your lawyer – contact them, they will definitely have a record of his being in touch, and the appointment in New York. You don't get to meet them without following the process. They will confirm the appointment, at least, and that will probably be enough. Especially if you tell them that you have remembered that he was going there."

"What: I just remember, just like that?"

No. She was right, it would look a bit strange. I hadn't thought about that. This was where I would give real value for the passport. "Okay. Did Brett keep a diary here?"

"No. We looked."

Of course. They would have done. "What about his mail? No letters from Page and Nash – the recruiters? I guess you went through all that as well?"

"No. I mean, yes, we did. No letters. Possibly it was arranged by phone. Look, couldn't you give evidence, make a deposition or something?"

Obviously, I was not about to appear before any investigation. But there could be a way.

"I guess I might have written to you to express my sympathies. Last man to see him alive, that sort of thing. I could mention where he was going, and when he was there, in my letter. I'd send it to you via his office. How about that?"

"A bit late, isn't it?"

"Maybe a bit, but I don't think so, really. It's only a few months, after all. And everyone's been traumatised. Not too late, anyway."

"Okay." She looked at me and thought about it. I couldn't tell what was going through that blonde head. "Okay. Let's work out that letter." She looked down at herself. "God, I'm still in my whites. I work as a beautician."

"I know. And you used to be a cheerleader. I can tell, anyway, but Brett told me."

"Did he?" She smiled, eyes distant for a moment. "I guess he wasn't all bad. But he couldn't keep his cock in his pants. That's not a problem for you, you said? Lucky for your wife, I guess."

"No wife. She had your husband's problem, you might say. Long gone now."

Mandy smiled, her first interaction with me as a human being, a fellow sufferer, I suppose. "I see. Well, why don't you work out a letter and I'll go get out of my whites. Use the bureau, there."

I worked out a letter I thought would do the job, and was reading it back when she appeared, showered, shampooed and smelling clean and fresh. She was wearing jeans and a blouse that showed her figure off very well. Too well, really. I wondered what her plans were.

She read the letter and suggested some changes. We sat close together and I breathed in her fresh smell as I wrote the last draft. She was sexy and knew it, and I was sure she was lining me up. I was fine with that. I looked into her eyes and smiled.

"Of course, I can't use this paper. It obviously comes from here. It's quality stuff. Traceable. I don't think anyone will check, but they might: we shouldn't risk it. So, I'll take this draft away and write you the same letter on different paper. It will have a vague address: I won't be traceable. But it will do the job for you. It only has to point you in a direction; it's not evidence in itself. You'll find the evidence when you look in that direction."

She looked at me with a quizzical expression. "I think you must be some sort of criminal. Or maybe a spy: James Bond, maybe? What did you say your name was?"

"Johnson. Bruce Johnson." As opposed to Bond, James Bond.

"Hmm. And where are you from, Bruce Johnson? Where are you staying in San Diego?"

"Good question, actually. I need to book a hotel." I smiled at her.

"Use the phone, there," She pointed at the bureau. "The Hyatt's good, by the marina." I found the number in the book and phoned the reservation desk. No, I didn't have my card with me to secure the booking, but I would be there within the hour. There were several rooms available right now. I did have ID, yes. That was okay, then. I rang off before they could ask my name. That would have been difficult.

"Okay, I'll be going. Don't want to set the neighbours talking."

"I don't care about them: not any more, anyway. Did you meet Mrs Rosencrantz next door?"

"Yes. An interesting lady ..." I smiled.

"Oh, did she sing? Poor dear. She used to be on the stage, you know. A singer. She's losing her memory and uses old tunes to prompt her memory. Sweet, really."

"Ah, I see. A bit odd at first, though. It threw me a bit to begin with."

"It would. Anyway, I'll soon be long gone, thanks to you. I have a sister in Phoenix, Arizona. We've talked about opening up a beautician business there. I guess we can do that now."

"Yep. I guess so." A thought struck me. "Will you keep the name? Foster?"

She thought for a moment. "I doubt it. My sister's just got divorced as well. We'll be the Holmes sisters again. Just like old times." She smiled to herself. So did I. Brett's wife was about to disappear as well. This was all good.

I stood up and gathered up my car keys and the draft letter. The passport was in my pocket. "I'll write this letter and mail it to the company early next week. I guess you'll get it or hear from them soon after they get it. I'd prefer you to throw the envelope away, but I can't make you do that. I don't think we'll meet again. Unfortunately." I smiled.

"Okay. I guess that would be for the best." She walked with me to the door. She opened it and turned to look at me. I couldn't read her face, but I'd have given a lot of money to know what she was thinking. In at least one way, I felt that she knew what I was thinking. "Well, goodbye, Mister Johnson. Or whoever you are. And good luck."

We shook hands. "And to you, Mandy", I smiled, and walked away down the drive and round the corner road to my car. I don't know why I felt unfulfilled. I'd got what I really wanted, after all. Pre-Sally, I might have followed-up on that half-offer, despite the somewhat caddish circumstances. So much had changed, and there were lots more changes to come.

Chapter 15

The Hare is Running

Sally and I spent a very happy Christmas in Sausalito. She was working at the bar and earning plenty of tips, and we invited her mom to Christmas dinner on the boat. I produced as close to a British Christmas Dinner as I could in the galley. I'd found a large duck in a specialist butchers in San Fran, and I even found some mince pies. I think it went OK. Sally certainly enjoyed it. New Years' Eve in Daisy's was great, with some of the locals I'd got to know quite well and a great band. New Years' Day was suitably subdued.

But it felt as if I was marking time now. The preparatory work was done, and I was ready to go. I gave about a second's thought to settling for the cash and forgetting about the Bearer Bonds, but that meant turning my back on far too much money. There was no point in half-measures now - I was already miles away from my old life.

So, it was time to move. I had an outline plan and a glamorous assistant. And viable ID – for a while, at least. I also had a boat that I had grown much attached to, and I was pretty sure I'd exercise my option to buy it when the arrangement came to an end. But that would be at the other side of the difficult process of getting my hands on the money at the same time as keeping myself – and Sally - invisible.

I discussed the next moves with Sally. She had arranged to take the first 2 weeks of January off work, and although there was some business involved, this was going to be 2 weeks or so in the Caribbean in January, which couldn't be too bad. Just in case, I arranged for Sally to have a debit card on my account, with a hundred thousand dollar line of credit, so that she had access to funds if she needed them. As I'd promised.

As Brett Foster, and using my new debit card, I booked a flight from San Fran to Owen Roberts airport, in George Town on Grand Cayman.

Sally, meanwhile, booked herself and me – well, Brett - on a 14-day vacation at a beach resort on the island. Our vacation was due to start a day after I arrived. I booked a room at the Marriott hotel, just north of George Town, for my first day, which was going to be purely business.

The selection of a Cayman lawyer had proved to be a slight problem. Obviously I needed a smart cookie who could manage the complexities of creating, buying and selling companies, but not a huge firm with lots of people aware of each transaction and over-developed sensitivity to the legal niceties. Or over-zealous record-keeping, for that matter.

Using Sally's computer, I went online and found a small firm with just 5 lawyers, based in George Town, and with what they called "Associate Firms" in other Islands, including Grenada, Grand Turk and also Zurich. I phoned and made an appointment – as Brett - to discuss "a new business registration", and kept the conversation as short as possible. My appointment was with Robert Garrido, a junior partner, the day after I was due to arrive.

I let Ken White know that I was going to be away from Sausalito for a couple of weeks or so, and he told me how to lock the boat up safely, and asked me to let George, the Harbourmaster, know. Ken asked me what my plans were – was I interested in taking up my option? I said I probably was, but that I'd discuss it after I returned. He seemed happy with that for now.

Of course, this meant that I was about to use Brett's passport. By now security was very much tighter than it had been - before what was now just referred to as "9/11." With the reading glasses, I was sure that I matched the photo well enough. I was fairly hopeful that the identity hadn't been flagged as void. I'd written the letter as promised, but that was less than a month ago. It would take longer than this to void the ID. Wouldn't it?

Sally drove me to up to San Fran airport in the Merc. She was excited about our plans and had quickly become very comfortable with her new-found wealthy lifestyle. I suggested that she did some shopping for holiday clothes, and she said that she would call in to a mall she knew of on her way home. She had arranged for Red to drive her back up to the airport the next day.

The first leg of my flight was internal – San Fran to Miami. Before "9/11", I could have boarded an internal flight like this with just a valid ticket, but things were changing fast. All I had to do here, though, was show "photo ID", and Brett's driving licence did the trick.

But I had to pass through proper passport control in Miami, since I was leaving the USA. I had read that some new "Bio-identity" processes were rolling out, and I had to register a fingerprint when I went through departures. So now Brett's passport records had my fingerprints attached. I was sure that there was no official record of my prints back in the UK to tie into these, although my flat would produce plenty of examples if anyone was sufficiently curious to pick them up.

That might prove a problem in due course, but there was no immediate problem with passing through departures as Brett, and I settled back in my Business Class seat to fly on to George Town, where I arrived around 10 o'clock in the evening.

The airport was chaotic, but it seemed to work, and my passport raised no comment. I didn't need a visa and I was in the taxi queue with my bags within an hour of landing.

I had taken the aluminium briefcase as hand luggage, with some clothes and books on top of the bonds, which were in several brown envelopes. The x-ray machine raised no objections to the documents. There was no restriction against bringing this stuff in, but I was relieved not to have to discuss them with anyone. No footprints. Sally was bringing my holiday clothes along with hers in a normal checked suitcase.

I got to the Marriott quite late, well after 11 PM, but my reservation was confirmed. Again, I showed Brett's passport at the desk, signed the registration form and took my key. I put the briefcase under the bottom drawer as usual, then sat down to a room service steak and bottle of wine.

I called Sally from my cellphone to tell her I'd arrived safely. She was fizzing with excitement about her holiday. She talked about her shopping trip and wanted to know about the weather, what people were wearing and so on. I said it was hard to say for sure at this time of night, but it all looked fine. I then got into bed and fell asleep quite quickly, despite my own excitement about what I needed to do in the next few days and weeks. Things were now starting to enter the critical phase.

Chapter 16

Building the New Life

The Marriott was a resort hotel, rather than a business centre. Sally had booked us into another resort for our holiday, but this looked very nice indeed. It was certainly a great place to do business – if you could concentrate on the job in hand.

My appointment with Robert Garrido was set for 12 o'clock. I phoned his office at 9 from the lobby phone and asked for him. I was put through at once.

"Mr Garrido?"

"Yes. Is this Mr Foster?"

"It is, yes. We have a meeting booked at 12, yes?"

"That's right. Is there a problem?" Garrido sounded young and keen. Good.

"No, not really, but I was wondering if I could buy you lunch and discuss my business somewhere more – erm – conducive ..."

"Oh, I see. Well, yes, why not? Where did you have in mind? There's a good place not far from here ..."

"Well, look, I'm in the Marriott Resort, and it's really very nice here. When's your next appointment after me?"

"Erm ... 3:30, in my office."

"Great. Can you get here for, say 12:30?"

"Oh. Yes, certainly, Mr. Foster. That would be nice. Thank you."

"Ok, I'll see you here then. Ask for me at the Solana restaurant desk. I'll book a suitable table."

"That's very kind of you. I'll see you there. Thanks."

"Great. 'Bye for now."

That would save me a taxi trip, I thought, and I didn't really want a conventional business meeting in a lawyer's office. After my breakfast in the beach bar, I went down to the Solana restaurant – it was the more formal one, with, I hoped, comfortable tables set a discreet distance apart. And so it proved. I found the booking manager and asked for a reservation for 2 on a table a bit out of the way "for a business meeting." He understood and suggested a table slightly removed from the rest. Excellent.

I spent the morning sitting on the terrace overlooking the beach, reading a day-old US newspaper and planning what I wanted to get out of this meeting – how much to say and what I needed back. The view was delightful, and I was looking forward to a few days' R&R with Sally alongside the business I needed to see to.

Garrido arrived on time and was shown to my table. I stood up to shake his hand and see what sort of chap he seemed to be.

He was about 5 feet 6, slight and olive-skinned. He had an eager air about him, a firm, dry handshake and a ready smile. He was wearing a lightweight suit and a confident smile. So far, so good.

We sat down and the waiter brought menus. Garrido ordered a mineral water and I asked for a beer. We studied the menus in silence for a moment. The prices were painfully high, but I expected that.

We exchanged small talk; he told me that he was 27, engaged to be married, and rented a small house just outside George Town which he shared with his fiancée, who worked as a bookkeeper.

After the waiter took our orders, I asked Garrido about his position in the law firm. He'd passed his law exams by correspondence course while working at the firm, and was offered a junior partnership a year after qualifying.

He had an ambition to buy a new house – they were building houses exclusively for residents as opposed to holiday renters, and he was hoping for a raise in salary or more shares in the partnership to help fund this before long. He wanted to get married and move with his wife into their own place. Then a nice gentle rise to senior partner and a comfortable retirement, I suppose.

It seemed that the senior partners had decided that my requirements as I'd described them were relatively trivial, or not hugely fee-paying, anyway, and could be dealt with by a junior. And that was just fine.

The starters arrived: Seafood salad for me and pasta for him. It was time for me to explain what I wanted.

"Ok, well, let me explain what I need from you. I assume that everything I tell you goes no further: it's privileged information?"

Garrido nodded. "Yes. Unless I need to brief anyone else to deliver the service."

"No. If you need to pass any of this on, please talk to me first. Well, what you can say without checking, and it's true, is that I want to set up a Company here in order to protect some funds derived from a previous enterprise, and I may need to move these funds across other new businesses in other territories to keep them secure."

He wasn't entirely happy, to judge by his body language – he stopped chewing his tagliatelli and his fork stopped in mid-air for a moment.

I added quickly: "I can reassure you that these funds are not taxable, and they're unknown to any tax authority or Government body. And I haven't stolen them."

"I see ..." Clearly, he didn't.

"Do you?"

He smiled and shrugged. "Well, no, not really – I have lots of questions. But I understand what you're saying. It just seems – well, unlikely, that's all."

I was warming to him. He seemed straightforward and honest. So far. "OK. Fair enough. I promise to tell you more as we go forward. If we do. But for now, what can you do for me? Could you create the right company structures?"

"Oh, yes, that's quite simple. We have companies already created that we can use – we just need to open a bank account and register the directors. One of these has to be a Cayman resident – a Nominee Director. That would be me if I acted for you – unless you have anyone else in mind...?"

"No, that would be you. And would I be an overseas Director?"

"You could be if you wanted, but the important thing is that you'd own all the shares. If I acted against your interests, you could vote me off, but then you'd have to appoint another Cayman Nominee. And if you're a named Director, you're visible. Are you OK with that?"

"Well, I'd prefer not to be visible, actually. So, no, keep me off the public record. OK? And the other companies? In other territories? What are they for?"

"Well, we'd create a complex web of companies, all owned effectively by another one elsewhere, so that the ultimate ownership is almost entirely obscured."

"Is that legal?"

Garrido made a 'kind-of' gesture. "It is now, if you get the details right. But soon, due to 9/11, there are plans to make this much harder, to impose more transparency."

As I expected. "So there's a network of companies in other countries? Who would be directors there?"

"The same would apply there. Local Nominee Directors. I have contacts – well, the practice does. But these companies are ultimately owned by the original core business as full shareholder."

"Hmm." I knew this was what happened, but hadn't expected to engage so many people in this chain – I had hoped I could simply choose someone I trusted and that would be that.

I decided to let some more information out. "Strictly between us, and I'm relying on your client confidentiality here, the important thing for me is to keep these funds away from prying eyes. I acquired them by accident, as it were, and, erm ..."

How to explain this? I paused and cleaned up my starter plate as I considered how much to divulge. The waiter arrived to take away the plates.

I put both hands on the table. Good body language, I thought. "Ok, I'm going to put a scenario to you. All theory, of course. Just a story. Hypothetical. OK?"

"Ok", he nodded, and leaned out of the waiter's way.

"Right. Imagine that you, erm, found, a large amount of money. Very large. And that you knew for sure that the owner – or holder, as it were - was dead. OK?"

"Right." He was hooked now.

"Then assume that you were sure that the money wasn't exactly stolen, but, well, it wasn't taken from widows and orphans. Or pensioners' hard-earned savings. But it has some less than savoury connections."

"Hot money, you mean?"

Hmm. Was it 'hot'? "Kind of. I think it belonged to very dodgy people before it landed in my hands. The people who, as I explained, are dead now. I don't know how they got it to begin with. I doubt it was completely above board at any point."

"OK ..." He still looked puzzled. He looked around him and lowered his voice to a whisper. "Is this the Mafia, do you mean?"

We went silent as the waiter returned with the main courses and checked us for drinks. We ordered the same again.

"Probably not them, but along those lines, I think. Anyway, as I say, the people who were looking after it are certainly dead, but their, erm, colleagues are going to want it back. By the way, this money is mainly in Bearer Bonds. Entirely, in fact, as far as this discussion is concerned." Obviously the cash element didn't need to be part of this process.

"Ah." He understood that. "Well, as soon as we make it liquid – pay it into a bank – they will know. Almost at once."

"Yes. Quite."

Garrido was on home turf now. "As I said, since 9/11, there have been lots of new rules proposed – some already passed – that will make it much harder to hide such funds. But if we act quickly we should be able to keep things fairly secret. Where are these funds – the Bonds - now?"

"Theoretically? Here. Hidden in my room." I smiled. He wasn't expecting that.

"What? You have the Bonds with you?" He was visibly shocked. "Exactly how much are we talking about here? Theoretically."

"Let's say enough to support a very generous lifestyle. And certainly enough to pay handsomely for a good job in setting up a safe haven for it. Maybe a big deposit on a new house."

He looked dubious.

I said, “You don’t need to know how much just now, do you? This is a theoretical conversation.” It struck me that I’d brought these documents all the way to the Caymans when I didn’t need to. They’d have been a lot safer if I’d left them in the bank. Ah, well. You live and learn, I guess.

Garrido looked thoughtful. “Hmm. Right. Tell me more, then. If you can.”

The waiter brought the drinks, and I set about my lobster as I thought about how much more I needed to explain. “OK. Back to the story. We agree that these bad men will – would - know very quickly that their Bearer Bonds have gone live, so to speak, and that their money has been cashed. Yes?”

He nodded.

I went on: “Well, they won’t hesitate to turn over every stone to find out where their money is.”

“Naturally. They’ll start with the bank that cashed them.”

“I guess so. But that’s not all. They won’t take kindly to losing this money, and they won’t be giving any rewards for finding it. Quite the opposite, in fact.”

“I see. No.” He was playing with his own lobster thoughtfully. “So we need to cover our tracks very carefully.”

“Yes. Can it be done?” That was the big question. I’d say the 64,000-dollar question, but that didn’t really cover it.

“Erm, I think so. I’ll need to do some thinking. And some reading. Are you sure you don’t know who these – hypothetical - bad guys are?”

“Not really, but I have some ideas. Does it matter?”

"Probably not at this point. Since we're being hypothetical." He resumed his disassembly of the lobster. "No. Well, as I say, since 9/11 ... Hold on, is this anything to do with that?"

I had been wondering when he'd make that connection. "No. Not as such. That is, this isn't Al-Qaeda money, I can promise you that. Not even hypothetically."

"OK. I guess I'll have to trust you on that."

"Robert, if we're going to do business, we'll certainly have to trust each other, I'd say."

He looked at me. "Yes, we will." He looked thoughtful.

I had one more question. "Right, I need to know there's no conflict of interest here, and I don't want you to construct anything from what I'm about to ask you – it's just a question, OK?"

"Er, OK, sure – what's the question?"

"Do you – or any of your partners – have any Irish clients?"

He considered this. "I certainly don't. And I don't think the firm has. In fact, I'm sure we don't. The partners may have some private clients – I can't answer for them. But I've never heard of any Irish clients. I think I'd know, but I can't be completely sure."

This would have to do. If this was IRA money, and that seemed to be likely, in the absence of any other indications, I didn't want anything getting back to them. I nodded my satisfaction.

"OK. Well, there is one other thing", I added, and waited till I had his full attention. "If you decide to help me with this, I'll pay well for a good job. Plus, let's say, danger money."

"Meaning?"

"Meaning that there is danger here. These people may well track you down and use you to find the money. They don't take prisoners. That should serve as a spur to getting this right, anyway."

Now he looked very thoughtful indeed. "I see. Yes, you're right. Lots to think about, then."

We concentrated on our lobster and salad and thought our own thoughts. Before long, the waiter reappeared to remove our plates. "Coffee?"

We decided against and I asked for the bill.

"How long are you planning to stay?" he asked.

"Here, just today. Tomorrow I'm going to another beach resort, further up the bay for a couple of weeks with my girlfriend. How long do you need to think about this?"

"Two or three days, I think."

I didn't want to do business at our holiday hotel – I thought it would spoil the mood, somehow. "OK. If you're free, let's meet here again in four days' time and you can tell me what you think. If you don't want to take this on, that's OK – this was just a theoretical discussion - and you might be able to recommend someone else. But if you're in, good. We'll discuss terms and you can tell me how you think we can bring this off. Remember, this needs to be a great job – mistakes could cost us more than money. And, as I say, if you don't want to play, I'll understand. OK?"

"OK." Garrido stood up and offered a handshake. Still dry and firm. "I'll see you on Thursday then. And thanks for the opportunity."

As he walked away, I thought about whether I had found the right man for the job. After all, I hadn't exactly done much research. None, really. But I liked his style, and I thought he had the right – well, profile. Young, but not completely inexperienced. Clearly intelligent and hard-working – anyone who qualified through remote study had far more determination and application than I had, that was for sure.

And he was ambitious, both personally and professionally, which I respected. I was about to give him a significant leg-up in both areas if he could do what was needed here. He had a fiancée, so wasn't likely to take too many risks. He didn't seem to drink at work, and he was sensible enough not to jump straight in without taking time to think.

Yes, I thought. I seem to have dropped lucky here. Again.

I had time to sit in the sun for the afternoon before I had to check out and get to the resort in time to meet Sally, who was due at about the same time as I'd arrived yesterday. I went up to my room, changed into swimming shorts, grabbed a towel and found a sunbed to doze on. I felt that I'd taken the next step.

As I relaxed in the January sun, I considered that I seemed to have become lucky – in getting into this situation in the first place, then in finding first Sally and now Garrido, both quite by chance, to support and guide me through the complex dance I was about to join. I hoped my luck would hold.

Chapter 17

Back in Ireland

"Mr. Edwards." Mary announced her visitor and followed him in with a tray of coffee and ginger biscuits, which she placed on a table between two not-very-comfortable sofas. The Lawyer thanked her and poured two cups, and wordlessly offered milk and sugar. The visitor shook his head. Mary left, closing the door behind her.

The visitor, Edwards, sat on one of the sofas sipping his coffee in The Lawyer's office, quite happy not to break the silence, as The Lawyer finished signing some papers at his desk. It was a miserable afternoon. The view out past the port to sea was obscured by a drizzly mist, adding to the overall gloom that was the mood in the room. It looked as if it might snow later.

Coming over to sit on the opposite sofa, The Lawyer spoke first. "I thought it was time to see what you were thinking about our missing money. So - any more thoughts?" He sat down and added milk and sugar to his coffee.

"No, not really. Unless the bills have been cashed. Have they?"

"No." The Lawyer shook his head and took a sip of coffee. He picked up a ginger biscuit, which he carefully dipped into the coffee. "I'd have called you at once if they had been."

"Well there was a large amount of cash as well, wasn't there? If – and remember, it's just 'if' – anyone has the funds, they can last a long time on that. Maybe they'll never cash the Bonds. Maybe they don't know what they are."

"True. True." The Lawyer looked out of the window at the miserable weather. "We checked on Richardson and Costello – it seems that they were lost – Richardson managed a mobile phone call to his wife before ..." he couldn't find the right word.

"Ah. Dreadful. How is she?"

"As you'd expect. This wasn't a risky mission – just office work really. If he'd been killed in action, she would have been prepared, but she was sure those days were over now. It was a shock. To say the least."

"And Costello?"

"Almost certainly with him. They both had to sign the agreement. And my colleague Finklestein must have been there as well. We made enquiries."

"I see." Edwards thought that was his job - enquiries.

The Lawyer could see that he was slightly put out. "My colleague knew the wives. We thought it was better that way."

"Fine. So that was a wasted journey, then?"

"Not exactly. We also talked to an expert in hiding funds – we've, er, had dealings with him before. We have a good idea what you'd do if you had those Bonds – where you'd take them and what to do. Of course, Finklestein was our best contact for that sort of thing, but now ..."

"Yes, I know. But nothing has happened yet?"

"No", smiled The Lawyer, grimly. "We no longer have the money, so we can't hide it. Any more news on the courier – Benson, was it?"

"Best. No, nothing. I spent a couple of days on your behalf. His office is managing things – the receptionist, I think. I phoned and spoke to her. I said I was an insurance man – about his household insurance. I'm quite sure he's not in circulation anywhere – he's almost certainly dead. That's the settled view at his office, anyway."

"No family, you say?"

"No. I didn't actually go to his office, but I went by his flat one evening and there's no sign of life. Then I posed as a relative and a neighbour let me have a look round. No sign of anything amiss. Just as he'd left that morning, clearly intending to return."

"Was he in the meeting in Finklestein's office?" asked The Lawyer.

"I have no idea. He wasn't reported as late, as you'll recall, and he should have been there by then according to his instructions, but you have more information from that room than I do ..."

The Lawyer looked at him. So, he was a bit pissed-off. "I explained that. And, no, we only have a short call from Richardson to his wife. I wouldn't expect him to list the Dramatis Personae in that scene, would you?"

"No," Edwards conceded. "So, we're no further on, then." He had a thought. "Was there anything else that Richardson and Costello had to discuss before signing the papers and handing over the cash and Bonds?"

"Yes, there were a couple of other items for the meeting. Nothing to do with this transaction."

Edwards was silent for a moment. "I see. So, if Best didn't arrive with the briefcase at the start of the meeting - if he was a bit late - the show would still go on for, what an hour or so?"

The Lawyer sat forward. "Yes, probably. Maybe longer. If he wasn't there yet, they wouldn't have been bothered – wouldn't necessarily have chased his office. Especially if he phoned to say he was running a bit late, perhaps."

They both sat in silence, thinking the same thing. The Lawyer topped up the coffee and took another biscuit.

Edwards spoke first this time. "So, there is a scenario that works, where our man Best is on his way, a little late, with the bag in his hand, he sees the first plane hit, and doesn't actually go into the building – the second Tower - with it?"

The Lawyer stopped mid-dunk. The biscuit collapsed into the coffee. "Yes, I think that's viable."

"So, our friend Best. No family, bit of a loner, no real reason not to scarper with all these millions. He had a good job in IT sales before he joined the courier firm, apparently, so he's no fool. Put yourself in his place – what would you do if the scenario is correct?"

The Lawyer answered at once. "Scarper. I'd take a look in the case – if I hadn't already looked – and decide that this was a lucky day for me, at least."

Edwards nodded. "I agree. Keep going – where would you go – how?"

The Lawyer pondered. "Frankly, I don't know. Not my, erm, area of expertise. What do you think?"

"Well, I don't think I'd use my own ID any longer than I had to. I don't see any suggestion that there was any use of his cards at any point after we suppose he was killed. We haven't checked that ourselves, but I think his office would have known. And probably mentioned it. But I don't see any evidence that he knew – knows – how to get a false ID. That's not easy, and most are, well, faulty."

"So, how could he do it?"

Edwards shook his head. "Look, the chances are that he didn't. His boss told him to report at half-eight. There was no report of lateness. I would think he was in the waiting room outside Finklestein's office and he's now been vapourised, along with the money and bonds. And he didn't return to the hotel as far as we know. They never saw him again."

"But we now have at least a glimmer of doubt?"

Edwards took a gulp of his coffee. He shrugged. "Just a possibility of a glimmer. But it's probably worth digging a bit deeper. I said that there hadn't been any sign of him – no cards used, no passport. But we haven't actually done any digging there, have we?"

"Why not – didn't you do that earlier?"

Edwards bridled again. "Because, a, there was no reason to, and, b, it was too early for there to be any data. And, c, that would take a lot of guile and patience, calling in some favours – it costs."

"Could you do it now?"

Edwards nodded. "Yes. If you think it's worth it. If his credit cards have been used, or the passport has shown up in a border check, it will be on file somewhere by now."

"Ok. Do that – get back to me in two weeks' time and let me know what you've found."

Edwards drained his coffee. "Please remember that I told you it will cost money. I need to oil some wheels and grease some palms. And that we agreed that it's only a tiny glimmer of a chance that he's alive and has your money."

"I understand. Will you have anything in two weeks, do you think?"

He shrugged. "Maybe. I'll be able to tell you what I've done, anyway."

The Lawyer stood up. "OK, we can decide then whether it's worth pursuing further. But we have to try."

Edwards stood up, shook hands with The Lawyer and nodded. "I'll see you in two weeks, then. 'Bye for now." As Edwards let himself out, a connecting door opposite opened. The Priest came in, uninvited, and sat down on Edwards's vacated seat. The Lawyer waited for him to speak.

"Mr Best," was all he said, and seemed to be deep in thought, examining his hands. The Lawyer knew better than to interrupt his musings. "He's the only way that this money could have been saved."

"A long shot, though", prompted The Lawyer.

"Yes, but you did the right thing. We can't leave any trail uninspected. Not even one this faint."

The Lawyer was relieved. He chanced another remark. "It would be a miracle if he survived – if the money did. The only real proof would be the Bonds going live."

The Priest looked up from his hands. "I'm supposed to believe in miracles. Let's see if there's been another."

He lapsed into thought, hands clasped in front of him. Despite the image, he was not praying. "I have some old friends in Boston. I may be able to give our Mr. Edwards some contacts and access to information he wouldn't find by himself."

The Lawyer sipped more coffee. "Up to you, of course, but let's wait and see what Edwards finds in the records. I think we have to accept that we don't know what we're looking for until the Bonds are cashed – assuming that happens. In fact, I'd say that if they aren't cashed in the next 6 months, a year at most, they won't be. And that would mean that they've gone for good. I can't see how anyone would have them but not cash them, can you?"

The Priest continued his musing. "I'm sure you're right. On both points – if they survived, they'll be cashed, and soon – within a year at most, yes. And if they're not, then they probably didn't survive." He nodded. "All right. I'll wait to see what Edwards finds out, if anything, before doing anything. Much as it pains me to sit patiently, I think I'll have to."

The Lawyer nodded. "Yes, I think the next move isn't ours to make." Then a thought struck him "Look, I'll talk to the bank to make sure they're aware of what happened. I should do that anyway. But they might – just might – reissue the Bonds after a period of inaction. Under these unique circumstances."

The Priest almost smiled. “That would be extremely beneficial. Please do speak to them. How long a period of – inaction – do you think they would regard as ample?”

The Lawyer shook his head. “I just can’t say. They may just not allow this. Probably not, in fact. After all, it would mean cancelling the Bonds, and the whole point of them is that they are as good as cash. You don’t just cancel cash equivalents lightly. It’s probably unprecedented. But at least a year – probably more. I suppose we’d need affidavits from Best’s employers, his social contacts ... we’d also need to explain where they were – and why.”

The Priest nodded. “Well, that transaction was above board, I think?”

“Oh, yes. And these depositions and affidavits would be as confidential as all the other details – that’s why we use these banks.”

The Priest stood. “Right. Do that, and we’ll meet again and discuss it after Edwards reports back. Meanwhile, I’ll try to be patient.”

After The Priest left, The Lawyer looked for the number of the contact at the bank which issued the Bonds. In George Town, in the Caymans.

Chapter 18

Warming Up

As I checked out, I asked reception to find me a taxi to the resort. Arriving about an hour ahead of Sally, I explored this new version of Paradise. This resort was much more holiday-oriented: the cabins were low-rise, clean, and pretty with a sundeck - and private plunge pool in our case, all set in tropical gardens. There was a huge main pool, several bars and restaurants and a long white beach and turquoise sea.

A small, shiny-bald and dazzlingly smiling porter called Pedro took me and my luggage to our cabin on a sort of golf cart. I tipped him, half-unpacked, and then walked the five minutes back to the main building and settled at a table in the lobby, where I could watch the check-in desk.

I saw her arrive in her taxi before she saw me, and I felt an unfamiliar but welcome thrill as I watched her busily organise the driver and doorman to take her luggage to the desk. Had I missed her in 2 days? It seemed so, and it must have been mutual, judging by her squeal, hug and big kiss when I got up and walked over to greet her.

She was even more impressed when she saw the cabin. It really was impressive, with high ceilings, a lazily circulating fan in the rafters, sitting and dining area and luxury bathroom. The view from the veranda and sundeck across the gardens and lawns led to where the sea was glinting in the background. Lovely.

We walked back hand in hand to the main building to explore a bit. We had a quick drink and a snack at the cocktail bar before a mixture of the combined effects of lust and a long day's travel for Sally took us back to the cabin. This was going to be a great fortnight.

The next few days were spent in typical holiday fashion – sunbathing, reading, eating, drinking and making love, in no particular order.

Thursday came around very quickly, and I found myself having to re-set my business brain after breakfast. I hadn't really said much to Sally about my meeting with Robert Garrido, so I filled her in over breakfast coffee.

"I like the guy. He's young, bright and keen, but thorough, I think. Likeable, but probably never going to be my best pal. I hope he decides to take this job on."

"Why wouldn't he?"

"Well, it's a bit unconventional and I'm not sure it's entirely legal round the edges. I mean, I should probably have handed the stuff in after the dust settled. The money isn't really mine, is it?"

"Too late for that now, isn't it?" She smiled.

"Of course, and I think it's better with me – us – than with the original, erm, owners or whatever. I think he'll be OK if I don't tell him the whole story. Garrido, that is"

"What will you tell him?"

"What he needs to know and no more. I said that I've ... fortuitously come by a large sum of money, which I want to keep hidden from the people who lost it, who I think are, erm, of a criminal bent. I also said that I didn't steal or embezzle it, and that there are no tax or other Government agencies looking for it. I think that's enough, don't you?"

She cradled her coffee with both hands and pursed her lips, musing. "Hmm. I guess so. Actually, some of that is guesswork, and so would anything else be. Does he believe you, do you think?"

"I'll find that out at lunchtime. He hasn't agreed to do it yet. But as a lawyer, he doesn't really need to believe me – it's more important that he can honestly say that he didn't know or have any reason to suspect that there's anything illegal going on."

"So, again, why wouldn't he jump at the job?"

"Well, it's dangerous, isn't it?"

She frowned and poured more coffee. "Why?"

"We discussed this." I lowered my voice, but the dining room was almost empty anyway. "In fact, I think there's an Irish connection here. Based on the contract that was with the money. And if this money did belong to the IRA, it must have come from rich donors in the States, or maybe Gaddafi – Libya. Now that it looks like peace is about to break out, all this money will need to be accounted for."

Sally frowned. "Peace?" I was a bit surprised that she hadn't heard of the Good Friday Agreement and everything that followed it – all the negotiations, the posturing, speeches and God knows what. But then, why should she?

"Yes, there's been a Peace Agreement. The fight is supposed to be over. There's a sort of amnesty and the IRA leaders can stand for office if they say and show that the terrorism is all over. Long story."

"Oh. I didn't know."

"Well it hardly affects you in Sausalito. But as well as putting their weapons beyond reach, I'm sure they shouldn't be left with a pile of money. Most of the IRA leadership on the ground were just mobsters. They'll surely have a better plan for this money than just handing it in alongside their weapons. And once we pay it into a bank, they'll know it wasn't lost."

"And they'll come looking for it?"

"Exactly. And they won't play nicely – they'll be much more, erm, determined than the IRS and so on."

"I guess so."

"Yes. And if – maybe when - they find the Cayman business that we're about to set up, they will find our lawyer – he'll be the local nominee Director."

She frowned. "But he doesn't know anything."

"He will. He'll know how we banked the money and then got it out of the system again. He'll know who had it – well, the guy he knows as Brett Foster, anyway. But no, he won't know who I really am, or where I am, by the time they catch up with him. Oh, and I hope he won't even know that you exist, by the way."

"What will they do to him if they find him?"

"Well, I'm paying him well to face that risk, and he has his eyes open – if he chooses to act for me. But it's my guess that they'll just shake the information out of him, and then leave him alone. They won't want to attract attention by making a mess. At least, not here. And I'll tell him to come clean at once, not to try to protect me."

She looked shocked. "What - you'll take them on? Come on, you can't do that, can you?"

"No, but I think there'll be a lot more distance between them and me by then. I just don't think it's worth him resisting. They'll just get nasty, and they'll get to know what they want anyway. No point in him being a hero. Assuming they get this far."

"How? What do you mean?"

"Look, let's talk again after my meeting with him. Don't worry – I think it'll be all right." I smiled and squeezed her hand. She didn't look terribly reassured.

We went back to the cabin and spent a couple of hours on the sun deck before I changed and set off back to the lobby to get a taxi to the Marriott. Sally was a bit subdued when I kissed her goodbye for the day. I hoped I hadn't spoilt her holiday.

Chapter 19

Garrido's Plan

Garrido was waiting for me at the same table in the restaurant when I arrived. "My turn to buy lunch," he smiled.

"Well, thank you. Does this mean I'm your prospective client?"

"I hope so, but I have some terms. And you may not like my plan."

I smiled back at him. Fair enough. "OK, well, let's order and then you can tell me what you think."

The waiter arrived on my gesture, and we ordered. Pasta and chicken for me; salad and grilled fish for him. Beer for me, sparkling water for him. The waiter shimmied away with the order, and Garrido started his explanation with a question.

"The Bearer Bonds – you still have them, I suppose?"

"Yes, they're safe in my hotel." For once, I had used the hotel's safe, after inspecting it carefully. I thought our cabin in the grounds was just too exposed, compared to a hotel room.

"Good. Now, what bank are they drawn on?"

I couldn't recall the bank itself – I hadn't actually seen them very often recently. "I don't know, but I do remember it's a Caymans Bank."

"Cayman National Bank?"

"Yes, I think so."

"OK, I was hoping against that."

The waiter brought our drinks and starters, and we organised ourselves accordingly. As we poured drinks and selected cutlery, I asked why.

"Well, you said these were bad guys – the people who would come looking for the money when we bank the Bonds?"

"Yup."

"Well, they possibly know their way around here, since this is where their money sits. Nominally, at least."

I hadn't thought of this. "Yes, I see. So what do you advise?"

"Actually, in that case, not a Cayman company. Probably Turks and Caicos, at first, anyway. Then Belize, then Guyana. And maybe back to the Turks. But that's my part to set up. Just not Cayman."

"So are you pulling out?" I hoped not.

"No, no. But I do need to introduce a colleague in whichever territory we go for. One in each. Unavoidable, I'm afraid."

My disappointment must have been clear to see.

"Please don't worry. It's probably a good thing, in fact. I can manage what the local Director knows – better than you can, in fact."

"Why's that?"

"Well, I know exactly what he needs to know, which isn't much, really. You may accidentally tell him more than that. Like you did with me, in fact." He looked at me and grinned. "I'll tell him – them - only what's necessary to set up the companies. No more. And I must also advise you to take the Bonds back to your bank until I tell you where and how to cash them."

I was somewhat taken aback. I finished my beer in a long gulp and waved the bottle for another. "I see. So I told you too much?"

He waved the idea away. "Oh, no. I needed to know most of what you told me, really. No more, though, please." He smiled again and put his hand up, palm to me. "And do, please, secure those bonds. But I want to be your legal advisor, not a Director of your Company. And as such, if you allow me, I'll create a series of companies whose Directors know nothing about what those companies do. Which is, of course, nothing." He looked quite pleased with that, and laid his cutlery down, almost with a flourish.

"All right. I understand all that." I had a thought. "If the Caymans is possibly unsafe, would the other territories they had companies registered in be a bad idea as well?"

He shrugged. "Maybe to some extent. If you knew where that was. But I don't suppose you do, do you?"

"Actually, I do. To some extent, anyway. I have the contract of sale that was associated with all this. It was in the same package as the money and the Bonds."

Garrido stared at me. The waiter arrived to remove our plates and serve the main courses and left us again.

"You have the actual contract? How on earth did you ... no, don't tell me that. Let me think a moment."

He busied himself with separating the flesh from the bones of his fish. He took a mouthful and seemed satisfied. "OK, so you have a large sum of money and a contract of sale, yes?"

"Yes, exactly."

"Is the amount on the contract the same as the money in the package – do you know?"

"Yes, it is. The whole amount is there, in cash and the Bonds. Was, anyway."

He paused and ate some more fish. "In that case, this was the final phase of getting the money out. The cash had been scattered and is now all back in one place. After this transaction, it would have been distributed to the actual shareholders – or shareholder - of the final company."

It was my turn to be startled. “So I’ve scuppered the share-out?”

“I think so, yes. If this was part of the smoke screen, just a step in the obscured trail, early in the laundering process, there would only be share certificates in the companies involved. I’m sure this is the reverse process – getting the cash out of the washing machine, nice and clean, if you like.”

We sat in silence. I ate my chicken and once again contemplated my extraordinary luck. I could have been carrying just a contract and share certificates. But in fact I had picked up the right job at the right time. “So what would have happened next?”

“Well, this is beyond my need-to-know area, really. But I’d guess they would bring the Bonds back here to the bank and convert them into cash. Or bank them somewhere else. Like Switzerland. In fact, that’s more likely. The trail back to where the original funds went into the system will be very complicated – probably only one person knows the full route it took.”

“I see. So they do know their way around here.”

“Quite possibly. They may be known to the bank, in fact. Their Lawyer will, anyway.”

“Hmm. And what would they do with the money after they cash the Bonds here – or wherever?”

“They probably wouldn’t need to turn it into cash at all. And anyway they needn’t come here to do that. They’d just end up with a company with lots of money in the bank. They’d give shares in that company to whoever was due to receive them. There’d be no connection with where the money came from. It’s just a large figure on a balance sheet and matching bank balance in whatever territory the final company is registered in.”

“Won’t it look suspicious, though?”

"It depends. There's lots of new legislation being rushed through most territories to spot this kind of transfer of funds, and make the banks report it to the authorities."

"So you'd never need to take the actual cash out?"

"No", he said, as the waiter removed the starter plates. "If fact, as your adviser, I'd suggest you simply moved the balance into your own personal account. But you could just take it out in cash if you wanted, given notice. Most banks would need to get that much cash from somewhere else, not the local offices – even Head Office. You don't need to, though, unless you intend to invest in something illicit."

This made sense, and backed up my understanding of the book I'd studied. I kept my limited knowledge and research to myself in any case. I was the amateur in this conversation. The waiter came to check on us and I asked for another beer. "No, I don't want a pile of actual cash. I just want to buy myself a nice lifestyle, really."

"Good." Garrido went on: "Anyway, withdrawing – and holding - lots of cash won't be so easy soon. I've been reading about the legislation they're bringing in. In fact I'm due to go to a conference on this, in Miami, shortly. But that's not in place yet, and anyway there are plenty of businesses who won't care about that, and would still want cash."

"Such as?"

"Oh ... mainly drugs, of course, but also smuggling, counterfeit goods, bribes to officials in some countries – all sorts of activities can use large cash amounts - especially US dollars. Very few of them are legal. And possibly terrorist activities, which is the driver for all this, of course."

"Hmm. So, overall, it's a good thing for the world that I've intercepted this money?"

"Yes, I suppose so. If this is dodgy money and otherwise it gets back into those sorts of businesses" He laughed. "Crime prevention, you might say."

"Right. Is there anything else I can tell you about the contract? Or do you want to see it?"

"No. Best not. But I'd like to know which territories are mentioned – where the companies in play here are located. I'll avoid them, to be on the safe side. There's plenty of choice. As soon as possible, because I'll start to create the companies today, if we agree terms."

"OK, I'll call you from the hotel when I get back. If we agree terms." I smiled. "What do you have in mind?"

"Well, as I say, I propose that you formally appoint me as your Legal Advisor, on a retainer, with your power of Attorney to create several companies in various territories. You will own all the shares in all the companies through a holding company; I'll appoint local Directors. I'll charge you a fee through the partnership and a separate fee directly."

It seems like my turn to comment. "I see. That seems fine in principle. How much?"

He looked directly at me. "In US Dollars, a hundred thousand for the firm's consultancy fee. Two-fifty thousand for mine."

"I see." I hadn't really known what he would ask. But I wasn't going to say yes or no yet. "And what will the other costs be – the local directors?"

"No more than a hundred thousand Dollars, I'd say. In fact, I can commit to that."

"When do I pay you – and them?"

"All except my personal fee, put me in funds at the outset and I'll deal with it all. Including my firm's fee."

"OK. And your personal fee?"

"As soon as you're in full control of your cash in a bank account in your name. Or another name. That's where you pay me from."

"I see. Are your senior partners in on this?"

"What – my personal fee?"

"Yes."

He smiled. "No. In fact, you'll be paying that part to my fiancée."

I grinned. I did like his style. That had been my only concern, really – did he have the cunning? He clearly had the professional skills and contacts, but he was going to need something extra. He seemed to have it.

"So, about 450k dollars, to place all these funds securely beyond the sight of the original owners?"

"And into your own control to spend as you see fit. Yes. That's it."

"I don't suppose you want to tell me how you'll do it?"

"Well, as you know, we'll be moving ownership of the money through several businesses in similar offshore territories. But no, you don't really need to know, do you?"

"I guess not. How long will it take?"

"All clear about two or three months from now, I expect. Maybe a bit less. But I need you to do a couple of things first."

"Oh." That sounded pretty quick to me. I said so.

"Well, with all this impending legislation, we need to move quickly. And we can do a lot of moves in that time. That's why it costs what it does – it's intensive work."

"Right. And what is it you want me to do?"

The first thing, of course, is to sign my papers appointing me as your Attorney, authorising me to act, and put me in funds, as I said."

"Fine. And the second thing?"

"Go to Zurich and set up a bank account. I'll tell you where, and of course you pay the Bonds into it. You'll have another personal account in a different bank at the end of the process, in your own name, or at least a name you can use to access the money. OK?"

"Zurich? Fair enough. I bet it's cold there right now." I grinned.

"I guess so," he chuckled. "But we can't wait until it warms up, as I said. Probably go in a couple of weeks' time. Do you ski?"

"Ha, not for ages, and I don't fancy it now. Do I need to?"

He shook his head and forked the last of his fish. "No, I just wondered."

"No, I'll make it an in-and-out trip. Where should I hide out, so to speak, while you're moving all these pieces around?"

"Oh, that doesn't really matter, as long as I can get you if I need you. You could stay here, but there's really no need."

I nodded, considering what he'd said. The waiter reappeared. I thought we may need a coffee this time – we had some way to go. I suggested this and we said we'd take them on the terrace by the beach.

That gave me time to think. Should I try to chip the price down a bit? It hardly mattered to me – I'd still have plenty of money – far more than I'd ever need, really. So, was it worth it? I was sure I was paying top dollar, and I could get this done for less. Again, see my previous answer. So, the real question was: Have I picked the right man for the job?

"Tell me, Peter. Have you done this sort of thing before – how often?"

"This sort of thing – moving assets between offshore businesses – yes, we do it all the time. Hiding funds from shady characters? No. But many of our clients want to maintain secrecy over their assets, whether from the taxman or indeed the press or an ex-spouse. I've done that several times, and my senior partners have been doing it for years."

"How much input will they have?"

"They'll check the company creations, ensure compliance and so on. But just the process, as a consultancy, not an execution contract. I'll be doing the actual work, and I'll be making the decisions."

I decided. I had to engage someone; I liked this guy and he seemed to know what he was doing. I couldn't see any reason why not, and I decided he should have his fee as he asked. If I didn't quibble now, I could make demands on him later if things got sticky.

I sipped my coffee, put the cup back in the saucer and looked out to sea. It was a perfect day. "OK, we have a deal. You're appointed." I put my hand out.

He took it with a huge grin. "Thanks. You won't regret it. It'll be my main task until it's done."

I laughed. "Good. I'm paying plenty. So, I'll get back to the beach and let you know what's in that contract that you asked about – the countries mentioned, and then plan that trip to Zurich."

He stood. "Great. Oh, do you have a reliable address in the US?"

I paused. "Reliable?"

"Yes, somewhere we can reach you, and where you can register your bank account. Or you can register that here in Cayman. Or wait a while – we don't actually need it until the money gets back to the destination business."

"Not really. I'm living on a boat." He smiled. "I'll figure out the best way for you to reach me quickly over the next three months. My cellphone, probably."

"Good." He stood up and picked up his jacket. "Call me at the office tomorrow morning, please. We can arrange for you to come in and sign some papers I'll prepare, and I'll arrange the meeting in Zurich for you. Have a good afternoon."

I stood up and we shook hands again. I held on to it for a second longer and added my other hand. "And you. Take care, now – I'm relying on you."

He nodded and turn to walk away to reception.

"Hey! I remembered something."

He turned back. "What?"

"Lunch is on you, isn't it?"

He laughed. "So it is. I'll deal with it. Bye for now."

I sat down to finish my coffee. So, that was that. It was out of my hands now, and before long I'd cash the Bonds and the alarm bells would ring somewhere – in Ireland, I was sure.

Chapter 20

Breaking Cover

I told Sally that I was shortly going to go to Switzerland, to deposit the Bonds, and thereby let someone, somewhere, know that they were not, in fact, reduced to dust or ashes. That act would have the effect of firing a starting gun for a race in which I had no idea who was chasing me or where they were. But, as Garrido had said, there was no doubt that they would come looking.

Garrido needed time to prepare the channels that the money would take once it was in the system, but once I'd signed his papers, I'd done all I needed to do. I'd given him the information he needed from the contract, but he was quite clear that this was all he wanted to know. So we were able to enjoy our holiday without any more interruptions. We took a taxi into George Town, the capital, where I dropped into his office to sign his appointment documents and transfer his initial fee from my Sausalito bank, and then Sally took me shopping.

After Sally and I had enjoyed another week in paradise, it was back to San Fran and Sausalito. I went back to Mystere, and Sally went back home to meet her mom and back to work the following evening. She was looking tanned and sexy, and I suppose I was sporting that winter tan that so irritates people who haven't been able to get away from winter blues. I called in at the bank and, in the private vault, took the case out of the safe, removed some of the cash to top up the account, and replaced the sheaf of bonds for the time being.

I needed clothes suitable for a trip to Switzerland in the middle of winter, so we went on the ferry to San Fran and up to Union Square, where we shopped for suitable clothing in a mall with the January sales still running. As well as a warm overcoat, I bought a "business casual" outfit of dark sports jacket and slacks, which I thought would be the right gear for a discreet visit to a private Swiss Bank. I wasn't sure what that was, really, but I didn't think it was Sausalito-style chinos and polo shirt.

A couple of weeks later, I received a message from Garrido. The companies in and around the Caribbean were all set up, with bank accounts ready for their share of the big money. And the Swiss account was ready for the bonds to be deposited. Quick work. I returned to the bank and collected the bonds again, and took them back to Mystere to pack them in my carry-on luggage.

Sally stayed with me on Mystere, and we had lunch in San Fran before "Brett Foster" took the BART up to the airport for the night flight to Paris. I had packed a bag for 4 day's travel and put the bonds in an attaché case which fitted in the larger suitcase, underneath my clothes.

I slept in the newly-fitted full-length bed seats all the way to Paris, sailed through immigration – Brett's passport was still working fine. I showered in the First-Class lounge, and took the short hop to Zurich. I'd done journeys like this before, but not right at the front of the plane, and I can say that this way was certainly better. The stewardesses were prettier, the food was better, and the ability to get proper sleep alone was worth the extra cost – if you could afford it.

I checked into the Zurich InterContinental around dinner time. I stowed the briefcase under the bottom drawer of the dressing unit as usual, even though I wasn't planning to leave the room. I ordered a steak on room service, and phoned Sally to say that I'd arrived – by now it was about 24 hours since we'd had lunch in San Fran. Duty done, I set my alarm and slept until 8 the next morning.

I dressed in my new business outfit, had a leisurely breakfast, and wandered out to see what Zurich had to offer the casual visitor. The answer was, very little, really – some astonishingly expensive shops, very clean streets and rather nice cafes. I wandered around more or less aimlessly, lingered over an overpriced lunch and generally wasted time. I found the street where the bank was located, then wandered back to the hotel. It was cold – really cold, compared with Grand Cayman and even Sausalito, and I was glad of my winter coat.

Eventually I'd killed enough time. Garrido had insisted that this transaction had to be done towards the end of the day at the end of the week, and that's what he'd arranged. He wanted it to happen after close of business in the UK and the Caymans, so it was half past three when I recovered the attaché case and set out to my appointment with one of the Gnomes of Zurich.

I don't know whether you've ever wondered what a Private Swiss Bank looks like, or indeed a Private Swiss Banker, but I had. And I was wrong.

The whole experience was something of an anti-climax, in fact. The "bank" was more like what I imagined a private clinic in Harley Street would look like than a major financial institution. Not that I'd ever been in one of those, either. There was none of the air of this being a hall of commerce, just an old but well-kept building in a quiet street away from the shops and bustle. I pressed the entryphone, looked up at the camera and was buzzed into a hallway with a pretty – no, beautiful - receptionist in a smart business suit waiting for me.

She showed me into what was once, I supposed, the library of a smart family house, and offered me a coffee. I agreed that that would be nice, and watched her pour it for me from a china pot on a sideboard in the corner. She was tall, slim, brunette and perfectly made up, and her suit hinted at what she would look like out of it. She wasn't dressed all that differently from those ladies in New York that last day of my old life, but she was so far on the right side of classy there was no real comparison. She put the cup down in front of me and turned to pour another as the door opened to admit a tall chap in a pinstriped suit, pale blue shirt and dark red tie.

"Ah, Good morning, Mr Foster," he said. I am Peter Carlson; Mr Garrido has told me that you wish to open a business account here?" The receptionist poured him a cup of the same coffee, black this time, and rather to my surprise, poured herself one and sat down across the table from me. We were seated around the end of a polished mahogany table that could have sat about 12 fat businessmen.

"You've met Francesca, I see."

"Yes," I smiled at her – but she didn't react to the charming, roguish look, it seemed.

"Francesca will act as clerk to these proceedings. It's necessary to have a third signatory to all the paperwork," said Carlson. Hmm. Some bank clerk. Some bank.

"Ok," I said. "That's fine. So what's the procedure now? I'm not familiar with this."

"Don't worry," he smiled. "I understand you wish to deposit some Bearer Bonds. I take it you have these with you? Ah, I see you do. I have the company documents, and I see that you are an authorised signatory as a Director. So, we can complete the paperwork."

As he was speaking, I'd placed the attaché case on the table, extracted the bundles of Bonds and placed them in 3 piles in front of us. I had sorted them into denominations to make counting easier.

"Well, we must now count these and ensure that the sums are what Mr Garrido advised us to expect. Twenty-three million, two hundred thousand dollars, I believe?"

"That's right," I nodded. "It's all there."

Carlson smiled. "I'm sure. But we must still count it to be sure."

He counted the various bills, reading out the denominations as Francesca tapped the values into an adding machine with a till-roll printout. I watched them work and sipped the coffee – excellent, of course. It didn't take long.

"Yes, as you say. Twenty-three million, two hundred thousand dollars. We must now check that we have entered each one." He counted up the number of bonds and checked them against the till roll entries. He was satisfied that nothing had been missed off – or double-counted. "Please initial this till roll to confirm that all is, as you say, 'above board'."

And that was done. Francesca gathered up the Bonds with the till roll, and left the room through a side door, returning with a sheaf of papers which she passed to Carlson, and sat down again.

"These are the documents that open the bank account for your company, Mr Foster. You will sign as the Director of, erm," he checked the document 'Pelican Investments' of Guyana. I will then countersign, and Francesca here can witness this transaction. The fact of the transaction itself will be known to the issuing bank, of course, as with our bank, but of not, of course, the name of the account or the signatory – these are entirely confidential. We will then give you the account numbers and the codes to authorise onward transfer to, well, wherever you wish."

"Or as Mr Garrido advises," I smiled.

"Just so. Will you require us to allow you privacy to make a phone call when you have the numbers?"

"Er, yes, that might be helpful," I said. I wouldn't have minded a private room with Francesca, either, but I didn't think that a mere twenty-three million, two hundred thousand dollars would impress her. And to my surprise, I wasn't actually all that bothered.

It took another five minutes to provide me with a printout of the account numbers and codes, with a balance statement showing all twenty-three million, two hundred thousand dollars. And then Carlson and Francesca left me to make the call to the Caymans.

It was God knows what time there, but he answered on the first ring. "Hello, Brett. All done?"

"Yes. Here are the numbers you need. The money's showing as full balance." I read out the string of numbers and he read then back. He had the numbers exactly correct, so we were done.

"Ok, that's good. I'll get to work. Can you get over here in a couple of weeks' time?"

"Sure," I replied. "Love to, in fact. It's damn cold here."

"OK, great. Use the same hotel, and I'll meet you for lunch as before. 14 days from now. Friday the – whatever it is - OK?"

"Yup, see you there. Thanks – bye for now."

"Goodbye." And he was gone. Francesca appeared within 30 seconds. They were probably listening in, but it hardly mattered. Our business was done.

Both Francesca and Carlson shook my hand, and showed me onto the street again. It had taken just twenty minutes.

Chapter 21

Alarm Bells

The smooth running of The Lawyer's office on Tuesday morning was broken by an interruption to a run-of-the-mill meeting about a mundane and above-board property transaction.

"Sir," said Mary, who had entered the office from her lobby area, "I've had a communication from the Cayman bank. I think you may want to see this. I'm sorry to interrupt," she smiled to the two slightly offended property development clients.

The Lawyer frowned and held his hand out for the note Mary offered him. His expression didn't change as he read it, but he went a few shades paler beneath his Barbados winter tan. "I see. Thank you, Mary. Can you call Mr Edwards, and, I think, our priestly friend, please? Ask them to meet me here or arrange to phone in as soon as convenient. Tell them it's urgent. Make space in my diary, please. You were right to interrupt me. Thanks."

"Trouble?" asked the older of the two developers, expectantly. He knew The Lawyer's history, or some of it, and was pretty sure his involuntary reaction might suggest a development that would have some gossip value, at least.

"Erm, no, not really. I must apologise. In fact, it might be good news. Something we thought might happen seems to be ... well, happening. Anyway, back to our business, yes? I really do apologise for the interruption." He was recovering his composure quickly. He was thinking very quickly, as well, but decided that there was nothing to be done right now.

He turned his best lawyer smile onto his clients and returned to the task in hand. The next quarter of an hour dragged by until he felt that he had discharged his duties effectively. He was advising on how to manage a planning application to turn an old warehouse into a café bar with executive flats above. Nothing new, and not that challenging, but this was now his bread and butter. And still, to some extent, his cover.

Eventually all three stood up and shook hands, agreeing the next steps. The Lawyer ushered them to the door, and Mary took them to the lift, seeing them safely behind the sliding doors.

She came back into the office. "The Priest can be here at three o'clock, sir," she said. Mr. Edwards is in London, but can join you by phone. I've warned your two-thirty that you only have half an hour now. Will that be all right?"

"Mary, that's excellent. Thanks. When's my next?"

"Ten minutes, sir. They're downstairs already."

"Ok, bring them up in ten minutes, but get the bank back on the line first. Don't bring them in until I ring off that call."

"Right, sir." Mary knew which bank. She went back to her desk, and a minute later, put the call through.

...

Exactly at three that afternoon, The Priest was shown in by Mary, and accepted a black coffee from the fresh pot on the table. The Lawyer asked for a new cup and a jug of milk, and some biscuits. "Shall I call Mr. Edwards now?"

"Not just yet," interjected The Priest. The Lawyer nodded at Mary and she left them to make the coffee.

"So," said The Priest, "Our money survived the devastation?"

"So it seems," replied The Lawyer. "It was deposited in a private bank in Zurich last Friday afternoon. That's to say, the bonds were. No names available, of course. And we don't know about the cash element, naturally."

"Last Friday? Why has the news taken so long to get to us?" asked The Priest.

"Quite. It seems that by the time the transaction happened towards end of day in Switzerland, Cayman banks were closed for human activity, then we had the weekend."

"Shrewd timing, then. But still, we should have known yesterday."

"Well, perhaps, but it hardly matters. The money would have been moving as soon as it hit the Swiss bank as a cleared balance. There's little we could have done yesterday that we can't do today."

"And what can we do today?"

Mary entered with the coffee. "Ah, Mary, thank you. Shall we call Edwards now? I think we need his – more practical – experience here." He looked at The Priest, who nodded.

Mary withdrew, and as The Lawyer poured himself a coffee and offered a biscuit, his speaker phone rang.

The Lawyer answered and switched to speaker. "Thank you for being so quickly available, Edwards. Did Mary brief you?"

"No, but I think I can guess. The Bonds have been cashed?" said the disembodied voice.

"Yes. Friday afternoon, in Switzerland. We only found out this morning. We called you at once."

"Good – thank you. Well, as I told you earlier, we now have something to work with. We know that the briefcase, at least, survived the catastrophe. And I'm prepared to bet that Mr Best did, as well."

"Could anyone else have taken the Bonds?" asked The Lawyer.

There was a pause. "Well, yes. But unless Best was robbed at some point before the handover time, or he was early and – what's his name – the US Lawyer, absconded with it ... well, I doubt it."

"No," The Priest interrupted. "Too much of a coincidence. We need to move quickly, and there no point in following anything but the strongest scent."

There were murmurs of agreement to this. "You're in London, I think?" asked The Lawyer.

"Yes, I am. I could get back to the courier's office, if that's what you're thinking. That's possibly the place to start. But I've already been there, so it might make sense to send someone else. I know just the right person, in fact, a lady friend of mine. She has the right approach for this, I think."

"Why?" asked The Lawyer.

"Well, do you remember that I said that the receptionist, erm ... Lizzie, seemed to have a soft spot for Best? She seemed to be quite cut-up about it – more than just a close colleague, I thought."

"Go on," said both the men in the office.

"Well, if there's anything out of the ordinary, I think she'd know. If my friend presented herself as perhaps a journalist, or maybe an insurance assessor, she might be able to get her to open up."

"Hmm," said The Lawyer. "It would be perfectly sensible to insure a valuable package, and then investigate its loss if there was a claim, quite usual, in fact."

"Was there any insurance?" asked Edwards. "We wouldn't want to meet a genuine investigation."

"No. The package was ... probably uninsurable."

"Mm. And if anybody did insure it, it would have been the owner – you - rather than the courier. OK, then, that's my best line. I'll contact my friend. Give me the rest of this week. How much can I tell her?"

"I suggest you advise her to use that story, in fact. Insurance. It's believable, and the less anyone knows, the better."

"OK. I'll get on to it now. It'll be one day for her on my usual rate and some small expenses, I expect. Then I'll report back and we can decide what next. OK?"

"OK," said The Lawyer. He looked at The Priest, who nodded. "That's all for now. Thanks again." He rang off, and looked to The Priest for comment.

"Well," said The Priest. "That should cover that end. I spoke to my American friends earlier, as I said. They also felt that nothing could be done until – unless – this happened. But now that it has, I think I'll pay that visit to Boston. I'll wait for our friend's report on Friday; I'll want to know what he has to say – but I'll make my plans. I'll tell you where you can reach me when we meet on Friday."

"OK," said The Lawyer. He paused. "You know, this is a positive development. The money wasn't destroyed, it was stolen. That means that it can be recovered, doesn't it?"

"Perhaps, Peter, perhaps. But it will be a mighty task, I think. We may need the help of some of those old friends I thought we'd said farewell to. It's as well they kept some souvenirs of the old days, just in case."

The Priest smiled his chilling smile and left without saying more.

Chapter 22

Careless Words

As arranged, at 11:30, two days later, a grey-haired lady of unremarkable appearance but remarkable intuition arrived at the courier company's office. Edwards frequently had to stop himself from calling her "Miss Marple" to her face, but that was how he saw her.

Lizzie was expecting her. She checked that she was indeed Mrs. Wilkinson from the insurance company – her ID was impressive, if fake – and showed her into Clive's office.

Tea was provided, introductions made, and the interview began.

"Now, I understand that Mr, erm ..." She consulted her notes "Best, was a reliable employee – excellent record, yes?"

"Joe. Yes," said Clive. "No complaints, ever. Always reliable, enjoyed the job, perfect employee. I wish I had a couple more like him, in fact."

"How long had he worked for you?"

"Two years or so, I think. Hold on, I have the records." He opened a ring-bound file. "Ah, yes. The first payment to him was exactly two years ago, in fact. He's on contract – paid per trip, not salary. Plus agreed expenses, of course. This first trip was up to Scotland. Aberdeen. An oil drilling company."

"I see." She made a note. "And did he usually know what was in the package he was delivering? Did he in this case?"

"No, not usually, and in this case, no. In fact, neither did I, or not in any detail. Actually, I didn't realise that the client had insured it. We were only told that it was a contract and some other documents. Papers. A carry-on bag – like a large briefcase. We don't need to be told. Or want to, really. The case was locked, of course, but I assume it went through the x-ray machines OK. We didn't hear of any problems at all."

"But he could have opened it?"

"Yes, he knew the code. That's necessary in case customs ask for it. But the client would have known – there's a small seal on the inside to show that it's been opened. It rarely happens, in fact. I guess that'll change now. After what happened, I mean." He took a sip of his tea and looked into the distance for a moment. "They'll want to look into everything on board, I suppose."

"Quite. Did Mr Best – Joe – usually open his packages?"

"I don't think so. I might not have known, but he would usually mention it if he'd had to, or the client might, but, as I say, that was unusual. And never without good reason."

"Ok ... When was the last time you heard from Joe?"

"When he left here. I wouldn't expect to hear from him until after the drop. He'd usually check in before he came home, to see if we needed him to go anywhere else."

"Was that usual?"

"What – another job? No, but it happened sometimes. It was the usual procedure. To phone in, I mean."

"But not this time?"

Clive stared at her for a couple of seconds. "No. Obviously not."

"No ... When did you expect him to complete the delivery? The impact on the second Tower, where the client's offices were was about 9 AM."

"Well, I told him to get there first thing. About half-past eight, I think. But he didn't call me at all after he'd set off to Heathrow. So, I can't be sure what he did after he left here."

“Would you have expected to hear from him?”

“No, not until after the drop. As I said. But he’d have called if there was a problem of some sort.”

Mrs. Wilkinson made notes on her pad. Clive tried to read it, but they were in shorthand. She looked up and paused for thought. “Tell me about Mr Best – Joe. What sort of chap was he? Outside the office, I mean – did you socialise at all?”

“No,” replied Clive. He paused. “I think he and Lizzie might have had a thing going – she was very upset when the – I don’t know what to call it – disaster happened. My accounts manager had to take her home.”

“It was certainly very upsetting, even if you didn’t know anyone in there, though, surely?”

“Yes, of course. We were all quite upset. Very. But it seemed to hit Lizzie worst of all.”

“Ok, and what about his life otherwise? Where did he work previously?”

“Actually, he had a high-powered job in IT Sales. With a customer of ours. But he quit and wanted a job with a bit less stress. And less bullshit, or so he said.”

“So, he wasn’t your usual type?”

“Well, I don’t think we have a ‘usual type’. We have four other couriers and all of them have had various previous careers – police, army … one was a travel guide. Most of them are quite well-travelled and familiar with the world and its ways.”

“But Joe was a bit different?”

“Maybe. He’d had more money than we pay, and had seen more upmarket places. But all that mattered to me is that he was reliable, organised and responsible. Resourceful, you could say. I think he was happy here. We were certainly happy with him."

"Family life? Was he married?"

"No, and no children as far as I know. Mates in the pub, some pals from his IT days, perhaps. We decided we should take care of his flat – we've let it out for now and I'm saving the money for, well, when we know what's going to happen. We thought it would be better than just leaving it empty. There didn't seem to be anyone else who was doing anything."

"I see. I'm sure you did the right thing. So, just an ordinary Joe, then?"

"You could say that, I suppose." Clive looked at his watch. "I don't think I can tell you anything else, really ..."

"Just one more question, if I may, then I'll be off. Is there any reason to think he might have survived what happened and gone to ground afterwards?"

"No reason at all. I do keep expecting him to walk in, in a way. But he hasn't. And I'm quite sure he won't."

Mrs. Wilkinson closed her notepad and stood up to leave. She shook Clive's hand. "Thanks for your time. I'm sure you understand that we have to ask these questions – to be sure ..."

"Of course. I hope I've been some help."

Lizzie was at the reception desk when Mrs Wilkinson came through on her way back onto the street. On an impulse, she stopped and smiled at Lizzie. "Lizzie, isn't it? Clive tells me you knew Joe quite well. Would you mind telling me about him? What he was like?"

Lizzie smiled and blushed. "Well, yes, I got to know him quite well, I suppose. What would you like to know?"

"Oh, I'd just like to get a picture of him – from a friend, rather than his boss, you know?"

Lizzie nodded. In fact she would very much like to talk about Joe, and this kindly lady looked like a sympathetic listener. "Well, I have my lunch break in half an hour," she said, looking up at the clock. "Would you like to wait? Or I guess I could go early. I'll let Clive know."

"Tell you what," said Mrs Wilkinson, "I'll buy you lunch if you like. Where do you usually go?"

"It depends ... there's a café in Marks & Spencer, about 10 minutes up the road. Shall I see you there?"

"Great. Lunch on me, then," smiled Mrs Wilkinson.

Once they we seated at a corner table among the shoppers, with a quiche and salad apiece and a large pot of tea, Lizzie opened up. "I always thought Joe was special," she said. "But a bit of a jack-the-lad on the surface, girl in every port, you know?"

"Mmm, I see."

"But underneath, he was really nice. Kind, you know? And he used to bring me silly little presents if he went anywhere interesting."

"Nice. So did you and he have a 'special relationship', would you say?"

Lizzie looked down at her plate and ate a piece of quiche. When she looked up, she sniffed and wiped her nose on the napkin. "I thought so. My situation is, well, complicated, but I used to think me and Joe could, well, one day ... Oh, I don't know. You'll say I'm being silly."

Mrs Wilkinson smiled. "No, I won't. I'm just trying to get a feeling for what kind of man he was. He seems like a nice chap."

Lizzie smiled. "He was, yes. He – I always looked forward to him coming in, you know? He cheered me up." To compose herself a little, she picked at her lunch again. Mrs Wilkinson did the same and they ate in silence for a minute or so.

"Might you and he have got together, do you think?"

Lizzie sniffed. "I don't know really. If he'd asked, well, maybe we could have ... but not now, anyway. No point in thinking about it, really, is there?" Lizzie was clearly on the edge of tears again.

"I'm sorry if I've upset you, my dear." Mrs Wilkinson laid her hand over Lizzie's and passed her a tissue. "Do eat your lunch."

Lizzie took the tissue and blew her nose. "I just can't get used to the idea that he won't walk right back in again, and give me some silly present. But he won't, will he?"

"Well, do you think there's any way he might have survived? Was he definitely there when the plane crashed into the building? Have you ever thought he might have escaped somehow?"

Lizzie ate some more quiche. "Well, I did at first. You see, he always used to call the customer and fix his own time, no matter what Clive had told him. Joe said he used to like to organise his visits to suit himself as long as the client was happy. He told me once ..." Unsure of what she ought to be saying, Lizzie ate some more of her salad.

"Told you ...?"

She decided that it was OK to tell this nice lady what Joe had told her. "Yes. He would arrive in whichever city he was going to and call the customer to find out exactly when he was needed. Clive just says 'get there at 9 o'clock' or something. Joe used to arrange a time that suited him better, that still suited the customer, as I say ..."

"So, did you think that he might have done that this last time? Set a different time?"

"Perhaps. But he can't have missed the crash, can he? Or he'd be here." Lizzie was crying again. Mrs Wilkinson passed her another tissue and nodded to herself. This was the real value of the visit.

Lizzie regained her composure as they finished the salad. Mrs Wilkinson bought them a slice of walnut cake each and poured some more tea. Eventually, they left the restaurant and walked back to the office. Lizzie smiled at the nice old lady, who patted her arm and smiled back. "I'm sorry for your loss, my dear. I hope Joe knew how much you cared for him. I'm sure he did."

Lizzie nodded and dried her eyes again before going into the office.

Job done, thought Mrs Wilkinson. She'd type up her report, email it to Edwards and attach her invoice for the day. Including an expense claim for two quiche and salad, cake and a pot of tea for two – a shrewd investment.

Chapter 23

Reporting

"Good evening, Mary", said The Priest, emerging from the lift. "Are the others here?"

"Yes, he had a call to deal with and I was waiting for that to finish. It just ended. I'll take you through."

"No need to trouble yourself." The Priest walked past her and opened the office door.

"Ah. Hello, Father. You remember Mr Edwards, I think ..."

"Indeed. Any news, Mr Edwards?"

Edwards was struck by the calm menace. "Yes, we've just been going through this report from my colleague. It seems that there's a perfectly sound case for believing that Best did indeed survive the collapse. That in fact he wasn't there when it happened."

"I see. How so?"

"Well, apparently, although he was instructed to get to Finklestein's office at about 8:30 AM, he was in the habit of making his own arrangements as to the time he was actually needed. In fact, he pretty well always did this, it seems. Unknown to his boss, but the office staff knew this."

"I see. We discussed this possibility, as I recall."

"Yes, we did, or something like it. So, if he did call Finklestein, he would probably have been told that he could be there well after the meeting had started – as you know, there were other matters to discuss."

"Indeed."

Edwards continued: "So, it seems at least possible that what happened was this: Best was on his way to the meeting at the new time he and your Mr. Finklestein had agreed – say 10 or 10:30 – and he saw the planes hit the building. If so, he'd presumably have turned around and taken the bag with him, possibly back to his hotel."

"I see. That seems credible."

"Yes, it does. It's guesswork right now, but it fits the facts. What he should have done is called his office for instructions, but he didn't. According to my colleague, they never heard from him at all after he left for the plane the day before."

"Was he reliable? Had this sort of thing happened before?"

"Well, obviously not on this scale. But yes, in fact they say he was very reliable. And quite resourceful, I think. He'd had a responsible high-level job before he decided to, well, opt for a quieter life."

"He may find his life will soon become very far from quiet." The Priest was clearly angry – he never shouted, but the tension was obvious.

The Lawyer stepped in. "Yes. Well, we assume that he must have checked the contents of the case – he was authorised to do that if circumstances suggested – customs examination, for example."

"And then decided to help himself to the contents, I suppose?" The Priest was struggling to contain his anger.

"And vanish with it, yes. It seems so." Neither Edwards nor The Lawyer wanted to catch The Priest's eye.

The Priest was silent for nearly half a minute. He seemed to be gathering his reserves of calm. "'Vanished', you say. That's very hard to do, don't you think?"

Edwards answered: "Ultimately, yes. But so far, nobody's been looking for him."

"Well, somebody soon will be. And we will find him. And he'll wish he'd phoned the office that morning."

The Priest stood up and walked over to the window. He stared out for what seemed like an age. Neither man wanted to interrupt him. He was very angry indeed. When he turned round, his face was a mask of calm again. "I'm going to Boston, as I planned. To see what information I can gather from sources you can't reach, Mr Edwards."

Edwards nodded. He couldn't think of anything helpful to add at this point.

The Priest went on: "And when I get that information, I'll expect you to follow it up at once. I think our Mr Best is trying to steal our money and he's damn well not going to get away with it. And he's bound to be leaving clues for you to follow, Mr Edwards. I'll get back to you in a very few days with some information to get you started."

And with that, he left the meeting without a further word.

Edwards felt as if he hadn't exhaled for about 5 minutes. "Whew. I really wouldn't like to be Mr. Joe Best if he actually catches up with him."

The Lawyer was slightly less shocked, having seen this sort of reaction before from The Priest in different circumstances. "He won't, not directly, but I do advise you to put everything you have into this next stage. Do you have any other business at hand right now?"

Edwards reached for a pocket diary. "I have a case I'm reporting back to my client upon, the day after tomorrow. That should close it off. Then I'm free."

The Lawyer nodded. "No, you're not. Please block out your diary for at least the next two weeks after that. Once our man of God has talked to his Boston people – I don't know who they are, but they are very well-connected – I'm sure you'll have a lot of work to do."

Edwards stood up and put his overcoat on. He nodded. “Right, I’ll do that. You know how to reach me. I can get back here any time after Thursday. Just let me know when you’re ready for me.”

Chapter 24

Back to the City by the Bay

Having checked out of my very efficient Swiss hotel, I set out to retrace my steps from Zurich all the way back to Sausalito. The only change was that the timing was different, so the Paris to San Fran stretch was daytime. Since it was a lengthy flight, with the return leg following so quickly - and because I could afford it - I'd forked out for First Class again. As before, being up front there made that a lot less tedious, even during the day – there was more drink, better food, and, it seemed, prettier stewardesses. Stewards too, I guess, if that's your thing.

Sally had offered to pick me up, but it made more sense for her to be at work as usual. So I took the BART to the ferry dock. It struck me once again that if I'd thought of that back in September, I'd have avoided one of those footprints I was so keen not to make. Ah, well.

I had just missed one ferry, so I dropped into the café and ordered a muffin and a coffee, neither of which I really needed. I then called Sally and said that I'd be back on Mystere in a couple of hours.

"Ooh, great. I hadn't expected you till tomorrow," she said. "Did it all go OK?"

"Yes, like clockwork. All very simple, really."

"And how was Zurich?"

"Boring, frankly. And cold. I was glad of the coat I bought. Any news on the home front?"

Sally giggled. "You've only been away a few days, you know." It felt like longer, but it was still Saturday evening and I'd only left on Thursday. "So, no. Same old same old."

"Hmm. So you didn't miss me, then?

"'Course I did. Shall I come round after work? Or will you come to the restaurant?"

"Actually, the last thing I need is another meal. Or drink. I'll unpack and take a shower, and look forward to seeing you when you finish. OK?"

"OK. And you can tell me all about Zurich."

"Really, there's not much to tell."

"Good," she giggled. "See you later."

As the ferry made its way across a choppy San Francisco Bay, I couldn't help but reflect on how lucky I'd been to find Sally so quickly after my new life had begun. Truth to tell, I hadn't needed an accomplice at all so far, from a strictly operational perspective. But just having this pretty, bubbly, giggly girl alongside me helped to give me perspective, or something. And she just made me smile. I only hoped that I could keep her out of danger.

By the time I'd unpacked, put a load of washing on, showered and settled down to watch TV, I decided that it was easily time for a glass of wine. I lay down on the sofa and shut my eyes for just a moment ...

When I woke up a few hours later the first thing I saw was Sally looking down at me with an indulgent smile. She leaned down to give me a kiss, her hair brushing my face.

"Well, there's a gentleman. Couldn't even stay awake until I get here. Come on, let's see whether you can find any energy before you conk out altogether."

I did, as a matter of fact. But then I slept like a dead man for 8 hours.

I woke to the irresistible smell of cooking bacon, and, for me, the only slightly more resistible sound of Sally singing along to an Eagles CD, off-key and missing some of the words. I crept up behind her and gave her a hug.

"Mmm. Morning. I wasn't going to wake you till the bacon was ready. How many eggs?"

"Three, scrambled, please. On toast."

"Very good, sir. OJ? Coffee?"

I hugged her again. "Please. I'll shower – I'll be five minutes."

We ate breakfast inside, as it had started to rain. Afterwards, Sally took full advantage of the easy access afforded by the towelling robe I was wearing, and we made love with, probably, a little more energy on my part than last night. It was an hour or so later when, the rain having stopped and with a feeble sun taking a tentative look at the day, we emerged onto the cockpit. It wasn't warm, but with a sweater it was nice enough.

"You know it's Sunday?" said Sally, for no reason that I could immediately figure.

"Er, yes. All day, I believe."

"So, I need to spend some time with my Mom. I didn't see much of her yesterday and we're going away again soon, aren't we?"

"Well, I probably need to go back to Cayman in about 10 days' time. "You don't have to come with me. I needn't be more than a day or two."

"Oh." There was a distinct air of disappointment in that short word.

"Well, you can, of course. It's up to you, really – but the whole thing is a business trip. Two nights, and lunch with Robert Garrido."

"Hmm. So, you don't want me to come with you?"

"No, it's not that. It's just in and out – maybe half a day by the pool. You can come along with pleasure, but is it worth it just for that?"

"OK, I'll tell you what. Come to lunch with Mom and me, and I'll let you go on your own. You're probably right."

So I was railroaded into lunch with Sally and her mom. I didn't really mind, but I had the feeling that I'd been manipulated rather cleverly.

The weather was still a bit British, but we all piled into Sally's Volvo – not the Merc – and went up into a vineyard near Sonoma, where we revisited a favourite restaurant, ate good steaks and listened to Sally's Mom tell us some stories of Sally's childhood – to Sally's blushing embarrassment – and bought 4 cases of mixed wine to bring home. All in all, not a bad Sunday, really.

Chapter 25

Waiting again

The next week or so passed unremarkably – even boringly. I was looking forward to my quick trip to the Caymans as a break in the fairly tedious routine as much as anything. Once again, I was feeling somewhat becalmed. But I was soon up and off again.

My flight to Cayman wasn't the same adventure as last time – it felt more like a routine business trip as I made my way to the airport, boarded, and found my Business Class seat. And most of my fellow travellers were evidently travelling on business, judging by the way they were dressed and the fact that they immediately opened up their laptops as soon as we were cleared to do so. I sat back and watched a movie and reflected that before long, I would only travel where I wanted, when I wanted. And, I hoped, with Sally.

As Robert Garrido made clear when we met again for lunch, the money I had deposited in Zurich had been having a very busy time of it. I met him at the same table on the terrace at the Marriott where we last met, and he was eager to show me how busy he'd been.

I insisted we order lunch before he talked, and I told him that I was paying. I persuaded him to have a lobster to keep mine company – he offered token resistance only - and I ordered a crisp Sancerre to go with it, which I was surprised to see on the wine list. I had a new favour to ask of him. But first I let him describe the mechanics of the money-washing process.

In between the garden salad's removal and the lobsters' arrival, he started to explain the process he'd been involved in on my behalf for the last couple of weeks.

"By the time you'd got back to your hotel that Friday – I guess – the money was moving in several directions. Apart from five thousand dollars, the whole amount was transferred in amounts between forty and seventy-five thousand dollars, all different, but none as much as a hundred thousand. Four hundred and seventy separate transactions, in fact."

This was more interesting than I expected, actually. I always enjoyed learning how specialists in apparently arcane areas of expertise operated. It partly explained why I was so good at my last job. "Why so many transactions?" I asked.

The lobsters arrived, and we organised ourselves around the salad, fries, sauce and Sancerre before he was ready to answer.

"Well, transactions are going through the International systems all the time – constantly. Until the monitoring systems improve – and the authorities are really moving quickly on this – it's only really necessary to avoid curious coincidences, such as a series of identical-value transactions, or values over, as I say, a hundred grand."

Interesting. "I see. So there's nothing to connect these transactions?"

"Oh yes. They've all come from the same account originally. But that's not unusual – monthly payment ledger remittances to suppliers, and salary or dividend transfers all look like this. It's the destinations which need to be different. They were to just under a hundred companies in ten Caribbean and similar countries. Which, ultimately, you own."

This lobster was even better than I remembered, and the wine was perfect. I remembered an idyllic spring holiday in France with my wife in the Ferrari, including a visit to a grower in Sancerre, a beautiful village on a conical hill. Looking round this different version of Paradise, I wondered whether he could imagine his wine travelling this far – or indeed, costing this much.

I came back to the present. "OK, I understand that," I said. "So, where are the funds now?"

"Right now, they're in bank accounts for those companies in those territories. There's no direct evidence of your interest in any of them. Just a local nominee director. Between a hundred and fifty and two hundred and fifty thousand in each, none the same. And none particularly remarkable."

"So, right now, anyone could abscond with the money and I'd have no record of it being mine – I'd lose it, yes?"

"Well, not easily – as I say, you ultimately own the businesses who have the cash balances. You're just not on the bank accounts. But anyway, you're paying me to ensure that this doesn't happen. And believe me, the reputations of the local nominee directors are worth far too much to risk those individual sums. Your money's safe. But anonymous."

"I see. Well that's the point of all this, isn't it? So, now what?"

"Well, now I need your instructions again. As I say, the money has been fragmented and distributed. Now we bring it together again."

We kept stopping the discussion to dissect and eat our lobsters throughout this discussion, which had therefore taken quite some time. The waiter was on his way to take away the wreckage, and offer more delights. I waited for Robert, who ordered 'just a coffee', so I indicated the same.

"So, what instructions do you need?"

"Well, where do you want the money to end up? It will be amalgamated into just one company in each territory, and then the sums transferred over time – say two weeks – to a central company with one bank account in one territory. Where do you want that to be? That's where your money will be, of course."

Ah. This seemed like the right question at the right time – This was where I needed my 'extra service'.

"Well, that's very interesting. Because I do have a, let's say, requirement that this could help with."

"Oh?"

"Yes. But first, we need to go completely off the record for a while. Are you OK with that?"

"Yes, fine. I'm used to that." He smiled.

"OK. Well, as you know, it's been a chap called Brett Foster who you've been dealing with so far. Me, in other words."

Garrido looked puzzled. "Yes, of course."

"OK, well now, for various reasons, I need to lose Mr Foster. As soon as possible, he needs to disappear, and never be seen again on any official systems, anywhere."

"Well that's no problem. In fact it helps – it's another connection between the, let's say the entry to the process, and the exit from it, broken. So, yes, I can do that. If you have credible ID for another name?"

"Well, I do, I have a UK passport in another name."

"Is it real? If I can ask that ..."

"Oh, yes, and it looks like me. It is me, in fact. But I don't want that to enter into any official system, either."

Garrido sipped his coffee and looked out to sea. His face showed the brain working behind it. Eventually he put his cup down and nodded to himself. "So, let's see if I have this right. You want a complete new identity in this new name?"

"New to you, but yes."

"But not using the existing UK credentials?"

"Exactly. I need a new passport in a new country, really. No connection to the UK identity."

Garrido nodded. "Ok. Some – quite a few - countries would grant residency status if you deposited this much money in a bank in their territory. But you need more than that, yes?"

"Yes. I want to become a citizen of wherever it is. But also to completely lose the old status."

He mused a moment longer. "All right. In fact I think I can arrange that. I have a contact, well, a friend, who's now the Foreign Minister in Turks and Caicos. You could become a citizen there if he was prepared to help. It might cost some money, but not a huge amount, considering the sum we're playing with here. Say quarter to half a million US. Would that be OK?"

I had no choice, really, and this would remove me one more step from any official trace back to my old life. There was no way I could keep using Brett's passport – in fact I was worried about it more and more now – surely the system would flag it up soon? And my UK passport had the same problem, but I hadn't used it so far, so it was still 'clean'. "If you can convince me it'll work, it'll be OK."

"I think I can, but I need to make a call first. I might not get straight through to him, and anyway I'll need to get your – your current – Foster - signature on some documents before you leave. Now we've agreed on the final destination. When are you planning to go home?"

"Tomorrow, but I can easily change that."

"If you can give me an hour, I'll make a call. At least that will tell me whether I need you to rearrange your trip. I don't think you will, though. OK?"

We agreed to speak again in an hour, and he left me with the waiter, the bill, and a coffee refill.

He phoned as I was back in my room, repacking my case for the return journey. The desk put him through. "Ah, good, I've caught you. I managed to speak to my friend in Providenciales. In the Turks and Caicos, that is, of course."

"Yes, I know", I laughed. "So, what did he say?"

"We can do this. He needs a favour from you – well, he has a project he wants to fund and if you help him, he'll help you. Those were his words. I think he was being overheard."

"Right. That sounds encouraging, if a bit vague. What do I need to do? I'm packing – should I unpack again?"

Well, if you could stay another day, I could get everything sorted out for you. I'm going to bring everything together in Providenciales, if that's your decision. It's a pretty safe haven, and quite secure. We can always move it elsewhere – Nassau, maybe, if we need to. But I think my friend will provide what you need."

"OK, I'll delay for a day or so. It's worth it if we can sort this out now. Are you sure you can have everything completed that quickly?"

"Yes, I think so. I do need a signature – a Foster signature - on a document to help create the Turks company now we've decided on that. I'll call round to your hotel for that on my way home, about 6:30, if that's OK, and we can discuss the passport tomorrow, assuming I can reach my friend."

"OK. I'll see you in the bar at 6:30, then."

We agreed on that and I went to reception to extend my stay – that was no problem - and then to my room to unpack again.

It was a short and sweet meeting in the bar. Garrido didn't want a beer, so I signed three documents and that was that. The Turks & Caicos company was created and the associated bank account all ready for the net total of the funds to be gathered up and paid in.

He put the documents back in his briefcase. “Right, that’s all I need for now – I’ll tell you where we’ve got to with the passport tomorrow. Oh, and the name on your new passport – you new identity. What name will you be using?”

“Best. Joseph Best. That’s my real name, in fact.”

Garrido smiled and nodded. “OK.” He wrote it down on a pad and showed me. “Like that?”

I nodded. “Yes, that’s it.” It felt strange to see it written down, but I was looking forward to recovering my real name. “Right, I’ll see you here tomorrow. Cheers for now.” We shook hands and he left with his papers.

Idling another day away by the pool and on the beach wasn’t too arduous, although I did miss Sally. In fact, I was looking forward to sorting out the new citizenship with Robert Garrido’s friend and getting back home, which was what I was now thinking of as Sausalito, Mystere, and of course Sally. I’d phoned to say I wouldn’t be back for another day and she seemed fine with that.

So I was hoping for good news from Garrido when we met over lunch as agreed. And he had made significant progress in the short time, as it turned out. Albeit expensive.

He was carrying a notebook, which he opened to consult. “OK, I think this will give you what you need, if you think the investment is worth it”, he said, as we browsed the menu again. It hadn’t changed since I was first here, and we both ordered the chicken salad again. “I can secure citizenship in Turks and Caicos – full passport. How would that suit you?”

“That sounds excellent”, I said. “A completely new ID?”

“Yes. Both citizenship and financial.”

“How do you mean?”

"Well, your new passport will have no connection to your old UK one - there will be no linkage at all. As if the UK one never existed."

I was impressed. This was ideal. "And financially?"

"Well, when we get the money gathered together again, you'll need to deposit a reasonable sum in a Turks & Caicos bank – which we would probably do anyway – and that gives you residency rights to start with. I can check how much, but you certainly have enough."

"OK. Then what?"

Garrido paused as the waiter brought our chicken and a beer each. "You'll have a credit and a charge card on the Turks bank. You can remove some of the money and deposit it anywhere you like – in fact I'd suggest you look at Antigua and possibly Nassau to spread your investment, and that could give you residency rights there if you wanted it. In any case, there's no actual connection between this, erm, financial profile and any previous identity. You can draw cash and spend against these cards perfectly legitimately until you run out, as it were. Anywhere in the world, of course. And of course you'll have a checking account for larger purchases. Like a house, maybe. And paying me", he smiled.

"OK, all good so far ..." I said.

"And, as I say, I've arranged for you to have a new Turks and Caicos passport. Not just residency, but citizenship. As I say, no linkage at all to your UK identity. Thanks to my friend in the Turks."

This seemed ideal. My own name back, but no identifiable link with the old Joe. There was a price to pay, though, I guessed.

"That's good. Very good. What's this going to cost?"

Garrido took a draft of his beer. "Actually, the only thing that's going to cost you is the Turks and Caicos citizenship. The passport, that is. The financial stuff is pretty well a given. It's the new passport that will cost you. Are you sure you need to do that? After all, you do seem to have two passports already." he smiled.

I laughed. "True. But neither of those are, erm, well, they're not helpful now. In fact the sooner I can stop using them, the better." I was pretty sure that Brett's passport was on borrowed time already. And I really didn't want to use mine at all if possible. I was looking forward to burning it, or something.

"Ok", he smiled. "You're about to be very charitable."

"Oh?"

"Mmm. My friend is very keen to extend the hospital in Providenciales and add a childrens' wing."

"Very creditable of him."

Garrido nodded. "Yes. It'll be named after him. His legacy if you like. The Fernando D'Souza wing. And you're going to pay for it, pretty much."

That was unexpected, to say the least. "Really? Is that the deal, then? A hospital wing for a passport?"

"Yes. Well, full citizenship as well as the document, of course."

I mused over this idea as the waiter cleared away and we ordered coffee. Garrido added: "By the way, I need to be back at the office before long. There are some transactions to check on."

"OK, but I need to get to the end of this discussion. Firstly, how much? I can't imagine a children's hospital wing comes cheap."

"Maybe not as much as you'd think. Half a million dollars. Well, a little more, but that's your, erm, contribution. Anonymous, of course."

So, more than I thought, but … I drained my beer and waved for another. Garrido shook his head. "Not for me, thanks."

I laughed. "You know, it's probably a good idea. It's a good use of the money, anyway. The kids get a hospital, your pal gets a huge amount of kudos, I get a nice new ID, and all in exchange for some cash I didn't earn and never expected to have. And can afford."

"Yes", said Garrido. "Wins all round, really, I guess. I can't write any of this down, of course. Well, not the hospital and passport part, anyway. I can give you the new passport within a week of giving my friend access to the money. He'll start the process now - if you're sure – the less we know about that, the better."

"OK", I said, "Yes - I'm sure. I'm trusting you anyway, so, yes. Tell you friend to start planning his hospital. Just as soon as the money comes back to us. And when he's ready to issue my passport, of course."

Garrido nodded, but seemed slightly ill at ease. He played with his glass and frowned. "There is just one thing – I hope I can speak frankly?"

"Of course – As I said when we met, I'll be as frank with you as I can, and I'd hope you'd do the same with me. What's on your mind?"

"Well, it's your new ID – the name. Would I be right in thinking that your British Passport is in your, can I say, real name – Joe Best?" He was still slightly nervous.

"Yes it is, and that's my real name – between us, of course."

"OK, well ..." It seemed that we were getting to the nub of this. "Is it a good idea for you to put that name back in the public domain? Are you happy that it's safe? I don't know – don't want to know – exactly why you were using the, erm, other ID – Brett Foster ..."

I felt he needed to feel more comfortable with this discussion – he possibly had a point. "It's OK, I see your point, I think. And I welcome your input. Really. Speak freely."

He relaxed a notch or so. “”Ok, well this is the thing – if you needed to keep your original ID out of the spotlight so far, well, why bring it back into play now? I mean the links between the two Joe Bests are not there legally, but, well, the name’s the same. If someone spots that, well, the legal distinction won’t count for much – it certainly wouldn’t stop anyone in their tracks if they wanted to find you.”

I nodded. He was right. I took a sip of my beer and considered. “I see.” I hadn’t thought of that, which was a mistake. “You were right to mention this – don’t worry.” I smiled.

He relaxed. “So, is there a logical reason for you to revert to Joe Best? Or is it just, well, sentimental – you want your name back?”

He was completely right. It was sentimental, and it was dangerous. “No, it’s not logical at all. I hadn’t thought that through. Thanks. So, I think I need a different name, don’t I?”

“I’d recommend that, although this isn’t my field at all – and as I say, I don’t know the background. You can be Joe – that’s easy - and safe – but not Joe Best, I suggest.”

I mused. “Yes I agree. Something close, though? Say, erm ... Joe Benson? Beswick? Brown?”

“All perfectly OK. Just a question of, well, not taste, exactly; it’s whatever you prefer. But Best’s out - unless you’re prepared to risk discovery.”

“Yes, I get that – it’s accepted. It’s really no big deal. And I think Benson and Beswick are possibly too close to Best alphabetically. But I do want the initials to be JB again. Brown’s too, erm, indistinct. Almost a cliché. Balfour? That might work. Biddle? Boodle?” I drank the rest of my beer and called the waiter over.

He came at once. “Another beer, please.” I looked at Garrido, who shook his head. “Just one beer, then.” On a whim, before he turned to go, I asked “By the way, what’s your name?”

"Roderick, sir. They call me Roddy."

"I meant your surname? Family name? Don't worry – it's just a silly conversation we're having – about people's names."

"It's Baldwin, sir. Like the old British Prime Minister, I'm told. I'll bring your beer."

Garrido and I looked at each other and suppressed a laugh. "Well, that's settled, then", I said. "Baldwin it is."

"OK, if you're sure," smiled Garrido. If you change your mind, let me know before you leave."

"Joe Baldwin ..." I mused. "No, I think that's OK. I'll need to get used to it. Well, thanks to you, I possibly just dodged a problem there. Thanks. And the money's on its way out of your laundry now?"

"Yes, a couple of weeks, I think. That's all going to plan."

And that concluded the meeting. We said our farewells and I went back to the room to pack again.

I was getting used to the journey back to Sausalito by now, but it was no less lengthy and tiring. I called Sally from the airport and by the time BART and the ferry got me back to Mystere, Sally was finishing work and she joined me just as I was undressing for a shower. Which was great timing.

She wasn't staying the night as her mom wasn't well, but as she left the boat, I said "Oh, I've just agreed to fund a new children's hospital. In Providenciales. It's in Turks and Caicos." All casual-like.

"What?"

"I'll tell you tomorrow", I grinned and waved her goodnight. She blew me a kiss and walked away. Still that sexy wiggle, and she looked back to see whether I was watching. Which I was.

Chapter 26

Southbound

It was now March, and the early Northern Californian spring was showing its first green shoots. That spring-like air of promise, and the fact that I'd nearly finished the process of getting the money through the banking system, giving me what I was sure would be untraceable free access, was making me restless. It being a Monday, it seemed to be an appropriate day to start work.

Of course, it made no sense at all to exercise my option and buy Mystere from Ken White, but I decided to do it anyway. I was really enjoying living on the boat, and rather relished the freedom it seemed to offer, even if I hadn't really taken advantage of it so far. I suppose some boats just seem to fit, rather like some houses or some cars. I knew that it wasn't really big enough to live on permanently, and it was very much in the wrong place – in fact on the wrong side of the continent if I was going to live in the Caribbean. That's to say, a continent whose coastline stretched pretty well from the Arctic to the Antarctic. But I couldn't be the first person to want to get across it with a boat, could I?

So, to resolve that problem I went to my best source of information, as I was trained to do in my old business life. I dropped into the marina bar one evening and asked George, the Harbour Master, whether and how I could get Mystere round to the Caribbean.

After I'd bought the necessary beers for each of us, and some opening niceties, I turned the discussion to my main purpose. It didn't start well.

"So, George, if I wanted to get a sailboat like Mystere round to the Caribbean, what would you advise"

George chuckled and took a long pull at his beer. "If it was me, I'd sell it and go to the Caribbean and buy another one. In fact, since you haven't bought it yet, you're halfway there, aren't you?"

He was right, of course. But I had plenty of money, and would soon have access to much more. I figured that I could do whatever I wanted. And if it was possible, I wanted Mystere in Providenciales. So there.

"Yeah, I get that. Of course. But if I was set on it, how would I do it? There must be a way."

George looked at me and then at his empty beer glass. "This is starting to look like a business consultation ..."

"Ah, OK. More beer?" I quickly finished my own and nodded to the barman. "Two more, please?"

When the new glasses were in front of us, George nodded. "Ok, if that's what you're set on, you have three, possibly four options. Three are more or less stupid, one's just a bit less so."

I laughed. "Ok, let's hear it."

"Well, here's the stupid ones. One, put it on a low-loader and drive it across country. It's a Hunter 460, so a forty-eight footer, isn't it?" I nodded. "OK, well you step the mast – take it off and stow it on deck – and load it up. With that keel, you'd need a cradle, so it's still an awkward load. You'd need to plan the route carefully. It's still tall, even with the mast down, so you'd need to avoid low bridges and power lines ... a decent haulage company could work that out for you, probably. But that boat – it's not just high, it's long, too. And quite wide in the beam. Definitely a difficult load. But I suppose it could be done. Not cheap, and not a job for cowboys. But yes, possible, if you insisted."

That did indeed sound stupid, if theoretically possible. I tried to imagine what Mystere would look like on a low-loader. It didn't feel right. And it would attract attention. "OK. And the next stupid idea?"

George downed half his beer, wiped his mouth and chuckled. "Sail her round. Round the Horn. It's been done, but there aren't many sailors could do it. Or would try it, more like. It would need to be summer down there by the time you attempted it, and I'd give you about a 50 percent chance of getting through unscathed. Assuming you did get through. Still. If you set off now, and employed someone who was good enough – and crazy enough – you might make it."

I shook my head. "No – even I can see that that's just crazy."

George chuckled. "Yes, and anyway, you couldn't do it at all. You'd need an experienced yachtmaster. Experienced and lucky, ideally." He mused a moment. "You know, 30 years ago, I might have had a go at that ... it would be quite a trip."

"Maybe. But this is about getting it there, not the adventure." I did see his point, though. It might be fun ... but I had less adventurous plans for the future, especially now that I had a fortune to enjoy, and, it occurred to me, Sally to enjoy it with. No, I wasn't going to brave the Southern Ocean. And neither was Mystere. "So, what's the next stupid idea?"

We needed more beer. I reflected that, although the American cocktails were simply lethal, their beer was pretty useless. I didn't really want another. I glanced up, and with that, the barmen was there. I ordered another beer for George and decided on a scotch and soda for me. With lots of soda, please.

"Well, the only sea route into the Caribbean that makes sense is the Panama canal. You could sail it through."

That didn't actually seem all that stupid. "That seems OK. Why is it stupid?"

George chuckled. “The canal is built for freighters. Nowadays some cruise liners do it as well. Taking your boat, it would be like riding a bicycle on a freeway. It’s not all canal; there are some lakes to cross, where you’d be OK, but most of it is canal. And there are 8 or 9 locks. It costs lots of money to take them solo, and you’d have to wait for a gap in the schedules. Otherwise, you’d be sharing them with those freighters. Not really safe. And it’s not much fun. By the way, I think about 20,000 people died building that canal. Half the workforce. Mostly from fever. Really, you don’t want to do that.”

I saw his point. It was obviously not a pleasure cruise. Not as bad as rounding the Horn, but certainly no fun. OK, three down, one to go. “All right. Possible, but not fun, and still risky. So, what do I do?”

George took another pull at his beer and came out with the only sensible idea. “You ship it. On a ship. A freighter. Through the canal.”

Ok, I thought. That might work. “OK. How do I do that?”

“Easy, really. 5-star shipping in San Fran - or they may be in LA, I’m not sure. Anyway. Sail it there, they’ll step the masts and stow it on the deck. They’ll take it down and through the canal and drop it somewhere on the other side. You fly down and pick it up in the Caribbean - or maybe the Gulf.”

“Gulf?”

“Yes. Gulf of Mexico. You could have it delivered to somewhere like Galveston, in the Gulf. Or maybe Miami. Or somewhere like Belize. On the other side, anyway.”

That seemed sensible. And a lot less scary, even if I wasn’t actually on the boat, I didn’t want to buy it and immediately have it wrecked. “I supposed it’s insured as well?”

“I guess so. Best go have a chat with them, or just phone ‘em. They do this a lot for motor boats, and I’m sure they’ll have shipped a sailboat plenty of times.”

"Do you have a contact there? A number?"

"No, not really, but they'll be in the book. In fact there'll be more than one firm. I just know of 5-star. Only thing is, you may have to go to LA; I'm not sure they have a boat shipping dock here in San Fran, as I say. But they'd tell you that."

"Right, Thanks, George. I think that's the answer. Another beer?" for answer, George drained his tankard and put it on the bar. The barman filled it up and I scooped up the tabs and paid up.

"Cheers. You've given me something to think about here." I left him to it and made my way down to Mystere. Sally was working late and staying with her Mom tonight, so I decided on an early night and sleeping the drinks off. And thinking through my options.

I hadn't changed my mind when the morning came, so I called Ken White once the hour seemed reasonable. I got his voicemail.

"Hi. This is Ken White. Please leave a message and I'll get back to you."

"Ken, it's, erm, Brett Foster." I was starting to have identity issues ..." On Mystere. I've been thinking about my option to buy the boat. Can we discuss that sometime soon?" I left my cellphone number and rang off. I didn't think it would take him long to get back to me. There were 245,000 very good reasons to reply, according to our agreement.

I was also aware that I needed to have a serious chat with Sally. I was close to leaving Sausalito and starting my new life as a citizen and probably resident of the Turks & Caicos – at any rate, somewhere in the Caribbean. I wanted Sally to join me in that. I'd never really thought anything else, I realised, but I couldn't recall the day I decided. I guess it had grown on me. Or snuck up. But I wasn't sure what Sally thought – we'd settled into a comfortable routine here, and I hadn't wanted to disturb that by discussing the future.

Well, I needed to sort that out now. We spent every weekend together and two or three nights during the week, but this wasn't a "last thing at night" sort of chat. I thought a trip into wine country in the Merc with the roof down and a lunch in one of the wineries might be a better setting. It struck me that I was nervous about this – I wanted to get it right. And I wanted her to say yes. What to, I wasn't totally clear yet.

What I could do at once was follow up on my discussion with George, so I got on with that. I looked up the address of the shipping company he mentioned and phoned them. They were based in Los Angeles. I explained what I wanted, and it turned out that they could indeed ship Mystere from this side of the Panama Canal to the other. There was a sailing from LA to Miami next week, which was too soon, but another in four weeks' time, which seemed about right. I'd have to sail it to LA, of course, but I thought I could do that, with help. But I wanted to see how this worked, and the shippers said that if I made an appointment, I could visit the docks and see how it would be done. This wasn't unusual, it seemed. I agreed to do that and they said that if I was happy, I could make the booking and pay for it at once, including insurance. That all seemed acceptable.

My last job that morning, allowing for the time zones, was to call Garrido for an update on the money transactions and the new ID. I got through quickly, and he called me back at once. I wasn't bothered about cost, but the pre-pay cellphone went through the credit so fast that an international conversation couldn't last more than 5 minutes.

"So, Peter, how's the project going?" I asked. He was nervous about using specific details on the cellphone – or in fact any phone. Probably quite rightly.

"Good morning Mr Foster. The project is almost complete. I'll have some final papers for you to sign next week, and that will be that. My friend in Providenciales is also looking forward to meeting with you. Have you made any travel plans yet?"

"Ah, good. No, I was waiting for your update, which is why I called. I also have business in Los Angeles, and I was hoping to make one round trip. It looks like that's feasible, then?"

"Yes, I'd say so. If you could meet me at the usual place, say next Thursday, I can arrange for you to go on to Providenciales the next day and meet my friend. I'll arrange the flights there and back, if you like. That should complete the whole, erm, transaction."

That was ten days away, which was fine. "OK, and that would give me time to open bank accounts?"

"Yes. In fact, the business bank account in Turks & Caicos is already open. You can open personal accounts any time, but the business banks will be, well, funded and functioning. You'll be the only signatory on those after I step down. As Joe Barlow, if we do this in that sequence."

This was good, and seemed very easy. I was within touching distance of several million dollars, and with it, a new identity and indeed a new life. I think this phone call was the first time it struck me that this really was going to happen. Chiswick seemed a very long way away, and last September felt like another lifetime. Which it was, really.

Ken White called me back just as I was contemplating what I was going to do for lunch. He was typically brisk. "Hi, Brett. Ken White here. So you want to buy the boat?"

I was tempted to play games with him, but in fact there was an agreement to buy in my lease document which meant that there wasn't much mileage in negotiating. For either of us. "Yes, I think so. Exercise my option, so to speak. That expires at the end of May, I think?"

"Sure. Of course. Look, I've just finished playing golf, and I want to have lunch with these guys. A bit of business ..."

"That's OK. I just wanted you to know that I've decided to buy. There is one thing, though …"

"What's that? We've agreed a price already … I'm not dropping the price."

"No, no, it's not the price. I need it sailing down to LA. Can you help me do that, do you think?"

"Hmm." I could imagine him having another root in his nostril. "Why, sure." A pause "If you can help me with something?"

"OK?"

"I need to keep the, erm, visible proceeds down as far as possible – my divorce, you know …"

"Ah. So you want me to pay less than we agreed?" I couldn't resist that.

There was a snort. "Hell, no! But if you have any more of that cash you paid the rent with …"

"Ah. I see. Yes, that could be arranged. My company will be buying the boat, but I'm OK with paying some in cash and, let's say, depressing the public price?"

"Yes, that's it. Can we say £25k in cash?"

"If you think that leaves a credible price, I could do that. If you could help me sail it to LA."

"OK, that's good. Look, are you around tomorrow morning? We can firm this up. And you can tell me why you need to go to LA."

"Actually, that's none of your business, is it? But yes, I'll explain. Tomorrow morning – or maybe you'd like lunch?"

"Great. I'll see you on the boat at 12, then."

"OK", I replied, but he'd already rung off and, no doubt, to his next deal. I wondered whether there was any cash involved with that.

Sally had been asked to help out by working some lunchtime shifts at the restaurant. The tourist numbers were starting to build, and they had a new lunchtime menu which was proving popular. I decided to pop in for a plate and a glass of wine – or maybe a beer. Sally greeted me with a discreet kiss. "Hiya! I wasn't expecting to see you today."

"No, I know. I thought I'd try your new lunch menu. And I wanted to ask you something."

"Ok, here's a menu. Sit there and I'll take your order – and you can ask me." She indicated a window table and winked. I really did like this girl. I also liked that feeling. I also fancied Fettucine Alfredo and a Peroni, but in a different way.

Sally greeted a couple of tourists – classic retired Midwesterners with video camera and ridiculous baseball caps with a team logo – and discussed the menu and specials board, then strolled over to my table. "So why don't I get the specials board description, then?" I grinned.

"Nah. I know what you're going to order."

"Oh yeah, smartarse? What's that then?" I faked a frown.

Sally giggled. "Tagliatelli Alfredo, green salad. And a beer. Right?"

I grinned. "It's fettucine, not tagliatelli. Or it should be. And I hadn't thought of the salad, but yes – top marks. And make that a Peroni. None of this American rubbish."

"Well I coulda guessed that as well." She wrote down the order. "So, what's the thing you wanted to ask?"

"I want to take you out for lunch. Are you free tomorrow?"

"Well, I said I'd work here again tomorrow, but the next day's clear, if that's OK. That would be nice. Any particular reason?"

"Yes. Well, I don't think we need a reason, do we? But things are happening. We need to talk, I think. I just thought a drive into wine country, roof down, alfresco dining - you know. Maybe that place we took your mom that Sunday."

She sat down in the spare seat. "Joe, is something wrong?"

"No. No, far from it. It's just that, well, as I say, things are moving forward ..." I didn't want to have this discussion here, but it seemed I was going to have to open up a bit. "Look, Sally. This adventure's about to move on to the next stage. I've ... well, I don't want to have that discussion now, but, well, I'd really like you to be part of that ..." I looked at her and smiled.

"Ok. Well I guess this was going to happen. I didn't realise it was happening so quickly, that's all, I suppose."

I thought I knew what she was thinking. I took her hand. "Sally, this isn't goodbye. It's a discussion about what we do next. You and I. I really do want you with me. But, like I say, we need to talk about what happens next in this adventure. And, honestly, I want you in that story. Really." I looked into her eyes and smiled.

She smiled back. "Good." She looked down. "So, I guess we do need to have that chat. And lunch at the winery does sound nice." She looked up. "I'll take your order in."

As she left the table and walked over to the kitchen, I realised how much I didn't want to leave Sally behind. I hoped I wouldn't have to.

Sally was calm efficiency for the rest of the meal, and I was somewhat edgy. But when I paid and made for the door, she caught up with me, gave me a lingering kiss on the lips – which shocked the Midwesterners – and said "I'll pick you up in the Merc on Wednesday, then? You book lunch. And we'll decide what our future looks like." She winked and I felt a lot better. I thought it was going to be OK.

As I was leaving, I remembered my offer of lunch to Ken White. "Oh, Sally."

She turned back. "Yes?"

"I'm bringing Ken White here for lunch tomorrow – that OK?"

"Why not? Shall I bake a cake?" she grinned.

I laughed. "No need for that, I think. But we might need a quiet table."

"OK. I'll put you over there, shall I?" She pointed to a corner table, furthest from the door.

"Perfect." I grinned and she grinned back. I thought, yes, it's going to be OK. Well, I hoped so.

Ken White was almost exactly on time next morning. I watched from the cockpit as he bounded up the gangplank and dropped into one of the seats. "Hi, Good to see ya." He stuck out his hand and we shook. "So, you've fallen for my baby, have you?"

I guessed he meant Mystere. It sounded odd – I'd got completely used to regarding her as mine already. "Well, I guess I have. I'm certainly keen to exercise my option, anyway. I'm glad I thought of that."

"Ok, great. I knew you'd want her once you'd gotten used to her. I can tell you, if it wasn't for this goddam divorce, I wouldn't be selling."

"Yes, well ... Do you still fancy lunch?"

"Sure. What do you have in mind?"

"The restaurant Sally works at – it's got a good lunchtime menu – she's expecting us. That OK?"

It was indeed OK, and we left the boat and walked down the dock and over to the restaurant. Sally welcomed us and showed us to the table she'd indicated yesterday. She sat us down and gave us menus as efficiently as if we were yesterday's Midwestern tourists. Then she winked and ruffled the back of my head as she left. White didn't seem to notice – he was scanning the menu – but I had a very nice tingly feeling. I found myself really hoping tomorrow would go well. I sort of liked that nice tingly feeling.

Sally came back for our orders. Chicken Caesar for me, pepperoni pizza for Ken and a bottle of local Pinot Grigio. Garlic pizza starter between us to take the edge off. Once she'd brought the garlic pizza and left us to it, Ken opened up as, after raising his eyebrows as permission, he poured chilli oil on the garlic pizza, and he tore a slice off. I did the same.

"Ok, so ... we've agreed a price, and you mentioned a trip to LA ...?"

"Yes, and you wanted some cash, yes?" Well, we'd already had this conversation, but it didn't hurt to have it again and confirm the set-up. We re-established yesterday's situation, anyway.

"OK, so it comes down to this," Ken summarised, as Sally swopped the garlic pizza for our main courses, and topped up our wine. "I'd like as much cash as you can manage, and you want some help in sailing down to LA. Yes?"

"Well, more than help. I mean, I know more than I used to, but I still couldn't do it solo."

"Well with your girlfriend's help you might make it. She's clearly done some sailing."

"I know, but 'might make it' isn't good enough, is it, really? Sally might come as well, I don't know – I haven't talked to her about this yet. But I'd be happier with an expert on board. I thought I'd sail and you can advise. From a sedentary position if you like. With glass in hand, so to speak", I smiled.

This conversation was more sporadic than it sounds. We were eating and drinking and generally lounging, and talking about our old days in the IT business. Of course, he knew me as Brett Foster, so I couldn't tell him that I actually knew, at some remove, some of the personalities he talked about. I kept my actual working history a little vague. But since he mainly liked to talk about himself, that wasn't really a problem.

I liked Ken, despite his nose-picking (thankfully not a feature today) and his bombastic approach. Like many bombastic people, once he'd settled down he was very good company. I'd learned that during our sailing days out with Sally. And after all, I'd once lived in his world of high-tech and quarterly sales targets, and for a long time, enjoyed it. His stories reminded me why that was, and also I was glad to be out of all of it, but I could still march to that tune, so to speak.

"Tell you what, Ken, let's get down to business. It's really very easy. I want you to sail down to LA with me. In fact, as I say, I want to sail it myself under your guidance. And you need some cash to squirrel away. Yes?"

"OK, yes. How much cash could you manage?" This was the first time he'd let me have the upper hand. "I mean, I need to make it look like a reasonable sale, credible to her lawyers, but cash is good for me right now." I explained that I wanted to complete this transaction before the option expired, but not right now. But that I could give him the cash element now if we could agree the deal. Maybe as a deposit.

The plates were removed and coffee was brought by the slightly bemused Sally. I hadn't discussed the details of this deal with her, and she probably thought this was just a price discussion. And couldn't see why it was taking so long.

I eventually told Ken that I could actually pay for Mystere entirely in cash if he wanted, so he needed to tell me what was a credible transaction for his wife's lawyers. I then said that I wanted to pay by company cheque or transfer for the "official" part of the price, but I needed about 3 weeks to get into position to do that, for reasons I didn't want to elaborate upon. I also explained, although I didn't need to, that once we got to LA I was proposing to ship Mystere to Miami.

We settled at $40k cash this week as a deposit on the sale, the sale to be contracted at the option price of $245k less the cash, full balance payment due on or before shipping, by transfer from my company. As before, we decided to create a memorandum of this deal. This would replace the rental agreement. The cash payment would be documented as a down payment for the full deal for now, but new paperwork would be prepared when the cheque for balance was paid, showing the balance of $205k as the purchase price. All other documentation would then be destroyed. Easy, really.

We agreed that Ken and I would sail down to LA in about two weeks' time. Ken thought that the trip would take 4 or 5 days. "There's a tidal push from north to south. If we were going north, that would take twice as long. I've done this a couple of times. If we sail for about 10 hours a day, we should be OK for that. It's daylight for at least that now. But we need to leave early on the first day to catch the breeze and get out of the Bay and into the ocean."

And that was settled. We flipped a coin for the bill and Ken lost.

That afternoon, I sat down and worked out my itinerary for the next two or three weeks. I was going to be busy.

I needed to visit LA to look at the shippers and satisfy myself that the transport arrangements were safe, and if so, book it. Then I needed to travel from LA to the Caymans, and, assuming Garrido sorted out the flights to and from the Turks & Caicos as he'd promised, I'd need to fly back from there to SFO. Being Business Class, the flights would probably be flexible, which I needed, especially on the return flight. Garrido had suggested I meet him next Thursday, so if I flew to LA next Tuesday and left for Cayman on Wednesday evening, that would allow a reasonable schedule.

For my earlier flights to Cayman, and indeed Zurich, I'd just called the airline and used my debit card, but this was more complex. I decided to find a travel agency and let them work it out. I didn't think there was one on this side of the Bay, so I needed one in San Francisco itself. I consulted Yellow Pages and found a travel agency that advertised "Commercial and Business travel a specialty." I figured that was what I wanted – this wasn't a vacation trip. I called the number and spoke to a helpful lady and explained my requirements. She didn't seem to find this unusual, and she was also able to deal with my hotel booking in LA and the Marriott in Cayman. I said that I wanted Business Class travel, with a flexible return leg at least, and she seemed to understand all that. She read back my instructions. "Mr. Foster, this is a fairly expensive itinerary. That's no problem, but I do need to know how you will be paying. Do you have an American Express card I can use?"

"Not Amex, no. But I do have a Visa debit card on my checking account. It has quite a high daily limit. How much do you think this will be, anyway?"

"I won't know until I work it all out. Possibly $5,000. No more than that, I'd say."

"OK. If you can start working everything out now, and I start out immediately, I can be with you in a couple of hours. Say 4:30 or maybe 5. I can collect the tickets and pay you then. Would that be OK?"

"Yes, but I can't confirm the flights or the hotel until we receive payment. I'm sure you understand ..."

"Yes, of course. But I'll be with you this afternoon anyway. I'll phone you if I'm delayed. OK?"

We agreed that would work, and as I grabbed my jacket and locked up the boat I called Garrido and told him in a very quick call that I'd be in the Caymans next Thursday morning. I suggested breakfast in the

Marriott, which was good for him. I rushed down to the ferry dock - there was a departure in 15 minutes, so I jumped aboard. As the ferry manoeuvred its way off the dock and out of the bay I phoned the winery and booked lunch the next day.

The travel agency was close to a BART stop, and I was in good time at the travel agency. As promised, the lady I'd been speaking to, who turned out to be a large black lady called Pauline, had everything ready for me to review and confirm. She showed me to a lounge area with low tables and comfy chairs and offered me a coffee, which I declined. As we worked through the itinerary, I was reminded what it had been like to work with a really efficient secretary. The whole trip was organised with just the right amount of slack between flights. She'd even identified back-up flight times and asked for my frequent flyer details. I admitted that I hadn't joined any schemes as yet. Pauline looked at me like a schoolmarm.

"You know, you should. With just this itinerary, you'd build up some really good points. You're missing out here. Really."

I said I knew she was right, and promised to pick up and fill in the forms in the departure lounge. I wouldn't of course – it was far too traceable, and anyway, what address would I use?

Pauline was slightly mollified at this promise, and I handed over my card. The total was just over $4,500 including the hotels and - of course – fully flexible Business Class seats. The only element not included was the side trip to Providenciales from Cayman. Once the payment had gone through, Pauline printed out the full itinerary, complete with flight and check-in times, hotel addresses and telephone numbers, and their own telephone number in case of emergency. I was impressed, and said so.

"Well, Mr Foster, perhaps you'll consider us for your next business trip. It's been a pleasure working with you."

"Well, certainly I would. But in fact I'll be moving away from the Bay area shortly. Nevertheless, I really do appreciate your work here. If I need to organise any travel before I leave, I'll be sure to call you."

Pauline smiled. "You make sure you do." She took a branded plastic document folder and placed the tickets and itinerary in various pockets, then handed it over. "You have a nice trip, now." We stood and shook hands and that was that.

That put me in midtown San Fran at what I still called teatime. Shops were still open, and I knew that Sally was working that evening and staying with her mom. So, I decided on some pointless retail therapy – not that I needed either therapy, or, frankly, any stuff. But actually, I thought, Sally might appreciate a present tomorrow. In fact, maybe some jewellery. I took BART to Union Square and found Saks not too far away. I strolled into the store and looked for the right department. I had no idea what I was looking for, but I felt that a generous gesture was called for. Not a ring - wrong message ... not a watch. Earrings? Were her ears pierced or not? I ought to know, really, but I didn't. I'd better check that, I thought, but for now, maybe a necklace? Yes, that would do it.

The sales assistant was only too happy to help me choose. She was distractingly pretty, and I knew I couldn't help but flirt with her. Old habits die hard, I guess. She smiled a dazzling smile and introduced herself. "Good afternoon, sir. I'm Saffron. How can I help you?" Saffron? Well, this was San Francisco. And she had that hippy-chick look they more or less invented here, although I did think it had gone out of style. Not here, though, and in fact I couldn't really imagine a 'Saffron' with any other look.

It was time to be English, I thought. "Hello, Saffron. Call me Joe. Yes, you can. I'm looking for a necklace, I think. Something discreet, but high quality."

"I see. And how much did you want to invest?" Invest – good line there.

"I thought I'd invest about 2,000 bucks or so. What do you have in that area?"

She seemed to think that was a bit low-rent. Maybe it was. "Well, we do have some items in that price area. Could you spend a little more? Perhaps if I show you something in that price range and also something around 3,000?"

She was good, but I think I was bewitched anyway. "All right. Let's do that. No promises, mind."

She smiled that smile again. "Very good sir. Now, are you thinking of gold, some diamonds? Or perhaps some classic pearls?"

Hmm. I hadn't really got beyond the idea of a necklace. I thought Sally would prefer something more contemporary. "Not pearls, I think. Something quite modern." I had a think. "Maybe white gold ... a diamond or two, maybe?"

She nodded "OK. Let's see." Turning to a cabinet behind her, she brought out 4 slender black boxes, about a foot long, and put them on the counter between us. "Ok. I won't tell you the prices here. You just decide which one you like. OK?"

Oh goodness. I was in expert hands. Never mind. I could afford it, obviously, but I didn't want to be too showy. Sally wasn't really the sort of girl who would like to be flash, in fact I thought she'd be embarrassed by that. Saffron opened each box to display the contents and stood back for a moment.

I looked at the range, and couldn't help mentally organising them in order of my guess at the price. In fact, I did rearrange them. "Is that right?" I asked her.

"Ah. Well, no, actually." She swopped the middle two around. "That's it." I looked at them closely and picked up the second one along. It was a series of 3 inch white gold rods, looped together at each end, with a diamond on the middle one and a smaller one on the clasp at the back. It had a reassuring heft to it – the rods were quite substantial.

The end necklace, the expensive end, was a white gold rope with a pendant diamond in a sort of claw clasp. I picked that up as well, and it seemed heavier. The single diamond was obviously bigger as well.

"OK", I said. "It's between these two, I think. Let's put the others away." She picked the boxes up and put them back in the display cupboard. Bobbing down very prettily, Bunny-style, she then took out a smaller box from a lower shelf and put that on the counter.

"I thought I should show you these as well. Matching earrings to that necklace." Meaning the cheaper – less expensive one. She opened it up and put it alongside the matching necklace. So now the two offerings were probably the same price again. Neat.

"Saffron, you're very good at this, aren't you? How long have you been working here?"

She smiled. "About a year. I'm really a jewellery designer. It doesn't pay – not yet, so I work here 3 days a week."

I smiled back "Ah, well, as an expert, which do you prefer? Which one would you like to be bought?"

She laughed. "Well, I design my own, so nobody who knows me dares buy me anything. Or in fact could afford it, come to think of it ..."

"Saffron, you need to take a good look at your choice of boyfriend." She grinned back. "But I'm buying this for my girlfriend, so, come on, which one? By the way, you still haven't told me the prices."

"Well, with the earrings, this one", she pointed to the one with rods and 3 diamonds, "is 3,150, and this one, on its own, is 3,000."

"Including tax?"

"Yes. State and city." She looked at me and waited.

I picked up the one with the rods. “I have to be honest. I can’t remember whether she has pierced ears or not.” I looked suitably embarrassed.

Saffron giggled. “You don’t know whether you wife has pierced ears?”

“Girlfriend, actually. And no, I can’t remember. We haven’t been together all that long …”

Well, you’d better not risk these, then. They only fit pierced ears. Most ladies do have them, but if not, well, she’ll say you should have known.” She looked me in the eye, “Which of course you should”, she grinned.

I smiled back. “I know, I know … but I can’t risk these, so put them away as well.”

She did so, doing that bunny-dip again, and turned back to the counter. “OK, this one, without the earrings, is 2800.” She looked at me, expectantly.

I picked up each necklace in turn. I put the rope one down and held onto the one with bars and 3 diamonds. “You know, I prefer this one. Not for the sake of the 200 bucks. I just like the detail.”

She nodded. “Me too, actually. It’s a bit more modern. Closer to what I’d like to design.”

“Good. I’ll take it, then. Can you gift-wrap it?”

She smiled “Of course. Let me take payment and then I’ll wrap it.”

I handed over my card and she swiped it. As I signed the slip, I reflected that this would normally be the point when I’d ask her for a drink. She was just too pretty and we’d created a toe-hold of rapport. Of course, it would have looked a bit odd, since I’d just bought an expensive gift for, obviously, a girlfriend who meant something to me. But some girls like a challenge. Or, in fact, just an adventure. It would have worked, I was sure. But things were different now, it seemed. I just watched her wrap the small parcel neatly, and hand it over with a smile. The new me thanked her and walked away. And I was looking forward to giving it to Sally tomorrow. In a manner of speaking.

Chapter 27

Boston Beans

The Priest had worn his clerical collar and dark suit on the plane and through immigration and customs at Boston airport. It had done the trick, and he was ushered through the VIP channel. “This way, Father”, whispered the security guard, all deference to the cloth.

“Thank you, my son”, smiled The Priest. And he was out into the taxi line before the last of the economy passengers were through immigration, and checking into the Sheraton before they were in their own taxis or buses.

He put a call through to the Congressman’s offices from the room and asked for a senior aide. He was about to start calling in favours. “Hello. Mr Sullivan, please. Father O’Callaghan here. Thank you.”

Silence, some clicks, then “Hello, Father. Are you in Boston? How was your flight?”

“Good afternoon. Yes, I am. It was no worse than usual, thank you. I’m staying at the Sheraton. I wonder if we could have dinner here, tomorrow evening?”

“Erm, yes, that would be … nice. Just you and me?”

“Yes. Just you and I. Shall we say eight o’clock? The matters we discussed on the phone late last year. There have been developments.”

“I see. OK, I’ll see you tomorrow. Anything I can do beforehand?”

“No, I’ll explain everything when we meet. Eight o’clock tomorrow evening.” He put the phone down.

…

The dining room in the Boston harbour-side hotel was designed to be a close representation of a London Club. Old Money and sleek businessmen were what it set out to attract, and it succeeded. In fact, the clientele looked very much like the British upper classes The Priest so despised, but possibly, secretly, even denied to himself, envied.

These patricians, however, had Irish roots. They had prospered over the generations until they resembled the hated Brits they were so keen to fight. The fight was vicarious now, though. It was fought from across an ocean, using dollars and rousing fighting songs from a safe distance. And now, the fight seemed to be over, although that was still being debated.

Many of these "Irish" had never been to Ireland, and those who did were treated there with the pragmatic reverence due to their spending capability rather than to their "Irishness." Previous generations had endured desperate hardships to escape even more desperate circumstances, but many of their great-great grandchildren were now wealthy beyond their ancestors' imaginings. And they used this wealth to wage a war that was driven by hatred of the Brits who, maybe rightly, they believed had forced them out after callously exploiting and neglecting them. But they were waging this war on people who were as far removed from those ancient landowners as they themselves were from their own previous generations.

For most, it had become a matter of honour, not to strive to bring peace to a land riven by hatred, fear and violence, but to pay to sustain what they saw as revenge on the British. And that is how The Priest came to be sitting in this opulent dining room with an ambitious forty-year-old from the Massachusetts Congress office. Mr Sullivan was running to fat and his once ginger hair was, at best sandy now, and thinning. But his ambition to be the next Congressman burned bright.

The support of the Irish "movement" and the money he collected on its behalf – a portion of which he retained, by tacit agreement – was a key element in realising that goal. The mutuality of interests – the Irish lobby in Congress and the Senate, and the money that could be raised and funnelled to the cause – had been a binding force. Now, however, the game seemed to have changed. How the new peace would play to his ambitions, he wasn't sure. So he was glad to have this opportunity to speak to The Priest, even if he still feared his aura. And lunch presented a civilising environment to do so. Or so he hoped.

They had ordered a Boston Chowder, followed by a steak for Sullivan and grilled flounder – Dover Sole – for The Priest.

Over the main course, Sullivan brought the somewhat one-sided small talk around to what he saw as the business of the day. "So, Father. Peace at last in Ireland, is it?"

"So they say, Mr Sullivan. So they say." He dissected his fish with painstaking precision.

"And what do you say, Father?"

"I say that we have signed a treaty with the British. And the Dublin government are supporting this treaty. We have had to accept that we cannot reunite the island of Ireland by force of arms. We must find a different way. Or accept the new reality."

"I see that McGuinness and Adams will be part of the new Belfast Assembly. Sitting alongside that lunatic Paisley. Who ever saw that as a possibility?"

"Certainly not me." The Priest sipped his wine. Judging by his face, it was bitter.

"Wine all right?" asked Sullivan, noticing the grimace.

"It's fine, thank you. Nice and dry."

There was a silence as both men dealt with their food.

"So," said Sullivan, as he cut another slice of his steak and dipped it in the béarnaise sauce, "Where does that leave our, erm, co-operative activities, would you say?"

The Priest turned his fish over and began fastidiously removing the white skin from the flesh below. "We still co-operate, and we still have funds to bring to bear. In fact, that is why I'm here."

"Oh?" This was more like it, thought Sullivan, picking up a handful of fries from the bowl in the centre of the table and dropping them on his plate. "So, how can I help?"

"We still require support for the Irish cause in the corridors of power in Washington. There is much to be done, and in due course, some – arrangements – may need to be rearranged. This is a time for subtlety and diplomacy rather than direct action. But the cause is by no means dead."

"Well, glad to hear it." Sullivan was cleaning the plate juices with a forkful of fries. The Priest did not choose to watch too closely. "So, how can I help at this time?"

The Priest placed his knife and fork carefully together and glanced at the waiter, which seemed sufficiently compelling. They remained silent as the plates were cleared, the table swept and menus were once again placed in front of them. The waiter made to withdraw, but The Priest held his hand up, as if in blessing.

"I'd like the Key Lime Pie, please," he said.

Sullivan wasn't really ready, but said "Same for me, then." And the waiter withdrew.

The Priest looked directly at Sullivan. "The problem we have is quite simple to explain, but quite difficult to resolve."

"OK," said Sullivan. "What can I do?"

"I will explain the problem in a moment, but since you ask, I need to gain access to some detailed records relating to the events in New York last September. And some other records after that event."

"9/11, you mean? What do you need?" Sullivan hadn't expected this – it seemed a long way from the Irish cause.

The Priest's response was delayed by the arrival of the Key Lime pies and an offer of cream or ice cream. When all was settled, he spoke again.

"Some of those funds you touched upon were being – shall we say – being brought into the open by means of a transaction in the World Trade Centre that very morning. We lost some good friends and our American lawyer. We also thought that we had lost the funds, but now, it seems not."

Sullivan was paying very close attention. This was certainly not what he was expecting. His brain was racing. What resources might he be asked to provide – what favours will he need to pull in? "So, you still have the funds?"

The Priest smiled – not a nice smile. "No. They have been – misappropriated. We now want two things – the first is to find out where they are so that they can be recovered and put to work as we all intended." He raised his glass an inch in Sullivan's direction.

Sullivan returned the toast. "Naturally. And the second thing?"

"We want to find the little bastard who thinks he can help himself to our money and get away with it, and show him that he cannot." This was spoken flatly, with no apparent emotion, which made it even more chilling.

Sullivan knew a little about how this priestly man showed his enemies the errors of their ways. He kept himself as unknowing as possible, but he knew enough. But he had no choice but to support this new vendetta. "I see," he said. So, what do you need?"

By way of an answer, The Priest asked a question. “How many people were reported killed in that event? Or – this is what I’m really interested in - how many bodies were not recovered?”

“Well, I don’t know. But it will be a matter of record by now. Is that the help you need?” He didn’t think that was it, but he hoped so.

“As you say, we can find that out easily enough. But what I want to do is try to find someone who *seems* to have died, but hasn’t.”

Sullivan nodded “I see”, he said, but wasn’t really sure what The Priest meant.

“This is what I need”, said The Priest. “I need to see a list of all bodies identified and named, and – most interestingly - a list of all names of the assumed dead whose bodies have not been found and identified.”

“OK”, said Sullivan, somewhat pompously: “that’s available to me as a concerned representative of the people. There’s a list of such names. They’re called the “Lost Souls.”

The Priest nodded. “Good. Nice to know. Now, I assume all the unidentified dead – these ‘Lost Souls’ - are simply assumed to have been in the building because of some circumstantial evidence? And there will be more names than unidentified bodies?”

“Ah. I believe so. That’s certainly the case now. Many of them will have simply, well, vapourised. Those actually in the planes or on the floors close to where the planes struck. There will be literally nothing left. We’re having to put new regulations in place to issue death confirmations for these poor souls. Lost Souls, as I say. To help their families deal with insurance and so on. We’re in uncharted territory here.”

“How many of these – vapourised – bodies are there? How many Lost Souls?”

"In New York? There are a couple of thousand names without bodies right now. It's still an unknown. There are many bodies which they still have to identify – very badly damaged, or, erm, incomplete. It's going to take years, but they won't find bodies at all for about half these names, I'm hearing. So we're moving forward with formal death confirmation on, so to speak, strong circumstantial evidence. It's the same in the Pentagon, on a smaller scale."

"I see. Is there a list of names for these Lost Souls? The ones in New York, I mean?"

"Yes, I can get that. Part of the special arrangements, you see."

The Priest was silent for a moment and addressed himself to his Key Lime Pie.

Eventually he nodded to himself. "I see. So, I also need to know any activity relating to the names on that list. Credit cards, bookings on airlines, trains, shipping ... anything. In particular, the name of Best."

Sullivan raised his eyebrows. "Really? Where do you suppose I can get that from? If at all?"

The Priest smiled. Not a nice smile. "I don't know, Mr Sullivan. But I'm sure there will be some records. To support these 'special arrangements'. Any strange, erm, post-mortem activity, so to speak, would be flagged somewhere, wouldn't you think?"

The plates were cleared and coffee was offered and accepted. And Bushmills. Sullivan was clearly working something out. "You know, I guess you're right. Someone would need to look out for that. The FBI, I'd guess."

"Good", said The Priest. Again, that smile. "And no doubt you'll have access to those people."

Sullivan looked aghast. "Well, I prefer to steer clear of those guys. They give me the creeps." Not as much as this priest, though, he was thinking.

"I think you could manage your, erm creeps, don't you? Given all those dollars you've had over the years? I think they'd really like to talk to you if they had any idea of that. Whether you like it or not."

The Priest had a point. And maybe it could be done. "OK. I have a contact in the BPD. That's the Boston Police ..."

"Department, yes. Is he safe?"

"Yes. One of us. A District Commander, in fact. He can introduce me to one of the FBI team responsible. It's a national team. There'll be someone here in Boston, I think."

"That sounds ideal. As I say, I need to know all strange post-mortem transactions against these so-called Lost Souls. Anything at all. Especially this Mr. Best. Is that clear?"

"All right. It could take a little time. When do you leave Boston?"

"Just as soon as you can answer this question for me."

Sullivan sighed inwardly. He would need to get onto this as a matter of urgency. He wanted this priest back home and out of his way as soon as possible. He was not a nice man to share a city with, let alone a dinner table. "OK. Give me 2 days. I'll contact you at your hotel."

"No, Mr Sullivan. We'll meet here again in two days' time. That way, you won't be able to spin me a line. I need that information very quickly. I'm a long way behind my fox here. I hope that's all right?" It was.

That closed their lunch with a bang. "I'll let you pay for this", said The Priest. "If you have news for me next time, I'll pay. For lunch, anyway." Again, that wintry smile as he stood and left. Sullivan resignedly called for the bill.

Chapter 28

A Word to the Wise

The following lunchtime, FBI agent Rose Meredith was making do with a Subway sandwich at her desk. She was re-running the conversation she had just had with a politician called Sullivan.

Before the meeting she had looked at the files the FBI routinely hold on all politicians, among others. This was standard procedure, but there were notes in the files she'd half expected. They related to his contacts with certain Irish names who were of considerable interest to the Special Branch of the British police. But there was no mention of his involvement with any formal organisation dealing with relatives of survivors of the 9/11 disaster. That didn't mean there was no such connection, of course – the records could be behind the reality. But still ...

She organised her thoughts. What had been the point of the meeting, really? Sullivan seemed to be looking for survivors who had slipped the net. Why might that be? Was there a link between the Irish situation shown on the file and this curious meeting?

She made a decision. Better to check than not. She opened a desk drawer and rifled through it for a diary. Two years ago, she thought. Ah. Now, it must have been April that year. A low-key conference on counter-terrorism and intelligence sharing. In London. She'd met a Brit there ... nice guy ... what was his name? Ah! She'd made a note – that's him. Olsen, Richard. Norwegian name, probably, but British through and through. Cute, actually ... and a phone number. His cellphone, she thought. She looked at the clock. 11:30 AM in Boston, so, what, 4:30 PM in London. She picked up the phone and dialled the UK code and the cellphone number.

"Hello?"

"Hi. Is this Richard Olsen?"

"Who is this?"

"This is Rose Meredith. We met a couple of years ago at the Hyde Park Hotel in London. It was a conference - you might remember. I, erm, I'm connected with your cousins here in Boston."

"Hold on ... sorry, I was just in a shop. I'm ok to speak now. Hello Rose. Of course I remember you. How are you?"

"Hi. I'm fine, thanks. Look, is this line secure?"

"Not really, no. Can you let me know what this is about? I'll set up a secure line in an hour if you like."

"Well, I've just had a rather odd discussion with a certain gentleman who is flagged in our files as having some interesting Irish friends. I thought you might be interested."

"I see. Well that's not quite so active an interest for us at present. But it's not a closed book by any means. Can I have a colleague call you on a safe line? Say tomorrow, about this time?"

"Yes. Thanks. I think it's worthwhile. I'll give you a secure number, and let's say 11:30 exactly -my time - tomorrow?"

"OK. I'll find the right person for you and I'll try to be there to set the call up."

"Thanks, Richard. I knew it was a good idea to get your number." They exchanged the coded numbers for tomorrow's secure call and rang off.

Rose tapped onto the chief's office door. He was on the phone but looked up and wordlessly waved her in and indicated a seat. Bingham was the name, but everyone called him Billy. She wasn't sure what his real first name was.

"... Sure, honey. You do that and I'll see you tonight. No, usual time. OK, 'bye now." He put the phone down and looked at Rose. "My daughter wants to go to a concert at the weekend. She's 16. I told Sheila to say we'll discuss it tonight. I guess she'll go anyway so we might as well say yes and organise transport ... Anyway, what's up?"

Rose smiled at Billy "Actually, I'm not sure. I'd like to know what you think." She summarised her conversation with Sullivan and his interest in The Lost Souls. She added "As you know, there are some transactions on credit cards relating to the Lost Souls. He asked me about that." He was asking about a man called ..." she checked her notes. "Best. He's on the Lost Souls list. But we have nothing on him. No activity at all. I showed him – Sullivan - the list of post-mortem transactions. As you know, there are about twenty of these. There are two sets of activity outside New York, one of which was nipped in the bud, and this ongoing Foster one. He took a note of that."

Billy stood up and went to his coffee pot. "Coffee?"

"Sure." Pouring coffee was Billy's standard way to buy some thinking time. He poured and gestured to creamer and sugar. Rose took a packet of sugar and a stirrer and say down again. Billy always managed to get decent coffee and proper cups. Privileges of rank, she supposed.

"What do we think about this Foster, then? Is he the one who's travelling to the Caymans and so on? From San Fran?"

"Yes. Well, we're almost certain that the real Foster is dead. He's on the Lost Souls list. It all checks out. His wife hasn't seen or heard of him, neither have his employers, or any of his social contacts. No previous interest to us."

"But he could be setting up a nice new life?"

"He could. But really, we don't think so. And why would he go to the Caymans?"

"Money. Lots of money. That's the only reason, really," answered Billy.

"Right", answered Rose. "But there's no way we can see that he could have got hold of a large amount of money that we can see. And we do think he's dead, of course."

Billy drank some coffee and exhaled. Coffee was a cigarette substitute but the shadows of the habit remained. "OK, let's say he's dead. Who's doing all this travelling in his name? Why haven't we stopped him and asked him?"

"We decided to let things develop and keep an eye on him. You remember, surely?"

"Oh, yes. Maybe to catch bigger fish ... And now you say our Mr Sullivan with the Irish connection is also interested?"

"Yep."

"Hmm. What have you done about it?"

"I've reached out to the Brits. I met a Special Branch guy in London, if you remember. He's arranging for me – us – to talk to one of their, erm, Irish specialists. Tomorrow morning."

"What did you tell our Mr Sullivan?"

Rose sipped her coffee. "Not everything. He could see some of what the file said. I said that we had evidence of Foster's card being used in San Fran, and a passenger of that name travelling there, but I didn't mention we were tracking the passport or the other flights –the ones to Cayman."

Billy looked at her. "Even so, was that wise?"

"I don't know, to be honest. I wanted to see where he was going with all this."

Billy nodded. "OK. And where was he going?"

"I'm still not sure, in fact. He took notes and asked for a copy of the names without bodies – the Lost Souls - and the names on the cards that had been used after the event - Foster's on both lists. I gave him copies. Was I right?"

Billy shrugged. "Probably not. But it fits in with the tactic of letting the Foster thing run for a while. It's all about finding the truth behind that. It's OK." He smiled.

Rose nodded. "Good. It was Best he was really interested in, to begin with. Then Foster's activities seem to catch his attention. But I got the impression that ... erm ..."

"Go on?"

"Well, I don't really think he knew what he was looking for. He was just taking down the information. Fishing. As if he was asking on behalf of someone else. Someone who might know more ..."

"Hmm. That all?"

"Well, yes. Apart from setting up this conversation with the Brits."

"OK. Tomorrow?"

"At 11:30, yes."

Billy drank coffee and doodled. Another cigarette substitute. Rose knew not to interrupt.

"OK", said Billy. "Let's see whether the Brits can move this on a bit. If there's an Irish angle to this, we need to involve them anyway. In fact, this could be the missing link we've been, well, missing. With the Foster thing."

"So, we'll call London from here tomorrow? Your office, I mean?"

"Yup." Billy nodded. "You got the number to call?"

"Sure." Rose finished her coffee and stood up to leave.

"You did right, Rose. This could be interesting."

Rose smiled and closed the door on Billy and his doodling.

Chapter 29

Picking up the Scent

At the same time Rose was talking to Billy, Sullivan was in a taxi to the hotel to meet The Priest. Entering the dining room, he saw him sitting at the same table as yesterday's meeting. It was in a sheltered corner, ideal for confidential business discussions. Especially less than legal ones.

"Good afternoon, Mr. Sullivan", said The Priest, who was drinking what looked like a Bloody Mary, which seemed somewhat appropriate. "I hope you have some good news for me. Would you like a drink?"

"I think I do", said Sullivan. And as the waiter approached, he added "And if that's a Bloody Mary, I'll have one of the same." He was sure what he had to say would please The Priest. Assuming that was ever possible.

You didn't really make small talk with The Priest. Sullivan tried, but eventually gave up as the waiter arrived with the drink. "Slainge", he toasted, in exchange for which he received a wintry smile, although The Priest took a sip of his drink, which he took for a reply to the toast.

The waiter was still close by, and The Priest summoned him with a glance. He ordered smoked salmon followed by ribeye steak. Sullivan ordered the same and a good bottle of Californian merlot with the steak.

The Priest took note of the lavish order. "So, I'm guessing that you think I'll be paying for this lunch. I hope that means you have some good news for me?"

"I do. Very interesting, in fact. I met the FBI woman this morning. My police contact told her that I was making enquiries on behalf of a victim's charity and we needed to know if the list of names of the missing bodies were all, erm, kosher."

"Interesting choice of words", mused The Priest.

"Yes, well, I needed something to say. I think she took me at face value, but I'm not sure there's not going to be any follow-up."

"I'm sure you can deal with that", said The Priest, as the smoked salmon arrived. They selected sourdough bread slices and the waiter withdrew.

"Yes, well. Anyway, it seems that there were some, what did you say – post-mortem transactions - in the immediate aftermath. Some scumbags seem to have found wallets in clothing and possibly even bodies, and used them."

Even The Priest was surprised, or at least he raised an eyebrow. "Dear me. Some people, hm?"

"Yes. Shocking, really. Anyway, the point is this. Most of these transactions happened in New York itself. All but two, in fact."

"That's two out of how many?"

"Not all that many, really. Nineteen. Most of these transactions happened very quickly, in New York, mostly Manhattan, and then stopped. The longest of these was ten days after the event. That was up in Queens. Presumably they decided they'd be too hot and dumped them at that point. Maybe even developed a conscience."

"Well, that's nice. So tell me about these two cards that were different."

"Right, well, as I say, there were two that were further away. One was in Miami and one in San Fran."

"I see. And the FBI see these as suspicious?"

"They did. They didn't seem quite so, well, opportunistic. The Miami one is easy to deal with. Some low-life was using it in a bar in the Coconut Grove area when the cashier suspected the signature. The name was Pennington, but the user was very Hispanic. It didn't feel right, she said. Very observant, actually. Anyway, eventually the police were called, and the guy was arrested. He confirmed he'd lifted a wallet from an office worker on the subway on the morning of 9/11. He swore he didn't realise that his victim went on to be killed. And to be fair, there's no way he could have known."

"Fair enough. So that victim is indeed a victim? One of the Lost Souls?"

"That's what the FBI have decided. The theft wasn't reported. He certainly isn't in Miami, anyway, and there's every reason to believe that he was in the South Tower. And of course that activity stopped with the arrest."

"All right. And the other? San Francisco?"

"That's a little more interesting. The name is Foster, Brett Foster. The card was used just once, in SFO airport - Alamo car rental. A week after 9/11. Just once, and no further appearance."

"Brett Foster, you say?"

"That's right."

"Did the name Joe Best show up?"

"No, I asked. Let's see - I have a full list of the names on the cards here." He pulled a sheet of computer paper out of his inside pocket and scanned through it. "No - no mention of any card activity under that name." The other pages are a list of the names of the Lost Souls, as I explained." He checked and then passed the list over.

The Priest glanced at the first page – the shorter list of card activity, then turned to the longer list of Lost Souls. The name of Joe Best was there, on the first page, since it was in alphabetic order, and Foster was there too, lower down. The Priest said nothing, but folded the papers and put it in his inside pocket. Sullivan wasn't altogether comfortable with that, but he didn't think he could ask for it back.

The waiter re-appeared and busied himself with removing and replacing plates, offering sauces and enquiring whether anything else was needed. The Priest waved him away. "All right. So tell me about Mr Brett Foster."

Sullivan added mustard to his steak and grabbed some fries. "OK, the first thing to say is that he's assumed to be dead - almost certainly is, in fact. He was due at a meeting in the North Tower and the FBI believe he arrived – almost exactly at the time the plane hit it."

"Assumed?"

"Yes. Apparently it was a job interview. It had been set up a couple of weeks previously and he stayed in a hotel up by Grand Central Station. He checked out using the express system, but was out in good time to get to the meeting. They visited his wife and the recruitment company and there was nothing – untoward. Either about Foster or the arrangements up to that morning." He stopped to taste the wine and nodded. The waiter poured two glasses and withdrew. Sullivan was pleased with himself. Untoward – lovely word.

"I see. Nothing – as you say – untoward. But there again, nothing to prove that he really did perish?"

"No. But the FBI are satisfied that he did. And that's good enough for me, anyway."

"Is it now? And is that the only exception to this list of the vapourised dead?"

"No, as I say, other 'dead' cards have been used. But this one – Foster's - shows an unusual pattern. And it was only used once. The exception point was how far away it got before it was used. It's outside the pattern, you see. But there's more." Sullivan paused for effect, catching up with his steak and the wine glass.

"More." The Priest cut a piece of steak.

"Yes. Although the credit card was used just once, the FBI found out how the card got to San Francisco. A passenger using that name flew from Philadelphia to SFO that morning. We think he showed photo ID – that was a new requirement – and we assume it was a driving licence. That would have been in his wallet. Foster's."

The Priest sat forward, his fork in mid-air. "I see. So we have a man travelling as Mr Brett Foster, looking enough like his driving licence photo to get through airport checks."

"Yes. For internal flights. Or one flight, anyway."

"I see. And what do we know about this Mr Foster?" asked The Priest, chewing his steak.

"Well, as I say, the FBI don't think it's him. But he works – worked - in the oil equipment business. Lived near San Diego, and travelled a fair bit. Married, no children. Nothing to attract the FBI's attention before."

"What did he look like? Or what does his impersonator need to look like?"

"I asked that. Passport and Driver's licence data says five feet ten, average build, dark hair, glasses on his licence photo. Nothing remarkable."

The Priest was thoughtful. As he recalled, this description would fit the man Best. Mind you, it would fit millions of people. "What are the FBI doing now? Are they doing anything, in fact?"

"I don't think so. The point of all this was to establish death for these missing people, or at least check reasons not to. And they seem to have accepted that Foster is dead. Job done, really. The credit card use seems to have been an anomaly. And a one-off. She didn't mention any other activity."

"All right, Mr Sullivan. Thank you. I'll take it from here. And I will buy lunch."

They fell silent and dealt with the steak. Sullivan nodded to the waiter who topped up his wine, then held up his hand while he took a large gulp and motioned for another top up.

Plates cleared, Sullivan made his excuses and left The Priest to the last of the wine, a coffee and his thoughts.

Chapter 30

Out to Lunch

I woke up on the morning after my trip to San Fran and my jewellery shopping feeling unusually nervous. I wasn't sure how Sally would feel about the next stage of this journey, and whether – or to what extent – she would be ready to join in. And it mattered a lot to me that she did.

It was a new feeling for me – well, I suppose a very old one, but not a way I'd felt for a long time. It wasn't totally unwelcome when I thought about it. I realised that I didn't want to leave Sally behind when I left Sausalito – to the extent that I felt that I might not actually leave without her. I was too nervous to stand still. As she pulled up in the Merc, with the roof down in the spring sunshine, I was already off the boat and, if not exactly pacing up and down, I was on the dockside waiting for her.

"Hiya!" she grinned. "You're keen – are you hungry or something? Would you like to drive?"

"No, stay there", I said and stepped into the passenger seat. Before I put the seat belt on, I leaned across and kissed her. "You're looking lovely." Which she was – just well-cut chino shorts that showed off her tanned legs and a baby blue cashmere sweater that suggested the rest of her figure. Simple and sexy, but classy. The whole look was topped off by the bright spring sunshine and the shiny Mercedes.

She smiled. "Thank you. You don't look too shabby yourself." In fact, I'd taken more care that morning and actually changed twice before settling on my linen trousers and shirt. I'd added my old Gap blazer, with my wallet and the jewellery box in the inside pockets. We must have looked like a happy and comfortably-off couple out for a leisurely lunch. Which is exactly what we were. And would, I hoped, remain.

“I’ve booked for 1 o’clock, but they’re fairly relaxed about it, especially midweek,” I said as Sally turned the car round and drove away from the town and into the spring countryside. She had selected a local soft-rock radio station and we cruised along in happy silence, except when one of us joined in and sang along with the music. Neither of us could sing, but it made us giggle. With the warm sunshine and the scenery, the smooth and comfortable car and the breeze in our hair, it was one of those perfect moments that stick in the memory for a long time. And I knew that I really did want to spend the rest of my life – the new life – with this woman. As I say, that was a new feeling. And I liked it.

Arriving at the restaurant, we parked the Merc close to the entrance under the shade of an evergreen oak tree, and pushed the button to raise the soft-top. The sheltering tree was a Californian speciality I’d never actually known about until I came here. Quercus Agrifolia, actually. I looked it up.

We strolled in, hand in hand, and approached the desk. Our reservation confirmed, we were offered a drink at the bar or the table. Sally suggested we go to the table. “I’ll drive, so you can have a cocktail if you like”, she said, but I said I’d stick to wine and the ubiquitous iced water.

The waitress brought menus, introduced herself – Petra – and poured us each a glass of iced water. She then went through a well-rehearsed recitation of the specials and recommendations. As usual, I wasn’t really sure how to arrange my expression to look suitably interested, and I simply didn’t take in what the specials were. It seemed I’d always be English – at least in that capacity for being embarrassed over nothing at all.

When she’d left us to think about it, I asked Sally what the specials were. She shook her head at me. “Weren’t you listening?”

“I was trying so hard to look as if I was listening that I didn’t take it in”, I answered, slightly embarrassed again.

She laughed. "Oh, really. You're so British sometimes. How did you guys ever build an empire? They're all on the chalkboard over there anyway." And they were, of course.

There was a Greek tendency to the menu, and when Petra returned we ordered a meze between us as a starter and I ordered a barbequed chicken and Greek salad while Sally ordered the Kleftiko lamb from the specials board. I ordered a Californian Pinot Grigio to go with it and Sally said she'd mainly stick with water.

The meze came quite quickly, with all the usual variety of dips and nibbles and pita bread. We dipped and shared and chatted - about what, I can't remember. But eventually Sally brought us round to the main business of the day, as it were. "OK, then. So, what is it we need to talk about?" She scooped a dollop of taramasalata onto her plate and looked at me with a quizzical look. And a morsel of tzatziki on her chin.

"Hold on", I said and wiped it off with my napkin. "Can't take you anywhere, can I?" I looked at her and smiled. Here we go, I thought. "Well, you remember I told you what I was doing with the Bearer Bonds – the trips to Cayman – and Zurich?"

"Of course", she said as she delicately dipped her pita into the taramasalata and popped in her mouth before it fell off again. "That's when the owners will know that their money survived the whole 9/11 thing."

"Well, yes," I said. "Well, the thing is that the system has worked. The money is now clear from the process and ready to collect, so to speak. Or it will be in a week or two."

"Ah, I see. So, now what?"

"Well, exactly. 'Now what'? Operationally, I need to go and sign the last papers and so on, but the money's all clear, pretty well. The original owners will probably never know where it went, only that the bonds were cashed and then the funds vanished."

At this point, Petra came to clear the table from the meze and set up for the main courses. So we sat in silence for a minute. Eventually, we had our main courses, and as usual, surreptitiously checked each other's to make sure we were happy with our choices. We seemed to be, and the meal resumed - as did our discussion.

"'Probably never know', you said", Sally queried. "'Probably'. How sure are you they won't find it now?"

"I don't think they'll be able to track the funds across the hundreds of transactions Peter Garrido set up, or the scores of companies and handful of countries it's passed through. I'm almost certain of that."

"Ok, so you're now a rich man?" Sally asked, with a quizzical grin.

"Erm, well yes. I haven't got the final numbers, but, well, I think I have over twenty million dollars to play with. So to speak."

Sally looked at me, her fork frozen halfway to her mouth. "That much? Really?" She thoughtfully put the fork back down. "That's a lot of money to, well, win. And lose, of course." She continued to eat, but was obviously thinking hard.

I nodded. "Exactly. I'm sure there'll be some very angry people somewhere, and they'll be doing everything they can to find me or the money. Well, to find Joe Best."

"And what if they find you?"

That was a good question, of course. I said so. "So, the point is that I need to lose Brett Foster – and, in fact, Joe Best - and take on a new identity."

Sally busied herself with her plate of lamb, and I let her consider this. She looked up "Another new identity? I was getting used to Joe – I like that. Who will you be now, then?"

I smiled. "Still Joe, but Joe Baldwin now. Citizen of The Turks and Caicos, with a genuine passport from there, and nothing whatsoever to do with Brett Foster or Joe Best. Whoever they are."

Sally nodded. "I see. So what was that comment about the hospital? I guess this is something to do with that?"

I nodded. "Yep. I'm paying for this new – apparently legitimate - identity by building a new wing for their hospital. Well, paying for it. A children's ward. It'll be named after the government minister who's arranging my new ID. But it'll be me who funds the actual building. I guess other people are paying for the equipment and so on."

She thought for a few moments and dealt with her lamb, while I attended to my chicken and the wine. "Well, I don't suppose that's what the original owners of the money were planning. And it's a nice story, really. Mr. Baldwin." She grinned. "Where did that name come from?"

"Well, it was the name of a British Prime Minister in the 1930's, in fact. But it also turned out to be the name of the waiter at the Hilton in the Caymans when I was arranging this with Garrido." I laughed at the ridiculous reason – so did Sally.

"Well, why not? Will it work – keep people away?"

"I don't really know, but to keep 'Best' would have been asking for trouble, really. It was Peter Garrido who advised against that, actually."

"Hmm. Good for him. He was a good find, wasn't he?"

"Yes – I was lucky there." This was an opening to the main business of the day as far as I was concerned. "And, to be honest, I was just as lucky with you – finding you in the first place I visited after getting to Sausalito." I smiled over our now empty plates, and raised my glass.

Sally raised her glass back to me and smiled. I went on "But we've come to a new chapter in this adventure, I think. That's why I wanted to come out here on our own and have this discussion. I think it's time to move forward. To sit back and enjoy the money and some sunshine, beaches, lazy days and so on. The whole point of the decision I made – and the one I didn't make - when I found myself in that situation. And I'm glad I made that choice. For lots of reasons."

At this point, as a sort of punctuation, Petra came to clear the plates and offer dessert. They had tiramisu, which we both decided was a no-brainer, and she went off to get two portions.

"Ok", said Sally. "So what's your plan now?" asked Sally. She grinned. "Actually, I don't think I know anyone with as much money. What's it like?"

I grinned back and then thought about it. "You probably do, in Sausalito, but they won't say so. It's odd, actually. It still hasn't sunk in. It's obviously a huge amount of money. I'd have to try very hard to spend it all – ever. And I can do whatever I feel like now. Well, whatever we feel like, if you want to be part of it."

That had brought up the main topic. Again with perfect timing, Petra came back with our tiramisu and spoons, and left us alone again. As she was setting these down, I reached into my jacket on the back of my chair and brought out the jewellery box. I passed it to Sally. "I nearly forgot ..." As if. "A present for you", I smiled.

"Ooh!" A present from a millionaire. Lovely!" she laughed and opened it, taking out the necklace and putting it on. I noticed as she did so that she didn't have pierced ears. Lucky escape there, I thought.

"If you don't like it, I can change it for you ..." I said, but I could see that wouldn't be necessary.

"No, no. I love it. You're very clever – it's exactly my sort of thing." She leant over and kissed me. She got up and walked over to a mirror near the bar area to admire it. I watched her and hoped again that she would stay with me on the next step in the story. Which we now needed to talk about.

The tiramisu held our attention for 5 minutes, although Sally kept touching the necklace. When Petra came to remove the plates, we opted for coffee on the terrace outside, under a vine which was just starting to produce leaf buds.

"So, the thing is, well, as you said, 'what now?'" I said, when we were comfortable and had admired the view over the vines and down into the valley. "I told you as much as I knew, really, back on Mystere that evening – as much as I had figured out. I didn't really have a clear plan then, but I'm quite a bit clearer now."

Sally was looking out at the view, and not at me. I didn't know whether that meant anything, and I carried on with the embarrassing part. I couldn't really leave it any longer. "Well, look, Sally. Thing is, well, I know I now have a small fortune and can just spend the rest of my life enjoying it, but, well, I wouldn't enjoy it as much if you weren't there with me. I really like you, and ..."

Sally interrupted me with a giggle. "God, you really are English, aren't you?" she laughed out loud. "I know you like me - and I like you. Obviously. We've had a lovely time together, and I'd like it to go on. Stop being so nervous." She squeezed my hand and kissed me again. And then laughed at me again. "But we do need to talk about what we both want out of this. 'What now' again."

I relaxed a little. "Well, I think I need to leave Sausalito. If I have left any traces of myself – as Joe Best – they will probably lead there. And my movements as the Brett Foster, erm, version of me are all out there if anybody cares to check. And they definitely lead to Sausalito. I don't think there are any links to me as Joe Best, but I can't be sure. But I'd say that Brett Foster is clearly active in Sausalito."

Sally looked very serious and didn't speak for a full minute. Which is a very long time in a conversation. I looked out over the view of the vineyards and hills behind and kept silent while I let her take this in. "I see", she said. "So, do you want me to leave Sausalito as well? And - am I in danger? After all, most people who know me know that I've been, well, with you - for a few months now."

"Well, in an ideal world, I'd like to sail off into the sunset – with you, of course, and break the trail completely. In fact, in a way, I've already made that break, by taking the money and, well, doing what I've been doing. But obviously it's a big decision – it was for me, and I had no real ties. You do, I know, and I'm not sure whether you'll want to do that."

Sally nodded. "You're right. I have my life here and I like it. And I have my Mom to think about. From what you've told me, your decision wasn't quite as difficult."

"Well, it wasn't easy. But once I saw how much money there was, and thought about the life it could make for me, then, yes. I wasn't actually leaving that much behind. Not as much as you would be, anyway."

The coffee pot had gone cold. "How about I get some more coffee and pay the bill? Then we can probably talk a bit more up here?" Sally agreed and I went over to the bar to arrange the coffee refill and sort out the bill. Since the coffee was proper ground coffee in a cafetiere, it took a while to get ready, and I went to the mens' room while Petra got the tray ready. She brought it out with clean cups and fresh cream, and took away the old one. Sally and I resumed our musings.

"Is there a way I can leave with you and still keep my life in Sausalito?" asked Sally. "Actually, what are your plans? You haven't really told me."

She was right. So, I told her about my slightly mad idea about having Mystere shipped over to the Caribbean, and my plans to live on her, mainly in the Turks, but also visiting the other islands. I explained that the money was going to be in a Turks bank account, but that other accounts could be opened elsewhere if it suited me – or us.

She sipped coffee as I talked, and I poured myself a cup and drank some as she took all this in. "Do you expect to live on Mystere the whole time? I mean, it's nice and all that, but you could afford a really nice house somewhere – a beach house, maybe, or a town house somewhere – more than one, actually. Why not do that?"

I nodded. "I probably will, in fact. But there's no rush – I can take my time to find a place I like. Meanwhile, well, I like living on my boat. More than I expected, actually."

She nodded. "Hmm. OK. And are you asking me to dig up my roots and come with you wherever you go? I mean, can't I split my time between you and wherever you are and here?"

That was perfectly possible, of course, and I said so. In fact, it was probably better, at least for the first year or so, as I got used to the new reality. Although I'd made the first huge shift in my life by seizing the opportunity, there were more changes to make.

"Yes, you're right. Actually, I need to complete the next stage – I've been focusing on this point – getting the money out and clean, a new clean ID, Mystere ... and you." I smiled. "I need to get some more, let's say clarity, on what happens now – 'what next', in fact."

She nodded. "OK, well I think we can say that we can keep going on the next stage, and I'm happy – very happy – to be part of that. I'll come with you to the Caribbean and so on, but I'll also regard myself as living here, for now, anyway."

I felt this was good - very good. "Yes - if you're cool with the travel, you can easily move between San Fran and, well, wherever I am – or we are - for the time being. And you can help me – us – decide on that beach house, town house ... whatever." I paused. "I'm happy with that. We can move as slowly as you like, but, well, we'll act as a team."

She grinned. "OK. Maybe regard this next stage as a – well, not a trial, let's say a transition. And I'll make sure you don't make any silly decisions", she smiled and kissed me as Petra walked over to collect the coffee tray. "Let's go now – we can take the long way home."

I was more relieved than I expected – meaning, I guess, that I was less certain and more concerned about the outcome than I'd realised. As Sally drove us through the wine country and back home, I explained where I needed to go during the next 2 or 3 weeks. Sally thought the sailing part of this – the trip down the coast to L.A. – might be something she'd like to do, which I was happy about. I stressed that Ken White would be coming along to ensure safe sailing, which she was relaxed about.

We talked about how she would need to talk to the restaurant about her working pattern. She seemed to think wouldn't be a problem, and I pointed out that she really wouldn't need to work anyway, as part of a wealthy partnership. But she said she'd prefer to keep working and I didn't really see why not. She also said that she was determined to keep up with her degree course, which I agreed with completely.

By the time we arrived back at the marina, we were completely in step with our view of the "what now" situation, and the steps I was – or, rather, we were - about to take. After dropping the car off, we walked back to Mystere and had a very enjoyable evening. Sally left the next morning and I got to work on fine-tuning my schedule for the next couple of weeks.

It had already struck me that I needed to discuss the possible dangers in case anyone was tracing my movements, either as Brett or Joe Best. But, not wanting to change the mood, I decided that that discussion would keep a little longer.

Chapter 31

Transatlantic Co-operation

It was early morning in The Lawyer's office. Present were The Lawyer, Edwards the Investigator, and The Priest. The urgency of yesterday's summons to attend was unusual, and this was only the second time The Priest was openly in the meeting. He thought he could guess why.

The Priest spoke first. "Mr Edwards. I hope you will develop a poor memory in respect of my presence in this meeting. Indeed, I hope you will forget we ever met. Is that clear?" He added a chilling smile.

Edwards had rarely, if ever, met such a force – evil in a dog-collar. He forced the thought away. "Quite clear. We never met."

"You never even heard of me. Believe me, it's for the best. But I need you to understand the importance we attach to this task."

"That's fine. And I do." He really wasn't going to find that a problem.

The Priest looked towards The Lawyer, who cleared his throat and said: "You said that there was little we could do before the Bonds were cashed."

"That's right. Until then, we had no proof that the ... package survived intact. And we now know that they have now been cashed."

The Lawyer took over again. "Indeed. So, as we know, two weeks ago, in Zurich, the bonds were cashed into a Swiss bank. Then it gets very complex. We're trying to unpick the connections now, but we don't expect to be able to do very much. This was done by an expert – it's almost impossible to unpick. But the important thing is that they did survive, as you say. So the money is at least theoretically recoverable, by starting at the other end – where the money emerges from the system."

"And, of course, our Mr Best seems to be alive", added The Priest. This didn't bring him any Christian joy, it seemed.

"I see. So, what do you want me to do?"

"Well", said The Lawyer, "This is what we now know. Never mind how. Firstly, someone flew from Philadelphia to SFO using ID belonging to a Brett Foster – the late Brett Foster, who the FBI believe was killed on 9/11. And he then rented a car for a week or so using his credit card – that is, Foster's, and presumably his driving licence. Secondly, thanks to your associate, we know that it's quite possible – likely, even - that our courier, Joe Best, had changed the delivery arrangements – so that he wasn't in fact in our – associate's - office when he should have been."

The Priest joined in. "And now – thirdly - we know that someone was indeed holding the bonds after we supposed them to have been destroyed. And has travelled to Zurich and San Francisco at least. That can only be our Mr Best, wouldn't you say?"

Edwards didn't like to challenge The Priest, but couldn't let this go. "Well. If those are all the facts you have, no. There's no real evidence that it was Best who travelled to San Francisco. And in fact, no need to look into that at all right now. You're connecting things that aren't really related. Why would you think that Best was using this ID? Why would he travel to San Francisco? And from Philadelphia, not New York? That could simply be a red herring. Nothing to do with these bonds."

The Lawyer nodded. "Fair enough. But who else would have the package with the bonds - and so on - after the, erm, catastrophe?"

"Hard to say, really. But Best could have passed the case on to someone else to deliver it – maybe someone who was going to the building anyway. Maybe, in fact, this Foster chap. Or if he – Best - survived somehow, with the package, as we now think he might, he could have passed them on after the disaster, if he felt that they were too hot to handle."

“OK”, interjected The Lawyer: “There are some other scenarios. But, as you say, he’s the favourite. By a long way.”

Edwards was silent, musing. “It’s circumstantial. There’s been nothing else, anywhere, to suggest that Best’s alive and using his own ID. So, if it is Best who cashed the bonds, he’s using someone else’s identity.”

“Yes - Foster’s, surely?” prompted The Lawyer.

“Could be. Probably is, in fact. But it’s not certain. And it’s only been used once, as far as you know. There’s absolutely no other connection. I mean, how did he get it? ... Of course, they may have met before this. I could do some more digging, but it doesn’t seem likely that they mixed in the same circles.”

“Well,” interjected The Lawyer, “didn’t you say that our man Best used to be something a bit more – what - high-flying, before he became a courier?”

“Yes – he was a Sales Manager in some IT firm. Quite a big hitter actually.”

“So, they could have met? What did you say Foster was? A Sales Manager?”

“Well, yes, but not in the same business, and not the same country. But I suppose, they may have met – maybe a sales course ...” Edwards rubbed his chin, briefly lost in thought. “I’m not sure how he could get the ID in any case – even if he did know him. There are lots of reasons – lots of ways ... Anyone might have found Foster’s ID and used it. With no definite reason to link it with Best.”

“So we could have a fake Mr. Foster, able to fly from Philadelphia to San Francisco for unknown reasons, and someone else paying the bonds into a bank in Zurich? Completely unconnected?” The Lawyer left that question hanging.

“Easily”, said Edwards. “As I say, purely circumstantial. In fact, I can’t see why you’ve focused on Foster. All you know is that his ID and credit card survived the 9/11 thing and so did Best, possibly – well, OK, probably - and certainly the package, and these ID items were last seen in San Francisco. There’s just no logic there. We have no reason to think that Best himself even went anywhere near San Fran.”

The Priest replied: “Philadelphia is a short train ride from New York. The trains kept running after the event, but there were no flights anywhere in the US - until the morning the flight was taken by Foster. Or whoever it was.”

“Well, OK, but how do you know that it was Best, and not some other, well, thief? Best could be anywhere in the world. Or, despite what we suspect, he could actually be dead.”

The Lawyer said: “Our sources are quite reliable. There have been no transactions of any kind under Mr. Best’s name at all.”

The Priest leant forward: “So, you see, Mr. Edwards, it comes down to this. The only anomalous activity after the event, but connected to it, and outside of New York, is this flight to San Francisco. If we accept the FBI’s view that Foster is dead, and add that to the fact that the money is at large, we come to the conclusion that there is indeed a connection here.”

Edwards didn’t like these percentage guesses, but he could see that there was a tempting logic. “OK, say I accept the possibility, maybe even a likelihood, that Best survived and used Foster’s ID to travel to San Francisco …”

“That’s our best guess”, said The Lawyer, not really spotting the pun until too late.

“… then Best is either still in or near San Francisco or used yet another ID to move on. I gather he returned the rental car to the airport?”

“Yes, that’s right. But we think he’s still there. In San Fran”

"How did the bonds get to the Swiss bank?"

"We don't know, but they will probably have been physically delivered. You wouldn't just pop them in the post, would you?"

"No ... Well, if that was Best travelling as Foster, and travelling to Zurich, he'd have needed a passport. Any word on that?"

The Lawyer looked at The Priest, who said: "We haven't been told so." He mused for a moment. "But our source may not have pressed for that information at the time."

Edwards nodded and was silent for a moment. "If we can find a passenger called Brett Foster arriving in Zurich on the day those bonds were presented – or during, say, the two days before, I'd say that might clinch it. Yes?"

"Can you do that?" asked The Lawyer.

"Possibly. I'd need to call in a big favour – maybe an expensive one - but yes, it is possible."

"Mr. Edwards." The Priest leant forward and held Edwards' eye. I don't care what it takes, you'll find us that link. I need to know whether this Foster is actually Best. And if so, where he is. Is that clear? I don't care how difficult it is, but it had better be as quick as you can make it. Stop anything else you're working on and get to the bottom of this. OK?"

Edwards didn't think there was anything else to say. "OK, I'm onto it. I'll need at least a week."

"You have 10 days at the most. Report to this office as soon as you have anything." The Priest stood and the two men followed suit. "Thank you, gentlemen." He left without shaking hands, and the tension eased somewhat.

"Hmm. Quite a priest, eh?" remarked Edwards.

"Yes, I know. I'd advise you to do as he says and forget you ever saw him." The Lawyer walked across and opened the door to the outer office. "Ah, Mary, good, you've arrived. Can we have … Coffee?" he turned to Edwards.

"Yes, thanks," Edwards confirmed.

The Lawyer returned to his place on the sofa. "So, what will you do?"

"Basically, look into the paperwork. I have a contact who can look at air passenger data for me. Not terribly legal, but it can be done. I think."

"If you can show that someone called Foster – or maybe Best – flew into Zurich and left again around the dates those bonds were cashed, that would be a huge step forward. Wouldn't you agree?"

"Mmm." They sat in silence, contemplating the scale of the task. Mary brought the coffee, poured for both of them and left them to it.

The Lawyer added sugar and broke the silence. "We're trying to track the money from the Bonds. But whoever cashed them has done a good job. The companies holding the funds are being sold and closed down very quickly. We know all about setting these smokescreens, but these guys are good. We can't find a name for the ultimate owner – not so far, anyway. Just a nest of companies. And obviously no name for the original Swiss account."

"It's always much harder to unpick these false trails than to lay them," added Edwards. "It might be easier to find our friend Best with the money – if it is him – than to track the money itself, as you said earlier."

The Lawyer nodded. "Find Best and you'll find the money, you mean? Exactly. Well, that's your job, then. I do know this will cost a lot. There's a lot at stake, as you will have gathered." He had another thought. "We last see activity around Foster's ID, in SFO – car rental, yes?"

"Yes, exactly - San Francisco. As The Priest's contact discovered. Rented a car for a week, and nothing after that, he said. But remember, it could be anyone. If Foster lost his wallet or something - or it was stolen - he wouldn't have had time to cancel it before he was killed. But anyone who had it would probably ditch it fairly quickly. It may mean nothing."

"No, I know", said The Lawyer. "But I think we should try to pick up the trail in San Francisco. I'm guessing Best's still there."

Edwards mused for a moment. "Well, if I can find a Foster – or Best – arriving in Zurich, I should be able to find where his journey originated – and probably returned to."

"I'm ready to bet that was San Francisco. If so, somebody needs to get there and look for Best."

Edwards nodded. "Let's cross that bridge when – if - we get to it. Meanwhile, I'll get started." He stood up, shook hands with The Lawyer and left.

The Lawyer sat down again, topped up his coffee and contemplated developments. It would probably have been better if all this stuff, and Best, had been destroyed in that holocaust. He prayed that Edwards would find the link between Best and Foster. And then find Best. There would be trouble, otherwise. In fact, there would be trouble for someone anyway.

Chapter 32

Transatlantic Alliance

Next morning, at 11:15 Boston time, Roseanne and Billy sat at the boardroom table in Billy's office with Billy's coffee pot and the speaker phone between them.

"Who's originating this call, Roseanne?" asked Billy.

"We are. This is their secure number. We'll call at exactly 11:30 our time and I'll confirm my ID with my contact." She handed Billy the London number.

"OK. Olsen, yes?"

"Yes, but he's not on their Irish desk – he'll introduce us to whoever that is."

"Right. What do you want from this?"

Roseanne considered. "Well, I think we're just handing this over. I mean, whatever's going on ..."

"If anything is ..." Billy interrupted.

"Yes – right - if anything's going on, it's not really our problem, I guess ..."

"Not unless they are planning something over here, anyway", added Billy. "We don't have any reason to think that, do we?"

"No. Nothing I've seen, but we haven't been looking, have we?"

"We're always looking, Roseanne. That's why there's a flag on Sullivan's file. That's why there is a file, in fact. But no. I spoke to some people who are – more involved with that situation. And they don't think there's any indication of anything going on."

"Right. So we're just helping our British friends?"

"That's what I think. And that's what I hope. Let's have that number and make the call." Billy dialled the code to get to the secure switchboard, then picked up Roseanne's note with the London number. There were a few clicks and buzzes, then the double-buzz UK dialling tone. The phone was answered after the first ring. Roseanne leant forward to speak.

"Good morning. This is Roseanne. Is that Richard?"

"Hello Roseanne. Yes, this is Richard. We're secure, yes?"

"Yes. For the record, this is Agent Roseanne Meredith. I'm in the office of Assistant Director Bingham. Just the two of us. Closed doors, and you're on speaker. And recording, of course."

"Good morning all – or good afternoon", added Billy. "Please call me Billy, everyone else does."

"OK, hello Roseanne, hello Billy", answered Olsen. "You're also on speaker here. And recording. In addition to me, you have Superintendent Richard Binner and Inspector Peter Page of our Irish desk." A chorus of "Good afternoon", followed by confirmation of date and times concluded the introductions.

"So, Roseanne, could you please tell my colleagues what you told me yesterday?"

Roseanne repeated her description of the meeting with Sullivan and his interest in the Foster ID.

"This is Peter. I see why you called us, and thanks for that. Why did Sullivan contact you – or why did he say he had?"

"Well, we're involved in an aspect of the 9/11 aftermath – specifically, dealing with the vanished bodies. As you can probably imagine, not everyone who died there is ... well, many bodies are simply not there. We think there are around a thousand or so on that site who will never be recovered. Simply destroyed, totally lost."

"I see. Go on."

"Well, what we need to do is look for any suggestion that these individuals may in fact have survived, and decided to disappear. It's been decided to allow their next of kin to deal with their affairs as quickly as possible. So we're looking for any evidence of survival, as I say."

There were murmurs of understanding from the other end. "Go on", someone said.

"Well, Sullivan told me that he was acting for an association of relatives of these missing dead. The thing is, I can't find any such organisation here in Boston."

"Ah." This was probably Peter Page again. "So what do you think he really wanted?" There was a hint of a Northern Irish accent there.

"To be honest, I can't really be sure", answered Roseanne. "And I'm not sure he really knew what he was looking for, either." She looked at Billy, who nodded encouragement. "As I said to Billy yesterday, I got the feeling that he was asking questions on behalf of someone else. Someone who knew much more about what was going on."

"This was yesterday, yes?" This from Olsen.

"That's right. Yesterday morning, our time. I phoned you when I reviewed the meeting. It didn't really make sense. And I saw that we had a flag on his file – some connections to the less salubrious members of our Irish community here."

"This is Superintendent Binner. We are aware of Sullivan, and we also know that there's a connection with a certain priest in whom we take an interest has visited Boston this week. Did Sullivan mention any other names he might be working with?"

"No. Just this vague victims' family group. Which we can't trace."

"Right. Never mind. And did anything you were able to tell him attract his particular attention?"

"Yes. We have a record of someone called Foster, Brett Foster, who we are almost certain perished in the first tower strike, apparently travelling from Philadelphia to SFO and renting a car there a week after the attack. Or at least, if not actually him, his credit card and probably driver's licence. I told him that - he was very interested. But what I didn't tell him was that we have also picked up his passport on some interesting journeys since then."

"Interesting - why?"

"Some trips from San Fran to Grand Cayman via Miami. And one to Zurich just recently."

"Hold on – we need to discuss this here for a moment ..." There was a conversation with snatches of audible speech and murmurs of what seemed to be agreement.

"Are you sure that the real Foster is in fact dead?"

"As sure as we can be. His wife was in touch with his company, who contacted us. They knew we were carrying out this programme and helped her in the process. She told us that he was in New York for a meeting in the North Tower at the time in question. And the company he was meeting – a recruitment company – confirmed the meeting and said they weren't informed of a no-show. The timing was tight, but we're sure he was there. No sign of him since, except this use of his driving licence and passport, which his wife said he'd have been carrying. He's clean in every way – certainly his wife is convinced. In fact she's just put her house on the market."

"And he's not been seen?" Page, this sounded like.

"No. We've only had low-level surveillance, but nothing at. In fact she's reverted to her maiden name – Holmes. She seems to be in no doubt, anyway."

"Ok. So we have an active ID, passport as well, misappropriated but in repeated use?"

Billy leant over to the microphone. "Yes. We could have closed down the passport but we wanted to see what was happening. This travel didn't suggest it was the real Foster – it didn't fit with anything we knew about him. But we didn't know what was happening, so we kept it live and waited. Are waiting, in fact. So perhaps you can help us with this?"

There was some more murmuring at the London end. Then Binner came back on. "Right. I'm sure you're aware of the – changes – that have happened in Northern Ireland in recent – well the last couple of years?"

"Sure", said Billy. "We're all very glad to see that."

"Indeed. Well, the IRA are supposed to put their weapons beyond reach – they refused simply to hand them over. And that process is happening – it's difficult, but it seems to be under control. More or less."

Billy was listening carefully: "This isn't about weapons, though? I hope?"

"No", said Binner. "It's about money. These people raised millions of pounds - and dollars - over the years. Some from your city, of course. But a lot more from other countries – our mutual friend in Libya, some from the Russians from time to time. And there were some very lucrative schemes going on in the province itself. There's a lot of money somewhere. And our friends seem even less willing to bring that into the open than they do their weapons."

"And you think our friend Foster – or whoever it is – is cleaning this money?"

"Actually, no. The cleaning, as you put it, has happened. The last stage in this process came through London and was on its way to a business account in New York. We've been watching this very closely. It involved a couple of your local Irish friends called Costello and Richardson and a lawyer in New York called Finklestein. Finklestein is probably clean, at least in terms of proving any knowing involvement. But Costello and Richardson are well-known to us."

Roseanne sat up. "Hold on. I think they're on the "vanished" list. Shall I get it?"

"Please", said London.

"I have it here, actually" said Billy. He stood up and went to his desk, picked up a file and returned to the table. "Let's see – Costello – Yes, he's here – we accept that he's dead – family contacted, no reason to doubt it. No post-event activity anywhere. And erm, yes – Richardson as well. Same thing. You're right, both from Boston. Erm ... also Finklestein, the lawyer – from New York, of course. Shall I check what we have on them in our main files?"

"Well there's no need right now. I can tell you, Costello and Richardson were IRA to the core. But not recently active. Back-room boys, really. We have nothing on Finklestein."

"So who's using Foster's ID?" asked Roseanne.

"Do you have the name Best on that list? Joe Best?"

"Hold on", said Billy, looking at the list. "Yes. He's here. But he's one of yours. A Brit, that is. So you'll have more details than we do."

"Yes. We know all about him, and all the evidence says he's as dead as Costello and Richardson. And the lack of subsequent activity. None at all."

"I think there's a 'but'", said Billy.

"Yes, Billy, there is", answered Page this time. "Best was a courier. He was carrying a lot of money. Cash and bonds. Best wouldn't normally know what was in the case. This was the cleaned money which would have emerged from the meeting as ready for use. And very difficult to trace, if the – beneficiaries – were sensible with it."

"How much was there?" asked Billy.

"To begin with, around 25 million, we think. US Dollars, that is. There would be costs, but still well over twenty million."

Billy and Roseanne gasped. "OK, said Roseanne. But why wasn't it wiped out with Costello and the rest?"

"We don't know", said Page. "In fact, we thought it was, until we noticed the bonds being cashed. In Zurich, about a couple of weeks ago."

"Zurich?" said Roseanne. "Which is where ..."

"Yes. Which is where your fake Foster was recently, it seems. So, we had this money and the bonds surviving the devastation, and now we have a name of someone who also appears to have survived, despite evidence to the contrary, it seems."

"But not actually Foster?" asked Roseanne, looking at Billy. "I'm sure he's dead."

"No, it's Best, we think. There's no history to go on, but he has no reason not to disappear. He's something of a loner – no family or anything. And there's more than 20 million great reasons to do so."

"Makes sense," said Billy. "And Costello and Richardson? Or Finklestein?"

"I think your research on them bears out. None of them would dare, anyway. I see Best as a chancer. But he doesn't realise who he's messing with here. The others do, and wouldn't dare run off, no matter what happened. They know all about who's involved here – they did, anyway."

Billy looked at Roseanne. She nodded. It all joined up. "OK," said Billy. "What would you like us to do?"

Binner answered: "Well, firstly, thanks for getting in touch. You've provided a missing piece to a puzzle that was starting to become insoluble. Could you keep that passport live, and let us know as soon as it's used again? Other than that, we'll look for our Mr. Best. And hope to find him before our Irish friends do."

Page joined in: "Roseanne, could you please send me the records of the Foster passport – where he went and the exact dates – please? I think email will be safe." He read out his email address.

"Done", said Roseanne. "Anything else?"

"Your Mr. Sullivan. Could you try to find out who he was working for, somehow? We're looking for a certain priest. We know he was in Boston this week, but he's just arrived back in Dublin, and we think he went up to Belfast by train. He usually uses the Marriott in the dockside area when he's in Boston. You know it?"

"Sure. Do you have any details on him? A picture, maybe?"

"I'll send you all you have. If we see him coming back, we'll let you know and ask you to keep an eye on him. But I think we're ahead of him now. Thanks to you."

"Hey, that's all part of the service", said Billy. "I'm glad we could help."

"Roseanne, this is Richard. Thanks very much for calling. This is a huge help. I'll see you soon. I hope? Are you due to visit us over here?"

"Maybe," said Roseanne. "If I do, I'll be sure to let you know."

There was a chorus of farewells from each side and the call was closed. Billy poured more coffee for both of them from the hotplate. "Nice work, Roseanne. Well done."

There was a reflective silence in the Special Branch offices after the encrypted line closed. Binner spoke first: “OK, Richard, thanks for bringing us in on this. Your hunch was good. And the same goes for your girlfriend in Boston.”

“Well, not actually my girlfriend ...” interjected Olsen.

“Yeah, whatever you say”, Binner grinned. “But she’s done us a huge favour. I think we have almost the full picture now.” He paused. “Look, Richard, it might be best if you leave this with us now. I know you’re cleared but I think you’d be better off not knowing any more than this. Or what we’ll do next. Need to know and all that, eh?”

Olsen decided not to be offended. “OK, that’s fine by me. I have enough on my plate already after this 9/11 thing – that could keep me busy until I draw my pension, I think. So yes, I’m happy to leave you to it. And wish you luck.” He stood up and shook hands with Binner and Page and made for the door.

“Thanks, mate”, Page added. “Oh, could you ask the lovely Debbie if we could have a pot of tea and some biscuits when you sign out?”

“Sure”, grinned Olsen and closed the door. He looked for the lovely Debbie and thought she must be the brunette in glasses and a red blouse at the desk near the door. He checked: “Are you the lovely Debbie? Your chaps have asked for tea and biccies if so.” She blushed and bustled away off to the small kitchen.

Binner sat back, hands behind his head. “Ok, Peter, what’s your take on this? How does it look now, do you think?”

“Well, like you say, I think we’ve pretty well tied the ends together, don’t you? This really does round the story off.”

“Erm, yes, but I don’t think the story’s actually ended yet, do you? I mean, the money is still moving around, for one thing.”

"True enough. But we know who's moving it - and of course we now know who took it in the first place, don't we?"

"It looks like it, yes. Question is, what should we do now? This Best chap – bit of a chancer, and certainly took a flyer with this. Did he decide to nick the money before the Towers dropped, do you think?"

"Hard to say for sure ... he seems to be, well, indifferent honest, up to this point. I mean the money involved here would be tempting, but there's nothing to say that he planned to do a runner with it. It doesn't really seem to be in character."

Binner pulled a face. "Yes, this does look like a spur of the moment decision. And that's easy to understand. If he knew what he was carrying ..."

"I don't think he did know at first", Page interrupted. "We got the impression from our interviews with the courier company that it was company policy to regard the package as just a package. Their couriers were, well, not encouraged to open the packages unless they had to – customs or whatever."

"OK, but it hardly matters. Best had a habit of, let's say, adjusting the delivery time, didn't he? In fact, that's probably why he witnessed the first plane hit ..."

"... instead of being hit by it, you mean? Yes. So what would he do in those circumstances – break the seal and look into the package, probably?"

"Yes, I'd say so. He'd have to, really. Of course, he should have phoned the office for instructions. The fact that he didn't says that he probably made a decision to abscond with the funds at about that point."

Page shrugged. "Well, he may just have decided to wait a day or so and think about it. Just didn't immediately decide to do the right thing, rather than positively decide to do the wrong thing."

"Well, ok", said Binner. "Either way, it doesn't matter, does it? As soon as he started to spend the cash – any of it – he was guilty of theft. If we brought him in, we'd have an open and shut case of theft by misappropriation."

"Yes, but that's really not the point, is it? That's not our brief, as I see it. What we need to do is recover the money."

The lovely Debbie brought in tea and biscuits and put the tray on the table between them. "Anything else?" she asked. "There's milk and sugar on the tray."

"No, that's fine, thanks Debbie", Binner smiled. Page winked. Debbie smiled back and closed the door behind her as she left.

Binner poured two cups from the teapot, took a biscuit for dunking and left Page to add his milk. "Actually, no. Our brief is simply to make sure the money doesn't get back to the IRA. I don't much care about what happens to it as long as it's not going back to that bunch of thugs. And I don't care at all what happens to Best. He's had a lucky break – or he thinks he has. But I think he might find out that it wasn't as lucky as he thinks."

"Ok", said Page. "So what should we do now?"

"Well, what have we learned? That Best is using this ID belonging to Foster, and that he's apparently got some professional help to clean the money from the Bonds ..."

"Yes, and that he's probably using someone based in the Caymans for that", added Page.

Binner nodded. "Looks that way. But I doubt we'll find the money unless we find Best. Now we know the name he's using. Foster. And we have the details of his journeys using that passport, or soon will have, thanks to our cousins in Boston. The thing is, he probably won't be paying cash at the desk for these trips. I'd bet he's travelling Business Class at least. You wouldn't fly all that way in the back of the plane if you could help it. And that would look very odd, paying in cash – these aren't cheap flights."

Page got it. "Ah. Yes. So, there will be some credit card transactions. Or charge cards. Linked to the bookings. And that would help us find the bank he's using."

Binner smiled. "Exactly. A debit card, possibly. Best would have to deposit the cash element somewhere and use a checking account, and that would probably come with a debit card if the bank is anything like up to date. Otherwise he's using cash for everything, or cheques, which would be a pain. And attract attention, more importantly. And of course it would mean stashing it somewhere. Which wouldn't be all that easy, either."

Page nodded. "Right, so let's assume he had a debit card or whatever, and used it for these tickets. He could book over the phone if so. And if we can find the card details, then track them back to the bank, we'll be lot closer to Best. The bank will have an address for him. Which might be false, but might not. I can do that quite easily, actually, once I have the travel dates. And, ideally the carriers and times, which I expect we will."

"Exactly, Peter. So, let's get onto that before anyone else does, eh?"

And that closed the meeting, except that there was some tea and biscuits left, so both men topped up their cups and took another biscuit back to their desks.

Chapter 33

Convergent Theories

The following morning, in his London office, located above a fried chicken shop in a shabby building in the main street running through Acton, Edwards the Investigator thumbed through an old desk diary and called a number he hadn't used for a while. The phone was answered on the second ring.

"Yes?" was all he got.

"Hi, it's Roy Edwards here. Long time and all that."

"Roy Edwards. Fuck me, I thought you'd died. What do you want?"

"Yeah, I know. Like I say, it's been a long time. How've you been?"

"I get by. Some people value my services, you know."

"'Course they do. So do I, when I need that sort of thing."

"So I guess you do now? Or did you just call to ask me out for tea?"

""I'll buy you a drink if you like. And pay well for what I need. Just up your street, I think. Poking about in someone else's computer systems."

Edwards could almost hear the ears pricking up at the other end.

"Explain."

"I need details of some flights taken by a, well, let's say, person of interest to me."

"What details?"

"I have a name, and a likely date for an arrival in Zurich – a likely range, anyway. Just few days. And a likely departure date. Inbound from the US, and back again, probably."

"Hmm. A bit vague. So what do you need to know?"

"As much as you can get me. Exact dates, point of departure and return, final onward destination, that sort of thing."

"Hmm. You don't want much, do you?"

Edwards was struck by a thought. Of course ... "Actually, I'd also like details of the credit card or whatever that was used. Mainly, the bank it was drawn on, if it was a debit card."

There was a sort of silence at the other end. Just breathing and a sniff. "I might need to get help on this. It's gonna cost you. Is your client paying well?"

"Well enough. How much, and how long?"

"Two grand. No, two and a half. That should cover my, erm, colleague as well. As for how long, I dunno. I'll need to ask my pal. Say a week?"

"Cash?"

"Of course fucking cash. Upfront, at that. Meet me at the Dove on Hammersmith Mall this evening at half-seven. I'll have spoken to my colleague. Bring the cash and a note of the name and dates. Usual arrangement."

"OK, I'll be there. With the cash."

The phone went dead. Edwards didn't think he needed to get clearance from The Lawyer for this cash transaction, so he called his bank to ask them to get the cash ready for collection, and typed up the details of the Foster ID and the likely dates. He took an over-large envelope and put the note in it, pocketed it and decided that he had enough time to do some much-neglected book-keeping.

At half past six, with the cash added to the envelope and all tucked safely in an inside pocket, he picked up his coat and walked down to Acton Town tube. He got off the tube at Hammersmith and picked up an Evening Standard outside. He then walked round the one-way system towards Hammersmith Bridge, turned right, walked along the river, past the Blue Anchor and on to the Dove.

Charles the Second and Nell Gwynne were reputed to have canoodled here, and if the old place had changed since then, it had been a reluctant and gradual change. There was a tiny bar to one side at the entrance from the narrow street away from the river, proudly claiming to be the smallest bar in the world. Too small for this exchange, anyway. Edwards had placed the envelope in the newspaper and folded the paper in half. He sat at the bar on the last but one seat and ordered a pint of London Pride. He put the paper in front of him.

He was halfway down his pint when a nondescript bloke with 2 days of beard and wearing a well-worn donkey jacket sat in the end seat and ordered a pint of Guinness. He took a deep draught, smacked his lips and noticed the Standard in front of Edwards.

"Finished with the paper, mate?" asked the donkey jacket.

"Sure. Help yourself", replied Edwards and passed him the paper with the envelope inside it. "I'm off now anyway."

"Thanks, pal", said the donkey jacket, and moved off with his pint and the paper to an empty table. And that was the handover completed. Edwards finished his pint and left without a backward glance, deciding to walk over to King Street in search of a curry. And another Evening Standard, to read this time.

As he sat in a corner table with his curry and the paper, he considered what to do next. Logically, the answer was nothing. There was nothing else to do but wait for the results came back from the computer snoop. A week, he'd said. That was when he'd need to make his plans, and this time he would need to clear the expenses. He was fairly sure he'd be visiting the City by the Bay. Which was rather a pleasant prospect, in fact.

...

So, exactly a week later, in the same seat in the Dove at the same time as before, Edwards had just started his pint of Pride when a slightly smarter but still nondescript chap walked in with what looked like a recent haircut and shave and a much smarter brown leather bomber jacket and what looked like new jeans. Edwards smiled inwardly – he could see where some of the two and a half grand had been invested. He hoped his own payback was worth it.

The new arrival put his copy of the Standard down on the bar and ordered a Guinness. He paid and turned round to look for a table seat, ignoring his paper.

"Hey, have you finished with this?" asked Edwards.

"Oh, sure, help yourself, pal", answered the bomber jacket.

"Thanks, mate." Edwards picked up the paper and downed the rest of his pint. He couldn't resist it: "Nice jacket, by the way", he said over his shoulder as he left in search of King Street and another curry.

Once the poppadums and pickles were on the table and a chicken dupiaza and rice were on their way, he took the envelope from the paper and started to read what his friend's colleague had dug out of the computer systems.

A typed covering note came first.

"Hi pal. You didn't give us much to work with, but I think this is what you need. We couldn't get actual images of the records, but these are the facts. As you thought, a quick in and out, but your man did pay by debit card and the flights originated in SFO - and then back again. Via Miami. Details attached. Good doing business with you."

He looked at the second sheet. Perfect. Dates and flight numbers and times. Plus debit card details, with the bank code and amounts. So it looked like he was indeed off to San Francisco, just as soon as he could look up the bank codes and clear the expenses. He dipped his poppadum in the lime pickle. In fact, he thought he'd ask for an expenses advance. No point in skimping yourself on a trip like this.

But first, he realised, he'd need to visit his clients in Londonderry. And probably meet that damn priest again. That wasn't such a pleasant prospect. Not to worry. His curry arrived and he ordered another beer.

Chapter 34

Round Trip

The day after my lunch with Sally, I set off on what I expected would be the last of my trips to Grand Cayman. This time, of course, my journey included a detour to LA to look at the proposed shipping arrangements for Mystere, and all being well, book the service, and also a side trip to Providenciales to collect my new passport and, well, become Joe Baldwin. I'd booked the whole trip as Brett, so I might have to complete it in that name, but then I could lose the Brett Foster ID – and Joe Best's as well, of course. That was going to be strange, but I was sure it was a necessary step.

Sally offered to take me to the airport, but I told her it wasn't necessary. We said our goodbyes on the ferry dock and I headed out across the bay once again. The short hop to LAX was quick and uneventful, and after passing through Domestic Arrivals, I took a taxi to the dock area.

I found the shipping company's offices and introduced myself. Simon, the manager, was expecting me, and after suggesting I leave my suitcase in his side office, he locked the door and took me down to the dockside.

If I was worried about transporting Mystere this way, I was soon completely reassured by what I saw on the docks. Simon was obviously well used to showing nervous owners how he did his business, and he clearly had a well-oiled system behind him.

Some sailboats like Mystere and quite a few motor yachts were lined up ready to be loaded, and a fair number already sat on the deck of the huge cargo ship. We went up to the cargo deck to see how the boats were secured and kept safe from movement or spray damage. Some of the motor yachts were huge – they would dwarf Mystere or anything on the Sausalito marina. In fact I doubt they'd get into the marina at all. Despite my new-found wealth, there was no way I could afford one of these.

As we stood on deck, a motor yacht about the same size as Mystere was swung up by the giant cranes and carefully positioned on deck. Teams of workers fixed the cradles, disconnected the slings and released the crane, and started to lash the vessel down to keep it solidly tethered and secure. I was convinced, and said as much to Simon.

As we made our way back to the office, Simon told me that they'd shipped about 500 boats on deck last year. "Most of them motor yachts" – he pronounced the a – 'yats', not 'yots', I noticed – "but about a hundred sailboats, like yours. No insurance claims at all. Not one." I was impressed, and said so. "Yup. That's why our prices are good. They include insurance, which is a big element, but our premiums are lower. You should still pay it, but we're very proud of our safety record. Yes, sir."

I smiled. "OK, let's look at your timetable. I'm guessing I need to empty the lockers and so on – what about the fuel? The power?"

"Yes," said Simon. "We'll give you a reference guide to all that, and what to do about customs and so on. Also what to tell Lloyds, if you're insured there, and how to follow our progress as we go to Miami. It's around 3 weeks sailing, by the way. I think she's in Sausalito now – you'll be sailing her down?"

"Yes. I have some business first, down in the Caribbean, then I'll go back and set off in her to get down here. Say about 10 days' time, maybe a little less, so I should be here in, say, 3 weeks."

By now we were in his office, and we checked his shipping timetable. "Ok, that should be good for this sailing here ..." He indicated a picture of a vessel just like the one we'd been on earlier, and a date 4 weeks out. "We prefer you to be here at least a week before we plan to sail, so that will fit if you can stick to that timing. We load and secure in an order determined by the size and shape of the vessels we're transporting, to maximise the space while keeping safe. So, the more we have here, ready, the easier it is to plan."

"OK. That works, then. Will I be able to off-load and so on here, and then just hand her over?"

That was OK: Simon told me that they could take care of stepping the masts, if I removed personal effects. That was fine. We agreed the date, the insurance details and the price, which I said that I'd wire over from the Caymans or Turks next week.

So, the first major transactions out of the new bank account would be one to buy Mystere and then one to pay for the shipping across to the Caribbean. And I needed to get my business completed in the Caymans and Turks & Caicos, get home and then sail back down here to L.A. - within 3 weeks. I needed to get a move on.

I phoned Sally from the hotel to bring her up to date. I asked her to arrange to pack up and remove all but the minimum of personal stuff from Mystere, or pay someone to do it. We needed glasses, plates, cutlery, most of the bedding and all of our clothing to be removed and packed up for transport to Miami, where we'd replace it once Mystere was safely off-loaded and ready to sail again.

Sally said she wouldn't come on the journey from Sausalito to LA with Ken and me after all, as she wanted to stay with her Mom and make sure she was OK on her own for a couple of months. That made sense, as it needed to be more of a business-like sail than a pleasure cruise, given the timings. In fact it was going to be very useful experience for me, if I wanted to be able to sail her without help, for days out at least, and possibly longer, out of sight of land.

One challenge we had was that the stuff we removed from the boat wouldn't be needed for about a month, or maybe a little longer. We discussed renting a U-Haul van of the right size and having ourselves a road trip across the southern states as Mystere was being freighted through the Panama Canal to Miami. We agreed that would be fun, as long as the van wasn't too slow or uncomfortable. The alternative – using Sally's Volvo estate – would leave the Volvo in Miami when we sailed off, which was a problem. Sally then suggested that we could rent a large SUV, estate car or minivan, which we could leave in Miami, which would be easier, and more comfortable. She said she'd check on that.

We decided not to book anything in terms of overnight stays, so that we could stay a bit longer if we discovered an interesting place, or keep moving if we wanted. Sally would take care of that as soon as she could find a map. We thought that we'd take 2 or 3 weeks to get to Miami and then stay somewhere on South Beach until the boat docked and Mystere could be unloaded.

Once we'd agreed on this, I asked her to contact Ken White and make sure he was ready to help me sail it down to L.A. in a couple of weeks' time, and tell him that I'd be completing the purchase transaction in about a week or so – that is, before we sailed.

It occurred to me that, apart from a couple of days preparing to sail down to LA, all this meant that my time actually living in Sausalito was drawing to a close. I was sure I'd come back with Sally from time to time, but my time as a resident was coming to an end. It had been fun, and it had certainly served its purpose as a bolt hole. It was only ever going to be a temporary hideaway, but I'd enjoyed it. And, of course, it had led me to Sally. I had a lot to be grateful to the little town for.

The following morning, I made my way back to the airport and boarded the plane to Grand Cayman, to meet Garrido and his friend in Providenciales, Turks & Caicos.

Chapter 35

Parallel Lines

Two days after the conference call with Boston FBI, Binner and Page were back in the conference room. The lovely Debbie had provided more tea and biccies, and Binner had administered the steaming brew.

"Ok Peter", said Binner, taking a biscuit. "What have you found?"

Page was grinning. "Gold dust, I think. Foster, or rather Best as Foster, booked over the phone and paid by debit card for all his flights. The ones to Cayman and the one to Zurich and back. The bank branch is in Sausalito. California Saving and Checking."

"Sausalito. Hmm. Nice place to lie low. And quite clever, in fact."

"Yes, I thought so. And I had an idea about how he might be doing it – lying low, I mean."

"Go on ..."

Page smiled, pleased with himself. "Well, I thought about what I'd do if this was me. How I'd keep off the radar for months, as Best seems to have done. If he'd rented an apartment he'd have appeared on some sort of city electoral roll or something. If he's in Sausalito there won't be any low-rent or cash-only, no questions asked areas - or trailer parks, I wouldn't think ..."

"... and why would you slum it, anyway? Why not splash the cash?"

"Exactly", said Page. "And how can you do that in Sausalito?"

"Do tell?"

"You rent a boat." Page sat back and sipped his tea.

Binner mused on this. "Yeah. Nice. Can you do that? Rent a boat? And live on it?"

"I think so. If you pay the right people. The only other explanation would be if he was living with someone – a girl, maybe, or an old friend."

"So why do we not think that?"

Page nodded. "It's possible, of course. Best was in the IT business – he'd quite possibly have connections there. Probably he'd know his way around San Fran – hence Sausalito."

"So, this is no more than a strong hunch?" asked Binner.

Page sat forward and dunked a biscuit. "Yes, I suppose so. But think about it. Why open an account in Sausalito if you're not living there or nearby? It's less than an hour's ferry ride from San Fran, or about that as a drive. Over the Golden Gate. It's not as if he's a professional, is it? He's just a chancer who got lucky."

"Well, he's done pretty well for a mere chancer. He's got away with 25 million dollars or so, so far. But I agree. It's very feasible."

Page sat back as Binner refreshed their teacups, took another biscuit and dunked it, following Page's example.

"Hmm", said Binner. I'm guessing you want to go to Sausalito and check this out?"

Page grinned. "Well, it's a dirty job ..."

"But you're prepared to do it" Binner completed the sentence. "And no doubt you've prepared a plan – and a budget?"

"Well, you know ... just in case. I think I'd need a week. Ask some questions, show some photos, see whether we find a match or a thread ..."

Binner mused some more. Sipped some more tea. Eventually he nodded. "Yes. I'd have to check upstairs for the expenses. But yes, I think it's worthwhile. When can you go?"

"Couple of days, I think. I can be in Sausalito on Saturday and back here next Friday."

Binner shook his head. "I think I'll need some time to put a case together to get sign-off on that. I'll need you to write this up – starting with the Boston call – then why you think Best's in Sausalito. And of course your research into the travel and payment details. If you can make that convincing, I think I can get you out there in a week or two. I can't see any screaming urgency, can you?"

Page hid his disappointment at the delay. "I guess not. It's Best we're looking for, not the money. If he's in Sausalito, he won't be too hard to find. If he flies anywhere, assuming he's still using the Foster ID, we can trace him. But I'd like to find him quickly. He's in danger, and he obviously knows where the money is."

"Ok, get me that report and I'll get the approval. But - and this is important – Do not, no matter what, follow any trail beyond Sausalito without getting further clearance. Gather the information – if there is any – and report back here, and we'll debrief."

"What if I come across Best? I mean - if I'm asking questions and showing photos, and he's living there, well, it's a small place ..."

Binner nodded. "Good point. It might be better not to engage until we know what outcome we want. I'll talk to the directorate about that before you go. In fact, it might involve the Home Secretary or Northern Ireland Office. We should probably update them anyway. That's why this will take a few days."

He paused to think and munch his biscuit.

"So, just talk to the bank and see what they know. I'll talk to our friends in Boston and find you a contact in San Fran who can give you some local authority. Just don't get outside that brief, not without talking to me, anyway. We don't want to spook anyone just now. I'd bet good money those Irish bastards are following the same path. I just hope they're a few steps behind."

Page nodded. "OK, I'll get to work on that report, and reckon on travelling in a couple of weeks' time."

"Well. It could take a bit longer. Now I think of it, I'm sure the Minister ought to know – that will add a delay. Better safe than sorry, though."

Peter Page resigned himself to a longer delay than he'd hoped, but he felt he could look forward to a trip to San Fran and an interesting assignment. The meeting closed and Binner and Page once again took their tea and biscuits to their respective desks.

Chapter 36

Orders to Travel

The view from The Lawyer's office showed a beautiful day, with late spring flowers and the trees coming into leaf, and both the sky and the water looked unusually blue and welcoming. Which could not be said of The Priest, who was sitting with The Lawyer drinking coffee when Mary showed Edwards in and set a fresh coffee cup in front of him. She left him to pour himself a cup and left the meeting to its deliberations.

"So, Mr. Edwards," said The Priest. "It seems that our best guess is looking likely. In other words, Mr. Best is alive and kicking, and helping himself to our money?"

"Well, it seems very likely - yes", answered Edwards. "We know that someone calling himself Brett Foster has a bank account in Sausalito, and is travelling, quite frequently, from there to the Caymans. He's also visited Zurich, and seems to have been there on the date the Bonds were cashed. Sausalito is a short ferry ride away from San Francisco. And your source is quite sure that Mr. Foster himself is dead?"

"Yes", The Lawyer said. "But I'd be inclined to try to confirm that first, if you're proposing to visit California anyway."

Edwards nodded. "OK then. You have the real Mr. Foster's address on the list you showed me, I think. La Jolla, near San Diego? If I fly direct to LA first, and then pop down to San Diego, I can clear that up quite quickly. Then it's a short hop up to San Fran and I'll see whether there's another Brett Foster up there."

The Lawyer looked at The Priest, who nodded agreement. "I think it's important to be certain that the real Foster is indeed no longer with us. That takes care of a possible loose end. But the real task is to find our Mr Best. Find him and we'll find our money."

Edwards interjected. “I’ll find him if he’s there. But I won’t be involved in any rough stuff. I doubt he’ll tell me where the money is simply because I ask him. Once I’ve located and identified him, that’s my job done. I want to make that clear.”

The Priest nodded. “Mr. Edwards, I know that this isn’t your, shall we say, skill set. But it might help all of us if you would explain to him – if you find him – that the consequences of retaining these funds will be extremely dire for him and those he holds dear. If this fails to elicit the information we require, you will let us know at once where he is. And we will take over with more, ah, muscular methods.”

Edwards nodded. “Understood. And I’ll make sure Best understands that as well.”

The Lawyer picked the discussion up. “OK, to practical issues. We’ll put you in funds to the tune of £5,000. That should cover your travel and accommodation costs and incidental expenses. Please keep all receipts, and we’ll pay your usual day rate for every day you’re away. Fair enough?”

Edwards nodded. “Yes – more than fair. I can be ready to leave the day after tomorrow. I’ll report by email – obscure but clear to you. OK?”

The Lawyer nodded. As Edwards rose to leave, The Priest added “I will connect you to one of our number based over in the US. He’s currently in Boston, but will make his way to San Francisco and contact you on arrival. His name will be Dolan. He’ll find you and make himself known. And he can take care of the more forceful discussions, as you might say.”

Edwards nodded his understanding and let himself out of the office. He was on his way.

Chapter 37

Becoming Mr Baldwin

Arriving in George Town, Grand Cayman, and taking a taxi to the Marriott was pure routine for me by now. The hotel reception staff all seemed to know me by name – or, at least by Brett Foster's name. I made a mental note that I'd better not come here again as Joe Baldwin, if I wanted to avoid embarrassment - at the very least.

After quickly unpacking, I phoned Garrido, who suggested that he could come over immediately after he completed his day's work. He also said that he'd get his secretary to make the arrangements for us to visit Providenciales as soon as his friend the Minister could be available for the hour or so that we needed. That was likely to be either tomorrow or the day after, and said he'd let me know when he got to the hotel. There were scheduled flights anyway, but he thought his friend might send us an official plane if one was available. That sounded like fun.

I freshened up with a quick shower, then went down to the lobby to wait for Garrido. He arrived just after 5:30, and suggested that we take an office rather than the outside areas, due to the confidentiality of the documents. I had a workspace in my room, so we agreed to use that. Before we went back up, I ordered tea and some sandwiches, since I hadn't eaten anything since breakfast.

Once we were suitably provided for in terms of tea & sandwiches and the waiter had left us, Garrido brought out the final papers from the money cleansing process. It was a small but, significant set of papers. Just six signatures, two as Brett Foster and the rest as Joe Baldwin, gave me – assuming "me" was Joe Baldwin - full control of the Turks company, a personal and corporate bank account, and a formal Turks passport application. I had access to over 20 million dollars in mainly corporate, but also personal accounts. That didn't take into account the balance of the cash in the Sausalito bank, of course. I hadn't checked, but that was probably another million or so. Loose change, really.

Garrido's company fee had already been taken from the account, according to the formal agreement, and I was happy to write him a cheque on the new bank account for the personal fee. "Robert, do remember that, although this transaction is now closed, and, by the way, I'm impressed with how smoothly it was done, there may well be a follow-up. I mean the original, erm, custodians of this money."

Garrido took the cheque and nodded. "Thanks. Yes, you did say that when we first met. You also said that I should not fight any, let's say requests for information, if anyone asks. Is that still your position?"

I nodded and swallowed a bite of my chicken sandwich with a sip of tea. "Yes, it is. Please don't try any heroics – it's not worth it. They'll find out what they want to know anyway." I thought for a moment. "But that depends on what they ask – what they want to know."

"How do you mean?"

"Well. They'll want to know what name I'm using, for example. You can give them Brett Foster – that's impossible for you not to know. And I'd guess, if they track you down, that would mean they know it anyway. But you wouldn't necessarily know my original name, or my new one. They'll know my old name – that's easy for them to discover, but it needn't mean anything to you, and it wouldn't help them anyway. But I don't think you do know it, do you?"

"Actually, we did discuss it, and I advised you against using it, if you remember. But I never actually kept a note of it, and I wouldn't ordinarily have a reason to ask, or even think that you had a 'previous name', now you come to mention it. In fact, I don't think I can recall it anyway. Except that it's Joe."

"Ok, good. So, you can simply say that you took me at face value – as Brett Foster. You can't pretend that you don't know the name and location of the final company in your process, but from what you say, and what I've read, there's no way the Turks would divulge anything about the beneficial owners. And in fact, you don't need to know the new name – Baldwin – at all. Unless they really press you, and even assuming they work out that there may be a 'new new' name, so to speak, there's no reason for you to know anything about that. The arrangements you made in the Turks were personal – off the record, I think?"

"Oh, yes, very much so. My friend – Fernando – is keen that it remains so, as well. Anyway, the transfer of ownership to, well, to Joe Baldwin, that's nothing to do with me. I don't appear on that transaction – I know nothing about it."

"OK, that's good. And the trip to Providenciales – is that a scheduled flight?"

"Ah, no. Fernando's sending a government plane. It's a 3 hour flight but he has one at his disposal with a free day tomorrow. I hope that's OK?"

That sounded excellent. "Oh, yes. That'll be a new experience", I smiled.

"For me, too", Garrido nodded.

"And of course, that journey won't be on the public record, will it?"

"Well, they'll have to file a flight plan and so on, of course, but no, no record of you and me as passengers on the flight there and back. Just an official return flight from Turks to Cayman and back. Nothing remarkable in that, at all."

"Even better", I said. "By the way, there's no certainty at all that anybody will come looking for me – or you - here on Cayman. But they might, which is why I've added the personal fee – for your extra confidentiality. It's usually quite easy to hide some facts if you divulge others, and you can certainly admit to dealing with Brett Foster in clearing certain funds carried in Bearer Bonds, via a bank in Zurich. And you can say that these funds ended up in a Turks & Caicos company with Brett Foster as the beneficial owner. You can even name the company."

Garrido nodded. "Yes, and, as I say, you – Joe Baldwin, who I've never heard of, has now bought that company and changed the name. That fact is completely unknown to me. The Turks company I set up will effectively vanish." He pointed to one of the forms. "But I can't say any more. As you say, I don't have to know any more. Neither your old name nor your new name. And even if they look for a company in the Turks, owned by Brett Foster, they won't find one – even if they pull strings, because there isn't one now. It's all rather neat, actually, although I do say so myself."

I picked up the papers to check. Of course, the new owner of the funds, and therefore the bank accounts, was Joe Baldwin. Brett Foster had sold the company to Joe Baldwin, who had changed the company name at once, and that broke the Foster connection. The record of that transaction and the corporate name change didn't show Garrido as having any input or knowledge of it, and that gave him plausible deniability, which is what we wanted. In any case, that transaction was effectively made in the Turks & Caicos, and would be lodged with all the company papers behind their solid barriers of confidentiality. First class stuff, really.

I stood up and shook Garrido's hand. "Thank you. You've done a great job. When we get back from Providenciales, I'll go back to the US and become Joe Baldwin, who you've never heard of, and you probably won't see me again. You'll never see Brett Foster, anyway. You've earned your extra fee, and I hope you won't actually need to do any more for it, but your deniability is at least plausible."

Garrido laughed. "Thanks. I'll pick you up here by taxi fairly early, then, tomorrow morning. Let's say 7 o'clock. That good for you?"

I said it was, and we said our goodbyes for the time being. I checked the time and phoned Sally to bring her up to date. She was very envious of the government plane flight, but was also excited about the plans she'd made for our road trip across country. She'd been on board Mystere to organise the packing, and was sure the contents would fit into a large SUV, such as a Cadillac Escalade, which cost a fortune to rent for a month or 6 weeks but was a very comfortable ride. Much more so than a van, anyway. I agreed and she said she'd arrange to hire one. Ken and I would need to travel light on our southbound sailing adventure, it seemed.

Chapter 38

Back in Boston

In the Boston office of the FBI, Roseanne opened an email from the team who were monitoring irregular movements connected to the 9/11 "Lost Souls." After reading it, once quickly and then a second time, more carefully, she printed it out and went to knock on Billy's door. She was waved in and gestured to sit as Billy finished a call. She checked the sideboard – there was coffee in the filter jug and some mugs arranged ready. Billy completed his call and almost instinctively reached for the coffee pot. "Roseanne. What's up?" He gestured an offer of coffee, but Roseanne shook her head.

"It's our friend Brett Foster. Or whoever it is. On the move again."

"Oh? Where to now?"

Roseanne read the details on the email. "Same again – the Caymans – but via LA this time. The debit card data shows him booking a hotel in LA and then the same one as usual – the Marriott – in George Town." She read on. "It also shows an open-ended ticket back to San Fran, with the outbound journey – to Cayman - booked for tomorrow. From LA, that is. He's in LA now, according to flight records. He booked all this on his Visa card via a travel agent in San Fran." She handed the printout to Billy.

Billy looked at it and slurped his coffee. "OK, I see. What do you think this means?"

"Well, if he's cleaning the funds the Brits talked about, it probably means that he's getting close to the end of that process. Maybe this is the end of the process, in fact. And I think we should let our friends in London know, if they don't know already."

Billy sipped more coffee and re-read the email. She also wondered how Billy managed to sleep, now that caffeine had replaced nicotine as his drug of choice. "OK, so let's get them on the line. What time is it there? Will we need an encrypted line?"

"It's early afternoon there – we can call them. And if we're not too specific, we don't really need to scramble or whatever. But you should probably open the call – you know they have a thing about protocol, the Brits."

Billy nodded. "Mmm. Best to pass it over to them as quickly as we can, really. Do you have the number for – what's his name – Binner, is it?"

"Binner, yes. It's on my desk."

"OK, go get it. Let's pass this ball on down the line."

Roseanne got her notes from her desk, returned and sat down again. "Here it is – the 44 code for the UK and the number itself."

Billy took it and dialled. After some clicking, the double-ring of the UK system sounded a few times, then "Hello? Binner here."

"Ah, Mr. Binner, good, er, afternoon. This is Billy Bingham from Boston – we spoke a week or so back."

"Yes, Billy, of course I remember. How are you? You were very helpful indeed. Do you have more news? Should we switch to a secure line?"

"Fine, thank you. No, I don't think so – it's a quick update. Roseanne is here as well. She tells me that our friend from San Francisco is on the move again. Caymans again, but via Los Angeles this time. He's in LA now, in fact, it seems."

"Ah. Interesting. Thank you. Do you have a full itinerary for him?"

"Open ticket, but onward from LA to George Town – the Caymans - and then back to San Fran. No timings yet, but a provisional booking to George Town tomorrow. We have an email from the monitoring team."

"Can you hold a moment? I'll see whether my colleague Peter Page can join me."

"Sure", said Billy, and took another gulp of his coffee.

There was a pause of a minute or so before Binner spoke again. "OK, Peter is here. For his benefit, our subject is in LA now, with a booking to Cayman tomorrow and an open return back to San Fran, yes?"

Roseanne leant forward. "Yes, that's it. We know his hotel bookings, because he used a travel agent and we've seen the entire itinerary, which he booked via the debit card on a single transaction. He's booked into the Marriott on Grand Cayman tomorrow, and an open return to San Fran airport – SFO – from Cayman. It's all on this email."

"OK, this is Peter. If this is an open return, I guess you'll get an alert when he books his travel from George Town back to San Fran, yes?"

"Yes – we'll know as soon as he firms up his booking, pretty well. Should I forward this email from our monitoring team?"

Binner came back in. "Assuming it's innocuous in itself, yes please, as soon as you can. I think we should wait until he books that flight, if you can notify us at that point. I'll move forward with our arrangements to get to Sausalito, which is where we think he's living. We're working on that now – paperwork, you know."

"OK," said Billy, and nodded to Roseanne, who took a note to forward the email. "So you don't want to get to the Marriott on Grand Cayman?"

"I don't really think we can be sure to get there before he leaves again. We don't actually employ James Bond, you know, or have his budget. And in fact engaging with Best himself isn't the very highest priority for us, really – it's more about ensuring our Irish friends don't gather these funds, and it seems that our mutual friend is doing a pretty good job at that. But we do want a word with him, if only for his own safety, frankly."

"Right," said Billy. "Roseanne will send you this email, and we'll keep an eye on the flight systems. We'll let you know when he moves on to the Caymans, and then when he books to set off back to San Fran. You can make your plans accordingly."

That seemed satisfactory all round, and, the call closed, Roseanne left Billy to his coffee and went back to her desk. The ball had been cleanly passed.

...

In London, the call completed, Peter Page was unusually animated. "Look, boss, assuming this is the end of the money laundering, we have to act quickly. He's returning to San Fran, but his circumstances have changed. There's no certainty that he'll just stay put in Sausalito, if that's where he is. He can afford to travel anywhere now. If the final company is in the Caymans, he'll probably go back there, and, well, who knows where else?"

Binner nodded. I know, but as I said to the guys in Boston, Best isn't actually a high priority target for us, is he? Not in himself. As long as he's cleaned the funds and squirrelled them away, our worst case is not happening, surely?"

Page shook his head. "Meaning the IRA getting hold of the money again? No, boss. Look, firstly, we don't know exactly who the, erm, pseudo-Foster actually is. I mean, we think it's the courier, Best, but we don't actually know that, do we?"

"So, who do you think it is?"

"Well, I think it probably is Best, yes. But I also think it could possibly be our Irish friends – maybe a double-bluff. In any case, I think we need to make sure that Best – or Foster - is just Joe Best, the courier. Just a chancer who got lucky, and not some cover story for, well, something else. And then we need to bear in mind that when – and I think it is when, not if – when the Irish find Best, then he's in serious danger physically. We need to make sure he's protected somehow. He's a British subject. More to the point, they might well recover the money from him, which is exactly what we set out to stop."

Binner nodded. "Yes, you have a point, I suppose. Best's personal security isn't our problem, to be honest, and that won't cut much mustard upstairs. Whatever trouble he gets into, he obviously brought it on himself. But if they do find him, they'll probably extract the money from him. And I agree – if we can find him, they possibly can as well. It's very difficult to disappear completely, and they have their contacts."

Page added: "Exactly. They were clearly fishing in the right pool when the Senator – Sullivan, was it – talked to Roseanne. They're getting close, and Roseanne inadvertently gave them some more information. I'd bet they're not far behind us. If they are behind. We do need to get moving, Boss."

Binner considered for a moment. "Hmm. OK. You've persuaded me. I'll get hold of them upstairs and move it on. Best's in LA now and then off to George Town. He's not likely to be back in San Fran until probably 3 or 4 days' time. At least. I think we can get you there in 4 or 5 days. That's the best I can do, I think."

Page knew he could do no more. "Right, thanks. I'll make my arrangements – I'll be ready as soon as you have sign-off." He left the office and started to plan the first part of his trip to Sausalito.

Chapter 39

She's Gone

Edwards shuffled forward in the immigration queue at LAX, Los Angeles International airport. He was aching and crumpled from his long journey in the back of the plane. He needed a shave and he wanted a shower. He'd booked a room at the airport Marriott, which he thought had an outdoor swimming pool, which might distract him from going straight to bed and to sleep too early. The client had been reasonably generous as far as expenses were concerned, but he was going to have to report back to The Lawyer every other day as a matter of course. He was due to collect a hire car tomorrow and drive down the couple of hours or so to La Jolla to try to find Brett Foster, or his widow, or any evidence of him. Then he would fly north on a domestic flight to SFO and head out to Sausalito.

Eventually it was his turn to hand over his documents and confirm his peaceable intentions. He said he was here on holiday – to do otherwise would add a complicated set of questions he didn't want to have to answer. "Visiting friends, down in La Jolla and San Diego", he explained. "Then a trip to San Francisco." This seemed to satisfy the unsmiling officer, and he went on to collect his luggage and find the airport bus. Once checked in, he found that his ground floor hotel room gave out onto the inner garden courtyard and the swimming pool, which also afforded significant mood adjustment in the form of a swim-up bar.

The following morning, refreshed and refuelled, Edwards checked out early and caught the shuttle bus back to the airport and then another to the Car Rental depot, where he collected a mid-range saloon and a map to the Foster address in La Jolla. This address was gleaned from public sources he'd accessed from his office before he left, and some less public information which his expert friend had found in the utilities and phone companies' records. They all confirmed the same address and zip code, which was now shown on Edwards' map as the end destination.

The route took the Interstate 405 and then 5, and once he'd joined it the Interstate system, his stress level dropped somewhat. After the first hour or so, the Pacific was in view on his right, sparkling blue, and he wished he'd pushed for the budget to secure a convertible.

Eventually he turned off the Interstate into La Jolla township and followed the map into the residential enclave and finally pulled up at the address his research had indicated. The Ranch-style house was as he expected. The most striking aspect, however, was a real estate company board with a "SOLD!" banner overlaid. That wasn't good, he thought, unless he had arrived before the Foster family – or what there was of it – was still living there, packing up and preparing to move.

Walking up the drive, he had a bad feeling. No car on the drive and the slightly neglected front lawn gave him a clue, but a glance through the windows to the family room and the kitchen revealed an empty house. The gate to the side was locked, so there was no access to the rear, and the front door was, as he expected, also locked.

Edwards took out his notebook and wrote the telephone number of the real estate company and started down the drive back to his car, thinking that this had probably been a waste of time. The real estate agent would tell him very little unless he could claim some sort of connection. He hoped he could at least get confirmation that this had been the home of Mr and Mrs Brett Foster if he had a credible story. Maybe an insurance company story...

He was reaching in his pocket for the car keys when a strange apparition in a nylon housecoat appeared in the next door drive. He stopped and she called to him.

"Hello, mister. Are you looking for Mandy? Mandy Foster?"

He thought quickly. “Well, yes. Mandy. Or, erm, Brett.”

“Oooh, Brett. No. He died, you know. In that awful thing in New York. He was killed there.”

“Ah. I did wonder …”

“Oh, yes. She was quite upset for a while. Mandy, I mean. She had no news, you see.”

“No news?” This was a bit off-centre, but there might be some value. “You mean she didn’t know?”

“Oh no. Not for weeks. Then that man came to see her. He told her.”

“Man? What man was that, Mrs, erm … ?”

“Rosencrantz. It’s Rosencrantz. I used to be on the stage, you know.”

Edwards was struggling to follow all this. “Oh. I see. Nice. And the Fosters – they’ve sold the house?”

“She has. He’s dead. I told you. She’s gone now.”

“Ah, yes. Where did she go? Do you know?”

“You’re English, aren’t you? I can tell. Like that other man.”

Ah. Interesting, thought Edwards. “I see. What other man? Who was that?”

“Well, how do I know? He came to see her and told her that Brett was dead. Weeks ago. Months, maybe. I forget things.”

“Oh. I see. He was English?”

“Yes. I can tell, like I say. We had lots of English people in the theatre. Nice boys. And girls. English.”

“I see … Did he tell you his name?”

The old lady stopped and thought. "Nope. Never knew that. He went in and talked to Mandy."

"And now she's left?"

"Yep. Put the house up for sale soon after your friend visited."

This was useful information, he thought. If it was true. It was hard to say ... "Where has she gone? Did she tell you?"

"Oh yes. She told me. Now wait a minute ..." Edwards watched her start to hum, then sing. It seemed to be 'Witchita Lineman'. "No, that ain't it. No." she kept humming, then singing in a thin but fairly accurate voice "Leaving ... midnight train to Georgia – yes! Atlanta! Georgia. She went to Atlanta, Georgia. I think she has a sister there."

"Ah, thank you. Atlanta. OK. Thanks." Edwards decided to get out while he could. He opened the driver's door and stepped in. Closing it and starting the engine, he lowered the window and waved. "You've been very helpful. Thanks again." He closed the window and backed out of the drive onto the road. As he looked back in the mirror, the old dear seemed to be waving enthusiastically, but he was glad to get away.

"Phoenix!" she shouted. "By the time I get to Phoenix. Not Georgia. Not Atlanta!" But Edwards was on his way back up the coast to LAX, and thence to SFO.

His journey wasn't wasted after all. He would check with the real estate agency that Mrs Foster was the only listed vendor and then ask his paymasters whether he should go to Atlanta on the strength of the old bird's information and look for Mrs Mandy Foster. Unless the real estate agency would give him a forwarding address, which he doubted, he didn't think it would be worth it. But the mysterious Englishman was interesting. He was prepared to bet that was Best. He had a worthwhile report for this side trip. He was booked into the

Marriott again and could write up and email his report before he left for San Fran. He thought it would make interesting reading, at least.

Chapter 40

On Her Majesty's Service

Binner stopped by Page's desk and spoke quietly. "My office, please, Peter." Page stood and followed Binner into his closed office and shut the door behind him. Binner gestured him to the guest chair. "I've had approval from upstairs for your trip to the City by the Bay."

Page grinned. "That's great, boss. Any issues?"

"Not really. They agreed with you that we need to ensure that the money is truly buried and safe from IRA hands. And they also agreed that if they find Best, if it is Best, he would suffer, let's say, irresistible pressure to let them have the money. Which we must avoid. That means that we need to deter them from trying to find him, but also let him know the risk he's running. He may hand over the money to us, but, in practice we probably can't actually make him, and I doubt he'll do that voluntarily."

"No", said Page. "Well, I don't think I would, anyway."

"Quite", smiled Binner. "We're working on a strategy to deter them from persisting in this search – the IRA, that is. Our colleagues in Northern Ireland will deal with that. But there's another thing. He needs to understand that he must never, ever, return to the UK, or to anywhere he could be recognised from his old life. Best being irredeemably dead, along with the money, needs to be a sustainable legend. If you do find him, he must be made to understand that."

Page nodded. "Fair enough. I'll make sure he does."

"Right. Make sure he understands this as well. He is, prima facie, guilty of the theft of 25 million dollars, the property of clients of his employer, which is a British company. Therefore, there is a warrant in place here in the UK for his arrest. If he appears at any border point, or in any other UK location where we can apprehend him, we will.

We'll have no option. And he will be remanded in custody pending trial."

Page hadn't thought of this. "Wow. But yes, you're right – it is theft. And it's a huge amount. No bail, and lots of time in jail, for sure."

"Exactly. We could put an extradition order out and have him recovered. In fact, we could provide you with one. But, as you say, our main objective is to keep him as safe as we can while the IRA are looking for him, until we can deter them, and ultimately to keep them and the money apart. If we can do that without arresting him, the general feeling is that we should do that. Actually, I think there's a lot of admiration for him upstairs."

Page smiled. "Yes - I'm looking forward to meeting him, in fact. He seems quite a character, if he's managed all this on his own." He paused. "Maybe we can use him ourselves …"

Binner contemplated this. "You know, you may have a point. He's apparently resourceful and self-sufficient, and obviously has no history anywhere in any of the intelligence systems. Maybe that's a trade-off we can ask for. In exchange for not extraditing him."

"Sort of a reservist, you mean?" asked Page. "To be honest, that was a throw-away thought, but, well, I'll take a view when I meet him, yes? Sound him out?"

"Do that," replied Binner, picking up a file of papers. "But it's not really likely, to be frank. Right. Here are your tickets and a credit card, and some dollars. You're lucky – it's Club - Business Class. The FBI will meet you at SFO and sort out accommodation for you. Report back to me on arrival, and then as we decide. The FBI officer can let you have a gun if you think you need one. I think you should, anyway. Make contact once you've reached your accommodation. But travel clean – as a tourist. No gun. You're under your own name. US immigration have your name and passport number. They'll move you though immigration without delay, but discreetly, using the normal channels. You fly the day after tomorrow, which should be OK."

Page took the file of papers and stood. "Thanks, boss. I'll tidy up here and then take tomorrow off to get ready, if that's OK?"

Binner nodded. "Yes, fine. Just remember to call me when you get over there and let me have your contact details. Close the door behind you, please."

Chapter 41

Project Review

Mary showed The Priest into the office and, as usual, followed up with a tray of coffee and biscuits. She set this on the table, and The Priest sat and poured himself a cup. "Thank you, Mary", said The Lawyer, and, closing the file he was working on, picked up a printed sheet of paper and joined The Priest at the coffee table. He poured a coffee, added milk and picked up a biscuit.

"So," said The Priest. "We have a report from our friend Mr Edwards."

"Yes. Emailed last night. Interesting." He handed the printed email over to The Priest and concentrated on his dunking biscuit. The Priest read it and placed in on the table.

"So, how do you see this information?" asked The Priest.

"I think it strongly indicates that this Brett Foster was indeed killed in the World Trade Center, and, apparently another Englishman has followed this up by visiting his widow. It also seems that, until that visit, the widow, erm ..." He picked up the printout "... Mandy Foster, was unaware of this fact. That Mr Foster was killed, I mean."

"'Strongly indicates'?"

"Yes. This visit isn't proof of that, but Mrs Foster apparently dealt with the sale herself, and there was a Government notice that she had inherited full ownership of the property under the special 9/11 arrangements. To me, that clinches it. The FBI obviously accept that he's dead."

The Priest recalled his conversation with Sullivan, and the list of 'Lost Souls'. "I agree. And this mysterious earlier visitor?"

"Has to be Best, I'd say. English, according to the neighbour. She seems a bit batty, but according to Edwards, quite reliable on that aspect. Who else could it be?"

“Well, there are plenty of Englishmen in California. But I have to agree with you. On the balance of probabilities, it’s going to be Best. I wonder why he’d visit, though?”

“I thought about that. Maybe he felt he owed the widow – Mandy – some closure. Or perhaps he needed something from her. And I think I know what that would be.”

“Do, please, illuminate my darkness,” The Priest smiled, icily.

The Lawyer went on quickly. “The passport. Foster’s passport. He clearly has it now - if he’s travelling internationally, he must have it, and I don’t suppose Foster had it with him in New York. I don’t know how he got any other documents, but I’d guess Foster carried his driving licence, which would be useful – the car rental, for example. But now, evidently, he also has his passport. This must be when he got it.”

The Priest contemplated that. “I believe you’re right. And – let me see the email again.” He picked up the printout. “Yes, Edwards says that, according to the neighbour, the property went on the market soon after this visit. Which suggests that it was during Best’s visit – assuming it was Best - that Mrs Foster learnt of her husband’s untimely death.”

Both men paused for thought and a reflective sip of coffee. The Lawyer broke the silence. “So, are we agreed? That, almost certainly, Foster is dead and that Best is alive, and using Foster’s identity, including driving licence and passport, and travelling in a way that suggests that he’s clearing these funds into an account under his control?”

“I believe so. I see little point in pursuing Mrs Foster to - Atlanta, is it – to establish that it was Best who visited, and that he somehow secured Foster’s passport. I think we should proceed on the basis of your reasonable assumptions. Which are that Best is alive, and calling himself Foster with formal ID to support that. And that he's busy hiding our money."

The Lawyer nodded. "I agree. So, Edwards is now proceeding to San Francisco. He'll look for Best in Sausalito to start with. What about the Caymans – do we look for the lawyer who acted for him?"

The Priest shook his head. "That won't be necessary if we can lay hands on Best. Maybe, if Best can't be found, we should have a look for him, but it's a distraction now. Time is of the essence. Best may not remain long in Sausalito." He paused and topped up the coffee cups. "But I think our Mr. Edwards could use a more, erm, aggressive assistant to support him. He's not an expert in extracting information that someone wishes to keep secret, is he? And he said as much himself."

The Lawyer grimaced. "Well, no. That's not what he does. I agree – he could use some muscle to help his persuasive processes, as it were."

"I'll make a call and send someone to meet him in San Francisco. We certainly have the right skills in New York and Boston, but probably not on the West Coast. Please let Edwards know that we're sending reinforcements. When we have his location in San Francisco, let me know and I'll pass it on. They can make their own arrangements for the liaison." He finished his coffee and stood. "Please let me have the next report as soon as you have it."

The Lawyer also stood. "Will do", he said to the departing priest. Mary came in to remove the coffee things, and The Lawyer went back to more conventional –and, so far, more rewarding business.

Chapter 42

The Only Way to Fly

7 o'clock in the morning had dropped out of my experience since my change of lifestyle. Nevertheless, at that time next day, after a quick standing-up breakfast of coffee and croissants in my room, I made my way outside to the drop-off area. The temperature was already heading towards the mid-70's, but the black Mercedes taxi was ticking over, keeping the aircon running. I said "good morning" to Garrido, who was waiting for me in the back seat, and climbed into the car. The Minister's plane had already landed, he said, and was refuelling for the return leg. We'd be through the airport and airborne within 10 minutes of arriving there.

There was, however, a slight hitch. "Unfortunately, the plane's needed for another flight this evening, and it may not be available for us to return. So Fernando has arranged our tickets on a scheduled flight this evening, and our seats are booked. In your case, as Mr Joe Baldwin – to match your new passport. He sends his apologies."

That didn't seem too much of a problem, and I said so. "I assume we'll have enough time to complete our business?"

"Oh, yes. That should only take an hour or so. We'll probably have time to have a look round your new country of residence before we catch the return flight. I think you'll like it."

I can tell you that airports are different places when you're using a private, or government, jet. We were escorted to a side office to check our passports, which took less than a minute, followed by a cursory glance into Garrido's briefcase. Then we were ushered onto what looked like a golf cart, to be driven to the steps of the jet.

The sleek plane looked very different from an airliner. It stood in a corner of the tarmac, engines humming and looking almost animal, rather than mechanical. Streamlined and gleaming silver in the sun, it seemed to be out of place on the ground. This was a creature of the skies, pure and simple.

The tail fin had a representation of the Turks & Caicos national flag, which included a familiar and, to me, slightly nostalgia-inducing union flag in the top corner, along with some rather odd shapes in a shield next to it, on a deep blue background. The steps were lowered as we approached, and we were greeted by a slim, smiling, black and beautiful stewardess waiting at the top.

We walked up the steps to the interior - which again looked nothing like a commercial airliner. The seating was sort of ruched tan leather, and the fittings were lacquered blond wood. There was a carpet of dark blue, to match the background of the flag, which was also reproduced on the bulkheads between the seating area and the pilot's cabin. Overall, I got the impression of a top-end Mercedes 'S' Class limo. Only a bit bigger. And airborne, of course.

There were 8 wide, comfortable seats arranged in 2 well-spaced opposing pairs with a table between each pair on each side, and a wide aisle down the middle. Behind these there were two more pairs facing forward on each side with fold-down tables on the back of the rearmost of the 4-group seats. I also noticed a door to the rear bulkhead, and guessed that there would be cabins back there. Very nice – but we would only be enjoying this luxury for about 4 hours.

The stewardess closed the doors behind us and indicated the seating. "Sit where you wish, gentlemen. We're clear to leave the ground in 10 minutes. I'm Naomi. We have some snacks and drinks whenever you're ready."

We each took a seat in one of the 4-groups on each side of the aisle and belted up for take-off. Naomi went forward to tell the pilot that we were all ready, and took her own seat at the front of the cabin. Almost immediately, the plane started to roll forward towards the runway. After a short wait for a couple of smaller craft ahead of us to take off and turn away from what would be the wash from our twin jet engines, we accelerated rapidly down the runway. Less than half an hour after alighting from the taxi, we were airborne.

As soon as we were clear of the airport air space and starting to level out, Naomi got up and opened what looked like a cupboard, but turned out to be a drinks cabinet with a small microwave oven. "Is it a little early for a glass of champagne, gentlemen? Maybe a Bucks Fizz?"

Garrido looked at me for a steer. "Never too early for that", I replied. "I think Buck's Fizz would be ideal. And I don't suppose you have a bacon sandwich?"

I was kidding, actually, but Naomi wasn't at all fazed. She smiled, "We do, actually. We thought you might like that." So she got busy, and in 10 minutes we were both sipping our Bucks Fizz, with a jug on the table in front of me and a plate of excellent bacon sandwiches on Garrido's table. I started to wonder what a plane like this might cost, and how much the staff like the unseen pilot – and Naomi – would require as salary. That was a 2-minute daydream, but I resolved to investigate private plane rental companies, if there were such things. This was definitely the way to travel, if you could afford it.

After our breakfast – my second; I'm not sure about Garrido – I asked Naomi if I could explore the rest of the plane – the bit behind the rear bulkhead.

"Of course", smiled Naomi, and, opening the door, stood back and let me through. There were 2 cabins on either side of the aisle, which was naturally narrower back here. I looked in one, which had a small, but large enough, double bed, and a shower and loo in a tight but serviceable en-suite facility. They were exquisitely fitted out, rather like a miniature version of Mystere's facilities.

"I guess all 4 cabins are the same?" I asked. Naomi nodded and opened the next door. "So you can seat 12 and sleep 8 – well, 4 doubles?"

"Well, we have to have all passengers seated for take-off and landing. So a maximum passenger load of 12, plus two cabin staff. These sleeping cabins are for longer or overnight flights. We can fly for 10 hours, so into Europe, western Africa, or pretty well anywhere in the Americas. The President and ministers naturally prefer to sleep overnight once we're airborne and they've eaten. But the seats you're in are fully reclining anyway. They're better than most first-class airline seats."

It's another world, I thought to myself.

Strangely, I didn't even consider making a pass at Naomi. It wasn't her immaculate exterior and efficient demeanour – in fact, that would normally be a real turn-on. And this was a classic opportunity. But it just didn't occur to me. Sally was obviously having a serious effect on me.

Naomi closed the bulkhead door behind us as we made our way back to the main cabin, and showed me how the seat reclined and the footrest extended. I relaxed – to the extent that I fell asleep for an hour or so. I woke up to the smell of coffee, and Naomi offered us lunch choices, including an excellent salad with cold meats and fish. We both decided against more alcohol, and settled for the coffee. I moved over to the window seat to take in the view.

I could see a sandy coastline and bright blue sea, with small offshore islands surrounded by white sands, way down below us, like tiny jewels. Naomi told me that we'd almost cleared Cuban airspace, and we were about an hour away from touchdown. I resumed my aisle seat, and must have dropped into a light sleep again; I was woken by Naomi asking me to raise the seat and fasten my belt for landing.

I slid across to the window seat and watched as we came over the blue sea, white sands and a range of scattered islands. Naomi had told me that our approach would take us over a National Park. It was certainly one of the most attractive airport approaches I'd ever seen, as we dropped past the palm trees into the small airport of my new homeland.

Chapter 43

Hello San Francisco ...

Entirely by coincidence, as Edwards, the investigator, strolled into SFO's chaotic domestic arrivals hall, Peter Page was rolling his bags through international arrivals. Page was noticed as he left the customs hall by a dark-suited, sunglass-wearing, close-cropped FBI man. He simply couldn't be anything else. Page, on the other hand, looked innocuous in jeans and an oxford shirt, wheeling a trolley containing his suitcase, a canvas bomber jacket and a shoulder bag. The FBI man held up a sign saying simply "Page."

Page nodded as soon as he picked out the sign, and pushed his trolley over to him. "Hi," he said, and put out a hand. "Peter Page."

"Bernie. Bernie Schwartz", replied the FBI man briefly shaking the offered hand. "I have a car ready for you, if you're all set?"

"Sure", said Peter. "Nice to meet you. Yes, let's go." If anyone was watching this, thought Peter, they'd think this was an FBI man meeting a British colleague. Not that anyone would be watching, he thought – hoped. The effect was heightened when Bernie showed Peter to an unmarked but dark and large saloon car waiting illegally at the kerbside, with a similarly sunglass-wearing and close-cropped driver waiting, engine running and parking wardens nervously hovering. "Subtle, it's not", thought Peter as the driver opened the boot – trunk – remotely. He dropped his bags in the cavernous space, closed the lid and stepped into the rear offside door, as Bernie closed the nearside one. The car then eased away from the kerb and headed for downtown San Francisco.

...

If Edwards had been able to see this encounter, he'd possibly have pondered on what was happening. But in fact he was through the BART station and on a train heading to the Embarcadero station, where a ferry for Sausalito departed every hour, and where he was expecting to meet The Priest's "more persuasive" colleague.

...

"OK, Peter," said Bernie, once they were under way. "We've had a briefing from our colleagues in Boston – I gather you're on the trail of some terrorist funds?"

"Well, sort of", answered Peter. "It's originally IRA funds, so that's pretty well right, but it's a bit more complicated than that." He explained the story in outline, and stressed that the main objective was to keep the money away from the IRA, rather than necessarily recover it. "We're working on deterring the senior players back in Belfast – well, Londonderry – from pursuing the money. My job's mainly to check exactly where it is and make sure it stays out of their reach."

"OK, I see. And you think there's a connection to Sausalito?"

"We think so, yes. Joe Best - the guy who stole the money – if we accept that he did actually steal it – he's been using a fake ID and a bank account in Sausalito in the name of Brett Foster. That's our first contact point. I want to find out everything they can tell me about their client. And eventually, to find him in person. That's where I need your help – your authority."

"This guy – Best, yes? He's obviously contravened a number of laws here in the US. We could throw him in jail for quite a time – is that what you want?"

"Well, you'll have to make your own decisions about it, but frankly, that wouldn't be ideal for us, no. We'd prefer to keep this whole thing under the radar – out of the press. If Best gets away with the IRA's money and they can't get it back, we're quite happy. And good luck to him – I doubt he'll do any harm with it. Like you, we could arrest and extradite him for theft of a huge sum of money. But really, we just want the whole thing buried. If the public knew that the IRA were stashing huge sums of money, and could still access it, that would open up a wound that's slowly been healing over. But rest assured, I'll be explaining the potential for charges both here and back home to our Mr. Best - when we find him. He'll need to behave himself from here on."

Bernie nodded. "Yes, I see. Well, we'll be guided by you on this one. I understand that you're booked into a hotel on Union Square. We'll drop you off there now, and collect you to visit the bank in Sausalito tomorrow, if that's good for you?"

Peter was now very keen on a quick nap before an early supper and, he hoped, a decent night's sleep, so he liked that plan." Yes, great. Thanks."

"And I think we should drive to Sausalito." Said Bernie. "This is an FBI car and looks like it. It adds a little weight to our visit – an official presence, if you see what I mean. We need the manager to tell us what we need to know, without having to take him into a more formal interrogation. After all, I don't suppose he's broken any laws – we just need him to back off on his client confidentiality procedures. We can force him, but that takes time and paperwork."

"Makes sense," said Peter. He yawned. "Ah, excuse me. What time in the morning?"

"Let's say 10. There's no point in getting involved with the morning traffic, and that will still get us there before lunchtime. We need to find him at his desk. And you'll need some sleep."

Peter nodded. The car swung into Union Square and pulled up outside the hotel. The driver, who hadn't spoken a word or been introduced, flipped the remote trunk release. One porter rushed to load Peter's luggage onto a cart, as another opened the nearside passenger door. Bernie shook Peter's hand. "OK, see you tomorrow at 10. Sleep well."

...

The investigator rolled his suitcase across the wide road from the BART station to a restaurant alongside the ferry dock and asked for the table booked by "Mr. Dolan." "Yes sir. Your friend is here already. Would you like me to store your case?" asked the desk clerk. "Walter here will show you to your table." Edwards agreed and, leaving his case at the desk followed Walter to the table, in the shade and in the corner.

Dolan, assuming this was him, was sitting with his back to the wall. He was remarkably unremarkable, thought Edwards, who knew a little about how to merge into a crowd. He was average height and build, his hair was unremarkably cut, mousy brown, and he was dressed in Levis and a black shirt. No distinguishing features whatsoever. It would be difficult to describe him again five minutes after you'd seen him, even if you remembered seeing him at all. That was a difficult feat to pull off – it wasn't an accident. He stood as Edwards approached and offered his hand. Edwards shook it. "Mr. Dolan, I presume?"

Dolan smiled. "Yes. And you'll be Mr. Edwards?" An unremarkable generic American accent. Edwards nodded and sat down. Dolan continued: "I thought we should discuss this situation over a late lunch before we make our way over the bay to Sausalito. I've booked us into a small hotel in the town. Goddam expensive for what it is. Anyway, I've booked 2 rooms for 2 nights. That should be enough."

Edwards nodded as Walter brought menus. "A beer – domestic – and a regular burger for me, please", he said, hardly glancing at the menu.

Dolan took a longer look. "Chicken salad and a glass of house white. And a bottle of water. Sparkling. San Pellegrino." Unremarkable again, thought Edwards. He handed the menu back to Walter, who walked away as Dolan turned back to Edwards. "So, I've had a briefing from my people in the 'old country', but I'd appreciate your take on this. How do you read it?"

Edwards gave his assessment of what had happened to the money, his researches into Best and Foster, and said that his reading was that it was now about 90% certain that Best had survived 9/11, absconded with the money and Foster's ID, and was almost at the end of cleansing it.

Dolan nodded. "Why only 90%?"

Edwards paused as Walter brought the drinks. "Well, that's quite a high chance in my book. It's a little short of certainty, but it makes sense that this is what we concentrate on as an investigation. That 10% uncertainty simply means that we have a chance of being wrong, which we mustn't forget."

"OK," said Dolan. "That's your job, I guess – investigating. Mine's dealing with what we – you – discover."

"Mmm," said Edwards, taking a draught of his beer. He thought he'd like to be some distance from that process if the 90% moved up to 100%. The food arrived, and he took the opportunity to break off the conversation as he removed the top bun from his burger and tipped most of the separate bowl of French fries onto the plate. "So, what's the plan tomorrow?"

"After this, we'll jump on the ferry and get to the hotel. We'll find the bank and get our bearings. I've never been to Sausalito, so we should familiarise ourselves with the place. If our man's there we'll find him. It's a small place."

Chapter 44

New Name, New Country

As we taxied over, we could make out a black Mercedes in a corner of the apron, with an attendant, probably the driver, waiting by the rear doors. "That's the Minister's car," said Naomi, looking out of one of the windows. The plane taxied over towards the Mercedes, and as we drew nearer I could make out what looked like the same representation of the flag on the driver's door as on 'our' tail fin. "We'll drop you close by, and the car will take you straight to his office", said Naomi.

So, the steps were lowered, we said our fond farewells and thank-you's to Naomi, walked down the steps and got into the back of the Merc. There seemed to be no need for formalities, as we swept out of the airport through security gates, being saluted as we went – I couldn't help but reply with a semi-regal wave - and down the palm-tree lined roads to Government House.

The 20 minute journey took us into the gardens of the 2-story colonial building, and stopped at the bottom of the short flight of steps up to the colonnaded entrance. An immaculately-uniformed policemen escorted us out of the car and up the steps. He handed us over to a sort of commissionaire, who greeted us in the double-height reception lobby with a smile and "Good day, gentlemen - this way, if you please." He escorted us down a carpeted corridor with large, open windows and potted palms into a well-appointed L-shaped office. That's well-appointed in terms of more palms in pots, a well-stocked bookcase and a large pedestal desk, with 2 armchairs set out for visitors and a swivel office chair behind it. But no Minister - unless he was hiding in the L-shaped area, which we couldn't see. "Please be seated, gentlemen. The Minister will be with you shortly", said the commissionaire, and left us to it.

The door opened again almost at once. "Peter Garrido! How nice to see you, old friend. And this is your client – Joe, yes?" This came from a large and smiling black man in a superb lightweight dark suit, light blue shirt, silk tie, and gold cufflinks on his outstretched arms. He enveloped the much more diminutive Garrido in a hug and slapped him on the back. Almost at the same time, he reached out and shook my hand, which I couldn't actually recall offering.

Like any good politician, he dominated the room. He took his seat behind the desk and rang a small bell, which seemed slightly out of place. It worked, however, and a small middle-aged lady appeared in the doorway. "Ah, Muriel", said Fernando D'Souza (for it was him), "Tea for our guests, I think. Yes?" Garrido and I nodded. "Thank you", I said, as I made a determined effort to appear as if meetings like this were an everyday occurrence for me.

"Good, good", said D'Souza. He smiled at me. "Peter, Joe. Welcome to Provo, as we call this island, and to the Turks and Caicos Islands. Now, I hope you enjoyed our little aeroplane? Did you have a pleasant flight?"

"Yes, Fernando, very nice indeed. Thanks for arranging that", answered Garrido. "And for arranging this transaction for my client here", indicating me, of course.

"Yes, a very enjoyable experience. And our thanks to the lovely Naomi. She looked after us very well." I added.

"Ah, Naomi. Did she tell you she's the President's daughter?" She hadn't of course. So, making a pass might have been a very bad call. "Anyway, it's our pleasure. And my thanks to you, Joe, for so generously agreeing to support our new children's hospital wing. Would you like to see it?" Without waiting for an answer, he leapt up and walked over to the alcove that formed the rest of the L-shape. "Come, you can see. We have a model here." There was a neat architect's model set out on a low table. "So, the new wing is here; this is the existing building on that side. This has been a campaign of mine for some time." He looked up to see Muriel setting a tea-tray on his desk, and waited until she left and closed the door behind her.

"My wife and I were not blessed with children – or we have not been so far." He smiled briefly. "But Muriel had a son. Justin was his name. He was just 5 years old when he became ill. We had no specialist facility for children, and no experience of diagnosing childhood illnesses specifically, or treating children as a specialised skill. We tried to treat him in the main hospital, of course, but by the time we worked out that he'd developed a blood cancer, it was too late. We flew him to the US – to Miami - but to no avail, sadly. Muriel was devastated, of course – still is, really. And I vowed to build this special wing to improve the way we treat our sick children like Justin. Your kind donation, Joe, will pay to build this area here." He pointed to the new area on the plan. "Once it's actually built, we're optimistic that we can equip and staff it from other donations. But it needs to exist – in bricks and mortar – first, you see."

This was an impressive story, and quite convincing. Of course, I recalled that it was to be named after him - the 'Fernando D'Souza Wing' - not after Justin, Muriel's unfortunate son. But that was none of my business. "Well", I said, "I'm delighted to be able to enable this. And of course, very grateful that you can help me to start my new life as a citizen of this country. Which looks delightful, by the way."

"Oh, yes", replied D'Souza, all smiles again. "So, let's have our tea and deal with the paperwork. Then I'll arrange for you to have a short tour of the island while we produce your new passport. As you know, I've arranged for you to fly back to the Caymans on a scheduled flight. I'm sorry, but we need the jet for the President this evening."

"No, please don't apologise", I said. "It's very generous of you anyway, and we really enjoyed our taste of the high life. Quite an experience." Garrido nodded in agreement.

"My pleasure", he replied. "Now, I'm sure Peter has the papers we need, and I have a passport application all ready for you to complete and sign. I'll ask Muriel to take your photo for the passport, if that's OK?"

The whole process, including taking a photo against a plain section of the wall, completing the passport application and, of course, writing a cheque to D'Souza's hospital fund for $500,000 in my new name on the new bank account for my new company, took a little under half an hour. I checked with Garrido that all the papers were correctly signed, and he nodded his approval. D'Souza held out his hand to me.

"Welcome to your new identity, Mr Joe Baldwin, and to the Turks and Caicos Islands", he smiled. I hope you'll be happy here, wherever you decide to settle. I understand from Peter that you'll be bringing your sailboat to begin with? Perhaps you should start your tour with a look at our marina? My driver is at your disposal for two hours – then your passport will be ready."

He slapped Garrido on the back again and saw us to the door, where he signalled for the same commissionaire – or whatever he was, who saw us to the steps and back into the Mercedes.

The tour of the island was much enhanced by the driver's droll but informed commentary, and the fact that this was a truly beautiful, unpretentious place. Garrido pointed out a rather imposing ex-colonial building in the main town square. "That's the bank where the funds are held. We have time to call in if you'd like to?" There was no need to visit the money, I decided, but it was useful to know where it was for future reference. I said as much.

After leaving the small town – the capital – we visited the pretty marina. In fact, our driver told us, there was another marina, further away from the town, but this one looked functional as well as convenient. We stopped the car and I took a little time to stroll along the boardwalk and look into the chandler, where I bought a series of large and smaller-scale charts and maps, and the two or three small cafes and bars. There were a number of sailboats like Mystere and some motor cruisers moored on the jetties. It looked like a smaller version of the marina at Sausalito. A perfect place to stay while Sally and I looked for a beach house. Helpfully, there were a couple of Real

Estate agencies, and I picked up one or two sample particulars. Really nice places didn't look ridiculously expensive, and it looked like Sally and I would enjoy house-hunting.

We also explored the nearby coves and beaches, and our driver pointed out some local bars away from the tourist areas. But, to me, this was hardly an over-developed tourist trap. There was a genuine local feel to it. I thought Sally would love it, and we'd be happy to spend a lot of time here, not simply out of duty as a new resident. I wondered how long this place could stay an unspoiled island paradise. I have to admit that I could also see a significant potential increase in property prices in due course.

All too soon, our tour brought us back to Government House. The same commissionaire opened the car door and escorted us up the steps into the main lobby, where he asked us to wait a moment.

"Ah! My friends!" We heard the minister's voice just before we saw him, coming down the main staircase with a beaming smile – and with a passport in his hand. "I hope you like our lovely island? And your new home?"

I couldn't help but smile back at him. "Yes, I did. I'm looking forward to returning and setting up home here. You have a beautiful country. A hidden gem."

He grinned back. "Ah, yes. Hidden. We're working on making it a little less secret paradise. Less secret, that is. Not less paradise." He laughed out loud at this. "All very upmarket, of course. You might like to look at investing in that. Anyway, ..." He held out my new passport.

I took it and looked at the photo and the formal detail pages, with my picture and the name of Joe Baldwin. "Thank you very much", I said, smiling nearly as broadly as the minister. "I'm very grateful for your help."

"As I am for yours", answered the minister. Please do hurry back, and if I can help you with anything, you know where to find me. I hope you can come to the opening of the children's wing. And if I see any opportunities to invest in that real estate development ..."

"Yes – please let me know", I said, mainly due to his infectious enthusiasm, but partly from a thought that this could actually make sense.

"And Peter – so nice to see you again. I'm sorry it was such a brief visit. You must visit us again. Do some fishing perhaps?"

Garrido smiled and shook his friend's hand. "I'd like that, and yes, it was good to see you looking so well."

"Indeed. Well, as I say, I've booked you on your flight and told the airline to treat you well. It's probably time for you to set off to the airport now. Of course, the car will take you, if you're happy with that?"

We said it was, of course. We shook hands once again and got back into the Mercedes. We were in the airport within the hour, and, being first class, with the ministry as the ticket purchaser, and of course my new name on the booking, we were installed in our seats within another hour. The return flight, nice as it was, was something of an anti-climax compared to the outward one, but it was a little faster, and we were back into Cayman by 10PM. Garrido was taking a different taxi, so as we shook hands at the conclusion of our business, it stuck me that I should thank him in a more specific way.

"Peter", I said. "This whole process has been remarkably simple for me, including today's trip and my new identity. You've done a great job – I'm very grateful."

"No need to thank me – you've paid me very well and it's been a pleasure working for you."

"Well, I think there is, actually. I'd like to celebrate the end of the process. Look, would you and your wife join me for dinner here tomorrow evening? It's too late for me to book a flight tomorrow, so I'll be here another night anyway. I think the main restaurant is rather good. How about it?"

Garrido smiled and agreed. He had indeed been well paid, but this was a personal thank-you, which I felt he deserved, especially after today. We arranged to meet at 7 PM tomorrow. It had been a spectacular and memorable day – a day I was looking forward to describing to Sally. But frankly, I was too tired for that lengthy conversation, and once I was back at the hotel, I went straight to my room, to bed and quickly to sleep.

Chapter 45

Looking for Joe … or Brett

Deposited by the ferry in Sausalito Marina, Dolan and Edwards looked in vain for a taxi rank. Giving up, Dolan asked directions to their hotel from the ticket office. It sounded quite close, round a corner behind the main street, so he and Edwards set off to walk. 10 minutes later, they were outside a small unremarkable 1960's motel. In another 20 minutes, having booked in and dropped their bags, the 2 men were walking along the main street, with the marina on their right and shops and bars on the left.

"What bank was it? California something?" asked Dolan.

"Yes – California Savings and Checking" replied Edwards. "I have the address, in fact – I looked it up before I left the UK. It's on this street."

Dolan nodded. "OK, well let's look for it. It shouldn't be hard to find. Do you have a number?"

"I'll check", said Edwards, reaching into his pocket for his notebook."

"Ah. No need", said Dolan. "I think that's it, there." There was a hanging sign in front of a modern glass building about 50 yards ahead.

Edwards looked. "Wow, you must have good eyesight. I can't read that from here", said Edwards, but as they approached he saw that Dolan was right. The bank was glass-fronted, with investment rates and other blandishments on posters in the windows. It was closed for the day.

Dolan looked at his watch. "Just gone 6 o'clock. Later than I thought. Anyway, we know where it is now." He looked at the 'Hours of Business' notice on the door. "They open at 9:30 in the morning. Let's be here, ready for them."

Dolan looked back down the street, the way they'd come. "OK, I think we should have ourselves a drink. Maybe talk to some of the locals. Do we have a photo of Best? Or Foster, come to that?"

"No, unfortunately. From the visit my colleague made to his office I have a bit of a description, but nothing exceptional. Average height, weight, etc. White, brown hair ..." He looked at Dolan. "But that could apply to you, or millions of other people."

"Sure. Ok, let's see whether anyone knows Joe Best. Or Brett Foster. If he's been living here for a few months, he'll have been eating and drinking somewhere. So we might as well do the same. See whether anyone recognises the name. Or names.""

They turned round and walked back towards the dock and marina area in the late afternoon sunshine. Edwards looked at the smart shops, the marina and the bright blue sky, and mused that this was a great place to lie low.

The first bar they came across was a wine bar called 'Barrel and Bottle'. There was a serving counter with stools and a handful of tables made from old barrels with the same stools. They approached the bar and looked at the range of wines available by the glass from a gas cabinet. Edwards hadn't seen this before, but Dolan seemed to recognise it. "The bottles are opened and the wine is poured, and a squirt of Nitrogen is added, to keep the oxygen away from the wine, so the rest doesn't spoil."

The Bartender smiled and nodded. "Yes, that's it. Have you seen this before? It's fairly new to us."

"Yes – in New York, last month", replied Dolan. "Very effective. I'll have a glass of the Chablis." He sat at a bar stool and pointed at the wine list entry, then passed it over to Edwards, who took the seat beside him. "Sancerre for me, please", he said, and watched as the Bartender poured a glass of each and then squirted a blast from a handgun connected to a gas cylinder under the display of bottles.

The Bartender set the glasses on the counter and Dolan put a $20 bill down. "Keep the change", he said. This would appeal to a friend of ours – Brett Foster. Has he been in here at all?"

The Bartender looked into space for a minute. "Don't know the name. Does he live here?"

"I think so. Haven't seen him for a year or two", answered Dolan. "We used to work together."

Edwards chipped in. "How about my pal Joe Best? I'm pretty sure he still lives here."

"Hmm – no, don't recognise that name either. If you find them, send them in", he smiled.

Thwarted, they sipped their wine in silence. The Bartender moved to serve some customers on the tables, and Dolan murmured "Drawn blank here. Let's move on."

They drank the rest of their wine as quickly as discretion permitted, said their farewells and moved off down the street. The next bar was livelier. The sign over the door said "Daisy's", and the country rock from the jukebox went well with the timber-clad interior. They approached the bar, where a tall redhead and a smaller, more rounded brunette were busying themselves rearranging some bottles behind the bar. The brunette turned round and smiled. "Good evening, gentlemen. What's it to be?"

"Two beers, please. Do you have Rolling Rock?"

"We sure do", she smiled. "Coming up." She produced the bottles from the refrigerated cabinet under the bar, which gave the men a tempting glimpse of what might be inside her "Daisy's" T-shirt. She opened the bottles and placed them on the bar top. "You need glasses?"

Edwards was momentarily embarrassed until Dolan said "No, we're good", and took a swig from the bottle. He put the bottle down on the bar top and smiled at her. "Nice place. We're wondering whether we might bump into a friend of ours. Brett Foster. Does he come in here?"

"Oh, Brett? Yes, sometimes. With his girlfriend. I think he lives in the marina. On a boat, you know. Mystery or something ..."

The redhead interrupted her: "Joanie, could I have a quick word?" This was supported by a fierce stare from what looked like a fierce redhead. The two girls disappeared into a back room behind the bar. Edwards and Dolan shared a glance. Clearly, they had struck a nerve.

"Hmm. We seem to be getting somewhere", murmured Edwards. The girls emerged from the back room and Joanie set off round the tables, collecting glasses and bottles. The redhead remained behind the bar. She didn't see inclined to share any more information, so the men took their beers to a far table. Edwards took a glug of his beer. "Seems we have a lead, yes?"

Dolan nodded. "Yes. And the redhead's protecting him for some reason." He turned to glance back at the bar. "Maybe there's something between them. We might be able to use that."

"Well, if she's not the girlfriend, she certainly knows him. Or her. Anyway ..." Edwards was facing the bar, where the redhead was serving a customer, and took a long look. "She won't take a lot of finding again if we need to press her for some details."

Dolan nodded and finished his beer. "OK, let's take a look at this marina, eh? See if we can find this 'Mystery' boat of his."

He drained his beer, put his bottle on the table and led the way out of the bar and across the road to the marina. They walked along the shoreline, but there was no way to get onto the jetties without a key to the gates at each access point. The names on the nearest boats were easy to see, but as they stretched away towards the bay, they were hidden by the neighbouring craft. None of the visible boats was called "Mystery", or anything like it. They turned at the end and walked towards a café or bar at the ferry terminal end of the run of jetties.

Edwards noticed an office at the rear, past the chandlery and souvenirs, and walked towards it. "Can I help you, sir?" asked a diminutive lady near the shop's till.

Taken slightly by surprise, Edwards and turned to face her. "Oh. Erm, yes. I'm looking for a boat in the marina. Belongs to a friend of ours. Brett Foster? Boat's called Mystery, I think?"

"Oh, Brett. No, it's Mystere, in fact. And it's not his – he just lives on it. Belongs another fella."

"Ah. Who is that? Is he here now?"

"Ooh, no. He let it to Brett. And I know Brett's away right now."

"Ah, thanks. Do you know where?"

"Not really. You need to ask George. The harbourmaster. That's his office, so you were going the right way. But he's finished for the day now. Might be back later for a drink. Might not."

"I see. So, erm, when does he get here in the morning?"

"Oh, quite early. Sailors come and go quite early, and there'll probably be some arrive tonight – he'll need to collect the dues. About 8, I should think."

"Ah. 8 o'clock. Lovely. Thank you very much."

As they left the shop and café, Dolan, who had been listening carefully as he browsed the charts, fittings and accessories, made a decision. "OK, forget the bank for now. This is probably a much better lead. We'll get here at 8 and see what we can squeeze out of him. Let's get back to the eating and drinking places. I think I saw an Italian restaurant just past that last bar. Fancy a pizza or something?"

Edwards agreed. It was a few hours since their late lunch, and a beer and a pizza did sound attractive. And the Italian restaurant was in a very prominent location, so it was almost inconceivable that Foster/Best hadn't been there – probably more than once.

Entering the restaurant, the two men were greeted by a pretty chestnut-haired girl with a fetching smile. "Good evening, gentlemen. Table for two? Did you have a reservation?"

They agreed that this was what they wanted, and confessed to not having booked. The girl picked up two menus from a pile on the desk and showed them to a corner table and placed a menu in front of each of them. "Maggie will take your food order. Can I place a drinks order for you?"

They ordered a beer each, and settled back to read the menu and take stock of the location. Edwards looked around the restaurant and then out of the window. The restaurant was starting to get busy, even this early in the evening, and the street outside the window was busy with both tourists and locals, as far as he could tell. "I'd be amazed if our man didn't eat here – if not regularly, then certainly much more than once", he said, as they studied the pizza section of the menu.

Maggie, who had clearly once been a classic West Coast girl, and still had the big hair, white smile and slender figure, and the dress code - faded denim shirt & shorts - of the late '80s, brought their beers and asked whether they had made their decision. They agreed that they had, and ordered one 4-Seasons and one pepperoni pizza. Maggie wrote the order down briskly, and moved off before they could ask after their friend Joe, or Brett.

In the 15 minutes it took to produce the pizzas, they had both drunk half of their beers, and after setting the pizzas down, Maggie asked whether they needed more. Dolan ordered two more, and asked "We hoped we'd find an old friend of ours here: Brett Foster? Do you know him? I'm sure Brett told us he'd moved here a while ago."

Maggie shook her head. "Oh, I'm sorry, I've just moved here from LA. I'll see whether Sally knows him, if you like?" They thanked her and started on their pizzas.

As Maggie passed the reception lectern, she spoke to Sally without stopping. "Sally, have you a minute? I need a word. Just let me deliver these beers and come to the end of the bar there. Where these two can't see us."

Sally was greeting a party of four. "OK, I'll just seat this party – give me a minute."

Maggie delivered the beers. "Sally's busy," she said. "I'll talk to her in a moment. Brett Foster, yes?"

"That's right, yes," replied Edwards. "No rush." He smiled and poured his beer.

Maggie waited for Sally at the corner of the bar, hidden from view by a partition from Dolan and Edwards' table. Having seated her party of 4 and provided menus, Sally joined her. "What's up?" she asked.

"Those two guys who came in earlier. They were asking about Brett – did I know him? They said they were his friends."

"Brett? Specifically Brett Foster?" asked Sally.

"Yes. Brett Foster. They said they knew he'd moved here. I just got a bad vibe about it ... I told them I'm new in town."

Sally sat down on the bar stool. "Thanks, Maggie. Thanks for talking to me first ..."

"Sally, you look dreadful. Are you OK?" Sally had gone very pale. Maggie waved the barman over. "Here, give Sally some water or something."

Sally drank some of the water and took several deep breaths. "OK, no big deal." She drank some more water. "Tell them I said that, erm ... that I think we did have a customer of that name, living on one of the boats. But he left recently. No forwarding address." She paused. "I think they're bad men, Maggie."

"OK," said Maggie. "Don't worry – you'd better get back to your station. I'll tell them that when I clear their table. Try to calm down – don't let them think you're flustered. I'll see that they get through here as quickly as I can."

A large party – a family of 6 – came into the lobby, and Sally stood up to go and deal with them. She touched Maggie's hand. "Thanks", and winked. By the time she greeted them, her smile was back and she was calm efficiency again.

The restaurant filled up, and Maggie and the other waitress were soon at full stretch. By the time Dolan and Edwards had finished their pizzas, and Maggie was collecting the plates, it was easy for her to cut the chat to a minimum. "Your friend Brett? Apparently he was living in the marina. On a boat. He was quite a regular for a while. But Sally says he's left now – she doesn't know where. Maybe he'll be back – who knows? These boat people tend to keep moving." By now she had the plates piled up and was ready to take them back to the kitchen. "I'll bring you the check, yes?"

"Yes, thank you", replied Edwards. Maggie smiled and moved off. "Not convincing, somehow," he added. "Look, everyone else has been offered dessert, or coffee. They want us away."

Dolan looked around and nodded. "Yes, you're right. And she and – what, Sally? – they had a discussion at the bar. Out of sight of us. There's something going on here."

Edwards nodded. "Yes. This Sally girl – she's clearly connected somehow. She's the girlfriend, maybe?" Maggie brought the check, and Edwards put cash and a tip on the plate, taking the check as his receipt. “Thanks,” he said. “Keep the change.” Maggie smiled a thank you, and took the plate and the notes.

“Ok,” said Dolan. “Let’s get out of here. We’ll get back to the hotel and send an email to the office in Derry. It’s what – very early morning there – we might get a steer from them by the morning our time, but we should plan to catch the harbourmaster first thing. This Sally girl isn’t going anywhere – she’s clearly part of the set-up here. We can come back for her tomorrow if we need to. I think we need to complete the picture – the harbourmaster and then possibly the bank. The harbourmaster is just a normal conversation – let’s hope he’s suitably indiscreet.”

Dolan pondered as they shrugged into their jackets. “But we’ll need to use different techniques on this Sally – and probably the bank manager”, he murmured. “And there’s that redhead in the second bar ... That’s raising things to another level - more complicated, so we should try to avoid that if we can.” Edwards was happy to agree with that, and they both made for the door.

As they passed Sally’s lectern, they took the opportunity to look at her with slightly more than a passing glance, to fix her face in their minds. Sally tried to distract herself, but she was fully aware of their interest. She felt she needed a drink. It was getting late, and there were no more bookings. She asked Maggie to keep an eye out for late arrivals and left early, walking round to Daisy’s.

As she approached the bar, she was relieved to see Red behind the bar. “Hi Red. I need a martini, please. Strong.”

Red nodded. “Oh, hi Sally. I was hoping to see you anyway.” She mixed, shook and poured the martini and gestured to an empty corner high table. “A quick word?” Sally nodded. Red grabbed a bottle of beer and they moved over to sit on the stools. Sally drank half of the martini at a gulp and put her head in her hands. “Busy night?” asked Red.

"It's not that. Two guys came in, asking about Brett. I don't know why, but they didn't seem quite right – it wasn't the casual enquiry about an old friend they made out. I'm worried."

Red took a pull at the beer. "Oh, I see. Well, I was going to tell you that they were here as well. I was going to call on you at the restaurant. They asked after Brett, and also mentioned 'Joe'. Joanie told him Brett was living in the marina – a boat called 'Mystery' – before I could shut her up."

Sally drank the other half of the Martini at a gulp. "God. I think I need another one ... please?"

"Sure", said Red, and walked back to the bar. Sally checked her watch. 10 o'clock, just gone. What time was it where Joe was? 2 hours ahead, she thought. Should she call him?

Putting a new, equally strong martini in front of Sally, Red said "OK, You're obviously spooked. I know you and Brett – or is it Joe? – have got pretty close, and he's been flying in and out of – where, the Caymans, was it? – and you've been with him on holiday. So, what's the story? How can I help?"

Sally sipped her martini this time. "It's best you know as little as possible, I think. Safer. But Joe – his name is Joe really – is one of the good guys. He's ... he's come across some money – a lot of money – by accident, and it belonged to some bad people. These are probably those bad people. Or they're working for them. Joe's been making sure the money is moved, sort of ... out of the way, so that they can't get it. He's away now, and I think he's finished doing that. He's probably coming back tomorrow. But as I say, it's best that you don't know too much – don't become involved ..."

Red nodded and took another pull at her beer. "That suits me, babe. But I'm bothered about you, not Brett – Joe, then. Are you safe from these people?"

"I don't know – I hope so. Joe did say something like this might happen. I think I ought to call him. What do you think?"

"I think you should do whatever will make you feel safer. And Joe might have some ideas on that, I guess."

Sally was calming down. Two strong martinis in 20 minutes couldn't fail to have an effect, and Red always seemed to Sally to have a store of strength and pragmatism, which she was able to pass on when needed. "Yes," she said, as she finished her martini, "I'll call him. It's not too late. And he ought to know these guys are here. He's due to fly back tomorrow."

"Use the phone in the back room here," said Red. "Then we can talk again."

Chapter 46

Midnight Call

When my cellphone chirruped in the middle of the night, I had just dropped off to sleep after a very sociable and enjoyable dinner with Garrido and his pretty wife. She'd been excited about the new bungalow they had agreed to buy, and wanted to thank me for making this possible. I told her it wasn't me she had to thank. "It's your husband's skill and experience that's made it possible, not my – what – generosity. He did a great job – easily exceeded my expectations."

Garrido was clearly happy to have his skills praised to his wife, but I refrained from saying that some of the money was a reflection of the possible danger from the – rightful? – owners of this money. Both Garrido and I were aware of this, although we didn't discuss it tonight. We said a fond, and possibly final, farewell in good time – I had an early flight to catch and he had a busy day – as did she. I'd lingered over a brandy but I was in bed and fast asleep by half-eleven.

Anyway, when Sally interrupted my sleep to tell me about the mysterious and inquisitive strangers, it wasn't a complete surprise. That's not to say that I knew exactly what to do about it. The first thing was to reassure Sally. I asked her to describe the two men. "Their accents: were they Irish, or American?"

"I don't think they were Irish. One was American for sure. I think the other one was English. I didn't speak to them directly. Well, only to show them to a table and take a drinks order."

"OK," I said, "Keep calm. What do you think they know?"

"Erm, well I told Maggie to tell them that you – Brett – had been living in the marina, but that you'd left now. I think Joanie in Daisy's said you lived on a boat called 'Mystery'. But then Red shut her up."

"OK. Give me a minute to think. I'm on a fairly early flight tomorrow, as you know ..."

"Joe, am I safe here? I know you did tell me there might be some danger, and I said I was cool with that, but this is a bit close ..."

"It depends on whether they think they know where I am. We need to get them out of Sausalito, for your sake, and following a trail away from there. Hold on ... Look, I have an idea ... You've got Mystere ready to travel down to LA haven't you? Is the Escalade loaded? Are you free tomorrow? I need you to do a few things to set that trail."

Sally said she had, it was, and she was, and I explained what I wanted her to do. I assured her, as far as I could, that this would flush these guys out and off on a chase away from Sausalito and San Francisco. It would be ideal if she could go over to the harbour bar now, and see whether George was still installed in his usual corner, and then over to the bank first thing in the morning ... She said she'd go straight to the harbour bar. Chances were that he'd still be there.

After we rang off, with Sally reassured, in part simply because we had a plan, I looked up Ken White's number. I checked the time in San Francisco, decided that it was unusual but not unreasonable to call him, and dialled his number. He was somewhat terse when he answered, but he wasn't in bed, and when I told him what I wanted to do, he was quickly amenable.

It took me a while to get back to sleep, but not because I was concerned about Sally – or not mainly because of that. I was reviewing what I'd arranged with Sally and looking for anything I might have missed. Eventually I fell asleep, although I'd have to say that I'd had better nights' sleep.

...

In the morning, after making a quick phone call to Sausalito from an airport payphone, I boarded the plane in good time, using my frequent flyer advantage as well as a Business Class ticket. I spent the flight back to SFO dozing and reviewing my plan, and hoping that Sally had been able to talk to George. I must have dozed more than I thought, because in what seemed less time than usual, we were buckling up for landing. Soon afterwards, I was heading for the Embarcadero and the meeting I'd set up.

Chapter 47

FBI Calling

"Sorry to interrupt, sir," said the secretary to the Sausalito branch of California Saving and Checking. There's a gentleman from the FBI asking for you. Well, for the manager. Two gentlemen, in fact."

This wasn't a regular occurrence in the California Savings and Checking Bank – certainly not in the Sausalito branch. "The FBI? Are you sure?"

"Yes, of course I am", she replied. "He showed me his ID and gave me his business card – here – and the car's parked outside. A big black cruiser. He looks the part, anyway."

The manager looked at the card. "Hmm. Well, best not keep the FBI waiting. Let's see him. Show him through, please, Cheryl."

Cheryl went back to the informal banking hall, where Page and Schwartz were waiting, looking slightly out of place and slightly off-putting, and gestured to the manager's office. "This way, please, gentlemen."

The Manager stood to receive his visitors and showed them to a sofa and coffee table. He offered a hand to shake "I'm the manager here. Ross. And you are ...?"

"My name is Schwartz, and this is my colleague from the UK ..."

"Peter Page", interrupted Peter. "How do you do?" They shook hands as Schwartz gave Peter an irritated glance. He intended to run this meeting, and was not planning to be particularly friendly. That wasn't the FBI way. They took the offered seats anyway.

Ross looked at his watch "Gentlemen, I wasn't expecting you, and I have a meeting at – 11AM. That gives us half an hour – will that be sufficient?"

Schwartz took over before Page could speak. "It should be, if you co-operate. We're interested in one of your clients – name of Foster. Brett Foster. What can you tell us about him?"

"Well, I know you've shown Cheryl your ID – may I see that?" Schwartz showed him the badge and replaced it in his pocket, showing the holstered pistol accidentally-on-purpose.

"OK, well, without a formal warrant I can't disclose very much, as you'll be aware. However, there isn't much to tell you. I know Mr Foster – he's not a typical customer. He opened an account about 6 months ago with a cash deposit and left some documents in a safety deposit box. He opened that two or three times and replaced it, adding cash to his account each time, as I recall. He's run the account quite normally otherwise, and we've had no reason to worry about him. We have his money in the account, and he draws on it as needed. As I say, he's topped the account up with cash once or twice, and made some cash withdrawals and payments with his card. That's all I can tell you, really."

"I see," said Schwartz. "I should tell you that his enquiry is connected to the 9/11 event. What ID did he use to open the account? What address?"

Ross thought for a moment. "I assume a driver's licence. In fact as I recall, he was staying on a boat in the marina. It'll be on the file."

"Could we see his transactions? And could we have a look at the documents he deposited with you?"

"Not really. Not without a warrant. I can't really see him as a terrorist, from my single meeting with him." replied Ross. There was a short silence while Schwartz gave him a cold stare. "Well, I can show you a list of the transactions, but I can't let you remove them - or copy them, and I certainly can't let you look at the contents of the deposit box. I'm sure you realise that."

"Can you ask for that, then? And do you have records of when he accessed the deposit box?"

"OK", said Ross. "But that's as far as I'm allowed to go without a warrant. Possibly a little further. These rules cut both ways, as you'll realise." He walked over to the door. "Cheryl, a moment, please?" He asked her for the file on Brett Foster and they waited in silence.

Cheryl came into the office and closed the door. "Here's the file, Mr. Ross. In fact, the account was closed today and the contents of the safe removed – both first thing this morning. So the file was already out on the clerks' desk."

"Oh?" replied Ross. "Well, Mr. Schwartz, here you are. It's still subject to the rules, even as a closed account, so you can't take it, but … well, take a look."

The file showed a series of cash deposits and withdrawals by cash, transfer and card, with a final cash transfer to an account in the Turks & Caicos Islands. The account was then closed, with a zero balance. There was a record of deposit box access, on a separate sheet. "Who authorised the final transfer? The closure?" Schwartz asked.

"That's not shown here – it was probably a passworded phone instruction, since we don't have a signed docket. Mr. Foster had a phone banking password."

"OK, and the deposit box? Who removed that?"

"I'll have to ask the staff. But, clearly, an authorised person in possession of the key."

"Clearly. So, can we get a description?"

Cheryl had remained in the office. Ross looked up. "Cheryl, could you ask whoever looked after - whoever took the box - to step in here?"

Cheryl nodded and left the room to another silence. Page studied the deposits and withdrawals, especially of the cash. From memory, the card transactions matched his recollection of the travel activity. He compared this with the record of access to the deposit safe, and back to the card usage. He felt sure that payment for the trip to Zurich and the removal of the box matched quite well.

Cheryl returned with a young clerk. "You wanted to know about the deposit box removal, sir?" said the worried-looking clerk.

"Yes", said Ross. "Don't worry, you're not in trouble. Please describe who this was, and what happened."

"Well, it was a young lady – well, a lady – and she had the key. I escorted her into the strong room, opened our lock and left her alone to open the customer lock and do whatever she wanted to do. As the rules say, sir ..."

"Yes, I know. As I say, you're not in trouble. What then?"

"The lady came out of the vault with a large briefcase. Well a sort of suitcase. Metal – aluminum, I think. She said that was all she wanted and the deposit box was no longer needed. Then she gave me back the customer key."

"And left?" asked Schwartz.

"Yes – she left at once. With this suitcase or whatever. I took the key back and entered it on the record."

Schwartz nodded. "Can you describe this woman? How was she behaving – did she seem nervous?"

"Erm ... mid-thirties, dark blonde hair, medium build and height. Local, I think. And no, she seemed to be in a hurry, but quite calm."

"OK. That's all. Thank you."

Ross nodded and the clerk left. Schwartz looked at Page. "Any more questions?"

Page nodded. "Yes - I see the address from the drivers licence is shown here – in San Diego – La Jolla, in fact – but his local address for correspondence is a boat in the marina. "Mystere." Isn't that uncommon?"

"Well, yes, but not unheard of", replied Ross. "We've had to tighten our procedures up recently - since that time, just a few months back. But at that time, no – well, not what you'd call irregular. Can I help you any further? Only my next appointment ..."

Page paused for thought. "No, not now. Thanks for your time. We'll probably be applying for a warrant to take these records – or copy them. But I don't think we can do much more now. Thank you for your help, Mr. Ross." He stood, which prompted the others to stand.

Back outside, standing by the car, Page summed up. "So, this very morning, our man closed the account, transferring the remaining funds to a Turks account, and an accomplice removed whatever was in the safety deposit box, and this is now a dead end, until we can examine the records."

Schwartz shook his head. "Well, not entirely. Let's have a look at this boat – Mystery, was it?"

"Mystere", replied Page. "Yes, let's do that."

Chapter 48

Embarcadero

I emerged from BART at the Embarcadero stop and hailed a cab on the street. Not that I minded walking a mile to the dock I needed, but dragging a roller suitcase all that way was tedious. Reaching the wharf I was looking for, I paid the cab off and looked for Mystere. There she was, 50 yards away, tied up close to the dock entrance, with Ken White in the cockpit. Sally was pacing nervously on the dockside. When she spotted me, she ran over and threw her arms around me, almost knocking me over. “Oh, Joe, thank God you’re here.” She hugged me close and then stood back and thumped my chest. “That was scary – last night. I hope you’ve got rid of them, you creep.” She was somewhere between laughing and crying. I hugged her again.

“I hope so, too. Did you get to George?”

“Yes. I just caught him. I told him what to say if anyone asked. He’s OK with that. And I went to the bank first thing this morning. The case is on the boat.” We looked across to Mystere, where Ken was messing about with ropes and sails.

He waved at us. “Hi, kids!” He seemed happy, anyway. Which was as it should be – he was about to receive a healthy pile of cash and a bank transfer.

“Right, and you’ve put some clean clothes in there for me?”

“Yes, you’re all set. Your suitcase and the bank one are in the big bedroom. Stateroom.”

“Great. And you?”

“Yep. The restaurant knew I was likely to leave at short notice. They didn’t think it would be as short as this, but they’re OK with it. I said I’d be back before long to collect my wages and say goodbye properly.”

"No, I mean - are you OK with all this? Are you still scared?"

"Well, yes, I am, but I'm a lot better now we're actually dealing with it. And we'll be away from Sausalito for a while, won't we?"

"Yes, for a few weeks at least. And I'm pretty sure they'll be away from there shortly anyway. I hope we don't see them again, but I can't be sure, to be honest."

"No, I guess not. But we'll be able to deal with that, won't we? I mean, we'll be together most of the time. And we'll see them coming – I've seen them as well as them seeing me. I'm OK."

"Well, good then. Is that the Escalade?" There was a huge gold SUV parked across the road. Sally nodded. "Bloody hell, it's huge. But you got all the stuff in?"

"Yes. The back seats are folded down, though – it's a two-seater now. There's a blanket over the load, but the windows are tinted – quite dark. I'll be sure to park safe, but I'm sure it's secure."

"Right. Well done. Now, you know where we'll be meeting in LA?"

"Yes – the Marriott dockside. I'll probably be there before you. I have a two-day programme at the uni in San Jose, then I'll drive down. I might do it in a day if I set off in good time."

I hugged her again and we walked up onto Mystere. Ken shook my hand and said "Hi, Joe. Ready for our sailing trip?" I smiled and nodded, but before I could answer, Sally took me through to the big bedroom and showed me my clothes suitcase and the familiar aluminium case.

I opened that one and checked the contents, which were now just the balance of the cash – still a substantial sum, packed as before in hundred-thousand-dollar bundles. I took a bundle and opened it, taking out what looked like ten thousand, and gave it to Sally. "Keep this for emergencies. You never know." Sally stared at the wad of cash and jammed it into her jeans pocket. "OK. I don't think I've ever had so much cash in my pockets. I'll stash it in the locker in the Caddy." I closed the case again and we joined Ken on deck.

"OK," I said. "LA, here we come. How's the weather looking, Ken?"

"Pretty good. The wind's perfect, and the tidal run's there, according to the gazette – and George agrees. We should have a great run."

All seemed set fair, then. "Right, so let's get under way. Ken, we should complete the sale paperwork here, before we leave, but Sally can set off to San Jose if you're ready?"

"Ha. You want rid of me already?" She laughed before I could protest. "That's OK, but be sure to call me on the cellphone each evening, won't you?"

I said of course I would, and walked her down the plank and over to see her safely into the massive vehicle. We hugged once more and kissed goodbye. I watched her climb in, dwarfed by the sheer scale of the Escalade, and watched her swing into the traffic, waving and smiling as the traffic parted. I felt proud of my brave partner and excited to be moving forward.

But there was one piece of admin to deal with before we could set off, and that was actually to buy Mystere from Ken. He had prepared a deed of sale, which I read and was happy with – it showed the "visible" price we agreed earlier, and I had the cash element handy. A handshake, a phone call to the Providenciales Bank to set up the transfer of the "visible" element, and, with the papers signed in duplicate, Mystere was mine. That's to say, Joe Baldwin's. I was delighted, and wished I'd asked Sally to put a bottle of champagne on board. I said that to Ken, but he thought not.

"Let's get under way and celebrate at our first stop, eh? We don't really want to be shipping out of here and into the ocean proper after a drink. But there's one thing more ..."

"Oh?"

"Yes – insurance. I ought to phone my broker and cancel my policy – I can't insure a boat that's no longer mine. I'd advise you to insure it through him at once. He insures in Lloyds of London, which is the top place. Up to you, but it does make sense."

It did indeed. I hadn't thought of it, which was a blind spot, but I was very happy to insure at Lloyds. It felt, well, right, somehow. Ken put the call in, and I took over when he'd cancelled his cover and introduced me.

It took 20 minutes to set the whole thing up. I had to explain the journey I - or rather Mystere - was about to undertake, including the transit as cargo through the Panama Canal, even though that was insured. The broker told me that if this was a permanent move, I would need to de-register Mystere from San Francisco and re-register her in Providenciales when I arrived. They were able to give me instant cover, with extra cover for the transit as a back-up to the insurance in the shipping agreement and also take care of the registration. The broker also reminded me that the cover would be void if the boat was at sea without a yachtmaster on board with a recognised qualification. I put that on my list of things to deal with. I thought I could spend some of my leisure time getting my ticket once we got to Provo.

The bill was steep, but as I called the bank again to pay it I knew that it was better to have proper cover, even if that meant I was over-insured. Once I got to Provo I could review the cover and perhaps scale it back, but for now it was one less thing to worry about, which was fine by me.

And so, suitably insured, and under Ken's expert – and certified - instruction, I took Mystere away from the dock under power, then switched off the motor, raised the sails and set off across the bay towards the Golden Gate Bridge and the Pacific Ocean – and LA.

Chapter 49

George Points the Way

Earlier that morning, two men had entered the chandlery shop and asked for George at the counter. He emerged from his office with his usual bluff bonhomie. “Morning, gents”, he greeted them, “What can I do for you?” One of the guys was wearing a sports jacket; the other was wearing jeans and a leather bomber jacket.

“Hi”, said one of them - the bomber jacket one. “We’re looking for a friend of ours. Lives on the sailboat called Mystery.”

“Mystere”, corrected his accomplice.

“Ah yes. Mystere. That’s it. In the marina here. He’s an old pal. We’re due some beers and catch-up. Is he still here?”

“Ah”, said George. “You’ve just missed him. Mystere set off this morning.” He smiled. No need to mention Ken White – he was aware of his domestic situation. And this wasn’t strictly a lie anyway. Plus, he liked Joe (he assumed it was Brett’s preferred nickname – and why didn’t these “friends” know that?). And he didn’t think he liked these guys, for some reason.

“Ah. Left just today?” asked bomber jacket.

“Yup. Early morning. Settled the fees and sailed away. Across the bay. On the way to the Caribbean, I think. Lucky guy, your friend, huh?”

“Huh. Why today? How long has he been here?”

“I don’t know why today. Just a coincidence, I guess.”

“Coincidence?”

“Yes – with his friends looking for him this very day, eh?” George really didn’t like the cut of this guy’s jib.

The two men looked at him, an assessing gaze. Instinctively, George felt he needed to make the message clear. The message being "Nothing to see here. Go away."

He didn't say that exactly, but he did say, "Well, very bad luck that you missed him. I'd say I'll tell him that you called. But I really can't say when I'll see him again. Or, you know, whether I ever will."

"Yes, very bad luck," replied bomber jacket. "And he's been here how long, did you say?"

"I didn't say. But Mystere's been moored here for a couple of years."

"Ah, I see. And has our friend been on her all that time?"

George didn't want to tell a direct lie. "No. More like 6 months or so. Maybe a little more than that."

"I see," said bomber jacket. "OK, thanks for your time. I guess we'll catch up some other time."

The two men turned to leave. Then one of them – sports jacket - turned back. "Sailing to the Caribbean, you say. But how does he do that? From here? Are you sure about this? I don't see how that can be true. Where's he really going?"

This guy was British, thought George. And he was challenging his word. That wouldn't do. "Of course it's possible. You can sail through the Panama Canal. Or you could freight it from LA to Miami and start sailing again – that's the expensive option. Safer, though. And easier. That's what I'd do. And what I advised him to do. Not difficult." That told the cheeky Limey, he thought.

The other guy – the American – stepped in. "I see. Well thanks. Maybe we'll catch him later, eh?"

"Sure", replied George. "Be seeing you." As they walked away, George had an uneasy feeling that he'd possibly told them too much. He'd been riled and reacted to that. Maybe he should have just said that he'd left, and not mentioned the Caribbean – and certainly not Miami. He wondered whether there was a way to warn Joe. Maybe he should talk to Sally. Warn her. Tonight, probably. He helped himself to a mug of coffee and returned to his paperwork.

But he was interrupted about an hour later by two more men. These guys looked a lot more serious, and he could see an official-looking black Crown Victoria parked just outside the gates. One of the guys had a buzzcut and a military bearing that struck a way-back chord with George, and one looked a little less stern – an ordinary guy.

Buzzcut introduced himself. "Hi, Bernie Schwartz. FBI. My colleague, Peter Page." He showed an ID with badge and photo. Either a good fake or the real thing. And the big black car also looked like the real thing. The guy called Page simply nodded on being introduced and leant on the bookcase. No ID shown, George noticed. But very self-contained. Almost certainly a spook of some kind as well.

"We're looking for someone we believe to be living here on the Marina. On a boat called Mystere, we think. Brett Foster. Do you know him?"

George decided to tell these guys the whole truth, or at any rate, more of it than to the other guys. They were the real deal, and he didn't want to cross the FBI. "Sure I do. But you've missed him. Sailed away today. Off to LA, then freight to Miami and the Caribbean, probably. I expect he'll fly to Miami and meet the freighter there."

"Today? You sure?"

"'Course I'm sure, I saw Mystere sail past the end of the dock myself. Into the bay and away." He still didn't see the need to involve Ken.

"OK, I'd better make a note of your name. You're the Harbourmaster, yes?"

"Sure. George Phillips. And there's something else you should know. You're not the first two guys to ask after him today. Did you know that?"

The two detectives – or whatever they were – looked at each other. "No," said the other one. "Can you describe these others?"

He's British as well, thought George. "Nothing memorable, really. But like you two – one US guy, one Brit."

"You're sure – one Brit? Like me? Not maybe Irish?"

George pondered. "Nope. One US – East coast, I think – and one Brit. Average build, nothing memorable. Average everything."

Buzzcut took over. "What did you tell them?"

"What I told you, pretty well."

"Here to LA, then Miami and into the Caribbean?"

"That's right. Or he could sail direct, through the canal, but I don't think he'd do that. He asked my advice, and that's what I told him. And he's probably southbound in the ocean channel by now, I guess. I'm sure I won't see Mystere again. Not sure about Joe."

The Brit came alert at this - he stood up off the bookcase he's been leaning on. "Joe?"

"Eh?"

"You said 'Joe'. Not 'Brett'."

"Ah, yes. His name was Brett – as you say. Brett Foster. I saw ID at one point. But he called himself 'Joe'. I thought it must be a nickname or something."

"I see," replied the Brit. "Did he have any friends here? Girlfriend?"

George didn't see why he should drag Sally into this. "Not really. Not that I saw. Friendly guy, though – we often had a few beers here in the bar on an evening. I explained how to get his boat into the Caribbean. By way of LA and freight to Miami. As I said."

"So he took your advice?"

"Guess so. He didn't actually say so, but I think that's what he's doing. It's what I recommended, for sure. Mind you, it's an expensive option - he might be sailing it through the Panama Canal. I don't know, but I warned him against that."

"Why's that?" asked Buzzcut.

"Well would you cycle down the Interstate? Even if it was legal?"

Buzzcut nodded. "Yes, I see. So, if you could afford it, you'd freight it."

"Yup. From LA. And I think he could. Afford it, I mean."

The British guy nodded. "Yes, indeed. Ok, thanks. You've been a great help." He looked at Buzzcut, who nodded.

"Yes, thank you, Mr. Phillips. We'll come back and see you if we have any more questions."

"I'll be here", said George, as the two men left the shop and made their way back to the big black car.

...

The email from Edwards and Dolan's hotel to the office in Londonderry was short, but to the point. "Our friend has sailed off, probably towards LA then Miami. Will then sail into Caribbean. Please advise."

...

The email from Page and Schwartz to London said much the same, but had more detail and more certainty, and was sent both to the FBI offices in San Francisco and Page's offices in London.

Both pairs then waited for a response. Edwards and Dolan decided to check out of the Sausalito hotel and return to San Francisco. They booked a hotel near the airport, just in case.

Chapter 50

Incoming Emails

The Lawyer had a busy day ahead. He arrived in his office at 8AM and turned on his desktop computer. Clicking on the email server, he couldn't avoid Edwards' overnight missive in the in-tray. He considered leaving it until he'd cleared his business to-do list, but it wouldn't be ignored. And once opened, the contents, short and sharp though they were, really meant that he needed to talk to The Priest. Mary arrived as he was re-reading the short email, and asked if he needed coffee. He did, but he asked her to contact The Priest first, and busied himself with organising his papers for the day until she put him through.

Once connected, and without small-talk, The Priest asked him to read out the email. There was a short silence. "That hardly tells us anything," was the comment. "Why has Best gone on this journey?"

"You know as much as I do," replied The Lawyer. "But if he's now sailing off into the Caribbean, I would assume he has his hands on the money and he's off into the sunset, so to speak." The Lawyer was starting to get bored with this project. There was a good fee agreed for clearing these funds, but the chances of that actually happening were diminishing fast. And, looking forward, rather than back to the grim days of strife and corruption, he could see a prosperous – and much cleaner – future, as the urban decay was addressed with huge scoops of government and EU money. Property was where the profits were now, and that's where he wanted to be. The Priest represented the old days, and whatever glamour and excitement those activities once held, the attraction was fast diminishing.

The angry reaction to his comment was clear, even over the phone. "I'm not going to allow that. 'Sailing into the sunset'? He's got my money, for God's sake. Now, why is he going to LA? What's Miami got to do with it?"

The Lawyer took a deep breath. "As I say, I know as much as you do. But I would have thought that, if he's got this boat in San Francisco, which he seems to have, and if you want to sail it around the Caribbean, I guess you'll need to get it through the Panama Canal somehow. I wouldn't know, but I guess there must be some companies who'll do that for you."

The Priest was silent for a moment. "Yes, that makes sense, I suppose. Can we find out who they are – whether Best has contracted with them?"

"Well, that's the sort of job we'd ask Edwards to look at. Right now he's still in San Francisco. It might make sense to get him back ...?"

"Yes. Get him back here, as soon as possible, and get him onto this at once – I want to know how and where he's getting this damned boat into the Caribbean. The email mentions Miami – is that where they unload it? If so, that's where we'll find him. Unless we can cut him off in Los Angeles. Can we do that?"

The Lawyer though for a moment. "Tight, I think. We'd need to know which company was doing the shipping, and the name of this yacht ... and since he's already at sea on his way to LA, I doubt we have time to discover all that. But we should be able to intercept him at Miami. That's the most certain plan. We'd be relying on luck in LA, and we'd be showing our hand. I recommend that we make a better plan to catch him in Miami."

The Priest's frustration was clear from his tone. "This man Best is making us look like fools. He's one step ahead of us all the time, and he's slipped through our hands again. I'll get a message to Dolan and you get Edwards back here as soon as he can get to the airport. First job, find out what company's bringing this damn boat to Miami. And when it's due to arrive. I'll talk to Dolan now. That clear?"

"Perfectly," said The Lawyer. "I suggest we meet with Edwards here in exactly a week's time. Does that work for you?"

"Yes. I'll make sure it does," said The Priest and the line went dead.

The Lawyer replaced the phone. He looked at the clock. 8:30 AM, more or less. He looked at a chart – 12:30 AM in San Francisco. Quite late, but ... he decided to phone Edwards' cellphone anyway. Better to get this out of the way, then get to work on some proper cases.

The phone made the single-tone US calling signal. Edwards answered after two rings. "Mm ... Hello?"

"Hello, Mr. Edwards. Sorry to wake you."

"Oh. It's you. That's OK. Is this about my email?"

"Yes. I've just spoken to our priestly friend. He is not a happy man. Not by any means. The instruction is to return to the UK as quickly as possible. Tomorrow if you can, which is why I've called you now. When you get back, you are to try to find out the name of the freight company carrying Best's boat to Miami. Do you know the name of the boat?"

"Yes. Mystere. But that's a tall order ... well, Best's en route to LA now. That means he must be planning to get to LA in, what – 4 or 5 days?" He paused. "So, yes, maybe I can do this – shipping movements, companies who do this sort of job. Hmm. OK, I'll phone the airline now and sort out my flight. What about Dolan?"

The Priest's talking to him directly. It's probably better you don't know about his instructions. Concentrate on finding that freighter, OK?"

"Yes, OK."

"Good. And we'll meet in my office a week from now. I hope you'll have some information for us by then. Goodbye now."

"Right. See you then."

The Lawyer went back to his daily grind, while Edwards sorted out a flight to London later that day, then tried to get back to sleep.

Meanwhile, The Priest was speaking to a contact in Boston, where it was very much the middle of the night.

"What the hell time is it, for God's sake?" was the immediate response to his call.

The Priest was icily calm, but his voice was instantly recognisable. "Here in Ireland, it's nearly 9 o'clock. It must be quite early over there. I do hope I'm not interrupting you?"

"Christ. What's happened? I was fast asleep."

"What's happened, Liam, is that the toe-rag Best has taken our money and is sailing off to a life in the sunshine. And I want him stopped. Now, your man Dolan."

"Yes, Dolan. What about him? He's in San Fran, isn't he? On this guy's trail."

"Well, he's been given the slip. This thief Best – he's off on his boat."

"Well, what do you think I can do about that? Now?"

"Liam. I want you to call Dolan, bring him home, and wait for an update. Then I want him to meet a certain freighter in Miami and ambush the thief Best as he collects his fancy sailboat, before he disappears on it, into the Caribbean. And make sure your man gets our money back, before he takes permanent care of him. Certainly code red on that."

"What freighter?"

"The one carrying this damn sailboat from Los Angeles to Miami. Whose details I will get to you in good time. This time next week, in fact."

"No, you won't – not at this time of the night. Make sure you call at a civilised hour. And I'll call Dolan in the morning. I'll give him the message. Now, let me get back to sleep." The phone went dead, leaving The Priest not much improved in mood.

...

Page's email was received more calmly in London. Binner called "upstairs" to check, but they agreed with his strategy – bring Page back, find out which freighter was carrying the yacht over to Miami, and intercept Best there. He waited until that afternoon and called Page accordingly, and then the FBI offices to ask for Schwartz's continued involvement. The FBI were happy to recall Schwartz and then re-engage in Miami.

There was, however, a major outstanding question which needed addressing, and it was the one that was challenging Edwards.

...

Edwards was back in London and at his desk in Acton by the following afternoon. He put in a call to his computer expert contact and arranged to meet him in the Dove on Hammersmith Mall that evening. "It's a complicated problem. I'm not sure whether you can do it. It might not actually be possible, but I can't think of anyone else who'd have a better chance than you would."

"OK, I'll take the bait. What's the problem?"

"I need to find out whether and when a certain sailboat – a big yacht - is being transported from Los Angeles through the Panama Canal to Miami, and when it's scheduled to arrive there. Is that possible?"

"Hmm. When's this happening? And do you know the name of the company?"

"No. But I know the name of the yacht. Mystere. It's probably happening next week. That's to say, leaving LA next week."

"Well, that's a start, I suppose."

"Yeah, well that's all I have for sure. Let's see what can be done. See you this evening. Usual fee?"

"Yes, but we need to discuss it as well. So I'll see you outside."

"OK." Edwards yawned. It had been a long flight back from LA and he had been in the back of the plane. He hoped he'd be alert for this meeting in the pub.

...

Towards the end of the day in London - a reasonable time in San Fran, Binner phoned Page. Page answered him at once. "Morning, Boss."

"Afternoon, Peter. All OK with you?"

"Yes. You got my email, I suppose? What do you think?"

"Well, I think we now know for certain what happened to the money, and who's got it now. This chap Best's our man, judging by what you've learnt over there. A pity he gave you the slip, though ..."

Page winced. "Fair point, I guess. But I think we can grab him if we want to. We just need to go to Miami and wait for him."

"Ha-ha. So the plan is for you to pop over to Miami and hang out until the freighter arrives, is it?"

"Erm, well ... It's probably too late to catch up with him in LA. I'm pretty sure the shippers will offload in Miami ..."

"Yes, if that's where it's going, and in about a month. No, get back here asap. Do some research and confirm the shipping line, the vessel and the schedule. Then get back out there and, yes, intercept our man. And make sure our Irish friends don't."

"Yes, OK. I do have an idea how to do that research, actually. I've been thinking."

"Oh, thinking, eh? Good. Go on."

"Lloyds of London. Maybe the yacht's insured there."

"Hmm. Really? No ... Lloyds - not from the USA ..."

"Oh, no, it's not at all unlikely. Lloyds is completely international. A huge amount of the world's insurance risk passes through. The US is a major market. And Lloyds was founded on marine insurance."

"Oh? How do you know this?"

"A pal from school. Came from a wealthy family – minor aristocracy. Third son. He's never been all that bright, so Lloyds was a natural home for him, according to the received wisdom – the estate, the army, Lloyds. In that order."

"I see. I think. Well anyway, get back, do the research, and, if you can get some hard information, get back to Miami. The FBI have told me that, all being well, Schwartz will re-join you in Miami once you've established the shipping details."

"Ok, boss, I'll sort the flight out. Tomorrow, I expect. But I'll contact my pal in Lloyds today – I'll buy him lunch as soon as I can when I get back. Nothing happens in Lloyds unless it happens over lunch."

"Ok, don't spend too much. I'll see you in a couple of days. Let me know the times when you've booked the flight."

"Right, boss." The line went dead, and Page looked up the number for the airline.

Chapter 51

We are Sailing ...

Ken had worked out a sailing plan for the journey to Los Angeles which would also work as a training programme for me. I intended to take the certification once I'd safely arrived in Provo. To help with that, I needed to become familiar with lengthy journeys behind the wheel – and using the technology, which was Ken's specialist subject. So, once we'd powered away from the dock and turned west, towards the Golden Gate Bridge, we put up the sails and I took over.

There were all sorts of private boats, both powered and sail, zipping around in the Bay, and there were ferries and freighters, all passing in and out and across, so we needed to be on deck and vigilant until we'd passed under the bridge and out into the Pacific Ocean proper. Once clear, we turned to port – south – and we were in a proper sea, with proper waves, which were running in the same direction as we were, and the wind was coming from over my right shoulder, brisk and apparently fairly constant. We adjusted the sails accordingly, set the wheel on a southerly bearing, and left the cockpit to look at the chart and the instruments.

I'd seen the "look, no hands" thing when we were out for the day earlier, but it still seemed a little odd. Ken had shown me more than once how the instruments – "great technology" - would let us know if we went off-course or got too near the shore or another vessel. I was about 85% convinced. But he showed me his plan on an old-fashioned paper chart – today's trip was relatively short, to Half Moon Bay, followed by a longer trip to Monterey, then the big one – day and night to San Simeon. That would be my baptism, if not of fire, then of cold and wet, and I wasn't really looking forward to that part.

I bought some fresh fish and salads – and cheese, which was not a big thing in the USA, I'd found – in Half Moon Bay town, and I intended to cook supper or lunch on the longer trips, but we ate on shore in Monterey, after a particularly challenging entrance to the harbour there, which I was quietly pleased to have managed without direct, hands-on help from Ken.

The overnight trip to San Simeon was about 100 miles (for some reason, that's just 80 nautical miles or so), and the challenge was to arrive in daylight. That meant leaving really early and arriving just before sunset, or leaving mid-afternoon and arriving after dawn in San Simeon, which we decided to do. Or Ken did. He felt that I needed to experience the "hell" part of what he said was the "heaven and hell" of open sea sailing. I'd seen plenty of heavenly days, earlier, in the Bay with Ken and, of course, Sally.

I thought of Sally, front or back of mind, most of the time. I hoped she'd be proud of my efforts at the helm – I was determined to sail every foot of the way when we were under sail. I was looking forward to our life in the sun, with days of heavenly sailing and a nice beach house, and with the Caribbean and Florida – maybe as far as the south-eastern seaboard – available for extended holidays. Well, it would feel like one extended holiday, really. In fact, I mused, I'd probably need something that looked like, if not work, exactly, business of some sort, to keep the brain exercised.

I decided I'd look into the property development plans the minister had mentioned. I'd need a lawyer, and notwithstanding that they were friends, I couldn't see why I wouldn't use Garrido again for that. He deserved the business. Maybe Sally would like to set up a restaurant in the Marina. All perfectly possible now.

The long overnight sail from Monterey down to San Simeon was certainly a challenge. Once it was dark, which was about 3 hours into the journey, I was relying on the instruments and technology to "see" where I was going. I could make out some shore-based lights, and the red and green lights of occasional fellow-sailors, but not having headlights was very strange. It was also cold and sometimes wet, with squally showers, and later, before dawn, it was quite foggy. But the sea and the wind both remained fairly constant, except for a larger swell in the middle of the night and the wind dropping during the foggy period. Overall, the elements were reliably driving us east of south, which was what we wanted. Ken slept in the cabin, in case I needed help, but I was determined make it without his help.

And I did. At around 10 AM, I took us into the mooring, and Ken and I tied up safely. I was suddenly bone-tired, and after a quick breakfast on board of scrambled eggs, tea and toast, I collapsed on the big bed up front and slept for 4 hours. Ken sorted out the harbour dues and spent time on shore, I think on the phone to his business contacts. I joined him on shore for a late lunch, and we agreed that we'd stay overnight to get my sleep caught up with, and set off in good time the next day.

There was a point where we passed officially into Southern California – Point Conception. Skirting this piece of land sticking out to sea was a challenge – the winds blew harder and less predictably, and as Ken put it, it required proper sailing. I needed his guidance, but I did the work – setting and re-setting the sails, and steering us slightly out to sea and back in towards land again. Ken's instructions on what to do seemed natural to me. I felt that I could have done it without him, but he was a reassuring presence, to say the least.

We made Santa Barbara in good time, and had a great – if astonishingly expensive - Italian dinner on shore in the upmarket restaurant district. Expensive, but superb. Veal chops in Marsala sauce, fried zucchini and broccoli, washed down with a couple of bottles of Barolo. I decided to ignore the price – I didn't think there was a downmarket district, in fact, and I was feeling pretty upbeat anyway. I felt I'd mastered this sailing business – something I'd never expected to care about when I first "met" Mystere – and I was enjoying it. This was a feelgood evening – nearly there, the overnight sailing test passed, and the tricky skirting round the Point accomplished.

Although this journey was mainly about getting Mystere to the shippers, and partly a training trip, there had still been plenty of time to enjoy the weather, when the sun shone, and also the marinas and towns where we stopped. For long periods the helm and the sails needed no adjustment – it was just a matter of sitting in the cockpit and keeping an eye open. Ken had regaled me with endless tales of his successes on the golf course and in business, and trips he'd made in Mystere and predecessor boats. Although we were only travelling at less than 10 MPH by land speeds, the time had gone very quickly.

We left Santa Barbara in good time next morning and made Los Angeles Port around 4 o'clock. We furled the sails and switched on the motor, found the wharf we'd been told to look for, and moored safely next to other deck cargo vessels, mainly big motor cruisers, but one other sailboat. We made ourselves known to the office, and they inspected the boat to ensure it was safe to prepare for shipping. Once we'd removed our clothing bags and my aluminium case, and disposed of the garbage, it was. I handed over the keys and left Mystere to their care and expertise with just a quick backward glance at her.

Ken had phoned the airport as I was completing the paperwork. I'd made the booking in the name of the Turks company, as I wasn't Joe Baldwin when I'd booked, and obviously I didn't want Foster or Best on the paperwork. I signed as Joe Baldwin, printed the name and put "Chief Executive" below that.

Ken found a return flight leaving in 4 hours' time with a business class seat available, and got the office to call for a taxi. He agreed to drop me at the Marriott. We said a fond farewell there, and I promised to have him visit us in Provo once we were settled. I was sure we'd enjoy more sailing together before long. Then we shook hands and went our separate ways.

Chapter 52

Chasing the Invisible Man

The Lloyds of London building was one of the ultra-modern buildings of the brash new City of London. It had the plumbing on the outside, as the critical press put it, and when it was built in the 1980s it stood out among the other buildings, all dating from the previous decades and indeed centuries, like a jet fighter on a WW1 airfield. It was, however, well served by lunchtime haunts which consciously emulated the old chop houses, coffee shops and taverns of those earlier decades and centuries. And one or two were the genuine article, with histories of two centuries and more of deals struck over veritable rivers of hock, claret and port.

It was in a small private dining room, or "office", that Peter Page bought lunch for his old school friend. The restaurant was a carefully constructed replica of a hundred year old chop house, built in the basement of a 1950's office block, with a separate entrance around the corner from the grand steps into the prestigious offices above. And those chop houses used to have lots of private offices, like this one, for confidential discussions. The pies, sausages, chops, mash and chips menu bore a distinct similarity to the school dinners they'd enjoyed in their teens; the difference being that, firstly, the food was produced with considerably more skill and better quality ingredients, and, more significantly, there was a wine list. And it had what Page's pal called "damn good claret for the money." After two bottles of this, it transpired that it also provided port by the pint jug, which, they decided, was the only reasonable way to conclude the meal.

Page's pal seemed almost immune to this sort of lunch. He summed up as Page called for the bill. "So, you believe you have a largish sailing vessel called Mystere, being freighted from LA to Miami, possibly leaving about now, and you want to know when it arrives in Miami, yes?"

Page was far from sober, and showing it. “Mmm, that’s it. Or at least, we think so.”

His pal topped up the port glasses from the pint jug. “Well, it’s a 3-week journey between LA and Miami, through the Panama Canal. That’s true for any sea cargo. So, if your man’s yacht is travelling as deck cargo, that’s when it should arrive. Three weeks’ time. Give or take about 3 days. Unless the Panama Canal is exceptionally busy.”

“OK, but I don’t know for sure whether it’s actually on there. The yacht, that is. Erm, Mystere.”

The waitress brought the bill and Page handed over a card. His pal acknowledged the payment with a raised glass salute. “No. So here’s what I’ll do for you. And thanks for lunch, by the way. I’ll look to see whether this Mystere is insured here, and I’ll also pull down a manifest for any specialist shipping firm leaving LA this week or next. I can get the manifest anyway, no matter where it’s insured. And that will show the names of the boats on board, and their owners. If it’s not directly insured here, the cargo might be. Or we’ll have reinsured it. Or maybe we’ve insured or reinsured the vessel itself. We’ll have records, anyway.”

Page was impressed, both with what his pal could do, and his pal’s apparent immunity to alcohol. “That’s great. I thought of looking at Lloyds List …”

“Well, if I can’t find it in our records, you could try that. But give me a couple of days and I should have something for you. Actually, give me a bit longer – you don’t know whether it’s sailed yet, do you?”

“No. Soon, though, I believe. If not already.”

“Ok, well, they may leave the manifest open until the last minute if they have some capacity left, but they’ll need to declare the final list before they sail. I’ll call you as soon as I have it. Shouldn’t take long.” He checked his watch. “Look, I have to be back shortly. I’ll have time to look for this information tomorrow, and if it's not there I'll look again the day after. OK? Thanks again for lunch. It's good to see you – been too long." He shook Page's hand and walked steadily out of the room, upstairs to street level and away. Page was wondering how he was going to get home without mishap. He was well out of practice at lunchtime drinking.

...

Edwards sat outside the Dove at Hammersmith, holding a copy of the Sun newspaper. He was nursing a pint of lager which he was finding a struggle. His body wasn't sure what time of day it was, but it didn't really seem to want a pint of lager. His contact arrived after 5 minutes and sat at the same table with his own pint. It was only midday, and despite the sunshine, they had the outside drinking area to themselves. Edwards put the Times on the table between them, and his contact pulled it discreetly to himself. "Ok", he said, "what is it you need this time? More airline flights?"

"No, we're on the sea this time," replied Edwards. "A freight journey from LA to Miami, carrying a sailboat as deck cargo. It should be leaving LA this week – maybe even yesterday or the day before. The deck cargo sailboat is called Mystere. It's all in there."

"A pleasure boat as deck cargo? That can't be a one-off – there must be firms that do that. Specialists." He took a draught of his Guinness. "LA to Miami. So through the Panama Canal, I suppose. Yeah, there must be a few boats needing to make that trip – that move. There must be some specialists. Is that what we have here?"

Edwards tried his lager again. It was getting a little easier. "I guess so. We know our target sailed off in his yacht from San Francisco about 5 days ago, and we're pretty sure he was on his way to LA, and it looked like he was planning to freight it to the Caribbean. Which means via Miami."

"I see. And this boat was called – what did you say?"

"Mystere. A proper ocean-going yacht, we assume. Our man was living on it for quite a while. As I say, it's in there." He pointed to the folded newspaper. "Along with your fee. The usual. Cash, of course."

"OK. I'll do some digging." He pocketed the newspaper into his leather jacket pocket. "You do realise that this could be public domain information? I mean, not necessarily buried in computer systems?"

Edwards yawned. "Sorry. Jet Lag. I flew back from LA yesterday. Actually, that's why I need your help – I don't have the time now, and it's urgent. I need some answers within 3 or 4 days. And I have some other stuff I've been neglecting recently. Plus I'm tired. And your costs are recoverable from my client."

"OK, that's fine by me. I'll start today – this afternoon. But don't be pissed off if I say that it didn't need any magic – no special skills. So, you want to know - what? The freight line, the name of the vessel, and the scheduled arrival at Miami? Anything else?"

"No, that's the main information we need. Well, and confirmation that this sailing boat – Mystere – is definitely on board. And quick. Two or three days' time?"

"Let's see. It's Tuesday today. You report when? Friday?"

"Monday, actually. But Friday or Saturday would be ideal, if you can."

"Should be OK. How shall I report? Same way?"

"Actually, no. I may be away on this other business – as I said, I've slipped behind on that. Can you drop the information into my office mailbox? Just write down the information – as you said earlier. And then phone me – or text – to say you've made the delivery. I'll collect it and send it forward. You do use text, I assume?"

"'Course I do. I'm no Luddite. As I say, I'll get onto it at once. If the information's out there, I'll get it quickly. And I think it will be."

“Great. Thanks.” Edwards tried a drop more lager, gave up and left half the pint behind as he made his way across the green and back to the tube station.

...

Page had decided against returning to the office after his lunch, and went straight home to sleep it off. So it was not until the following morning when, restored to health, he got back to the office. Binner saw him passing and called him into his office. “Good morning, Peter. Long lunch, that. Fruitful?”

“Erm, yes, I think it will be. It might take a day or two to get the information, but it’s certainly available. I expect I’ll be able to get the shipping line, the vessel name and the arrival time in Miami within a few days. I’m also hoping that the manifest shows the ownership of this sailboat. I’m sure we can greet the boat – and the owner – on arrival in Miami. About 3 weeks; maybe a bit less.”

Binner seemed impressed. “Good. A useful contact. I’m guessing this lunch was a bit – liquid?”

Page nodded. “Not half. God knows how they survive if that’s the usual behaviour. It hardly seemed to affect him. I decided not to come back here afterwards.”

“Quite right”, said Binner. “Do you have the bill on you?”

“Yes ...” Page took the bill out of his pocket and handed it over. “I was going to submit it along with my US expenses ...”

“Binner looked at the bill. “OK, hand-written scribble, headed paper, but the VAT number’s provided. And the food is, what, 20% of the total? ... Well, less than 25%. You’ll not get that signed off. Go back and get another one. Make the food and the drink the other way round. And write it neatly.” He handed it back.

Page put it back in his pocket, slightly embarrassed. “OK, boss.”

"So, what happens now? When will you know what's what?"

"Two days, maybe three. Lloyds is all a bit old-fashioned, but their computer systems seem pretty good. And there's always Lloyds List. But I may not need that."

"Right. Let me know what you learn. And go and get that bill sorted out."

That seemed to be all, so Page left Binner's office. He decided to write up the American expenses and revisit the city restaurant at lunchtime. But not, this time, for lunch.

Chapter 53

Road Trip

The Harbourside Marriott was located on the side of the marina for pleasure boats and yachts, about 5 miles by road from the commercial docks. When I arrived, at 6 o'clock, there was a long line at reception, which I hadn't had patience for. I took out my cellphone and called Sally.

"Hello, Joe", she answered. "Where are you? Have you moored up for the night?"

I laughed. "Sort of. We've arrived in LA. Ken's left for the airport and I'm in the Marriott. There's a long line at check-in, so I thought I'd by-pass it, assuming you've already checked in. Have you?"

"Ooh, great. Yes, I got here this morning. I'm in the Marina, window-shopping. Wait there and I'll come back."

"Well, hold on. Is there a decent-looking bar or restaurant anywhere near you? I'll leave my bags and come to you, if you like. I'm hungry."

"Erm, yes, well, it looks decent. A Chinese restaurant. Or there's a steak house. Which do you prefer?"

"Steak, I think, if that's OK with you. What's it called?"

"Hold on, I'll check ... Ah. Tony's. Tony's Steakhouse. You'll need to walk round the marina, alongside the car park for the golf course. 10 minutes, I think."

"OK, well, if you can stop window-shopping and get us a table, I'll drop my bags and walk over. What's the room number?"

"440. OK, great. Can't wait to see you ..."

I smiled. "Likewise. 10 minutes, then."

I rang off and walked over to the bell desk. “Hi”, I said. Could you please have these bags taken up to room 440 for me? No hurry.” I found a $5 bill in my chinos and passed it to him. He seemed OK with the deal, so I turned back to the entrance. A porter stood at the foot of the wide steps, shaded by the large roof to the turning circle. I asked him for directions to Tony’s, and he pointed the way.

In all, it took me 15 minutes to get to the corner table Sally had secured. She jumped up and hugged me for what seemed like a full minute, but probably wasn’t. We kissed for about the same amount of time, while the waiter hovered with the menus. I apologised to him as we sat down in the banquette, still somehow holding hands. He smiled and gave us the menus and a wine list. “I’ll give you a moment to read these and come back and tell you the specials,” he said, and left us to it.

“Wow, it’s good to see you. And you look so tanned! Sailing must be good for you – you look great,” she said.

I laughed. “Well, you’re a welcome sight as well. But it’s been less than a week. I can’t have turned into a rugged sailor in that short time, can I?”

Sally giggled. “I guess not. But you’ve gone a bit – ruddy. It’s the sea and the wind, I guess.” She touched my face. “And you’ve got these lines here, around your eyes. From squinting. Quite attractive, actually.”

“Thanks”, I grinned. “I sailed it all the way, you know. Ken didn’t need to do anything. We did an overnight as well – I did all that.” I felt childishly proud of myself.

“Oh. So you’re a real sailor now?” She grinned back.

I chuckled. “Yup. But a hungry one. And then, well, you’ll see what fresh sea air can do to a man’s other appetites. Let’s order.”

"Mmm. Good. OK, steak first. Then we'll go to the room." She kissed me again and we concentrated on the menu.

The steaks were tender, the wine was good, and the walk back to the hotel was just long enough to walk off the effects a little. We went up to the room and fell into bed, leaving most of our clothes on the floor.

...

Sally had parked the Escalade in the underground parking garage, and after a leisurely breakfast, we dropped the room key into the auto-check out, retrieved the enormous vehicle and added my own bags to the boxes and cases under the blanket in the huge rear section, then set out into the seemingly endless LA morning traffic. We had no plans beyond getting out of the city and finding the first nice-looking place to stay once we'd left LA behind. As we drove, I told Sally about my sailing adventure, and she told me about the residential course she'd been on for the first three days of the week and the long drive down from San Jose. We seemed to talk non–stop.

It was mid-afternoon by the time we felt we'd truly left LA and were in rural Southern California. This felt like the start of our road trip. We knew that not every evening and night would be spent in pretty tourist towns or smart chain hotels. And we were actually looking forward to that "real America", although we knew we'd probably have the occasional dodgy experience. We had a rough route in mind – through Phoenix, up to Flagstaff and the Grand Canyon, across to Dallas and Southfork, down to Houston and New Orleans, up to Memphis and Nashville, down through Atlanta and across to the South Carolina coast, then down to Orlando and eventually, by way of Naples and the Gulf Coast resorts, to Miami.

We intended to book each night on the morning we moved on, using a map and the major hotel chain web sites as a default. We had more than 15 nights to spend, so we weren't in any sort of hurry.

Our first night was in a motel outside Palm Springs. We arrived quite late, eating at a diner a short drive away from the motel, and left early, having breakfasted at the same place. We were on the road before 9, and pointed the huge vehicle eastwards.

…

As we approached Miami, heading towards South Beach and our art deco beachside hotel, we discussed our trip. The biggest disappointment was Southfork, outside Dallas, which looked far too small and unremarkable to be the glamorous setting for the scenes apparently shot there. And the interior had never been used anyway – just the outside, mainly around the pool. The biggest jaw-dropper was the Grand Canyon, which neither of us had seen close-up. Lots of cities and overnight stops had sort of jumbled together, but we had lots of photos, which we could review later.

But the big surprise – for me, anyway - was that we'd genuinely had not a single row – never even a cross word. This was despite a couple of very disappointing overnight stops, and many miles in the Escalade over sometimes utterly boring scenery, if you could even call it scenery. This felt like a good sign for our new life in the sun, by the sea. And, of course, on the sea.

I'd booked us into a very striking hotel on South Beach in Miami – one of the newly-restored art deco hotels dating back to a more glamorous age. We arrived at lunchtime, parked the Escalade in the secure park, and took our overnight bags up to the lobby. This area and the public rooms were spacious and airy. Large doors at the rear led down to the garden area, with subtropical shrubs and trees, a huge pool and bar & grill, and, according to a map on the wall by the open doors, a path down to a large public beach and the Atlantic Ocean. The sun was beating down, and the pool looked irresistible. The pool bar was a welcome added bonus.

We took our overnight bags to the room and changed into poolside clothes. Before we went back down to take advantage of the garden, pool and bar for lunch and a lazy afternoon, I phoned the shipping company. The timing was good –the freighter would dock in four days' time and start to offload the deck cargo – the boats - the next day. So, we had a few days to relax, sunbathe, and enjoy Miami South Beach.

Chapter 54

Critical Information

Around mid-morning, two days after the Lloyds lunch, Page received a phone call. “Hi, Peter. I hope you’ve got a notebook and pen there. I have your shipping information. Everything you needed.”

Peter grabbed a notepad and pen. “Oh, hi. Great – thanks – everything, you say?”

“Yup. Full details of the freight carrier and timings – and your yacht, erm, Mystere. Wonderful things, computers. They’ll put us out of work eventually.”

“Maybe - when they can eat and drink huge lunches,” laughed Peter.

“Haha. Good point. Anyway, you ready for the information?”

“Sure. Fire away.” Peter wrote quickly as the details were read out. Shipping line, date of departure, estimated time of arrival, confirmation that the manifest showed a Hunter 460 sailboat named Mystere, owned and booked on board by a company registered in the Turks & Caicos. “Wow, thanks. That’s exactly what I needed.”

“There’s a bit more – on the sailboat. You want that as well?”

“Sure, let me have it.”

“OK, well, it is insured here, in fact. It’s just changed hands – a week or so ago. The original owner was insured here. That’s now cancelled, but the new owner insured immediately, using the same broker, who’s placed it with the same syndicate. Change of owner and notification that the boat is being shipped from LA to Miami. But also a change of home port registration, from San Francisco to Providenciales, Turks and Caicos.”

Page was writing fast. “And the new owner – the Turks company?”

"Actually, no. It's personally owned. By a Mr. Joe Baldwin. But his address is care of a bank in Providenciales."

"Ah. Baldwin? Not Best?"

"No, Baldwin. Joe Baldwin. Is that right?"

"Yes. I'm sure it is. This is really great stuff – thanks a lot. Oh, the name of the bank?"

"Erm ... Caicos Securities and Deposits." He gave the full address. Page wrote all that down as well.

"Fantastic, that's really helpful," said Page. "Thanks again." He thought for a moment. "Actually, who did he buy it from? Do you have that?"

"Erm, it'll be here somewhere ... Yes. Name of Ken White. Here's the address we have ..."

Page scribbled that down as well. "I'm seriously impressed. And extremely grateful. Thanks a lot."

"No problem. Look, it was good to see you. We have a spare slot on some hospitality. About 6 weeks' time. The Lords test. First day. A box, of course. Fancy it?"

"God, yes. That would be great. Thanks."

"I'll send you the invitation today. Reply at once and you're in. See you then."

"Well, thanks again – this is all great stuff. Cheers."

Page put the phone down and grinned to himself. That was a great phone call, he reflected. He re-wrote his scribbled notes into a more coherent thread and took it through to Binner's office, not including the invitation to Lord's. He knocked and entered.

Binner noted Page's ebullient manner. "Ah, Peter. You seem to have some news, yes? Your expensive lunch bearing fruit?"

Page grinned. "Ooh, yes. Look at this." He handed over the neater version of his notes.

Binner was clearly impressed. "Yes, I have to admit, that lunch bill is looking like a good investment. This is solid stuff. And our man's new identity as a bonus. Baldwin, eh?"

"Yes. I'm sure it's him. Still Joe, and same initial. Can't be anyone else, can it?"

"Well, it could, of course. To be fair, we really don't know for sure that this is our man. It's just strongly circumstantial. Compelling, but not utterly conclusive." He paused for a moment. "But OK, I'm fairly convinced, given what you learnt in San Francisco. And it's the right boat." He re-read the notes. "But it's a new owner. Why's that?"

Page nodded. "My guess is that he was borrowing it before now. Or renting it, probably, unless he knew the owner ..." He looked at his notes. "This Ken White. He'll have paid cash, presumably. Below the radar – quite a smart move, really. But if he's decided he likes it, and wants to move it to the Caribbean – well, he can afford it, so why not?"

"Hmm ... OK. I'll ask our American colleagues to quietly check out this Ken White chap, just in case. Look, write this up, including the San Fran trip, and I'll recommend to those upstairs that we send you to Miami to meet the freighter. We have a couple of weeks, even if they have a quick journey. Let's make sure we give them a good report with a strong conclusion, and it'll be all right, I think."

Page nodded, took back the notes and returned to his desk to prepare his report, looking forward to a trip to Miami - and a day at the Lords test when he got back. He whistled quietly to himself as he opened his computer and signed in.

...

Edwards was sitting in a window seat in a café in Turnham Green Terrace, Chiswick. He'd ordered a coffee and a Danish pastry as he watched a hairdressers' salon over the road. He had a clear view of a lady whose movements were of interest to her husband. She was reading a magazine, waiting for the stylist. He was reading the Times, expecting to sit there for an hour or so. On the table in front of him, his phone buzzed to announce the arrival of a text. He picked up the phone, flipped it open and checked the screen. *"Got what you needed. Left you a note at office as requested."*

He considered his best course of action. His target was a well-dressed and well-built blonde lady in her mid-40s, and so far entirely blameless as far as he could discover. She had arrived by taxi from a large detached house in Grove Park, the part of Chiswick across the Great West Road, towards the river. Edwards had followed the taxi in his own car. He'd waited in the traffic, 2 cars back, as she paid off the taxi and entered the hairdressers, then he'd parked on a convenient meter two streets away, paying for the maximum 2 hours. His office in Acton was just 2 stops away on the District line - easily reached and returned from within an hour. And he knew that a session with the hairdresser could easily take that long. Unless this was a quick tidy-up job.

He sipped his coffee and dunked his Danish pastry while he watched the salon. He had a clear view of what was happening in the reception area and most of the chairs in the salon above about 3 feet from street level, which is where the wooden plinth and inscribed frosted glass gave way to clear glass. Within 5 minutes, he could see his target, sitting in a chair in front of the mirror, as a hairdresser chatted to her and examining her hair. Eventually they agreed on a course of action, and another, younger, girl rolled over a trolley, which he assumed contained bottles and foil strips; in other words, this looked like a full colouring session.

He waited another 5 minutes, during which time he drained his coffee and finished his Danish. The younger stylist was starting to wrap sections of his target's hair in foil, and the older one seemed to be preparing the chemical dye mix. He decided. She was going nowhere for at least an hour. He left coins for the bill in the saucer and walked out of the café and down to the tube station.

He opened his office door and collected the mail from the basket attached to the letter box. He sifted the conventional mail and put it on his desk for later review. There was an A4 envelope with a handwritten scrawl saying just "Edwards", which he opened and saw that it was the one he wanted. He replaced the contents and stuffed it in his pocket as he walked back to the tube station.

He reviewed the contents as he rode the tube back to Turnham Green. There was a covering note, handwritten, and a list of facts - exactly the information he'd asked for. The note said *"This was quite easy, mate. I looked for shippers who'd take boats as deck cargo on this route. There are 3. I pretended to be a British copper, and phoned them all. I found one which had just had a vessel depart for Miami. A bit of chat to the bird in the office, and she told me that that the sailboat I was interested in, Mystere, was on its way on their boat. They couldn't give me the client's name – it was booked in by a company. In Providenciales, which is in the Turks & Caicos Islands. I said that fitted in with our investigations, and asked her to keep my enquiry confidential. She was quite impressed - thought I was from Scotland Yard, which I let her believe. ETA and contact details are in the notes. If you phone them about a week in advance, you can get a definite date for docking. Cheers" ...* and a scribbled sign-off.

Easy work for a grand, then, but Edwards knew his Irish clients would cover the cost. He reviewed the information on the summary sheet. Yes, it was all there. He could email it to The Lawyer once he'd seen his lady target get safely home, as he assumed. He'd then hand over the watching brief to his assistant. Unless she went off somewhere else. The tube slowed down and he stood to leave.

As he walked slowly past the salon, he saw that she was still there, and the assistant was picking the foil off her hair. He quickly walked to where he'd left his car and drove back to a stretch of road where, although there was no parking, he could sit with the engine running until a warden wandered along. He had a clear view of the entrance to the salon, if not the inside. He was lucky – he had been undisturbed for 10 minutes when which she emerged and hailed a taxi. He slid into the traffic a few cars back, and as he expected, the taxi took her back across the High Road to Grove Park.

He parked up further down the road and waited an hour, but saw no more movement. He looked at the dashboard clock – 1 PM. It was a quiet street and very little was happening during the day. Then another taxi arrived and disgorged two more ladies of similar age and style to his target. They went into the house and the taxi drove away. He looked in his mirror and saw a grey Nissan pull in behind him. He picked up his phone and briefly described his morning – except his detour to the office and back – to his colleague in the Nissan, including the arrival of her guests. He then raised his hand and eased away, leaving the afternoon shift to keep an eye on the house. After 3 days of this, he was fairly sure there wasn't anything untoward happening, but he'd agreed to watch her for a week. And of course, he would. This was a well-paid assignment. Meanwhile, that email to Londonderry ...

Chapter 55

Unexpected Visitors

The Lawyer had asked Mary to contact The Priest and meet him as soon as possible to discuss the email he received late yesterday afternoon. Despite The Priest's demands, The Lawyer refused to read out the detailed information on the unprotected phone line, but he said that as far as he could see, it was clear that the information in there was everything The Priest was looking for, and he said so, leaving at that. The Priest tetchily said that he'd visit the office at 3 o'clock that afternoon, and rang off.

Now, as he waited for the meeting, he hoped this might be an end to the whole affair. He was heartily fed up with the whole episode, and, in truth, he admired this Best character to some extent. A chancer who'd won through. It was difficult to share The Priest's hatred of him. In fact, it was impossible. But he had to see this through, at least to hand over this information. He hoped he wouldn't have to say so in as many words, but he wanted nothing more to do with this.

Mary showed The Priest in, and as usual, had organised a tray of coffee. As they waited for her to bring the coffee in and pour two cups, The Lawyer printed off two copies of Edwards' email and joined him on the sofas, taking the one directly opposite him, with the coffee table between them.

The Priest read and re-read the email printout. "Ah! This is excellent. We have him. I assume this is reliable information?"

"No reason to think not, is there? He's been right all along. I suppose you could telephone the shippers and check, but I'd rather not. Not from here. I wouldn't recommend it in any case. But I think this is what you and your friends need to know, isn't it?"

The Priest noted the distancing implied in that question, but said nothing. He was more focused on immediately passing the information over to his Boston contact. He looked at his watch and did a quick calculation. Liam would be up and about – he didn't want to cross him again by calling in the middle of the night. He knew The Lawyer wouldn't allow the firm's phone to be used to make the call, so he reached into an inside pocket for his mobile phone and called the international number.

It answered after 3 rings. "Hello."

"Liam. It's me. I have some news for you."

"Oh. Will I be needing a pen?"

"I'd say so. Please find one."

There was a pause. "Right. So what do you have?"

"These are the details of the shipping line carrying the sailboat that your man Dolan missed in San Francisco. Times and contact details. Are you ready?"

"Yes. I said so."

"Right ..." The Priest read out the salient points from Edwards' email, verbatim. "Please read that back."

Liam did so. "Is that it?"

"That's it", replied The Priest. "You have all you need, I think. Please pass all this information to your man Dolan and tell him to make sure we intercept this – this man Best - in Miami. Secure access to the funds and then deal with him. Is that clear?"

"Yes, perfectly. I'll call him now. I'll let you know when he reports back."

"Right. Just make sure he doesn't fail. Goodbye to you." The Priest rang off.

The Lawyer looked at The Priest. "You made that call out of my hearing. Please remember that."

"Of course. Thank you for the information. I'll leave you to your work now. I'll be back in touch when appropriate." The Priest left without waiting for a reply, and The Lawyer sat down and refreshed his coffee.

He was thinking about whether and how to avoid The Priest's next contact when his door opened with a bang and a flustered Mary entered in company with two men. They were wearing matching dark suits, shiny shoes and short haircuts.

"I'm sorry, sir, these gentlemen were most insistent they see you. I couldn't stop them."

The Lawyer looked up and assessed the two visitors. He folded the email printout in half to hide the contents. "That's all right, Mary. You can leave us now. No, no more coffee, thank you ..."

At about the same time, two rather larger men in similar clothing met The Priest as he stepped out of the lift on the ground floor. They walked either side of him, one with a hand behind The Priest's back, and one discreetly holding his arm just above the elbow. Stifling any resistance, they quickly escorted him into a dark blue Range Rover, which pulled away from the kerb as soon as the three of them were installed into the rear bench seat. The whole process, from lift to car and away, had taken just 30 seconds.

As his guests left his office, The Lawyer followed them to the door and spoke to Mary. He saw them get into the lift and watched the doors closing. "Don't worry, Mary. They were just checking some details on a property deal for their boss. I'm sorry if they were a little rude. Can you please get me Edwards on the phone? His mobile if he's not in his office."

Mary didn't believe a word of it, but got hold of Edwards and put him through to The Lawyer's desk.

“Hello,” said Edwards. “Something wrong with my information?”

“No, no, I don’t think so. But this investigation is now closed. Can you email me a final invoice for your time and any new expenses beyond your trip to the States?”

“Oh. Well I was just bringing that up to date when you rang, as it happens. I can do that right now. It includes my colleague’s costs in securing that last set of information. Wait a moment ... There, you should have the email now. The latest invoice is attached.”

The Lawyer brought up his email inbox. With a ping, the email arrived, with the invoice attached. He opened the attachment. “I have it. I will transfer those funds to you along with payment for the last one – the American trip - when I close this call. Once the funds arrive, please delete and destroy all your records in connection with this project. Please then confirm that you’ve done that.”

“I see. Is this a reflection on my services, may I ask?”

“Absolutely not. You’ve done a great job, in fact. No, we’re, erm, cutting our connection with the client, and we feel that the files are somewhat sensitive. We’ll be doing the same here – shredding them.”

“I see. Right, well, as soon as those funds arrive I’ll regard the case closed as well. And shred my records. But I’ll need to keep the financial details – the invoices. For the tax man.”

“Of course. Let me know if they’re enquired about by anyone else, please. And this firm will be sure to contact you again if we need your special services – as I say, you did a great job.”

“Ok, thanks. And goodbye. For now, anyway.”

“Indeed.”

The line went dead.

A considerable sum arrived in Edwards' bank the next day, including a £5,000 bonus. He immediately fed all his case notes and reports into his shredder, deleted the email and Word files he'd opened for the case. He then sent a short cryptic email to The Lawyer confirming the deletion and the receipt of the funds "With thanks." Somehow, he felt a little cleaner after that.

Chapter 56

Miami Gathering

At Page's request, the FBI had been following the freighter's progress through the Canal, then north through the Caribbean and across the Gulf of Mexico. The journey had obviously passed without incident or delay, and a phone call to the shippers confirmed that it was due to dock in 2 days' time. It would start to unload, starting with the deck cargo, on the next day – three days' time.

So Peter Page was now patiently making his way through immigration in Miami International airport. Once through, he took the shuttle to the airport Holiday Inn. Schwartz was flying in from California and, all being well, would make his way to the same hotel the next day. The hotel was as close to the docks as any other chain hotel, and, like all airport hotels, anonymous and bland. Page was planning to rest up tonight, then rent a car and take a look at the docks, as discreetly as possible. When Schwartz arrived, they'd be able to use his FBI credentials to get closer to the action, and Schwartz had also insisted on using his FBI clearance to bring a second handgun for Page. It seemed likely that this is where they'd converge with the bad guys ...

...

And the bad guys, specifically Dolan, were also up to speed with the freighter's arrival and unloading dates. It was now public information if you made a general enquiry – there was no need to pretend to be the FBI or Scotland Yard.

Dolan had booked himself into a cheaper hotel, handy for the docks, and had hired a Honda Acura for a week, which he collected at the airport. Liam had given him a clean credit card with a few thousand dollars available and matching driving licence in the name of Andrew Sutcliffe. He'd also given him instructions which were - almost word for word - The Priest's message in his phone call.

Dolan was in no doubt of what he had to do here, and had no qualms. This guy was a chancer and a thief. He'd stolen money that was supposed to support the nationalist struggle, and frankly he'd been taking the piss so far. That couldn't be tolerated. This guy was going to be very sorry he'd crossed this organisation. Then he was going to be very dead.

...

Sally and I were enjoying the luxury of staying in the same place for more than a couple of nights, and it was great place to spend time. We left the huge unwieldy Escalade in the hotel's secure car park, and – to hell with the expense - rented a convertible Chevrolet Camaro to explore the tourist areas of Miami, including Coconut Grove and the marina on Biscayne Bay as well as the mainly Hispanic area around South Beach outside the hotel. We ate some interesting food and danced to salsa music in Tequila bars. We sunbathed and drank beer by the hotel pool and we played chicken in the Atlantic rollers at the bottom of the grounds. The past few weeks' road trip fell away, and we started looking forward to the sea journey to Providenciales.

On the day the freighter was due to arrive, I left Sally by the pool and took the Camaro down to the docks to find the shipping office. It was in a modern block just inside the gates, and the staff were very helpful once I'd introduced myself as a valued customer. The big ship had picked up the pilot, and was making its way between the bottom of South Beach and Fisher Island. It would dock this evening and start to unload first thing in the morning.

The deck cargo – the boats – would be first off, and they suggested I came back the next day around lunchtime to check that it had travelled safely. They would re-step the mast tomorrow evening, and have it ready to move away from the cargo wharf under its own power by the following morning. I told them that I'd do that - return to see Mystere in the water next day - and that I'd get organised to move her away as soon as she was ready on the following day, which was fine.

This meant that, officially, I needed a qualified Yachtmaster to move her up to the marina, and I certainly needed one to sail on to Provo, although I intended to do most of the actual sailing. The office suggested that I went to the Yacht Club Marina further back on the same island. Although it was visible from this dock, it meant that I had to drive back to the mainland and back over a different bridge. By water, on Mystere, it was about half an hour under power. I didn't think I'd really need a supervisor for that, especially with Sally as crew. But the insurance wouldn't stand for an unqualified trip all the way to Provo.

The marina office looked like a larger version of George's office in Sausalito, although the Marina manager was younger and more efficient. I arranged a mooring for two days' time, and asked about available qualified Yachtmasters for a leisurely journey to Provo. The harbourmaster made a couple of calls, and told me that there was a married couple available for such a trip, if I was OK with taking the two of them. I had no objection, of course, and agreed to meet them that evening in the hotel. That would allow Sally to check them out as well – we'd be in close company for a month at least; maybe longer, if we decided to take the odd detour.

I returned to the hotel, and updated Sally. We decided we'd go to the docks together tomorrow lunchtime to check that Mystere had weathered the journey without mishap. It also made sense to wait until we had moved it into the Marina before loading up with all the stuff currently safely stowed in the Escalade. We settled down for a few hours in the sunshine by the pool bar before we met the Yachtmaster and his wife, and I ordered beers and burgers to keep us going until dinner. We thought it would be a good idea to ask them to join us for dinner, unless one of us took an instant dislike to them.

I was waiting in the vast reception area when the couple arrived at the hotel right on time at 6:30. It was obvious at once who they were as soon as they walked through the wide glass front doors. He was slightly older than I expected, but had the unmistakable look of a sailing man – tanned, fit, dark hair and a short beard, wearing chinos over deck shoes, and a polo shirt which was clearly faded by the sun to a gentle pale blue. His wife was not what I was expecting, though. She was tiny and oriental – I wasn't quite sure exactly where from. She was dressed similarly, except that her chinos were neat shorts, and her polo shirt was faded pink.

I walked up and introduced myself, asking if they were looking for me, which of course, they were. He introduced himself – Robbie, and introduced "my wife, Mae. We just got married." He smiled, and she beamed and said "Hi, nice to meet you." He was clearly Australian, from the accent, and Mae's accent seemed to be pure California girl.

"Well, congratulations", I said. I couldn't help grinning back. I liked them at once. As we moved over to a sofa area, I suggested coffee and said I'd call the room to ask Sally down. I gestured at a waitress, who came over to take the order, and I walked over to a wall phone to dial the room.

Sally answered at once. "They're here", I said. "Have to say, I like them, at first glance. We're in the lobby, so let's have a coffee. Give it half an hour, and if either of us has doubts, say that we'll let them know later. But if neither of us does that, we'll move on to dinner. OK?"

"Yes, Great," Sally replied. A pause. "What are they like? Is she pretty?" she giggled.

"Yes," I replied, laughing. "And he's a good looking Aussie. But they're just married – first thing he told me. Should I offer them the big bed?"

"No, you bloody shouldn't", Sally replied, giggling.

"'Bloody'?"

"God, I'm turning British. I'll be right down."

As I expected, we all got on very well indeed. After confirming Bob's credentials, we moved on through to a very sociable dinner in the hotel dining room. Bob and Mae told us how they'd got together – in Vancouver – and travelled the West Coast crewing for sailing and motor yachts, with Mae doing cooking, cleaning and general crew work, before getting married in Las Vegas, en route for Miami to look for work in the Caribbean.

Sally and I gave them a potted version of our story, with some creativity on my part. We discussed terms, and I explained that I wanted to do as much of the sailing as possible, learning as much as I could to help get my qualification. I agreed to include a flight from Provo to anywhere in the Caribbean, within reason, at the end of the trip, and the deal was done. We shook hands on it.

Sally and I saw them into their taxi and went up to bed very happy with our new crew, looking forward to the journey down the Florida coast and out into the Caribbean. It looked likely to be a lot of fun.

However, the next day turned out to be the very opposite of fun.

Chapter 57

Reunited

Dolan was having a late breakfast, comprising of eggs over easy on toast with bacon, coffee and a cigarette, in a diner near his hotel. His Glock 19, loaded with all nine 9mm Nato rounds, was in an inside pocket of his leather jacket. The Glock 19 was promoted by the manufacturer as “ideal for carrying as a concealed weapon”, due to its “reduced dimensions.” And they were right – he’d also chosen the jacket for its slightly larger inside pockets, and the automatic pistol fitted easily, leaving no external indication of its presence. For close work, which is what he was anticipating, this was the ideal weapon.

His table was away from line-of-sight from the counter, and he kept his face behind the Miami Herald, which he browsed with very little interest as he lingered over his breakfast. He’d checked by phone that the freighter had indeed docked last night and was due to start unloading the deck cargo in the early afternoon. That would probably mean that he could complete this job and make good his escape today, with luck. He was reckoning on being back in Boston for his next breakfast, never apparently having been away. But his first problem was identifying this man Best.

From a visit to the docks the previous afternoon, he saw that there was no real chance of closing in on the target there, even when he’d identified him. There were far too many people milling around, no easy cover and no secluded corners to lure or drag him into. It was also built like a trap – there was only one land access in and out, which would be very easy to close off if there was trouble. But, dressed in jeans and his leather jacket, with a baseball cap pulled low, it should be easy enough to observe while remaining unobserved.

He thought it would be easy to identify his man by watching the sailboat, Mystere, being unloaded, unpacked and put into the water. He was sure that Best would make himself obvious by being the one who was generally fussing over the unloading, and inspecting the boat as soon as it was accessible, but not a docker or manager. Dolan reckoned he could then follow the asshole until a chance to close in on him and complete the mission presented itself. This plan, such as it was, called for spontaneity and improvisation, but this wasn't the first time for that. There was, of course, a chance that Best wouldn't show at all today, but would wait until the boat was re-assembled – masts back up – and floating, ready to move under its own power. In which case, Dolan would return tomorrow. No problem.

...

As it happened, that wasn't much different from Page and Schwartz's plan. They had a photo of Best, courtesy of HM Passport Office, but they needed to look for the live version of the typically lifeless passport photo. And, like Dolan, they thought that Best would want to see his boat safely off the deck of the freighter and into the water. They expected that, once his boat was ready to sail, he'd be off, and they'd be playing catch-up. This discussion had to happen here, on dry land – in Miami. But in private.

Like Dolan, they didn't see the dock as the right place for their discussion. But they were quite confident that he would be staying in a hotel in Miami, and that they could easily follow him - an unsuspecting civilian - back to wherever that was. In the unlikely event that he gave them the slip, they could always wait for him on board his boat tomorrow.

Unlike Dolan, however, they knew that they weren't the only party interested in Mystere and Best. The Priest had, so far, disclosed nothing after his abduction in The Lawyer's office, and The Lawyer was, naturally, deliberately ignorant of the plans laid by The Priest and his associates. But, since the contact from the FBI in Boston, Page knew that this theft, and this money – which was what it was all about – was a high priority for those associates. And it was likely that these guys also saw these two days as a unique opportunity to be where their thief was. Whatever else the IRA were, they weren't stupid.

So the forces of Law and Order were carrying FBI-authorised handguns in concealed holsters under their suit jackets. Unlike Dolan's lightweight weapon, these were heavier Smith & Wesson 9mm semi-automatics. In competent hands, they were accurate over a longer range. Close up, they were devastating. But they gave away their existence, even under a jacket. Of course, that wasn't a problem, if you were also carrying FBI ID.

At around 12:30, Schwartz parked the plain rental Ford saloon outside the shipping offices and he and Page approached the reception desk. They showed their ID and explained that they were just here to observe. "Nothing to worry about – you're not in any danger. We're just interested in one of your clients. Please don't alarm anyone – we just wanted to make you aware. We'll find our own way from here." The receptionist took all this in her stride and pointed out the way to where the freighter was tied up, with the cranes and deckhands already preparing for action. Schwartz asked her when they would start unloading, and she replied that they had already started. Given the FBI connection, it would be OK to drive over, as long as they kept out of the way and didn't leave their car unattended. So, that's what they did.

...

Dolan also parked near the offices. Without bothering reception, he strolled over to the berth where the freighter was tied up, dwarfing the motor cruiser which had apparently just been swung off the deck and into the water behind it. He stood among a small crowd of sightseers and watched the dock workers and supervisors carefully disconnect it from the crane harnessing and the protective buffers which had kept it safe from damage on the journey from LA.

This seemed to be at least the second boat off, judging by the presence of a large cruiser already manoeuvring its way from the dockside and out into the main channel. Looking up at the deck of the freighter, he could see at least 6 more boats on the deck from where he was standing. There were probably more on the other side. Dolan looked around for a better place to wait without being too obvious. There were some benches about 30 yards away, outside an official-looking shed. In fact it was the US Customs offices, according to the sign painted above the door. He could sit there and keep an eye on the berth.

From there, he would easily see which boat was swinging off, and pick out the concerned owner. The owner of the motor cruiser currently being unloaded right now was certainly easy to spot, in his silly sailing cap. He was pointing and waving his arms while the dock workers carried on, discreetly ignoring him. There was a scattering of vans and cars near the customs building, but these were of little interest to him. He took an empty bench, sat back, lit a cigarette and watched the buzz of activity around the freighter. He noticed the Ford saloon which drove slowly past and parked at the end of the customs shed, facing the freighter, but paid it no attention.

...

Page and Schwartz parked to the side of the Customs building and watched the unloading. Both men scanned the small crowd, but nobody looked much like Best's passport photo. This meant very little, and it was clear from what the office had told them that the sailboat was still on deck, so there was clearly no hurry. They left the engine running to give them air conditioning and watched proceedings through the windscreen. After 10 minutes, Page reclined the seat a little and closed his eyes. "Jet lag", he explained. "I need a quick nap." Schwartz nodded and watched the proceedings on the dockside.

...

I'd called the shipping office again at 8:30. They were remarkably patient, really, and told me that Mystere would probably be the third or fourth boat to be unloaded. About 2:30, they told me, and I'd be most welcome to watch and generally get involved. Just as long as I didn't get in the way. That last bit was unspoken, but very clear nevertheless. Sally persuaded me to get back into bed, and eventually, after breakfast in the room, we went downstairs and collected a local paper to read by the pool.

There wasn't enough time to go anywhere, but there was too much time to kill. I was likely to be irritating company. Sally seemed to have worked this out, and booked herself a spa treatment for a couple of hours. That left me restlessly swimming lazy lengths and sporadically reading a paper I had no possible interest in.

It was past midday when Sally reappeared. She looked great, in shorts and a sleeveless shirt, and the spa treatment had given her a glow. Her finger and toenails were varnished a bright red. She kissed me and threw herself into a chair beside me. "I enjoyed that," she said. "I've never had the full treatment before – steam bath, massage, hair, manicure and so on. I feel like a new woman."

"I was quite happy with the old one, really", I replied. "But you do look, well, rejuvenated."

She smiled again and waved to the Bartender in the cabin. "Let's have a beer", she said. "Then we'll go down to the docks. I know you can hardly wait to see your mistress again." If she meant Mystere, well, she was right.

Eventually, it felt like a reasonable time to set off for the docks. We collected the Camaro from the underground car park and joined the southbound traffic.

We parked the Camaro near the offices and introduced ourselves at the counter. I showed my paperwork from the LA office, and we were introduced to the manager, who came out to greet his valued customer and shook our hands. "Hi, nice to meet you. The sailboat Mystere, yes?" I confirmed - yes, and he looked at a list on the reception desk. "Ah, OK. We've been releasing the crating for the last half-hour or so. I think it's nearly ready to come off. Would you like to go and watch?" Of course we would, or at least, I would. He offered to escort us to the dockside. I said there was no need, but he seemed to want to stretch his legs, so the 3 of us walked together across the concrete towards the side of the freighter.

A huge motor yacht was backing away from the dock, presumably to make way for the next offload, which I hoped would be Mystere. We watched this for a few minutes, and then the dockside crane started up and swung a huge harness rig upwards towards the deck of the freighter. There was a period of about 10 minutes during which all the activity seemed to be happening on deck, out of sight to us on the dock.

Suddenly, we saw the huge crane swing the dark blue hull and keel of a sailboat – my yacht - over the side and down towards the water. My heart was in my mouth as it swung out, dwarfed by the huge mother ship, and slowly dropped into the water, with more of a ripple than a splash.

Mystere looked very odd, with her masts missing and a cluster of dock workers busy disconnecting her from the various ropes and harnesses. But before long she was tied up, side-on, and the manager invited us to go aboard. One of the team had obviously remained on deck as she was swung off the deck, and now he unshipped the gangplank and lowered it onto the dockside. The manager indicated that we should climb aboard. Remembering my manners, I ushered Sally on board in front of me. The dockhand aboard helped us down into the cockpit and we walked forward and down into the main cabin, and he walked back onto dry land behind us.

...

Meanwhile, Schwartz nudged Page awake and indicated the dockside. "I think that's the boat, and that must be our man. Best. Or Baldwin, now. And look - there's the girl."

Page was awake in an instant. "Ah. Yes. I can't read the name, but that must be it. I got some information on the Hunter 460 – that's almost certainly what that is. Yes, it must be them. He matches the passport photo, I think."

"They've gone aboard. Want to go over?"

"No," said Page. "I don't think so. Too many people around – and they'll be distracted. We need to get them somewhere more private. And we need their undivided attention. Let's watch them a while."

The manager walked back towards the office, and the dockworker stepped off the boat and casually chatted to a colleague. They seemed to be waiting for the go-ahead from the owner to start to re-step the masts and restore the profile and dignity of the sailing boat. Eventually, the couple emerged from the interior and stepped back onto the deck. Best had a word with the senior dockworker, and they walked off to one side, apparently looking at the masts and spars, lashed to the deck, spoiling the sleek lines. They seemed happy with what they saw, and eventually the couple stood back and took a last look at their de-masted sailboat before walking back to the offices.

...

Mystere had actually travelled very well, with no internal evidence of the loading and unloading or the journey. Sally and I checked all the rooms and found nothing untoward. The wheel had been removed and safely stowed in its cradle in the cockpit, where the table was folded down safely. Nothing to worry about here. It was as I'd left it in LA, internally.

The outside wasn't, of course. The masts were safely lashed to the deck, and the mastless profile was very peculiar - both the view from the cockpit, and, after we stepped down, from the side. The office manager introduced us to the senior dockworker, who told us that he was a hobby sailor himself. He assured us that he would have the masts back up and the rigging in place by tomorrow morning. I said that I'd bring the Yachtmaster along around 10 AM to check everything and set the sails; we shook hands and Sally and I left them to it.

We walked back to the office and set off in the Camaro back over the Bay and up South Beach towards the hotel. As I drove, I asked Sally to call Robbie, the Yachtmaster, to check that he could join us at the dock tomorrow at around 10, to oversee the rigging and refitting the sails and run it up to the marina under power. Yes, they'd see us there. Looking forward to seeing Mystere, he said.

That was all we could do at this point. "So, what shall we do this afternoon? Shopping?" I asked.

"Let's have lunch in the garden and then decide", she said. "I don't think I have any urgent shopping, but we might need to get provisions and maybe some clothes once we've got Mystere put back together."

"Yes – shipshape, as it were. OK, lunch and a beer in the gardens, then we'll decide."

...

"Who's that, do you suppose?" asked Schwartz. "The guy in the baseball cap?" He'd been watching the manager as he headed for the office, and noticed a man wearing jeans, a leather jacket and a baseball cap pulled down low, halfway between the customs shed and the water's edge. This guy was standing back, watching the unloading process, clearly paying close interest, but just as clearly, had nothing to do with the docks.

Page looked across to where Schwartz was indicating. He saw what the man was watching, and noticed him paying particular attention to the couple as the disembarked. He nodded. "I think that's our man – the Irish guy. Can't really be anyone else, can it?"

"Could well be", replied Schwartz. "He's watching all this very closely. But he's nothing to do with it, is he, the boat and all? He's not a wharfman. So, he must have another reason to be this interested." As they watched, Best and the girl turned and walked away from the dockside, back towards the office. So did this guy, keeping his cap low and looking disinterested. He kept his distance, but was clearly tracking the couple.

"I think he's the bad guy, for sure", said Page. "He's obviously following Best – assuming it's Best. Which I'm sure it is. Let's keep them both in sight." They eased the car forward to face the exit, past the office, ready to move off as soon as either the Irishman or Best and the girl did so. In fact, both parties climbed into cars and headed for the dock gates. Schwartz moved off to fall in behind.

...

Dolan had watched the sailboat swing out from the deck of the freighter and down into the water. It was easy to spot the nervous owner, standing with the manager, and anyway he'd watched the three of them walk down from the offices. There was little doubt that this was the thief Best. He looked at the girl by his side. Hmm. She looked familiar, somehow. Now, where had he seen that girl?

He stood up and walked from his bench towards the water, stopping well short of the activity around the sailboat, but with a clear view of the couple who were the centre of attention. The girl turned round, and for a second, looked straight in his direction, before looking back to Best. He had it! The restaurant in Sausalito. She was the waitress – no, the greeter; he was certain of it. Sally, was it? He cast his mind back – the marina, the bars and the Italian restaurant. Edwards – the Brit ... he took his mind back and pictured the evening by the marina ... yes, this was the girl in the restaurant. And yes, she was called Sally. He'd spoken to her, not realising her part in this deception. Well, she'd picked the wrong customer here.

He stood still as the pair walked back towards the office until he was behind their eye-line, then he followed. They unlocked a Camaro and climbed in, and he quickly jumped into his Acura and followed them out of the gates, allowing a Ford Pickup to come between them. The Camaro swung north and took the lane for the bridge over Biscayne Bay, and he followed it, keeping two or three cars behind. It was working out as he'd hoped, assuming they were heading for their hotel.

...

Schwartz and Page followed the two cars, allowing one or two vehicles to come between them and the Acura. It was almost certain that the Acura was following the Camaro, so there was no real need to keep an eye on that, but Page watched it anyway while Schwartz concentrated on not being seen by the driver of the Acura. This was basic training stuff, and as the traffic swung left onto South Beach it seemed likely that Best and his girl were staying at one of the newly-restored 1930's hotels on the right – the beachside.

...

Dolan thought so, too. And that was a good thing, because most of the hotels gave onto the public beach at the rear, behind their gardens and pools, which was a way to vanish after the job. He was hardly dressed for the beach, but he only had a T-shirt under his jacket. Jacket off, he thought he'd pass for a tourist taking a stroll along the beach path. There were frequent access points between the large hotels back to the street, where he could either collect his car, or find another way to return to the hotel, collect his things and get back to the airport. Sweet.

...

I swung into the hotel grounds and dropped down the ramp into the car park. The Escalade was still there, of course. Maybe it would be a good idea to return the Camaro this afternoon – or have it collected, if I was having another beer. We locked it up for now anyway, and headed for the elevator to the lobby to go through to the garden and pool.

...

Dolan was right – halfway along South Beach the Camaro turned right, into a large, very smart 1930's style hotel. A nice place to stay, he considered, especially when paid for by stolen money. As he drove past, he saw the Camaro drop down the ramp to the underground car park. Dolan carried on and spotted a parking slot about 40 yards further on. He parked and walked back towards the hotel. He strolled confidently past the doorman, who wished him a good afternoon, and sat on a sofa with a view of the elevator doors. Best and the girl would either go straight to the room from the parking garage and come down to the lobby later, or simply come up to the lobby and then perhaps go straight out to the garden and pool area. Either way, he'd wait here until the elevator delivered them.

...

Schwartz and Page saw the Camaro pull into the hotel, and as they drove by, watched the Acura park up, a bit further on. They drove on slowly, and Page turned round to watch the driver leave the car and walk back and enter the hotel gates. "Ok," he said. "He's parked up, and followed them in. I think it's time we got involved."

In response, Schwartz u-turned across the traffic at the next intersection and drove back towards the hotel. There was nowhere else to park, so they u-turned again lower down and turned into the hotel grounds. There was a small car park in front, with signs restricting waiting to 20 minutes. Schwartz put an official-looking FBI notice in the dashboard and collected some gear, including FBI-badged caps, and they walked into the lobby.

Chapter 58

Death in the Garden

Dolan watched as Joe and Sally left the elevator and turned towards the gardens, hand in hand. He couldn't see far into the gardens from where he was sitting, but he was sure that there were very few other people in there, if any. It was, after all, mid-afternoon and midweek – if there was ever a quiet time, this was it. He gave it 5 minutes to let the couple sit themselves down, then stood up and walked to the sliding doors to the garden, standing wide open and welcoming.

He immediately saw the couple, sitting at a table beyond the pavilion style bar, and confirmed that there were no other guests out here. Great. The perfect scenario. He strolled into the garden and up to the bar, and called the Latino Bartender to him as he leant over the bar. He showed him the pistol's grip in his inside pocket, then closed the jacket again. He looked at the Bartender's name badge: Luis. "Now, Luis, I need you to do something for me. I'm sure you speak English. Are you listening carefully?"

Luis nodded. He'd seen the gun and wasn't inclined to argue. Or even speak.

Dolan reached over to the side wall, where a wall-mounted telephone allowed both staff and customers to call the main building. He unclipped the main cable from the bottom of the phone and dropped it on the floor. "What I want you to do is leave that phone alone. I also need you to stay here, behind this bar, with your hands on the bar, where I can see them. Is that clear?"

Obediently, Luis placed his hands on the counter, palms down, and nodded again.

"Exactly like that, yes. Now, I'm going to join my friends over there at that table." The table was in full view of the cabin, but Sally and Joe were facing the other direction, across the gardens towards the large pool. “Now, whatever happens, you didn’t see anything. If anyone asks, you were in back. Now, is that clear as well?”

Again, Luis nodded. Dolan lightly slapped Luis’ face. “You’re a good man, Luis. You’ll go far.” Dolan went behind the bar, took a bottle of Cerveza Corona from the cold cabinet and opened it on the counter edge. “Put this on their bill. When I’m gone, of course. Now, remember, I’m watching you. Hands where I can see them. All the time.” Luis nodded.

Satisfied, Dolan nodded back, and walked over to the table where Joe and Sally sat drinking beer and considering the afternoon. He sat next to Sally, facing the cabin, and put his beer on the table. The couple looked surprised at the interruption. Off-balance. As he’d expected. “Good afternoon, my friends. I believe you have some money that doesn’t belong to you. A lot of money. Around 25 million dollars, I believe. Or there was, when you stole it. I’ve come to take it back. You’re going to dig it out of where you hid it and transfer it right back to where it came from. Or else your girlfriend will pay the price.” He stroked Sally’s knee. But not in a nice way.

…

Strolling through the main doors, Schwartz and Page sized up the lobby. Page immediately saw the guy from the dock – mainly thanks to his slightly scruffy jeans & leather jacket outfit, which looked slightly at odds among the smart clothes of the wealthy guests and holidaymakers. He indicated him with a glance to Schwartz, and took up a seat where he could keep an eye on him, while Schwartz quietly showed his ID at reception and asked for the manager.

Page could see past Dolan to the gardens, and saw a couple at a table towards the far end, on the corner of the pool. He wasn’t certain, but it looked like Best and his girlfriend, based on his view of them on the docks. As he watched, Dolan finished his coffee, stood up and made his way towards the sliding doors. Page looked for Schwartz, who was talking to the manager. He walked across and pointed towards Dolan, who was approaching the bar cabin.

"I think this is it. Time we stepped in." Page automatically checked his holster, and unclipped the safety strap.

"OK," replied Schwartz, looking towards where Page was pointing. He turned to the manager. "I need you to close those doors. After we step out there. And keep them closed. Put a maintenance sign up or something."

The manager nodded and called a junior over from the Bell desk. "Get me a maintenance sign. Now." The youngster recognised the urgency in his voice and scuttled back to the desk, returning with a yellow A-frame board, saying "closed for repairs." The manager took it and followed Page and Schwartz to the sliding doors. They stepped out, and he closed the doors behind them, putting the sign clearly in view in front of them. He waved the junior bell boy over again. "I want you to sit here," he pulled over a hard backed chair from a nearby writing table, "and don't let anyone into the gardens until I tell you it's OK. Say there's an emergency maintenance issue. OK?"

The boy nodded "Yessir", and sat down, facing the lobby.

Page and Schwartz spoke in low voices. They were shielded from the bar and the tables by vegetation here, but there was about 30 yards of wide open concrete path alongside the right hand side of the pool leading to the bar cabin and tables. Anyone approaching the tables would be in full view for some time. Page looked left, to the far side of the pool. There seemed to be a path through the planting which would afford some cover. Page quietly suggested that he would move round that way to the far side of the tables, while Schwartz watched the Irishman from here.

Schwartz nodded, but said "OK, but be quick. If he pulls a gun we'll need to be ready to move in. Get behind him as soon as you can." Both men took their guns out of the shoulder holsters and quietly chambered a round. Page walked quickly and quietly to his left, in front of the sliding doors and picture window, then up through the shrubbery towards the far side of the pool.

...

This was as big a shock as I'd had since the events in New York, back in September. I felt the blood drain from my face – the impact was a physical jolt. Surely I'd covered my tracks properly? Suddenly, it seemed not. And this guy and "friends" – who were they? I thought I could guess.

I tried to bluff it out. "What money? Which friends?" I managed to ask.

"Ah, now. Don't try that one. You can't kid a kidder. A couple of mill in cash – dollars – and all those bearer bonds, eh?" He took a swig of his beer. Sally switched her horrified gaze between the two of us. "Greedy, you were. If you'd stuck to the cash, we'd never have known you'd survived. You'd probably have got away with it. But I guess those bonds – what, 23 million bucks? I guess that was just too much to leave alone. Can't really blame you."

I was speechless now. He really did know everything. Where had I gone wrong? I drank some beer – my throat was suddenly very dry.

He went on: "Now, I'm sure you've spent a bit. You've bought yourself a nice sailboat, haven't you? I've seen it – very nice. And I'm sure you'll have spent more on nice hotels – like this one." He looked around him, and back towards the bar. "Very nice. But I'm sure there's most of it left. Squirreled away in some Caribbean paradise, yes?"

I nodded. My world was falling apart here. I tried to imagine how this would end. Would I have to return home, to London? Would I be allowed to? What about Sally – what would she do? I realised with another jolt that I'd actually let it all go if I could keep her. No time to process that thought. I wondered if there was room to negotiate. "Look," I said. "OK, I took the money. If it wasn't for me, it would have been burnt - or smashed to atoms. Your friends must have thought that was what happened, surely. Perhaps there's a compromise here. There's a lot of money. Enough to share ..."

He laughed. "Bargaining now? We've had denial – you'd better get to acceptance, as soon as you can. It's over. There's no deal on offer. Now, where have you put the money?"

"It's well hidden. You'll never find it on your own. Surely a deal's the best way to do this?" I wasn't really expecting he'd agree, but I had to try.

I thought I was getting somewhere when he smiled. "OK. Here's my deal for you." But then he reached into his inside pocket and took out a very business-like automatic pistol, and showed it to me, rather than pointed it at me. "Now, I need you to put your hands in your pockets while we talk. Go on. In your pockets. That way, I know you can't snatch this piece of precision engineering."

I did as he asked, and he placed the gun on the table in front of him. He then put his hand back on Sally's knee. She sat upright and then winced as he squeezed her knee. Nice legs, your girlfriend. Sally, as I recall, yes? Nice ..." he looked down "... very nice knees. I think I noticed that in your restaurant. In Sausalito, Hmm?"

I wasn't following this – how did he know that? Sally knew, though. "You. You were asking questions ..."

"I was indeed. And you were lying to me, weren't you?" He patted her knee.

Page had worked his way round to the opposite side of the pool. He saw the gun appear and watched as Dolan placed it on the table. He looked back at Schwartz, who nodded. He'd seen it, too. This was moving up a gear. Schwartz signalled Page to keep moving round.

The gunman continued. "Now, knees, they're quite useful. Imagine if we didn't have them. Or if one – or both – were seriously fucked up. It's hard to walk after that, Sally." He squeezed again and Sally let out a whimper. I was transfixed, horrified. I remembered the stories about the 'kneecapping' punishments in the very bad old days of the Irish 'Troubles'.

"Ah, I see you understand me." He'd seen the horrified look on my face. "Back in the old days, we used a drill. A Black & Decker – you know, an electric drill." He smiled an awful smile at Sally. "With a woodworking bit. Slow, but effective. We never had to do both knees. Well, sometimes we did anyway. But by then our – guest – would be unconscious."

He paused to take another swig. Sally and I stared at each other, beyond horror, or words. "The smell was awful, you know. Not just the bone burning, but the shit. They'd always shit themselves. Sometimes as soon as we plugged the drill in, sometimes later." More beer. "Anyway, as time went on, we used a gun. Like this one. Much quicker, and in fact much harder for the hospitals to mend. The Royal Victoria Hospital, in Belfast - they got to be the world's number one at knee injuries. All that practice. But if you use one of these ..." he picked up the pistol "the damage was worse. Pieces got lost. Quicker, though, as I say. Mind you, I don't suppose the hospitals here have much experience of that sort of thing. You'd probably save the leg. Well, possibly." He picked up the gun and stroked the muzzle against Sally's knee.

Page eventually reached the end of the pool, eased across the end out of sight from the tables and stood on the corner. The three people at the table were clearly focused on each other, and nobody had seen him or Schwartz so far. Page watched as the bad guy picked up the gun again. It was time to break cover.

I'd had enough. Obviously there was no dealing with this guy. "OK. I get it. So how do we do this? Let the girl go – she's nothing to do with ..."

"FBI! STAND CLEAR. PUT THE GUN DOWN!" Page stepped forward and walked rapidly towards the tables, closing the distance as he shouted his warning. Dolan turned to face him. Schwartz quietly moved out of cover, walking with his pistol held in a two-handed grip, pointing at Dolan's back. Instantly, or so it seemed, Dolan stood and dragged Sally to her feet, his gun held to her head, as he faced Page down.

"No," said Dolan, clear and calm. "You drop your gun, or the girl gets this." Unseen by Dolan, Schwartz kept his gun up, but this was now a dangerous shot. Dolan kept behind Sally, gun to her head. "Right, Mr Best, or whatever you're calling yourself, come with me. We're leaving the hotel. That way." He nodded towards the beach path, past Page. "We'll take a walk on the beach, the three of us. You – I said drop the gun. And lie down. NOW!"

Page placed the gun on the ground and lay down on the concrete as Dolan started to edge towards him, dragging Sally, towards the beach exit.

"DROP THE GUN! RELEASE THE GIRL!" Schwartz had used the distraction of Page responding to Dolan to close to within 15 yards of the group, and was pointing his gun at Dolan, two-handed. Dolan now had armed opponents on both sides, 180 degrees to each other and 30 yards apart. The one at the top of the pool was lying on the floor, though.

So he turned towards Schwartz. He threw Sally to one side, into Joe, who caught her and pulled her down to a squat. Three shots rang out within as many seconds. Schwartz fell down and rolled into the pool. Then Dolan wheeled round as a mist of blood erupted from his shoulder, and then dropped in a heap as the side of his head exploded and threw blood, bone and brains over Joe and Sally. Sally screamed.

Dolan's body dropped into the pool, blood already starting to stain the water.

Page had shot from a lying position, ironically helping his accuracy. He jumped up and checked the floating body, then went to pull Schwartz out of the pool. Joe put his arms round Sally and hugged her closely. She was sobbing as if she would never stop.

Schwartz was floating on his back, coughing and trying to swim. "You OK?" asked Page, who was shrugging out of his bullet-proof vest. Schwartz coughed a bit more and said "God, that was some punch. But I'm OK. I'll get out at the shallow end. Look after the civilians." He winced as he stood up in 5 feet of water to remove his own bullet-proof vest.

Page turned back to Sally and Joe. "Hello," he said. "Peter Page, Special Branch. You'll be Joe Best, I expect? Nice to meet you." He offered his hand to Joe, who shook it.

"Yes, well, Joe Baldwin now, actually. Pleased to meet you. Very pleased, in fact." They smiled at each other and Page helped Joe to his feet.

Sally had started laughing, slightly hysterically, but with some humour showing through. "God, you Brits. So fucking polite. 'Nice to meet you'. Jesus."

Joe looked at her. Her newly-coiffed hair was covered in blood - and worse, and her face was pale and streaked with tears. "Sally, I'm so sorry. If I'd known that would happen – any of that – I wouldn't – well, I wouldn't have brought you here. I mean, well ... that was the worst moment of my life. I thought he was, well, I didn't know what to think."

Sally thumped him on the chest, hard, several times. "It was your fault. You took their money. You must have known what would happen. And you brought me in to this – this fucking bloodbath." She was crying again, a steady stream of tears. "Why didn't you just take the money back to London?"

"If I'd known, well, I would have done. But ..."

"But what? You'd have had to go back to your boring life in London? What was so wrong with that?"

"Nothing. And I nearly did. But ..."

"What? But what?"

Joe looked down. Deep breath. "But I'd never have met you. So, even without the money, it was worth it. Even if this had been the end, and I'd had to hand it over, it was worth it for this last year. Truly." He looked up, into her face. "Truly."

Sally sniffed. She smiled. "Christ, you Brits. You're full of it, aren't you?" She thumped him again, but gently, and then hugged him. The blood in her hair smeared his face, and her tears were wet against his cheek.

Schwartz sploshed his way down the path from the shallow end, wincing as he walked. He glanced into the bar cabin, where Luis was standing transfixed, palms still on the bar. He must have seen the whole thing, Schwartz realised. "It's over, buddy. Relax. Get yourself a drink. But stay there. We'll need to talk to you." Once more, Luis nodded.

"OK, you guys," said Schwartz. "Time you weren't here, I think. We have some cleaning up to do here." He looked at Dolan's body in the pool, floating feet-down, with a red stain spreading across the deep end towards the extraction filter. "You're safe now. You need to clean up as well. Go up to your room and tidy up. And stay there. Get some rest if you can. That adrenalin takes it out of you. We'll come up and talk to you in an hour or two. We'll need a statement, but we also need to fill some gaps. For you as well as us – well, for your cops." He looked over to Page.

"Yes, good idea", said Page. "I'll see you as soon as I can. Have a nice cup of tea?" he winked at Joe.

Joe and Sally walked away from the carnage, through the sliding doors which the astonished bell-boy opened for them. They didn't notice the horrified stares as they waited for the elevator and pressed their floor number.

Chapter 59

Filling in the Gaps

Back in the room, Sally and I sat on the bed and looked at each other. "Christ. I'm sorry, Sally. I didn't think that would happen. Well, obviously. Christ." I had no words. I was suddenly exhausted.

Sally sat on the bed, sobbing noiselessly. I didn't know what to do. I passed her a tissue from the desk.

"That was the guy who came to the restaurant? God, I had no idea ..."

Sally reached out for my hand. "It's OK. I know you didn't. And it's over, it seems." I smiled at her. She was still bloodstained.

"Your nice new hairstyle. It's ruined. "Sorry."

She sniffed, then blew her nose. "OK, first thing. Never say sorry about this again. You didn't do this to me, or threaten me. That dreadful man did. I'm with you because I wanted to be. You didn't make me come with you."

I nodded. "OK. Thanks."

She blew her nose again. "And second. Did you really mean it back there – that you'd give it all back if we could stay together?"

"Yes. I only realised it when it seemed obvious that I'd have to give it back. I thought – if I can keep you, they can have the money." I paused. "And the boat, if they must." I smiled. "I mean, I hadn't seen it as a choice before, but, well, it was obvious, really ..."

She kissed me. "Good. I'm sorry I beat you up. But it is over now, isn't it?"

I shrugged. "I think so. Well, I hope so. Let's see what the Special Branch guy has to say. Page, was it?"

"Mmm. 'So pleased to meet you, Mr Best'." She giggled. "I think it was that that brought me back to myself. So, I don't know ... normal - and British. Calm."

I laughed. It helped. "Good. Well, my dear, you look a bit of a mess, frankly. How about a shower to get all that mess out of your hair?"

We shared the shower, and that led to a reviving lovemaking session in the bed that meant we needed another shower. Adrenaline seemed to be quite an aphrodisiac. Anyway, by the time Page knocked at the door, an hour and a half after we got to the room, we were much cleaner, and if not exactly restored to normal, certainly a lot calmer.

Page sat down in the lounge area and we phoned down for coffee and cookies. As we waited for room service, he asked how we were after our ordeal. We said we were surprised how well we seemed to have recovered, and he warned us that it might give us some problems for a few months – maybe longer. "The medics call it Post-Trauma Stress or something", he said. "You might get nightmares or sudden panic attacks. Although, looking at you now, I think you'll be OK. But be sure to look after each other." I picked up a faint Belfast accent. Not surprising, really.

Sally and I looked at each other solemnly. "We will," I said. Sally nodded.

The coffee arrived, I signed the check, and we poured coffees and settled back.

"OK," said Page. "Now, listen carefully. Here's how it is. This money you stole. It belonged to the Provisional IRA. It originally came from a number of sources, and it was managed by a Priest, working with a Lawyer in Londonderry. When the peace – such as it is – was signed, this Priest decided to put this money out of sight. We're not sure what he intended to do with it, but we think he was planning a cosy retirement."

"Yes, I was told by – let's say an expert – that the money I was carrying was the outcome of a laundering operation", I commented. "And based on the contract that was with it, I thought there was an Irish connection."

"Yes. Well, we'd been monitoring the Priest and his Lawyer for a time, and we noticed them setting up this meeting in New York. All it needed was that contract of sale completing and witnessing, and the money was clear. Your delivery was the ticket to a few people's comfortable old age. Which was thwarted."

I considered that. "Bad people, though?"

"Oh yes. Very bad people. By the way, I don't suppose you still have that contract – the one you mentioned?"

"I think I do, actually. And the case it all came in."

"Ah, good. That could be very useful for us. If we could collect it from you?" I nodded.

"Thanks." Page made a note in a small pad he took from his pocket. "Now, it's very important that you realise a few things." He looked at Sally. "Both of you."

We looked at each other. "OK", I said.

He sipped some coffee. "Right. You've been lucky. Lucky and clever. You've been playing with the big boys, and you've got away with it. You've been in shark-infested waters. And you've broken a lot of laws, both here and back home. I could decide to arrest you - at least for theft, and then take you back home and straight into a very dark hole. Plus, my FBI friend downstairs could take you down on a number of charges – false identity, fraudulent use of a passport, money laundering ..."

I looked down. He was right, of course. How had I thought I could really do this and get away with it? Hubris, that's the word that came to mind.

Page nodded as he saw his message going home. "OK. Now, the good news. We want you to keep this money. It's theft, and as I say, we could certainly take it from you, but if you co-operate, we don't need to."

I shrugged. "Well, as you probably know, it's been re-laundered and invested anonymously. Hidden. But I'm happy to know I can keep it anyway. What do you mean by co-operate?"

Page smiled. "Yes – in the Turks and Caicos, I guess." My surprise showed, evidently. "We do have our methods. I'll admit, we don't know right now whether it's all in the same bank, but we know about the payment for the boat, and the Lloyds insurance. And the intention to register it in the Turks. If we were to dig, I think we'd find it. But, as I say, we probably won't."

"Why not?" asked Sally.

Page replied: "Good question. Mainly because we don't want it generally known that the IRA had all this money and retained it, even after putting their weapons out of use. It's highly sensitive, politically. The whole Northern Irish question – it's always volatile. To a great extent, it's no longer violent, but it doesn't take much to blow on the embers. This money – it's a lot, of course, and we'd like to bury it. And it seems that you've buried it very effectively. If we took it back from you, people would know."

"The less said, the better, then?" I added.

"Exactly. So here comes the main co-operation point." He looked me in the eye. You must never, ever, return to the UK. If you happen to meet an old acquaintance anywhere else, walk right by. You must, if you want to put it this way, be dead and stay dead. As you so nearly were. Both in New York - and today."

"I see. Hmm." This was a surprise. Not that I had any plans to return – hadn't even thought about it, but still ...

"And if you're tempted, remember this. If you appear at a border control, as Best, Baldwin or anything else, we'll know. And you'll be arrested for theft of the 25 million dollars consigned to the care of your employers. You'd go straight to a police cell, and for that amount of money, there'd be no bail. You'd go straight to remand and then to jail proper. For many years."

I sat back. They had me, really. And there was no room to negotiate, or not at this point, anyway. "I see. OK, I can live with that. What else?"

Page finished his coffee and topped up. He smiled, at last. "Well, Joe, frankly, as well as being very lucky, you've actually done a great job here. You're obviously resourceful and intelligent. You've cleaned and hidden 25 million dollars. And you've created a brand new identity with no previous record. You're a natural."

"Oh. Well, it wasn't that difficult," I said, more embarrassed than modest.

"It was, Joe. Most people wouldn't know where to start. And you did it alone, even though you had the sense to find a lovely sidekick", he smiled at Sally. "But with respect, it was all your own work, wasn't it?"

Sally nodded. "It was, Joe. I was just a supporter. You figured it out, and you made it happen."

"Well, OK, assuming I accept that, so what? What's the 'co-operation'?"

"I'm not sure, specifically. But you have those personal characteristics – especially this capacity for ingenuity – and a completely clean identity. And with all this money, you have the leisure – you have time – possibly - to help us - from time to time."

I was intrigued. "Help? How?"

"Well, you have a new Turks and Caicos ID, I think? How did that come about? Did you meet the Foreign Minister, Fernando D'Souza?"

"Well, I did, yes. Nice guy, I thought. Larger than life, you might say. He's building a hospital wing. I helped him with a contribution, and he managed my citizenship application. So, is he of interest?"

"Well, we think he's genuine about this hospital wing, but he'll need a lot of contributions along the same lines as yours. Some, let's say, interesting people, will possibly look to gain citizenship the same way as you did. We might well want to know about some of this."

"I see." I didn't really. "What would I need to do – how would this work?"

"D'Souza's a sociable sort of bloke, I think?"

"Yes, I'd say so. I got the feeling that he has receptions and parties and so on, and he's clearly ambitious. I have to say, I like him."

"Good, good. Well, my people might need to know whether certain people turn up there. What we want to do is send you photos sometimes, and ask you to tell us if they surface there, and what they're up to. Not really demanding, but it needs a degree of discretion and resourcefulness. Can you do that?"

I pondered a moment, topped up my coffee. "Sally, what do you think?"

She shrugged. "It seems fair enough. Just report back? I can't see any real danger. Not like this morning."

I nodded. "OK, but on that point – how do we know that these guys – this Priest and so on – won't have another go at me – us? When you're not there to shoot the buggers?"

Page smiled. "Ah, yes. You should know about that. Well, we've had a word with this Priest and his Lawyer friend. A quiet word – again, we don't want any of this to get into the public domain. By the way, I need you both to sign the Official Secrets Act. It would be hard to bring it to bear, but my bosses insist, if that's OK?"

We nodded.

"Right, well, under the terms of that Act ... The Lawyer was easy. He was fed up with The Priest and his people anyway, and could see that this money was lost, barring violence, which he wanted no part of. All he wants now is to pursue his quite lucrative post-Troubles career, which we've allowed him to do. In exchange for telling us what he knows, and telling no-one else."

He sipped his coffee. "But that Priest. A nasty piece of work. How he called himself a man of God is beyond me. He was involved – at arms' length, but only just – in some very bloody business. He knew and sometimes decided what was going to happen. Very bad things – you'll probably know about some of them from the press, Joe. A real piece of shit, that man." He laughed. "I'm very glad that he doesn't have that money, and you do."

Sally touched my hand "So am I", she smiled.

Page nodded. "Well, this is what we did. We lifted him from The Lawyer's office, just after a meeting there, and spoke to The Lawyer at the same time. As I say, The Lawyer was co-operative. But The Priest – he was like a cornered rat. Even spat at us. Appalling man. He just wouldn't accept that it was over. So we hit him where it hurt – his pride. His self-respect. Reputation.

"The Irish Police – The Garda – had investigated a particularly nasty paedophile ring, based on a catholic orphanage, just over the border into the Republic. This was about 2 years ago. The Priest had nothing to do with this, obviously. In fact, it disgusted him."

I nodded. These scandals were hitting the headlines back home. People were universally appalled.

"Well, we added something to one of the statements. From the caretaker of the unit, who'd since died. This man was deeply involved, but knew he was dying. This was a sort of deathbed confession for him, and he spilt the beans completely. All the names. As a result, we interviewed the other main perpetrators, and they all - nearly all - confessed and gave statements. So we never used the caretakers' statement in court. But we used it for this. The extra passages we've added now clearly implicate our Priest.

"I'm not proud of this, and it wasn't my idea. But it worked. We showed the Priest these false allegations. They were quite explicit. He was enraged. He knew what we'd done, and he knew he was beaten. We said that if he so much as thinks about looking for this money, we'd 'accidentally' publish this document – leak it. No amount of money would compensate for his lost reputation – or his disgrace. He accepted defeat. In the end."

"Bloody hell. You do mean business, don't you? Can you really get away with that?"

"Probably. But he won't risk it. It won't need to come out, and the caretaker's dead now. We wouldn't actually need to prove anything – the exposure is the threat. So, yes, you're safe."

I looked at Sally. "OK. Good. And yes, I'm happy to help if I can. It's the least I can do. And thanks, of course." On an impulse, I reached over and shook his hand. "It's been quite a day, really. I'm very grateful – we both are – to you and your colleague for, well, saving us down there. I guess neither of would have got away uninjured."

"Sally might, if you'd co-operated, but I'm sure he'd have killed you. His instructions seemed to have come from the Priest, and he – the Priest - almost said as much. We tracked his phone calls to Boston, but there was nothing conclusive. That's where our man this morning came from. We've got him out of the pool and we're putting together his ID just now. You wouldn't be the first person he'd bumped off, here or in the UK. By the way, they're having to drain the swimming pool. The blood, you see. Good job you'll be sailing off soon – I expect?"

"Oh, I see. Well, yes. We'll get all shipshape tomorrow, probably check out of here and sleep on board ..." I looked at Sally, who shrugged, "and then, yes, put all this behind us. Sail away."

"Right, that seems to be that, then. I'll call in tomorrow morning and collect that briefcase. And you can sign the Official Secrets Act, then you'll be free to go. Oh, here's my card. Please let me know when you get to Providenciales, and we'll establish a way to stay in touch. I don't think we'll keep you very busy, mind you. But you owe us. Never forget that." He stood to leave and picked up his jacket.

A thought struck me. "What's happening back home? I mean, with my stuff – my flat, my car?"

"Ah, yes. Well your office are looking after your flat for now. I think they may have let it. I think your car's in a lock-up somewhere. According to your office receptionist – erm ..."

"Lizzie? Yes, that's just like her, looking after things. Look, if I had a will, would it be actioned now? I mean the disposal of the assets?"

"Well, not immediately. But your executor could apply to manage them pending an inquest, which would probably confirm your death. And the executor would need to ask for that, I think. Why - do you have a will?"

"Well, no. But, look, if I wrote one now, you know, dated as of before … and it was discovered, could you see to it that it was carried out? I hate loose ends, and, well, I think I can do someone a huge favour."

Page pondered for a moment. "I think so. I could get one of our tame legal practices to 'discover' and act on it. Do you know how to write a will?"

"Not really. But I can have a good go at it. And if it's clear enough, there's nobody to challenge it." I looked around. "I can't write it on this headed paper – from this hotel - though."

"Yes, you can", said Sally, who picked up a sheet from the desk. "The heading's quite small, just one line deep, right across the top. I can cut it off with my nail scissors. Look." She showed us, making a neat cut below the heading, leaving a usable page clear of identification. If I used both sides, I could say what little I needed to say on it.

I left the flat and all its contents to Lizzie. I hoped she'd use it to escape from her worthless husband and start a new life – she deserved better, as I said when I started this account. And I left the convertible BMW to my friend from the pub down by the river who'd always admired it. That would have been wasted on Lizzie. Page agreed to get a London witness to my signature and have a lawyer discover and act on it. There was a fee involved, of course, but there was money in my bank account to cover that.

The next day, after signing the Secrets Act and handing the contract and the aluminium case to Page, and transferring the contents of the Escalade back into Mystere, we checked out of the hotel and had both hire cars collected. We then settled ourselves and Robbie and Mae on board the re-rigged and relocated Mystere. We planned a route out of Miami, down past the Keys and out towards the Caribbean. And, eventually, our new future - in Providenciales - and wherever our adventures might take us.

The End

Acknowledgements

This is my first book – it's my first-born, if you like, but the next one is available now. Writing this one took me about 12 years, although it was a neglected project for much of the time. That it got finished at all is entirely thanks to the support and encouragement of a group of very good friends, and their friends and contacts. I couldn't have got anywhere near the end of this without the following people – they know who they are; I hope they realise how important their input, advice and encouragement was for me at various times.

So, to Anne, Annette, Elizabeth, George, Guy, Harry, Hilary, Jamie, James, Julie, Michael, Mike, Richard, Sue: my eternal thanks. And to anyone else who's name I've forgotten, my apologies – and again, my thanks.

Thanks also to my friends in Malton: in Chapter 2 and Maison du Vin for their encouragement and support, and to Hoppers of Malton for agreeing to stock my books.

And to you – the reader – even more thanks, especially for reading to the end. This, ultimately, is why I persevered - for you to read it. Feel free to tell me whether you enjoyed this – please give it a rating at amazon.co.uk or, better still, a review. And please be kind to a novice!

By the way, if you think you have a book in you, I'd encourage you to get it out – write it! I did, and I'm glad I did.

David Hoggard, Malton, September 2017.

https://www.facebook.com/groups/2941446919470012/

Here's the opening section of my next book ... out as a download or e-book from September 30th 2019 on Amazon.co.uk

SUDDENLY, KATYA

By David Hoggard

Prologue

This big old farmhouse is nobody's home any more. There are no carpets or soft furniture; in fact, there's very little furniture of any kind. There's a bed in this upstairs room, but nothing else, not even a rug on the floor. The bare bulb in the ceiling light is still on, even though it's been full daylight outside for several hours.

The girl gets out of the bed. She's small, with dark spiky hair - and naked. She moves almost silently as she walks carefully downstairs to find a weapon. There's nothing in the kitchen that would do – no knives, nothing at all really. It's deserted outside, although it's past 9 o'clock. Outside, across a small courtyard, there's a shed. Treading gingerly in her bare feet, she walks over and pushes the door open. She sees some old garden tools. This looks promising. She picks up a spade. Swings it like a club, two-handed. Yes. This will do.

She checks the track back up to the main road. Nothing. She looks the other way, towards the new buildings. Nothing moving there, either. They must be at work already. Good. She carries the spade back into the house, pauses to listen, then walks carefully up the stairs with it. One stair tread creaks. She stands stock still for a few seconds, listening carefully. Nothing - just regular snoring.

OK, then. It's time. Here, now. At last.

Silently, she walks into the bedroom she just left and kills the fat guy who was in the bed with her. First, she smacks him very hard, flat in the face, with the back of the blade. He bucks on the bed, then gives a loud gasp that sounds more like a lengthy snort. There's blood everywhere, spurting from the smashed face. That's cured his snoring, anyway, she thinks.

Then, in case this hasn't killed him, she turns the spade edge-on and swings it, like an axe, straight into his naked chest. She puts all her strength into it, plus a little extra from somewhere. Despite his layers of fat, his ribs cave in with a crunch. She pulls it back and swings again, hitting the same spot. This time she hits softer tissue, and instead of cracking bones, she hears a softer, chopping sound. She's smashed his heart. She leaves the spade embedded in the mountain of flesh.

She looks at the fat man, now clearly dead. Blood is running off the bed onto the floor. Gallons of blood, but after all, he was a big man. She spits on him, then leans back against the wall to gather her thoughts, staring at him. At last. Time to go now. She looks down at herself. She's spattered in blood. Quite a lot of it.

Still naked, she goes downstairs and washes herself in cold water in the kitchen, head to foot. It feels like a religious cleansing, although she gave up on God ages ago.

Her clothes are in the downstairs room. There's a battered armchair in the corner where the fat man sat last night, a large old-style TV on a low table, and half a dozen empty cans of Special Brew, but absolutely nothing else - except some of her clothes, scattered about on the floor, or in a burst plastic bag. She empties the bag onto the floor and selects a relatively clean yellow sundress and underwear. She picks up a jumper, some jeans and some more underwear, spilled out of the plastic bag. She sees a rucksack, which is much better than a carrier bag. It's behind the door, which has swung back a little. She grabs it.

Quickly now, she shoves the clothes into the rucksack. She looks round for her notebook. There it is, half-hidden under the fat bastard's jeans. She shoves it into the top of the rucksack and straps the cover tightly closed. She finds her boots, on the floor next to the chair, and pulls them on. She looks round again, but there's nothing else in this place for her. She shrugs the rucksack over one shoulder and sets off down the farm track towards the main road.

Printed in Great Britain
by Amazon

53826431R00255